Latitudes *of* Longing

Latitudes
of
Longing

a novel

Shubhangi Swarup

ONE WORLD
NEW YORK

Copyright © 2018 by Shubhangi Swarup

All rights reserved.

Published in the United States by One World, an imprint of Random House, a division of Penguin Random House LLC, New York.

One World is a registered trademark and its colophon is a trademark of Penguin Random House LLC.

Originally published in India by HarperCollins Publishers India in 2018.

Hardback ISBN 978-0-593-13255-5
Ebook ISBN 978-0-593-13257-9

Printed in the United States of America on acid-free paper

oneworldlit.com

2 4 6 8 9 7 5 3 1

First US Edition

Book design by Andrea Lau

to my parents, Sunanda and Govind,
to the value of words and the wisdom of silence

Contents

ISLANDS

S ILENCE ON A TROPICAL ISLAND is the relentless sound of water. The waves, like your own breaths, never leave you. For a fortnight now, the gurgle and thunder of clouds has drowned out the waves. Rains drum on the roof and skid over the edge, losing themselves in splashes. Simmer, whip, thrum, and slip. The sun is dead, they tell you.

Seeded in the sounds is an elemental silence. The quietness of mist and the stillness of ice.

The newly married Girija Prasad and Chanda Devi have resigned to their fate—strangers in a bedroom damp with desire and flooded with incipient dreams. And Girija Prasad dreams furiously these days. For the rains are conducive to fantasies, an unscientific truth.

One night, when the downpour suddenly stops, it wakes him up. His ears had adjusted to the tropical cacophony like a spouse to a snoring partner. Rising from a wet dream, he wonders what happened. Who left the room?

He peeps down from his queen-sized bed to Chanda Devi's rustic mattress on the floor, where she sleeps facing the open window instead of him. Aroused, he gazes at the curves of her silhouette in the darkness. When the two of them were united for several births by walking around the sacred fire seven times during their wedding ceremony, she followed his footsteps meekly, firm in her conviction that destiny had brought them together once again in a new avatar. Yet in this avatar, he would have to find a place in her heart once again. "Until then," she informed him on the first night, "I will make my bed on the ground."

She's wide awake, distraught because of the accusatory cries emanating from the other side. It is the ghost of a goat. The ghost escaped countless realms to come wander on their roof. And now its restless hooves have descended to stand under the open window, filling the room and her conscience with guilt.

"Can you hear it?" she asks. She can feel his eyes on her back.

"Hear what?"

"The goat bleating outside."

His forlorn erection withers away. He's alert now to Chanda Devi and the predicament she poses.

"There's no goat roaming in our house," he replies in exasperation.

She sits up. The bleating has grown louder, as if to tell her to convey to her dreamy husband, "You took away my life, but you can't take away my afterlife, you sinful meat-eater!"

"It's just outside our window," she tells him.

"Does it scare you?"

"No."

"Are you threatened by this goat?"

"No."

"Then perhaps you could ignore it and go back to sleep." He meant to say "should" and not "could," but he doesn't have the courage to be stern. His wife, he has realized, doesn't respond well to dialectics or coercion. In fact, she doesn't respond well to most things. If only she were less attractive, he could have ignored her and gone back to sleep.

"How can you sleep?" she asks. "You hacked the innocent creature, minced its flesh, deep-fried it with onions and garlic, then ate it. And you left its restless soul to haunt our house!"

If the souls of all the various kinds of animals he had consumed returned to haunt him, his home would be a zoo and barn combined, leaving no space to move, let alone sleep. But mild-mannered Girija Prasad cannot say that. Two months into his marriage and he's resigned to his wife's fecund imagination. It is a willful act of hope, attributing her behavior to her imagination and not some mental illness. For the sake of his unborn children and the decades they have to endure together, he announces, "If it helps you sleep, I will stop eating meat."

That's how carnivorous Girija Prasad turns vegetarian, much to his wife's and his own surprise. For the sake of a few hours of rest, he says goodbye to scrambled eggs, mutton biryani, and beefsteaks forever.

At the first hint of sunrise, she leaves her bed. She enters the kitchen to prepare an elaborate breakfast. There is new life in her movements and a smile lurking in her silence. Now that the killings have stopped, it's time to stretch out a white flag in the shape of aloo parathas. Two hours later, she serves them to him and asks, "How are they?"

Girija Prasad can't help but feel unsettled, and for all the wrong reasons. The sun is finally out. His wife, who has cooked him breakfast for the first time, has been bold enough to place a napkin on his lap, brushing past his shoulders, spilling her warm breath on his skin. He craves the comfort of grease mixed with flesh, but he can't find it on his plate.

"How are they?" she asks him again.

"Who?" he asks, disoriented.

"The parathas."

"Perfect."

She smiles and pours him a second cup of tea.

Chanda Devi, the clairvoyant one. She feels for ghosts and enjoys the laconic company of trees. She can sense them, his unexpressed cravings. But she knows he is better off giving up flesh. The kingdom of flesh is as ephemeral as it is unreliable, especially when compared to the kingdom of plants. Chanda Devi has seen it all, even the rivers of blood that will drain out of her body one day. It makes her obstinate, this knowledge. It makes her a demanding wife.

When Girija Prasad went to Oxford, it was the first time he had left his home in Allahabad by himself. After a four-day journey in horse carriages, ferries, and a train, when he finally sat on the ship that would carry him to England, he'd abandoned jars of pickle, ghee parathas that could outlive human beings, images of assorted gods, and pictures of his family, including a portrait of his mother that he had painted himself.

While he was relieved to leave the gods behind—especially Rama, the dutiful son who left his wife for no good reason, and the riverbank baba who was no god, just a senile, starving man—discarding his mother's portrait had seemed impossible to do without breaking down. But so would staring at her face, oceans away. To face the separation, he would have to start a new life. A violently different one, the mere thought of which gave him piles. Lost in an unending ocean, he spiraled into a shell of silence. Stillborn tears expressed themselves as stubborn constipation. A diligent documenter of the plant kingdom, Girija Prasad carried kilos of isabgol husk for this very purpose. He also carried dried tulsi, neem, ginger, powdered turmeric, cinnamon bark, and ground pepper to counter other physical ailments. When he arrived at Dover, the customs officials mistook him for a smuggler of spices.

Within a day of his arrival at Blimey College, Oxford, Girija Prasad Varma became "Vama," christened thus by tutors untrained in Hindu names. On the very first evening, he tasted alcohol for the first time and also broke the generations-old taboo of consuming things *jhootha*, or "contaminated by the mouth of another." When the colossal mug of beer was passed around among the freshers, he was presented with two options: embrace this culture wholeheartedly or languish forever at the crossroads. There were no portraits or deities on his desk to admonish him. The next morning, he would taste eggs for the first time, nudging at the globe of salty yellow with his fork, watching it quiver. He would soon acquire a taste for how complex and unpredictable life could be.

Girija Prasad Varma, India's first Commonwealth scholar, came back home after five years with a doctorate thesis that he concluded with two native words: *Jai Hind*. "Victory to the Indian nation" is how he translated the words for his supervisor. At the behest of the young prime minister of India, he was tasked with setting up the National Forestry Service in the first year of independence, 1948.

Most evening conversations among the tea-drinkers in Allahabad involved far-fetched theories linking them to the illustrious bachelor. But why would he choose to be posted to the Andamans, the aunties wondered, a place known only for exiled freedom fighters and naked tribes? It was rumored that there wasn't a single cow on the island and that people had to resort to drinking black tea.

One of the tea-drinkers, a gold medalist in mathematics and Sanskrit, Chanda Devi, was relieved. Her medals clutched her like a chastity belt. Only a man more qualified would dare marry an intelligent woman. If she could have had it her way, she would have married a tree. She disliked men and women equally, meat-eaters even more, beef-eaters the most. But in 1948, even misanthropes were married off, if only to increase their tribe.

The task of bringing them together was left to the starving, stooping baba who sat on the banks of the Sangam—the confluence of the Ganges, the Yamuna, and the mythical Saraswati. The sandy banks were forever crowded with devotees wailing, singing, and praying loudly, fooling local frogs into believing that it was mating season the whole year round.

Girija Prasad's ghunghat-wearing mother visited the baba and offered him bananas and a garland of sunshine marigolds. She touched his feet and her worries came tumbling out. Her son was exceptionally intelligent, exceptionally qualified, with an exceptionally bright future. He was exceptionally handsome too. He retained his mother's features and borrowed only his father's chin. A prying devotee asked, "Then what is the problem with your son, behenji?"

"I can't find him a worthy wife!"

"But what is the problem?" the baba asked as well.

Girija Prasad's mother was about to repeat herself. But when she saw the baba smile, she stopped. Holy men were in the habit of speaking in riddles and half-uttered sentences. He ate half a banana in silence, took the garland, and flung it in the air. It swirled several times and landed around the shoulders of a perplexed Chanda Devi, who had been lost in hymns. And that is how the marriage between the man who studied trees and the woman who spoke to them was fixed.

"But, baba"—it was Chanda Devi's father's turn to complain now—"my daughter doesn't speak English; she is a strict vegetarian. And this man you've selected, he has done a doctorate in the English names of plants and . . . and . . . I hear that he has tasted beef!"

The baba peeled another banana. "Child, you see only the present," he said, and handed the peel to the father, to confront metaphysical truths with.

The truth is, it was the islands that brought them together. Chanda Devi dreamed of her escape from a stifling household into the company of trees. For Girija Prasad, it was a little more complicated.

Although the islands gave their name to the surrounding Andaman Sea, that was as compliant as they got. Hens here behaved like pigeons, roosting in mango trees. Airborne butterflies drifted into sleep, floating down like autumn leaves. Ascetic crocodiles meditated on the banks of mangroves. In the Andamans, species lacked names. For the longest time, no one could colonize the islands, for the impenetrable thicket hid more than just natural history. It hid tribes left behind by the original littoral migration across the Indian Ocean. People who preferred to read minds over the obfuscations of language and clothed themselves in nothing but primitive wrath. Who were equipped with only bows and arrows to fend off the syphilis of civilization. Their world was a giant island held together by mammoth creepers, not gravity.

On this knotted thread of islands, Girija Prasad hoped to live the life he dreamed of: a life of solitude. An intrepid bachelor and a simple academic creature, he addressed every woman as sister, sister-in-law, or aunt. He failed to see that the allure of the virgin forests wasn't simply one of the unexplored. It was also the allure of consummation.

Here, his world experienced an earthquake. Tremors ran through his body on a forest excursion when he saw a tree that was actually two trees entwined. A peepul tree had coiled itself around the trunk of an Andaman padauk, sixty feet high. For the first time, he saw two full-fledged trees growing in a coital position, blocking the sky with their embrace. Parasitic orchids found footing in the entanglement. A cancerous growth high up on the trunk obtruded upon his thoughts with its almost human visage, leading him to believe that the trees were staring back at him. Exposed claw-like roots crept upon the ground like pale pythons. He could feel them inch toward him and halt at his toes. Standing there, Girija Prasad felt like an ant, shuffling around, tempted by the impossible.

So later, when his mother began searching for a bride for him, he didn't object. Science had taught him that all creation demanded male and female investment. And the islands seduced him by the beauty of it all.

A month into the monsoons, the four walls and roof that are supposed to keep the couple dry are reduced to a mere symbolic gesture, a warm thought left behind by the British. For the rains have flooded deep into their beings. An invisible wall has caved in, filling them with curiosities and preoccupations from another time.

When Girija Prasad first came here, he arrived believing in half-truths like "no man is an island." It has taken him a year to realize that no island is an island either. It is part of a greater geological pattern that connects all the lands and oceans of the world. Half a mile away from his home, he found a living plant that was previously only seen as a fossil in Madagascar and central Africa.

On the day that would later mark the end of the downpour and his trysts with beefsteak, Girija Prasad spent his office hours researching the ancestor of all continents: Pangaea. A supercontinent, a single entity that splintered into all the pieces of land that exist—a possible explanation for the plant near his house, as the Indian subcontinent broke off from Africa and rammed into Asia. He studied the world map spread out in front of him. "An impossible jigsaw," he said aloud.

The day's efforts were rewarded in his dreams that night. The belly of Latin America slept comfortably in the groove of West Africa. The jigsaw fit so perfectly—Pangaea came alive. What in the daytime had seemed like bits and pieces breaking off and floating now felt like a living being. He was ecstatic to see her stretch her arms wide, from Alaska to the Russian Far East, to see her lift her head and stand on her toes, poles apart. Pangaea, blooming with the grace of a ballerina. He was aroused. But when the downpour suddenly ended, it woke him up. Left to ruminate on half a dream, he wondered why the continents had drifted apart in the first place. Water swept into the cracks, a trickle turned into a stream, streams turned into rivers. And then there was no turning back.

Overnight, the rivers revealed cracks only oceans could fill. It is in water's nature to absorb the void, made jagged with crevices, peaks, and other irregular symmetries. Only a fool would consider the shores of continents, sandbanks, and parched patches the ends to the unbroken surface of water. At best, they are breaks and pauses. Or mindless chatter. Islands are mindless chatter in a meditative ocean.

He peeped from his queen-sized bed and looked at his wife's silhouette. He wondered what the continents were thinking. Perhaps Pangaea dreamed of being a million islands. Perhaps the million islands now dreamed of being one. Like the ridiculously dressed sailors sent forth by mad queens, perhaps the continents also discovered that the end of one's world is another's beginning.

How does it matter, he thought. Even if we had the answers, we'd still be lonely. Like the island he lived on, he was too far into the ocean to change paths. Only god could help him endure the loneliness created by their separate beds. For a brief moment, the atheist wanted to believe in god.

Brought up a devout Hindu, Girija Prasad's atheism wasn't an act of rebellion. He was just stretching his belief system, the way Pangaea stretched her arms. All the languorous ship journeys he'd made between England and India, Calcutta and Port Blair, had changed him. "When you stand on a ship's deck and meditate upon the blue-green, it's the closest you come to staring into infinity," he once wrote to his brother. "Standing alone in the face of infinity, it's not your beliefs but what you have rejected that bothers you."

It was the closest they would get that night. Continents apart in their beliefs, god was the precarious isthmus connecting them.

And, at that moment, the devil was a goat.

"Can you hear it?" she asked. "The bleating." And Girija Prasad lost his erection, the ninety-ninth one in the first two months of their marriage.

I T IS NOT THAT GIRIJA PRASAD kept track of all his lost erections, but the phenomenon had swiftly turned into a symbol of nervousness and unconsummated love, the way roses were a celebration of love itself, of announcing that invisible, intimate thing two people shared.

As an adult, Girija Prasad had never lived with a woman and could only imagine the onslaught brought about by having a lady in one's life. He emptied out half his wardrobe, giving her the higher shelves and hangers. But after observing the wives of other officials, he realized that his wife might also possess a different sari for each occasion, with matching bangles and sandals. Accordingly, he had a new wardrobe constructed in Burma teak. Intoxicated by the beauty of a face he was yet to see, he had a full-length mirror installed on the wardrobe door. There was also the problem of curtains. He didn't have any. Privacy was a female issue and, more important, Girija Prasad didn't have any neighbors to hide from. So he hung his lungis, the only suitable pieces of cloth he possessed, over the windows.

Before setting off on the difficult and hopeful journey most animals make in search of a mate, he thought of her. Although he had prepared his lair in anticipation, how could he show her his gratitude? Shakespeare and the Romantics had taught him that women loved roses, or at least being compared to them, so he ordered a crate of the most beautiful ones he had seen, found on the distant blue hills of Kalimpong. When they arrived a month later, after an arduous journey over mountain passes and sea, only one had survived. He opened the crate to confront the mangled stems and withered buds of what should have been gigantic fuchsia-pink roses. He took it as a sign—an ominous sign. He was determined to nurse the only sapling that survived. He would keep it in his office to protect it from the harsh sun—only the gentle rays of sunrise and sunset for this one—and use a drip to water it. A recent study in the *Oxford Journal of Applied Aesthetics* proved that plants were fond of Western classical music, especially Mozart, so he lugged his gramophone to his office, needling his symbol of love continuously in order to revive it.

When he returned with his wife, Girija Prasad was ecstatic to find a solitary rose bobbing in the air, staring back in shades of pink. The bungalow was finally, truly, good enough for his bride.

Popularly known on the islands as Goodenough Bungalow, Girija Prasad's residence had been constructed in the 1930s to house the visiting Lord Goodenough during one of his voyages. As was the case with most visiting dignitaries, no one really knew the purpose behind his excursions to far-flung corners of the empire, especially to an upcoming penal settlement like the Andaman Islands. After decades of failed attempts and shifting sites, the jail and its headquarters had finally been completed. Two out of three laborers, mostly prisoners, would die—by tribal arrows, centipede bites, crocodile attacks, hanging, torture, and good old homesickness—while the jail was being constructed, and the remainder would perish inside its stone walls. Their deaths would be no loss to the empire.

The isolation of the archipelago would spur the colonizers' imaginations to create elaborate methods of torture, dedicating entire islands to specific methods. It would also inspire Lord Goodenough to do more than just inspect masonry and dance with the natives. A secret desire propelled him to visit the newest acquisitions of the Raj. It was the desire to name. His own name had forced him to develop a sense of humor early, one that he'd waited all his life to unleash on unsuspecting creatures, objects, and lands. From the dull comforts of his ancestral manor, the lord kept a close watch on developments in the Indian Ocean, littered with squiggly islands. Islands, intuitively speaking, made the perfect canvas for practicing the art of nomenclature. The heightened isolation would cause species to become endemic, sooner or later, demanding a unique name. The only exceptions to the rule were the British themselves. They had broken most laws of nature by leaving their island to multiply on others without losing any of their original characteristics—only their marbles.

Lord Goodenough believed that proper nouns ought to marry languages, the same way colonization forced distinct cultures to. When he sailed into an undiscovered bay while eating breakfast on a luxurious ship, he named it Breakfast Bay, and the landing spots around it he named Marmaladeganj, Baconabad, and Crumpetpur.

The lord spent a week in the house in which Girija Prasad now lived. Built on a formidable mountain peak, the location was a popular crossing point for tribals going from west to east, until political prisoners were forced to hack down the thicket to the threatening sound of guns being fired into the air. The bungalow was built on stilts to survive heavy rains and earthquakes. A machan was set up as well, three stories above the ground. It was from this fantastical height that he espied what he would go down in history for spying upon.

Through his binoculars, he saw a group of naked tribals with significantly bigger breasts and buttocks than all other recorded groups. Distracted by their enormous assets, he did not notice the extra thumb they all possessed. Lord Goodenough would spend weeks searching for the perfect name for them, one that was simple yet reflected the glory of those buttocks and breasts.

The name found him much later, on the voyage home, as he sat in the ship's dining room, cutting up his bacon into six equal parts—a morning ritual that he found therapeutic in the boredom of the high seas. Trapped as he was in his childlike attempts at playing god, the name brought him closer to finding god. And that is how the island's most dangerous, six-fingered tribe was christened the Divine Nangas, or the Divine Nakeds as the Oxford Dictionary later translated it.

Five years after Lord Goodenough's visit to the Andamans, an earthquake would mock all its colonial constructions, splitting the very island the British headquarters sat on in half. Goodenough Bungalow too would come down, and the machan would slip off the mountain as if it stood on a banana peel. The earthquake was a harbinger of bigger catastrophes, World War II in particular.

During the war, the Andaman Islands would be the first to claim independence from the British, only to be captured by the Japanese. While the white people ate with forks, knives, and spoons, the short people used only two sticks. This simplicity of thought was reflected in their methods of torture. Why shackle someone when you could twist their legs and hands until they broke? Why hang someone when you could behead them with an efficient swish of the sword? And why force the locals to part with their produce when you could drown them mid-ocean to end food scarcity?

While the British viewed the destroyed bungalow as a pack of cards strewn across the lawns, the Japanese saw in it an opportunity. Like a professional cardsharp dealing out a new round, they would put the house back together and declare it their headquarters, building bunkers on the surrounding slopes. They would introduce the gigantic snail, a native of Malaysia and a high source of protein, to the island. When the British ships surrounded the islands and cut off all their supplies, the snail would become their savior, a ready snack that didn't even need salt. A decade later, decrepit bunkers would be the only reminders left of the snail-eaters. The number of snails would sharply increase, making them one of the most destructive garden pests, second only to the barking deer introduced by the British for game.

When the tide turned in favor of the Allied forces, Lord Goodenough would create a new committee in the House of Lords to bring the islands back into the fold. But the joy of winning World War II would be as short-lived as a sunrise. For the sun had set on the British Empire. The Andaman Islands would now be part of an independent India. He couldn't help but feel betrayed. Despite his position as an influential aristocrat in the biggest colonial power the world had ever

seen, he couldn't go back to the place that had brought him close to
god.

Caught between the starving snail-eaters and the retreating sahibs,
the island remained a no-man's-land for almost two years. In that time,
four drunken Karen youth—a community the British had imported
from Burma to work their farms—declared themselves supreme rulers
of the land and made Goodenough Bungalow their palace. They spent
their evenings on the patio, doodling mustaches over King George's
image on the British rupee and fashioning flags from tablecloths.
Hours would go by as they debated the national symbol of the free islands. Would it be the ferocious one-foot-long centipede, or the tiny,
gentle swiftlet that made her nest out of her own spit? By 1948, the
Forest Department would be the newly founded nation's sole outpost
on the islands, like a frayed flag fluttering on a treacherous snow peak.

When Girija Prasad decided to move into Goodenough Bungalow
without knowing any of this, he did so for the very reason the Divine
Nangas, the British, the Japanese, and the Karens had been drawn to
it. From this peak, you could see the sun glisten on a deceptively blue
sea. It made you feel like the king of the world.

And while Girija Prasad contemplated bringing his bride here,
Lord Goodenough contemplated moving on. He plotted a voyage
across the Pacific Islands instead. As the couple spent the first month
of their marriage cocooned inside the furious layers of a storm, the lord
resumed his journey toward god. Touring in the Pacific, he realized
that all names, no matter how unique or new, were ultimately synonyms for a universal yet elusive truth. The nature of life, the struggle
for survival, it all remained the same, no matter how many fingers a
creature possessed.

Soon after, he died.

S HE MADE ALL THOSE who called the bungalow their home, living and dead alike, nervous. Like the bachelor Girija Prasad, the place was jittery on its stilts. Her presence confused the ghosts of freedom fighters, the perpetually starving snail-eaters, and Lord Goodenough himself, who shuffled between the Pacific, the Andamans, and his ancestral manor, chasing warm currents.

Life as ghosts had been liberating, until Chanda Devi's clairvoyant gaze reminded them of their tattered presence and uncouth ways.

"It is impolite to enter a lady's bedroom," the lord warned the Punjabi mutineer who was in the habit of lolling upon beds like a dog. "And, you, get yourself a new uniform. I gather you died in a blast that blew your brains out and clothes off, but the lady will be shocked if she sees a naked man roaming in her garden, especially one of such diminutive proportions," he ordered the Japanese soldier. But the man didn't understand English. So Lord Goodenough took the liberty of wrapping the British flag around his waist himself.

The soldier was confused. Then he was grateful.

I T IS ONLY AT TEATIME that the two of them are compelled to sit face-to-face. For Chanda Devi runs out of things to serve and must force herself to be still. It is an art the bungalow has mastered. It has endured storms, earthquakes, and wars by simply not budging from the pinhead peak surveying the ocean. Sitting in the garden, watching a hibiscus sun set over an emerald-green archipelago, leaves the couple unsettled. It forces them to swim in the solitary world of thoughts, preoccupations, and visions. Yet it doesn't feel lonely.

"Everything is here for a reason." He tries to break the spell, pointing to the garden. "The lemongrass you brewed the tea with," he says, sipping on his cup, "I planted it to hold the loose soil on the slope, to prevent flash floods in the rains." She smiles. He is encouraged. "The lemon too . . ." he goes on. "To value a lemon is to value the wisdom of all creation. In the jungle, you can squeeze it over leeches that have latched on and they shrivel instantaneously. You can squeeze it over bites and wounds as an antiseptic. And when you are dehydrated, nothing revives you more than an entire lemon, especially the rind."

She is blushing now. Her cheeks are fuchsia pink, like the rosebush in front of them. He is perplexed. How can this talk of lemongrass and lemons transform the mercurial lady into a shy bride? There is an awkward silence, so he repeats himself. "I planted everything in the garden myself. It is all here for a reason."

"Thank you," she blurts out. "The roses are beautiful. Had it not been for your will, they wouldn't have survived."

It is his turn to blush.

It is only much later, as he's whiling away the hours in his office, that he wonders: How did she know? She had arrived after the rose's revival.

———————

Days give birth to a new sky, harboring both the sun and the rains. Under the bright gaze of late morning, a weak drizzle endlessly wets the islands, fomenting mushrooms and fungus wherever it falls, on bark and skin alike. It is one of those days when you find yourself looking up at the sky, hoping to catch a rainbow. The air is heavy, and the heart is heavier still.

When the harsh sun and raindrops pour down like colored sand in the same hourglass, the phenomenon is called the "hour of the wedding." In different folklore, depending upon the tellers' longitude, latitude, dreams, dispositions, and eating patterns, different creatures are forced to tie the knot—foxes, snails, monkeys, ravens, leopards, hyenas, bears, the devil too at times. For hell, like everything else, is built by the domesticated few. The bachelors may keep the world spinning, but it's the married ones that keep it grounded.

On the islands, the hour of the sun and rains belongs to someone else. Far from folkloric unions, it belongs to Goliath centipedes. Creatures one foot long with claws that can snatch men out of reality, taking them back to that moment when they left their mothers' wombs, howling like newborn babies. The centipedes have no interest in settling down, least of all with humans. The islanders know this, for they've been bitten.

Crawling out from their sunless subterranean lairs, all these invertebrates seek is to bask in the sun and feast on the flurry of insects that dance after the first rains. But human beings, obsessed with mythic unions, cannot understand such a simple desire. When someone comes too close, they bite out of fear. And the schism grows deeper. Humans: once bitten, twice shy. Centipedes: shy once, biting twice.

Girija Prasad sits on the steps of his porch, dedicated to the act of sunning his toes. Often, officials find mold growing between their digits when they remove their jungle boots. It is his worst nightmare. A staunch academic, he fears turning into a specimen himself. But this morning, the ritual is an excuse to sit outside and gaze at his wife, busy in the garden.

Chanda Devi is out in the vegetable patch, plucking out the day's menu under the drizzle. She is the picture of grace and balance. As she sits on her haunches, her center of gravity seems to be her voluptuous derriere, which hangs in the air, precarious and unsupported. She holds on to an umbrella between her shoulder and cheek, using both her hands to weave through the growth.

She picks tomatoes with the same intensity with which she combs her hair, serves him his meals, and treads the unpaved inclines of the islands. It makes him nervous. He doubts the strength of his own hand when he offers it to her. He questions the virility of his appetite when he cannot finish the fifth roti she places on his plate.

As he watches her, the picture of all his yearnings takes a blow. Suddenly, Chanda Devi is on the ground. His wife has fallen in the mud. She is shielding herself with the umbrella and is using her hands to fend something off.

He runs toward her, barefoot. He's afraid she's seen a centipede or, even worse, been bitten by one.

"Where is it?" he shouts out. "Don't be afraid, I will kill it!"

"Kill what?" she asks him, baffled. She doesn't need his hand as she gets up and brushes the wet mud from her elbows.

"The centipede!"

"Where?"

"Where did it bite you?" he asks, anxious to get her back into the bungalow and squeeze a lemon on the wound before she faints from the pain.

"But I'm not bitten."

She returns to picking tomatoes, unruffled. Why must he talk about killing all the time, she wonders.

He stands still, shocked. She definitely looked like she was in trouble when she fell. He couldn't have imagined it, for he had been staring at her all the while. He returns to the porch, confused. He gives up on the idea of sunning his toes and heads inside. The ship that arrived this morning has brought him important mail—a journal that carries the map of the hypothetical Pangaea, an apparition he is eager to see.

But the master illusionist, the Indian Postal Department, has been up to its tricks again. Seated at his Andaman padauk table, he finds all the pages of the journal stuck together, bark-like in texture. He picks it up to sniff out the culprit. Someone, it seems, has literally spilled milk over his parcel. A can of condensed milk, to be precise. On a milk-less island like this, such cans are worth their weight in gold. Adamant and armed with a paper knife, Girija Prasad attempts to peel the pages apart one by one, a tedious and delicate task that could swallow up his entire morning.

Even in the inexplicable world of his wife, what happened outside doesn't make sense. Perhaps she is too embarrassed to show him where she was bitten, he suspects. Perhaps it was just an insect, not a centipede. Perhaps the trauma of picking the vegetables, of murdering what could be plants and trees one day, gets to her at times. It isn't something to fret over, he tells himself. Most women are oversensitive, which makes his wife just a faithful representative of her species.

The more he observes the female species from a distance, the more this hypothesis gains credence. As an adolescent growing up in Allahabad, Girija Prasad would keenly note the moments when the audience wept the most during the retellings of Tulsidas's Ramayana. The men were forced to disguise their tears as sneezes and other discomforts, while the women were encouraged to turn their tears into a theatrical display of faith, though he never quite understood the timing of it. While it made sense to feel overwhelmed when Sita was reunited with her husband, Lord Rama, after her gentlemanly abduction by the ten-headed Ravana, or when she was banished from the kingdom by the very same husband only to prove an incidental point to a washerwoman, nothing could explain the timing of their biggest outburst. It would be after the book had been closed and the discourse had ended for the day. The women cried for no rhyme or reason.

Outdoors, Chanda Devi is relieved to be alone again. It was a close call for her. She used her umbrella to fend off the emaciated ghost wrapped in a flag, who has been following her through the patch, pointing out snails and playing dumb charades. Using twigs as chopsticks, he gestures to her to break the shell and gouge the soft flesh out for him, rubbing his belly emphatically. Death, the soldier had hoped, would rescue him from his weeklong hunger. Instead, it stalks him in the afterlife. Though surrounded by fat snails, the Japanese soldier cannot break a single shell and scoop the flesh out with his faint limbs and brittle, glass-like nails. He implores Mrs. Varma to help him. As does the Punjabi mutineer, sitting on the dining table beside her husband, insisting on his right to be served the hot malpuas first, before the "traitor who dresses and talks like the British."

It isn't she who is crazy. The place her husband has brought her to is a madhouse. But she is afraid to share her predicament with him. Men aren't comfortable with their wives interacting with other men, especially naked, desperate strangers.

The time Chanda Devi takes to handpick, wash, chop, cook, and serve the vegetables for lunch along with freshly made rotis is the time Girija Prasad takes to unpeel all the pages of the journal from one another and confront the new hypothesis of his existence: Pangaea, under the influence of milk and salt-laden winds, has turned into a giant multicolored blot that resembles the female genitalia.

Chanda Devi knows she distracts him. It is evident in the way he fidgets in her presence, the way he restlessly shakes his leg. She knows she makes him nervous. She can smell it in his sweat, for she sniffs his laundry daily. His socks smell of hooves. His shirts have a heavy, earthy fragrance, like that of leaves, grass, and fruits crushed into the dark earth by the movement of animals, rains, and wind. Even in his smells, she senses no respite. Despite the pleasantly cool nights, the bedsheets smell of nervous sweat mixed with tropical humidity.

Added to the mix today is a new, lethal fragrance emanating from a single drop of mango that dripped onto his sleeve last evening. A ship from the mainland had arrived with a crate of the finest mangoes for Chanda Devi, ordered by her husband from the opposite end of India, the red soils of the west coast. The entire nation is up in mangoes in the month of June, from the southernmost tip to the edges of the plains. And Girija Prasad is eager to taste the royal variety of mangoes, especially after the rechristening. Previously called Alphonso mangoes after a Portuguese general, the newly elected representatives of the free nation renamed them Shivaji mangoes after the regional hero who valiantly fought off all invaders. Chanda Devi is touched. She washes and wipes the mangoes and displays them in glass bowls like a centerpiece.

She watches him tuck in a napkin like a bib, roll up his sleeves, and work through the mango with a knife and fork, dexterously dividing it into cubes. Still, an errant drop slides down his fork to his little finger and then to his sleeve. Left to herself, she would have bitten the stem off, used her fingers to peel the skin and sunk her teeth into the naked fruit, all without staining her sari. But she feels self-conscious in his presence, so she picks at the cubes her husband has cut instead.

"When I ate it last, it was Alphonso. Now it is Shivaji," he says. "Who would have thought that even mangoes would change their identity after independence."

Chanda Devi, trained in the straightforward ways of Sanskrit literature, is oblivious to the English obsession with wit as a higher form of intellect. She interprets her husband's remark in earnestness.

"We are the children of the soil, but they are the fruit," she says. "They are more sensitive. Changes in government, affronts to their faith, it all affects them deeply, even more than locusts or worms." She senses his surprise. "When I eat Hindu vegetables, fruits, and pulses, I don't feel as bad," she goes on. "Unlike Muslims or Christians, who only live once."

"But all beings must die, irrespective of their religious beliefs," replies Girija Prasad. "Muslim mangoes can hope for resurrection on Judgment Day, just as Christian mangoes can look forward to heaven. In all theological discourses, man can only speculate, never judge.

Only the subject of the study—the formless, genderless almighty—bears that privilege."

By defending Muslim mangoes, Girija Prasad is making a case for himself, especially the dietary habits he was forced to abandon.

Though she sits perfectly composed, a tidal wave of emotions has hit Chanda Devi, refusing to let her surface. He may not see the ghosts that sit beside him, he may not recollect the other times the two have shared a mango in their various lives, but he too sees things she doesn't.

Later in the day, when her husband leaves her alone with the ghosts of Goodenough Bungalow, Chanda Devi closes the door to their bedroom for privacy. Old-fashioned in their ways, the ghosts will never enter a room when the door is closed or peep in when the curtains are drawn.

Alone, she retrieves the mango skin her husband had so carefully peeled half an hour ago. It reminds her of the bright-orange flesh the two had shared, the thoughts they had exchanged. She caresses the skin with her fingers, rubbing it and sniffing it in turn. Fibrous and wet on the inside, smooth, glistening, and fragrant on the outside. Is this what human skin is like? she wonders.

As an eight-year-old child, Chanda Devi once asked her mother, "Ma, how are babies born?" Her mother turned red. She reprimanded her daughter and told her never to repeat the question, least of all to her father.

Lost and alone in her worries, Chanda Devi's mother visited the riverbank baba for guidance. This was a time when he was still considered young, only 102 years old.

"Baba," she said, after offering him fruits and flowers, "my little daughter asks me shocking questions. The other day . . . How can I tell you? I feel embarrassed to even repeat her question." She adjusted her sari to cover her hair and turned around to ensure no one was eavesdropping. "How are children born, she asked me. As a mother, I cannot give up on her. But who will marry her, baba, if she continues to ask such questions?"

The baba was engrossed in arranging the flowers and fruits in order of size. One marigold turned out to be bigger than an apple. It made him smile.

"Beti," he replied, "this is Kali Yuga, the age of evil and immorality. All men and women must do is hold hands to bear children, such is the blinding power of Kama! A time will come"—his eyes widened, and his voice vibrated with the power of prophecy—"when boys and girls will hold hands before marriage. They will hold the hands of many boys and girls in plain sight. For everyone to see!"

Though it didn't really ease her plight, Chanda Devi's mother returned to instruct her children to never, ever hold hands with the opposite sex before marriage.

Exhausted by the enterprise of raising six children, she was secretly relieved by the baba's words. What had rattled her the most about her daughter's question was her own ignorance. She herself didn't know how children were born. But now there was hope. She avoided holding her husband's hands, especially when he lay over her.

Though much has changed in Chanda Devi's life since she asked her mother that question, she hasn't found the answer yet. There is more to it than holding hands, she suspects after three months of marriage. Why else would her entire body erupt into goosebumps in his presence, and not just the skin on her hands?

For her husband, an accomplished scientist, it is the bigger, unresearched questions of the time that trouble him. Though there is no evidence to suggest that *Homo sapiens* have a mating season, there is not enough evidence to suggest its nonexistence either. The lack of clarity on the subject has put him in a spot. The tropical climate heightens the ambiguity. Even tigers, with their clearly designated mating rituals—which begin with a tigress roaring to attract attention and sometimes end with her punching the partner—find the tropical heat confusing. A study showed that, in temperate regions, *Panthera tigris* went into heat seasonally, but in tropical climes they were documented to mate throughout the year.

If only human beings went into heat like other mammals, displaying specific behavior, colors, or sounds to signify readiness, Girija Prasad wouldn't have to spend his days twiddling his thumbs, pontificating on theology and mangoes.

I N THE EXCRUCIATINGLY limited social life of the islands, Mrs. Varma's presence has created a storm. She is a popular subject of speculation in gatherings, much to the relief of the officers and their wives. Before her arrival, the biggest scandal to hit the islands was when the postal department secretary's dog ran away to pursue the doctor's pet mongrel. The secretary accused the doctor of luring away his handsome Labrador in a bid to gain another pet, and the doctor retorted by accusing him of torturing his pet, for why else would he escape? As salacious as the entire episode was, with elements of elopement, torture, the mail, and a standoff, how long could it sustain their gossipy evenings?

Mrs. Varma is a blessing to their bored lives. She perplexes them. She may not have been to Oxford like her husband, but she's far more learned in their eyes. She has studied Sanskrit, the language of the gods, and is an expert on Hindu scripture. Such is her divine prowess, they say, that she can calculate the astrological positions of planets while buying groceries in the market. Once, she even caught an errant vendor overcharging her by two paisa. "The moon in the house of Cancer makes people vulnerable," she was overheard saying, "but that does not mean you can cheat them." Her aura of conviction tempts some to bow down in her presence and exclaim, "The goddess, she's arrived!" But they are afraid she might shoo them away like dogs.

The couple's presence in social events is marked by a dramatic entrance, side by side. She doesn't leave him when he joins a group of men and discusses serious topics like inflation affecting the islands' subsidized rations, or the weather. Nor does he leave her when she exchanges culinary tips with the ladies. In fact, he always has something useful to add, like the scientific name of the herb they speak of and how best to cultivate it.

If Girija Prasad is accused of displaying feminine traits for suggesting alternative ingredients in recipes, his wife is accused of being a man by virtue of her knowledge. Their oddities complement each other. If only they could peer into the Varma household to see how a marriage of equals thrives in a world of unequals. For now they must satisfy themselves with observations from a distance and wonder: When they eat, does she serve him before she sits down, or are they brazen enough to serve themselves? Who decides the menu? It is whispered that Girija Prasad turned vegetarian to please his wife. Though it is Girija Prasad who posts the letters to their families, is it Chanda Devi who writes them? What about the curtains they recently put up? Who decided their pattern and why were they put up? Is it to hide what the soon-to-come-into-effect Indian Constitution will term "unnatural sexual acts"? Born of generations interlocked in the missionary, it seems impossible to imagine sex among equals.

The life of an equal couple in the latitudes of longing and the longitudes of trepidation has hitherto been a rare, undocumented phenomenon—like a whale giving birth in Antarctica or white elephants mating in south Asia.

Both Girija Prasad and Chanda Devi are quick to realize that the phrase "falling in love" is a euphemism. Romance isn't as straightforward as diving into cool waters on a hot afternoon, nor is it instinctive, like learning to walk. It's not a treasure trove of superlatives like Sanskrit poetry or the "sweet sorrow" the Romantics spoke of.

The struggle of an equal couple isn't just the subject of ethnography. It is multidisciplinary. Intimacy and distance operate like the tide—high during the day, peaking at mealtimes. The moon is a cup of tea; it pulls them to the zenith of their interaction. The nights are parched. Unconquered land separates their beds.

Communication among birds relies heavily on unintelligible sounds and tilts of the head, displays of plumage, and actions like dances or formations. So do the exchanges between the Varmas. He clears his throat to signal his entrance into a room. Since he doesn't make demands, she has learned to read his desires by his actions. When he looks at the horizon with vacant eyes, he yearns for tea. If he is famished, his belly emits cub-like growls. If his forehead is wrinkled and he has a mild frown on his face, he is deep in thought. His head droops when he is tired. It tilts to one side when he is sleepy. If he sits or stands upright, his attention is on his surroundings, observing perhaps the call of a bird, a shift in the winds, or an increased smell of chlorophyll. A scientist studying the environment looks very much like an animal on the alert, alive to potential predators and prey. Long visits to the loo imply that the meal she cooked was too spicy for his delicate constitution. Though she has never seen him sketching, she often finds her husband returning from work with a lining of lead in his nails and pencil shavings on his clothes. It is the equivalent of a man coming home whistling away to himself in a cheery mood.

Chanda Devi, her husband has discovered, is a complex study that demands the skills of a botanist, an ornithologist, and an astronomer combined. She moves around in her cotton sari like leaves rustling in the breeze. She breathes as imperceptibly as a tree, sucking in all the room's air and spilling it back, fragrant. Like a bird, her gaze is intense, unblinking. With a single nod, it shifts from the metallic blue eyes of a fly perched on her wrist to an Andaman padauk trunk toppling somewhere on the archipelago, to a pod of dolphins entering the bay. Though Chanda Devi sits in the same room, Girija Prasad often suspects she is constellations apart. He wonders if she finds herself alone in that different time and universe. But he is hopeful. One day, he too will travel across time to reach the end of Chanda Devi's gaze.

There is not a single straight line in her being, a sinuous landscape. At work, he tries to capture her in the margins of office files. Her curves, her eyes, the geometrically precise division of the sari pleats fanning out from her navel, all impossible to sketch. It is in the relentless exercise of sharpening, drawing, erasing, and reworking that Girija Prasad experiences something no sonnet or ode can convey.

———

Only the dead can sympathize with the couple's plight. Ever since her arrival in the month of centipedes, in the season of the monsoon, the ghosts of Goodenough Bungalow have been alive to their predicament. Like the invertebrates, the couple fear their desires may be misunderstood.

It is difficult for the ghosts to just sit and watch. Had the Varmas been in their north Indian homeland instead of the Andamans, the Punjabi mutineer claims, Chanda Devi would have conceived by now. He blames Girija Prasad's sissy ways on his British education, especially the Raj-era clothes he wears. Like a concerned mother-in-law, the mutineer advises Chanda Devi to serve Girija Prasad hot milk with almonds at bedtime to strengthen his libido.

Lord Goodenough has studied love in its extremes, with hindsight afforded only to ghosts. Among the isolated peoples of the Pacific Islands, he'd chanced upon a cannibalistic ritual where the mourning lover consumes the heart of the deceased beloved—the ultimate act of union. But with his own heart, the lord had exercised typical Victorian restraint. He would admire his muse—his brother-in-law—from a distance. He could only caress the engraving on a Grecian urn with his fingertips: the image of an older, bearded man entering an adolescent boy. If only he could, he would tell the young Mrs. Varma that when some men are in love, they doubt themselves. They fear they are not good enough.

As for the Japanese soldier, he prefers to fold his palm into a tunnel and penetrate it with his finger to get Chanda Devi's attention. He is not being lewd. He's just showing her how it's done.

But fear succeeds where desires do not venture, the inhabitants of Goodenough Bungalow are soon to find out.

Chanda Devi sits under a palm tree, searching out her husband in the crowd. He turns around once in a while and acknowledges her with a nod. All the officers and their families have gathered at Sir Mowgli Beach for a Sunday picnic. The men are content with standing at the surf instead of swimming. The children, ever willing to pick shells, pull out crustaceans and proclaim themselves the new kings of the conch. The women chatter away like parrots as they drift with the shifting shade. How they wish they too could frolic in the surf with abandon and look at their toes through the glassy water. But a small matter prevents them: They would rather drown with shame than step out in wet clothes.

Girija Prasad, an awkward social animal, has been trying to extricate himself from the crowds, in vain. He wants to go for a swim with the snorkel and mask he'd acquired in England, but the gear generates talk wherever he goes. A few colleagues even call him Jules Varma.

If only she could join him—for she is a proficient swimmer too. Sitting on a beach full of women who couldn't float to save their lives, Chanda Devi considers her ability a boon from the goddess herself. Chanda Devi had grown up near a temperamental river, and her grandfather had insisted that every child learn how to swim. He'd been conceived in a home the river would eventually swallow and delivered during the seasonal floods, half submerged, so every year he would make all the family members, young and old, male and female, dive off a boat to visit the clan temple that now sat at the river bottom. If they didn't, the river would shift course again. Chanda Devi took her role seriously. She would dive deeper than the others, using the temple's dome to pull herself farther down to the door and hang on to the temple bell, swaying like seaweed.

Lulled by the breeze and incomprehensible chatter, Chanda Devi closes her eyes. Girija Prasad has left the picnic behind to swim to the corals farther out. In her thoughts, she is swimming by his side. Her skin tingles with the cool touch of the ocean while her back heats up under the sun. In her mind, she sinks into the world of corals that her husband swims over. And as he swims over the coral mounds, Girija Prasad is a bachelor again. Lost to the world, nothing prevents him from following the star-backed turtles to the edge of the horizon, with fish nibbling at his toes.

On the shore, Chanda Devi is jolted out of her reverie. A stab of fear pierces through her trance, pulling her by the hair. A premonition has surfaced, like a prehistoric creature swimming out of the abyss. She is quick to sense that Girija Prasad isn't alone in the water.

Amidst the corals, Girija Prasad turns around to identify the cause of the approaching ripples. He's delighted to find Chanda Devi tugging at his leg. He's impressed by her strokes and her courage to swim in a sari. But she's tugging at him with such urgency that he is forced to follow her back. Chanda Devi, he realizes, isn't here to swim along but to take him back to the shore. As they begin to walk in the shallows, she shouts over the waves, "We must go home immediately." The rest of the picnickers are shocked to see her in a wet sari, but Girija Prasad doesn't even notice. He cannot look beyond her panic.

"Did anyone do or say something to upset you?"

"No."

What would it take for you to trust me? he wants to ask. Instead, he says, "You can trust me. I'm your husband."

"I'm your wife," she replies. "You can trust me too. We need to leave this place immediately, that's all I know."

He's resigned to the futility of inquiry, for when she chooses to withdraw, only she can bring herself back. Girija Prasad hands over his snorkeling gear to the head of felling operations to experiment with. The picnic is over for him and his wife.

All through the long drive home, Chanda Devi sits on the edge of her seat, holding on to the door handle, ready to fling it open and jump out at any minute. Restless, shivering, suffering in the cage of her bones. Girija Prasad is disturbed. He wants to stop the car, look into her eyes, hold her hands, and convince her that whatever it is that alarmed her is gone, she is now with him. Like the distance between their beds, the terror in her eyes pierces his heart.

Back at Goodenough Bungalow, Girija Prasad looks at Chanda Devi weaving through the vegetable patch, plucking at nothing in particular—or possibly everything—to avoid his company.

A little while later, a forest ranger brings the news: Soon after they'd left the picnic, a crocodile from a neighboring swamp swam away with the head of felling operations, holding him in its jaws. Intrigued by the clear sight the snorkeling mask offered, the officer had ventured dangerously close to a creek at the end of the beach.

Girija Prasad immediately puts on his boots, loads his rifle, and leaves without a word. The terror in his wife's eyes has flooded into his own.

When Girija Prasad boarded the ship to the islands for the first time, he brought with him eight elephants he had personally selected at an animal fair in Bihar. In Calcutta, they were herded like cattle over the ramp leading to the ship's deck. But in Port Blair, they had to be lifted onto land by crane as the jetty wasn't sturdy enough. Hovering over the harbor, the crane gave way and the first elephant plunged into the inky-blue depths. There was nothing Girija Prasad could do to rescue the drowning elephant. Until his last days, he will never forget the mammoth's face, just as he will never forget the fearful eyes of the crocodile he encounters while searching for his colleague.

The flashlights and torches of the search party ignite the darkness, terrifying the twelve-foot creature that has sought refuge in the mangroves. Blinded by the light, the crocodile hides behind the corpse but doesn't abandon it. Crouching at the helm of the dinghy, Girija Prasad's eyes meet the crocodile's.

With a leg, pelvis, and abdomen missing, the corpse looks barely human, even less like his fellow officer. It terrifies the men on the boat more than the crocodile does. They decide to return the next morning with harpoons and traps.

He reaches home in the indistinguishable hours of night, to find her seated in the darkness of the porch, gaping at the sky. The rains have painted the steps with moss. Girija Prasad slips but keeps his balance. Shaken, he sits on the steps. Black-and-white mosquitoes feast on his flesh and buzz near his ears, setting the tone for the thoughts swimming in his head. The moon hangs exceptionally low, peering through the night, looking him in the eye.

He'd never been so nauseated before, vomiting into the receding tide as soon as the dinghy hit the shore. The stench of a man's entrails, the sight of an intestine trailing in the water like anchor-less rope, were enough to bring forth every undigested morsel and unpalatable fact. When the elephant had plunged into the harbor, it hadn't surfaced even once, as if it had surrendered all its instincts to the ocean. As for the crocodile, Girija Prasad saw fear in its eyes, even as the creature saw fear in his.

"Please don't kill the crocodile." Chanda Devi breaks the silence. "We can't punish beings for acting out their nature when we are the intruders."

Girija Prasad tries to retrieve his last real memory of the now-dead man, but he can't find anything. No last words, no lasting impression, besides the commonplace gesture of saying "thank you" for lending him the snorkeling kit. Nothing makes sense. The bliss of a languorous swim, the panic in his wife's eyes over something yet to happen, the ripped-up corpse of a colleague who happened to swim to his death, a man-eating crocodile.

"Do you also know how we will die?" he asks Chanda Devi.

That night, Chanda Devi draws the curtains and crawls into his queen-sized bed.

GIRIJA PRASAD IS DISILLUSIONED with all the knowledge he's spent his youth collecting and hoarding like an ant preparing for a long winter of reflection. Science, as he knows it, has no space for premonitions. Darwin's proclamation—"survival of the fittest"—has let him down. Had the man traveled to the Andaman Islands instead of the Galapagos, would he have formed a different view? One where sacrifice was as crucial as survival? If Chanda Devi could sense danger in the waters, why did she risk her own life?

Girija Prasad is adamant on creating his own map of the archipelago. It is a portrait created with the same earnestness he pours into sketching his wife. It is his engagement with the memories, curiosities, and emotions the landscape evokes. The map may look like that of the Andamans, but it is equally the artist's portrait of himself.

The blank sheet of paper spread out upon his table is the Indian Ocean. The tip of his pencil is a force of nature, carving islands out of the blue. An equilateral triangle represents Mount Harriet, the highest peak in the South Andamans. A creek separates it from the Middle Andamans. Girija Prasad is certain that this peak is the highest point, for he has witnessed numerous sunsets here and nothing else rises to obstruct his vision. Next to the triangle, he draws a tiny circle filled with purple and orange strokes. In Girija Prasad's personal history, Mount Harriet will always be the place of sunsets. He had read about this obscure peak while studying at school. It was where Lord Mayo, then the Viceroy of India, had been murdered.

The sunset on Mount Harriet had been described in such vivid language in a Christmas periodical that it intrigued Lord Mayo. He made a mental note of it. On a visit to the islands to inspect the notorious penal colony called Kala Pani, or "the dark waters," he made a detour for his evening tea. "Ah, how beautiful! It's the loveliest thing

I've ever seen," he exclaimed as he witnessed the sky turning crimson, gold, and purple. He wished Lady Mayo were with him to enjoy this rare sunset. When he died two hours later, stabbed by a convict hiding in the bushes, he left the world still preoccupied by the vision. It was such a shame: He had no words to describe what he'd experienced.

Only another lord could have sympathized with Lord Mayo's plight. His voyages had shown Goodenough that inventing new names didn't completely solve the English language's crisis of inarticulacy. His mother tongue, he suspected, was incapable of expressing the complexities that lay dormant in a single word. It could not, for instance, describe snow the way the Eskimos did with their dozen synonyms. It did not see the diversity that fell with each flake. Nor had the English language experienced rains in the way the people in the Straits of Malacca had. Their word for heaven meant sublime rain, and hell was rain that drowned. All life was an oscillation between the two. No word—certainly not the innocuous "love"—could be used to describe the all-powerful, all-consuming force Lord Goodenough had encountered in the Pacific. It wasn't mere cannibalism, the ritual of eating the beloved's heart.

In the same way, it wasn't solitude that one experienced on Mount Harriet. In the presence of a purple sun, the nature of solitariness itself seemed to expand until it included everything on the island, all the life forms, mountains, rivers, lagoons, beaches, forests, even the boulder peering down from Mount Harriet's peak into the rain forest's abyss. It was the solitude of an archipelago. Separated from all lands by an ocean bigger than any continent. Sitting under a sky bigger than all the oceans and continents combined.

As vast as the universe, the solitude transformed into the meditations of the universe.

Girija Prasad and Chanda Devi sit on the rock protruding from Mount Harriet's peak and are transformed into a pair of birds, hidden from the ocean by the highest branches of the tallest trees. All they can hear is the babble of other birds and the crashing of water. It is a peculiar feeling. To sit at a height and in a fog evoking the Himalayas. Yet to be lulled by the sound of waves.

"If it wasn't for the waves breathing," says Chanda Devi, "I would have mistaken this for an evening in the mountains."

"It may just be a possibility," replies Girija Prasad. "I read an academic paper that claimed the volcanic islands of Indonesia and the Andaman Sea are a continuation of the Himalayas. We are sitting, so to speak, on mountain peaks arising from the ocean floor. I find it hard to believe, though it is plausible."

She smiles at him. He smiles back.

Sunlight sieves through branches and falls on Chanda Devi, creating geographical patterns on her skin. On her forearm, he can spot a ridge. On her feet, a river. Her throat, a restless waterfall created by her hair. Soon, the sun will move farther west, drowning all the rivers, ridges, mountains, and waterfalls of her body in darkness. The evening will come to an end. The only way to recapture it will be to travel along with the sun, experiencing the sunset again and again in the topographies of different longitudes and latitudes, in the Mongolian steppes, the windy passes of the Hindu Kush, the sand dunes of the Kalahari, the isles of Crete, the Black Forest in Germany, and the Norwegian fjords. By the time Girija Prasad reaches the Scottish Highlands, he is distracted by a memory. In the humidity of the tropics, he is dreaming of snow.

"Have you seen snow?" he asks her.

"No. What is it like?"

It is impossible to describe snow while sitting in the Andamans. The cacophony of the monsoons drowns out the silent drift of snowfall. Girija Prasad's thoughts have returned to a solitary walk that he took in a park covered with snow, as a student in Oxford. A layer of the softest white had transformed the ordinary into a dream. Nothing—not the lake, not the sky, not even the sun—remained untouched. Ice clung like moss to the bare trees. Snow hung heavy on the leaves that remained; his footsteps fell heavy on the snow. The crisp air scraped his nostrils and chafed his throat. Perched on the highest peak of an archipelago, pinned right between the Equator and the Tropic of Cancer, Girija Prasad yearns for the impossible. He yearns for a similar sunset in a landscape of snow.

"I cannot describe snow to you," he tells her. "We tropical creatures are incapable of grasping its beauty, even in our imagination. But I can show you the sun setting over snow. We could visit Kashmir in winter."

"These islands," she says. "We may never want to leave."

"In that case, another lifetime."

As easy a target for ridicule as it may be to Girija Prasad, he must admit that the theory of rebirth has a lyrical appeal—it might allow him to enjoy another sunset in another land with his wife.

She blushes. So does he. Girija Prasad reaches out for her hand.

Chanda Devi entwines her fingers with his.

The entire island rises up to the occasion. The birds, insects, trees, waves, and the setting sun all play their part in a larger symphony, orchestrated by the fingers in communion.

Girija Prasad's love affair with snow could have been a long and fulfilling one, had it not been for his academic interest in rain forests. Sensing its fleeting presence in his life, he spent every opportunity observing its fragile existence and delicate temperament, until his fingers turned numb and icicles formed on his lashes.

Reminded of snow, Girija Prasad finds it hard to sleep that night. He spends his hours in bed dredging all the snow from his memory and placing it on the island where he sleeps. In his reverie, this verdant land is blinded by snowfall.

Canopies droop, spilling the snow onto the sticky tropical soil. Insects have turned into fossils trapped in ice. Unable to break through, earthworms, centipedes, and snakes are forced into hibernation. The cold-blooded crocodiles find it difficult to scramble over the icy creeks, skidding sideways like crabs. Muffled by the cold, the cuckoos sing sore-throated songs. Girija Prasad is tempted to paint the brightly colored parrots and kingfishers a radiant shade of white, for the whole world is white on a snowy day. The night sky glows in its reflection. The moon and stars pale in comparison. Encouraged by the frozen expanse, pigeons stroll on ponds and streams, laying eggs wherever they please. The rain forest shrivels. Leaves and fruits wither instantaneously. The beach is a mosaic of ice, sand, and snow. Turquoise waves pound chunks of ice onto the shore. The naked tribes are forced to retreat to the warmth of caves and fires. In their refusal to desecrate their bodies with clothes is obstinate belief. The snow will melt as mysteriously as it appeared. Nothing, not even the reveries of an insomniac, can last on the islands.

Girija Prasad's own home, Goodenough Bungalow, resembles a cottage in the Alps. It sits comfortably on stilts over a bed of snow. A makeshift fireplace warms the potted ferns and flowers. For a change, the water flowing from the drainpipes hangs frozen, midair, diminishing the patter of the monsoons to the slow drip of melting ice. His bed remains the only warm spot on the islands. Girija Prasad proceeds to cover his sleeping wife with snow. Her skin turns pink, bursting into gooseflesh. Her navel sinks into her belly as her chest heaves with the shock.

When Chanda Devi wakes up the next morning, her throat is sore and her nose clogged. She is annoyed with her husband. "The next time you dream of snow," she tells him, "dream of a blanket too."

Nine years after Girija Prasad stayed awake to adorn the islands and his bride with snow, he will find himself sinking into the white magic once again, this time as a father. Strolling with his daughter on a beach, he will hold her hand to prevent her from running into the tide, for she is as unpredictable as her mother.

"Where did you find me, Papa?" she will ask, mildly annoyed by his grip. "Why did you bring me home?"

Girija Prasad will weave a story from the embers of twilight to pacify her. "It was a beach just like this, an evening just like this, when your mother and I came across an empty bottle, half buried in the sand. We opened it to find a note inside: 'Please put all the ingredients of your dreams in this bottle and shake vigorously.' And so we did. Using a prism, I trapped sunlight in the bottle. I closed it with a cork and shook it vigorously for hours. Then your mother opened it. She took a deep breath and exhaled into the bottle. That was your first breath." For the ingredients, Girija Prasad will concoct a fantastical list to arrest her wandering imagination: golden sands from the dunes of Rajasthan and white sands from Havelock Island; shreds from the swiftlet's nest and petals of a fuchsia-pink rose; a piece of bark from the oldest padauk tree on the islands; ash blessed by the riverbank baba; a crocodile's tooth, an elephant's eyelash; and drops of the monsoon mingled with Himalayan snow.

When the story ends, the father and daughter will walk in silence. The effort she puts into digesting the story will be palpable. He will sense his daughter's thoughts rush all over the place, tossing in the tide's foam, sinking into the uneven sands, wandering lost among the rocks that mark the beginning of the jungle.

"What is the difference between melted snow and raindrops?" she will ask. "Papa, what does snow look like?"

I F CHANDA DEVI CAN SEE GHOSTS, transform her beef-eating husband into a vegetarian, and predict crocodile attacks, she can definitely speak to god, the islanders believe. Rumor has it that Girija Prasad is married to a god-woman who controls crocodiles and elephants the way she controls her husband.

People arrive at her doorstep with fruits and garlands as offerings. A mother-in-law brings in her pregnant daughter-in-law. After the disappointment of eight granddaughters, she appeals to Chanda Devi to use her divine powers to give her a *kul deepak,* a "torch-bearing male," to rescue her lineage.

Chanda Devi examines the old lady from chin to toe and from ear to ear.

"I'm not the one who is pregnant," the mother-in-law wants to say. "I'm not the problem." But she doesn't. No one can risk the ire of god-people.

"The Devi has blessed you with all her nine avatars," Chanda Devi says. "Should you ill-treat any of them, her wrath will know no bounds."

"But why must my son work to feed a son-less family, especially this pregnant cow?"

"You can think of the answer in your next life, when you are born as an earthworm. All earthworms are eunuchs. Male, female, it makes no difference to their lives. That's why the goddess makes all those who torture women earthworms in their next life."

That night, it is the mother-in-law who cooks dinner for a change. She serves all her granddaughters and washes their feet as penance. She asks them for forgiveness. She had decided to do so when she stepped out of Chanda Devi's porch to find an earthworm on the slippers she'd left outside, shriveled black under the sun.

The Forest Department also seeks out Chanda Devi, to cure an elephant who has trampled two mahouts in three weeks. Though the elephant is a raving lunatic, it is easier to replace mahouts than a productive animal. Left to deal with a psychotic pachyderm, Girija Prasad's juniors turn to his wife for guidance.

"I only speak to free spirits," Chanda Devi announces before unshackling the elephant, frightening the officials further. She spends the afternoon stroking the animal's trunk and belly, feeding her bananas, and giving her buckets of water to drink. On her way out, she tells them that the first mahout had been drunk on country liquor and that the second one had stubbed out a bidi on the elephant's foot. "If there is a next time, your shackles won't be able to stop her."

No one drinks or smokes at work anymore. Girija Prasad laughs in disbelief at this new development. His wife has achieved what he couldn't in a year.

Chanda Devi finds her schedule busier than her husband's. In the morning she is pacifying the souls of men who drowned on Mollycoddle Beach. In the afternoon she is inaugurating a mithai shop. And amidst all this, she is accosted by the gravest appeal of them all.

The administrators of the islands fear that errant ghosts of British officers, generals, hangmen, clergy—in short, all the villains in the soap opera of colonization—may have cast evil spells on their project of building a new nation. That is the reason why everything is going wrong: Files get mysteriously misplaced and bad decisions are implemented despite the high caliber of officers (men who find it difficult to work for more than four hours without taking a nap). They want her to visit Ross Island, the erstwhile British headquarters, and chain the evil-eyed, curse-uttering, cake-eating, cigar-smoking ghosts to the sinking island.

Life at Goodenough Bungalow has trained Chanda Devi in the art of turning a blind eye to ghosts of all nationalities, just like Girija Prasad has learned to turn a blind eye to his wife's eccentric behavior. But she cannot refuse the administrators' request. It may cast a shadow on her patriotism.

Ross Island is a tiny island, replete with swimming pools, ponds, bakeries, movie halls for silent films, ballrooms, and churches. It even had a marketplace where the memsahibs could buy native fruits alongside Marmite and fresh scones.

As with most ideal plans, this one too fell apart. The earthquake that destroyed Lord Goodenough's inspection bungalow in Port Blair also cracked Ross Island into two. Like an iceberg, the majority of the island sank, tilting the rest toward oblivion. When the Japanese bombed it in World War II, it was for the sheer pleasure of aiming accurately at a speck, as the place was ravaged already.

It is on this bombed-out speck that Chanda Devi confronts some of the palest ghosts of her life, waltzing unhindered through their daily rituals. Unlike the intrusive ghosts of Goodenough Bungalow, the ones here are too proud to acknowledge her presence, giving her the luxury of watching them, wide-eyed, for hours. It isn't the passage of time that they document but the exact opposite. They have practiced their routine for decades, defying events like death and India's independence. They have even learned to ignore the ghosts of the present—the living.

An elaborately dressed couple catches her eye. The woman, in a velvet gown and lace gloves, holds a parasol in one hand and her husband's arm with the other. The man is covered from head to toe in befitting finery, complemented by a waxed mustache. "In this heat!" Chanda Devi exclaims. The couple climbs up a spiral staircase, flowing from one level to another with an ease that comes from several lives spent in practice. But the staircase leads nowhere. It broke off with the island. The banquet the couple had dressed to attend now lies upon the seafloor. Chanda Devi stands agape as the couple steps off the cliff and floats down into the sea, like leaves caught in a breeze. She sees them swim back to the shore and walk out in clothes as dry as their expressions.

In the garden by the miniature lake, Chanda Devi sees a man wipe imaginary dust off a chair. He then stands on it and ties a noose to a tree branch above. He slides his head in and knocks down the chair with his feet. Even though Chanda Devi knows that he is a ghost, the sight of his body swinging from the rope sends a shiver up her spine. Gradually, his eyelids ease, his mouth closes, and the wrinkles on his forehead vanish. After a while, he squeezes his head out of the noose and falls down like a clumsy monkey. He gets up, dusts his pants, and sets the chair straight. He wipes the seat once again, ties the noose once again, and hangs himself once again. Dying, it seems, is a hobby for some.

While other souls moved on to new identities and continents, these souls clung on to rituals and moments like kids hanging on to their lollipops. They had experienced the futility of change. Lives could change, but their preoccupations would remain the same.

Some had found the loneliness of a hundred births in just one.

When she comes back home, Chanda Devi inspects herself in the mirror. She pulls the skin below her eyes down with her fingertips. The viscous pink around her eyes is comforting. She pinches her flesh hard. She is relieved to find that it leaves red bruises. These are all signs of life.

Later that night, Girija Prasad is dreaming of ostrich-sized peacocks running in a desert of sand and gold when, suddenly, huge hands appear from the sky and grab one of them. He wakes up, startled, only to find Chanda Devi hugging him in her sleep with all her strength. He lies awake, trying to read the tremors on her face. He wonders what they may be, the visions her eyelids hold back.

Chanda Devi lives in a painting, and each day the artist adds more white to her complexion. The rhythm in her womb is new to her. It follows the father's heartbeat. Like the father, it yearns for something heavier and fleshier than the leafy fare she consumes. Ever growing, ever demanding. She cannot keep up. She can only look at the tattered Japanese ghost and empathize. She is perpetually hungry.

There is only one doctor in Port Blair, a senior English gentleman who survived the World War and independence and continued to live here for a very simple reason: He was the only doctor on the islands. On his insistence, the Japanese had sanitized parts of Cellular Jail and turned it into a makeshift hospital. On his insistence, the Forest Department is bringing a veterinarian from the mainland, since he cannot cope with the treatment of both humans and elephants.

The doctor gives Chanda Devi's paleness a name: anemia. "The water in the islands reduces the iron content of the blood somehow," he tells her husband. "That is how most of the women and children perished on Ross Island, even some of the men. They died of a mysterious condition called death by paleness, later shortened into 'pale death' for telegrams. It was just good old anemia."

"My wife didn't suffer from anemia earlier. She's enjoyed good health since she arrived."

"The pregnancy has made her vulnerable."

The paleness forces Chanda Devi to hold the armrest when she gets up. She often feels dizzy. Girija Prasad doesn't allow her to cook anymore and assists her in her baths. He is afraid to leave her alone, so he works from home.

Though he should be overjoyed, he is afraid. The only one he can look to for assurance is the one he is most concerned about.

"What do you see when you black out?" he asks Chanda Devi.

"I see red. Flesh red. When you close your eyes under the strong sun, your eyelids look like they're on fire. I see something similar."

The doctor suggests she eat red meat and chicken soup, but even Girija Prasad will not entertain the suggestion. Instead, he picks tomatoes, spinach, and beetroot to make fresh juice for her twice a day. He feeds her a spoonful of black sesame seeds. There is nothing in nature that nature itself cannot cure, he believes.

By her fourth month, she is less pale, observes Girija Prasad, who maintains a daily chart of her complexion, dizziness, nausea, weight, and moods. She manages to squat over the Indian-style toilet without fainting, but her mood is still somber.

"This complexion suits you." He tries to cheer her up. "I could put in a request with the goddess to keep it this way, but I'm afraid I may not be entertained. My carnivorous past will not go down well with Hindu deities."

Chanda Devi smiles. He means it in jest, but he means it nonetheless. Her husband, she can see, is in anguish. He wants to pray, but he doesn't have faith.

She sits on the bamboo chair with her legs slightly apart to make space for her belly. Though she is firmly seated, with her back against the cushion and her elbows on the armrests, nothing stops the dizziness. The pull of the earth is stronger than ever. It compels her to leave everything aside and lie down until she loses consciousness. She has begun to have a peculiar nightmare: She is sprouting roots as she sits in the garden, unable to extricate herself from the soil.

She wants to respond to Girija Prasad's compliment. She wants to be witty enough to bring a smile to his face and faith to his heart. But words have leaked out of her thoughts, like the energy that bleeds out from her womb onto the ground. As she sits, she sinks farther. Her eyes well up even as she smiles.

Girija Prasad plucks out a handkerchief, ironed and bleached, from his pocket. He leans forward and dabs away her tears. He takes another look. Her eyes have welled up again. He dabs at them once more. This time, the tears are large enough to leave a wet patch on the cloth. So he uses another corner. He wipes his wife's tears with all the corners of his handkerchief until there are none left and her eyelashes are dry and stiff like hay. He waits. He watches. Only after Chanda Devi has regained her composure does he fold his handkerchief three times and place it back in his pocket. He leaves the room to pick vegetables for her evening glass of juice.

To extract an entire beetroot without harming the plants growing in its proximity or ripping the stem off is always a challenge. One must use a sickle to unearth the root before using force. A meticulous and patient gardener, Girija Prasad is immersed in the enterprise. Yet he can't help but dislike the uncertainty descending upon him this evening. Seeking solitude, only to find in it the value of companionship. Sowing seeds, only to uproot. The purpose of life, Girija Prasad had hypothesized early on, was to be purposeful. But if Girija Prasad cannot claim confidence in his role as a husband, how will he be as a father?

Fatherhood, even as he stands at its brink, still seems as distant, formless, and incomprehensible as the moon on an early winter's evening. It exists light-years away in a cosmic space, where books, academia, or natural history cannot go, only raw strokes drawn in charcoal.

Girija Prasad has begun to draw imaginary trees. Their trunks have a waist-like slenderness, bulging at the knots. Branches as delicate as human fingers soar in all directions, some joining the land to sprout again, others reining in the clouds. All sorts of fruits and flowers can be found on a single tree, from daffodils and lotuses to orchids, from apples and watermelons to the humble coconut. Anything is possible, because everything is.

When Girija Prasad holds his son, he cannot discern his features. The head is the biggest part, followed by the slightly bloated belly. His eyes are slits, stitched together. As for the hands and feet, they are minuscule. Girija Prasad has seen bigger sepals on flowers. Both the feet fit in his palm.

His son is a shriveled, pale raisin with the skin of an aged being. One so ancient, it is difficult to ascertain whether he is at the beginning or the end of his life. Girija Prasad holds his son's miniature hand in his own.

He was alone with Chanda Devi when her waters broke, five and a half months into her pregnancy. He was alarmed to find a spot of blood on the mattress. The spot grew into a patch in front of him. The patch spread farther. Soon, the bed was drenched with blood. He picked his wife up and placed her in a tub of lukewarm water. He held her hand throughout, even after the doctor arrived. When it had all ended, when there was no doubt that their fragile dream had evaporated, he left her in the doctor's care. He threw the bedsheet and mattress away. He scrubbed off the blood that had seeped through to stain the wooden frame. He brought her back to a clean bed. Once she had closed her eyes and entered a world where she ventured alone, Girija Prasad picked up the infant and cradled him.

He holds his son's hand. He counts all his fingers and toes. All twenty of them. He seems to have developed beautifully.

"Miscarriages are common. As common as childbirths in these islands," the doctor tells him. "But the blood loss, if not addressed, could further her weakness."

Girija Prasad makes vegetable juice for his wife, like on any other day. He leaves her semiconscious to drive up to Mount Harriet with his son in his lap. He fears that once Chanda Devi wakes up, he will be forced to give his child a traditional Hindu cremation. As his father, it will fall upon him to set his fragile body on fire.

Alone, he uses his hands to dig a small pit near the rock where they first held hands. He buries his son in a womb of soft, wet earth—the kind one strives to sow seeds in. He covers him with a blanket of soil.

But he cannot bring himself to cover his face. What if he opens his eyes and lets out a cry, choking on the soil?

Girija Prasad's shirt is drenched with tears. Tears wept for everyone and everything he has ever loved and will love.

AFTER THE MISCARRIAGE, Girija Prasad doesn't return to work. Instead, he brings his office desk into his bedroom. Chanda Devi is yet to regain her strength. Her hair falls like autumn leaves. She cannot bathe without tiring herself out. She slips in and out of consciousness, stumbling into shadows that are both inviting and intimidating.

Even the ghosts are concerned about her health. Lord Goodenough, her English mother-in-law, sits by her bed, fanning her on stuffy afternoons, protecting her from mosquitoes. "Abstinence is advisable" is all the advice he can muster.

The ghost of the Punjabi revolutionary is busy being a father-in-law to Girija Prasad, indifferent to his indifference toward ghosts. "Only four of my seven survived," the ghost lectures him. "The rest of them didn't make it to adulthood. One was bitten by a scorpion when he was an infant; another died of high fever. My favorite daughter got lost in the Kumbh Mela. I prayed to god to take my mother and return my daughter. But he didn't answer my prayers, so I stopped going to the holy fair. More people get lost there than find god."

Focused on the file he is reading, Girija Prasad has nothing to say.

"Son, I know that you support the British. Look at you—you dress like a jailor. But deep down you are an Indian. Listen to your forefathers. As a man, you cannot give up. The only way to ensure your legacy is to keep producing children. If one wife tires, find another. Don't just sit on your family jewels. Polish them and put them to use!"

The room feels claustrophobic. Girija Prasad gets up to open the windows. He notices that Chanda Devi is awake and sits beside her.

Even in her weak state, she can see that her husband is as fragile as a porcelain doll with cracks running through it. Sometimes, when he reads a newspaper, his fingers tremble in the silence of his heavy breaths. Often, she notices a wet patch on his pillow in the morning. She plays with his fingers. Her husband's flesh is soft, his fingers podgy like a child's. She wonders if her son had them too, but she cannot recollect his hands.

"Whom did he look like?" she asks Girija Prasad.

"You," he replies.

Girija Prasad uses his handkerchief to wipe her tears. He doesn't go back to work for the rest of the day.

That evening, Chanda Devi makes an effort to dress up. She discards the nightgown for a sari and styles her hair with jasmine oil. She enters the kitchen after two months. They share a pot of tea in silence. By the end of it, both have reached the same conclusion. Neither can make it alone.

A month later, Girija Prasad takes his wife along on an official tour. The couple set sail from their home in the South Andamans to the neighboring group of islands, the Middle Andamans. It is where independent India will construct its first town from scratch, bringing development to the jungles. If the British could get the Burmese to build ramshackle villages on those islands, surely the new government can make a town.

As simple as the thought is, the plan is even simpler. The Indian government has leased the timber-rich neighboring jungles to a businessman from Calcutta to exploit unconditionally. All they want in return is a township. Like all great visionaries, the fat businessman names the timber township after his muse, his even fatter wife, Savitri. He calls it Savitri Nagar.

Girija Prasad and Chanda Devi must spend an entire day trailing the shores on his official boat, the *Ocean Whore*. They must cross the turbulent currents where Division Creek meets the sea and avoid all encounters with the tribes on the Sea of Dying to reach Savitri Nagar, the sole harbor in the Middle Andamans.

The *Ocean Whore* is a sturdy boat with a living room, bedroom, office space, kitchen, room for the captain, and enameled decks from which to admire the flying fish, dolphins, and turtles. It is Girija Prasad's headquarters at sea. When exploring distant, desolate settlements, the *Ocean Whore* is the only place he can hold meetings accompanied by milky tea—the fundamental feature of all government offices.

Though they will arrive at Savitri Nagar by morning, Girija Prasad finds it difficult to stay in bed. The waves keep him tossing and turning, reminding him of a loss that he never forgot to begin with. He gives up on sleep and decides to complete his correspondence instead.

He sits at his desk at sea, waiting for the words to appear. "Respected brother," he begins. "I write to give you terrible news."

Or is it injustice? Is it tragic? "Your nephew was stillborn in your bhabhi's fifth month of pregnancy. She is very weak now, not the vibrant lady you may remember her as."

Girija Prasad can't go on. His tears have turned the letter into blotting paper. So he crumples it and begins on a new page.

"My dear brother," he writes. "I buried your nephew in a garden. While my mind may have accepted his death, my imagination still grapples with the nightmare. I lie awake in fear. What if he opened his eyes after I covered him with soil? What if his lungs decided to inhale twelve hours later but choked on the soil instead? What if I buried him alive? Was I responsible for his death?"

Girija Prasad begins to howl. Playing man of the house is an act that has broken him down. He heaves, he sobs, he swallows his sobs. He cannot stop crying. He doesn't want to wipe the tears. As he crumples the letter and throws it on the floor, he sees her shadow. She stands at the doorway, with the dawn behind her.

Though she has seen him cry before, she has always pretended not to notice. Girija Prasad, like all respectable men, isn't supposed to cry—in public or in private. He is supposed to hold back his tears. He removes his handkerchief to wipe his face, his neck, his collar. He clears his throat.

"I couldn't sleep, so I tried completing my correspondence. I believe the post leaves Savitri Nagar only on Mondays, two hours after we reach it."

Chanda Devi nods. Her husband, like the ghosts that live with them, is at his weakest moment. There is no point reasoning with such people. She has learned this lesson time and again.

According to the British, a creek separates the South Andamans from the Middle Andamans. Hence, they named it Division Creek. Its longer, horizontal arm is called Long Division Creek, and the shorter bit that turns south, Short Division Creek.

Had they lived their lives naked, draped in nothing but colors of the earth, interacting with their surroundings in the same way they interacted with their lovers, they would have known that the Middle Andamans are a world apart from the South Andamans. The creek, like a sinuous snake, just happens to sleep between the two.

The soil of the Middle Andamans is some of the best in the Indian Ocean. It is an enlightened soil. It is indifferent to the cycle of life and death. When trees or plants are satisfied with the lives they have led on the island, they willingly fall down, shedding leaves as nourishment for new growth. The air is light, free of regrets and loneliness. Here, hens fly as high as crows do on the mainland. They build their nests on mango tree branches. Some even compete with eagles in their flight, clucking in desperation to fly higher, faster. Easily flustered, they lay eggs mid-flight or perched on branches. Hens here are birds of ambition, not mere poultry.

The neighboring kingdom of Indonesia is a civilization that thrives and feeds at the feet of its imposing, short-tempered rulers: the volcanoes. Even an ordinary grumble will force the islanders to bow down to their will and whims. In the Middle Andamans, though, the fury of the volcanoes is reduced to a whimper. They lie hidden in the jungle, overshadowed by anthills and bushes. Destiny has given them a raw deal. While their cousins rule like gods, instilling fear, faith, and everything in between, these are almost cute. They are baby volcanoes, rising no higher than a foot—proof that even the creator loses interest in tasks midway.

For the longest time, the Andaman Islands had been on the fringes of the empire. When the British did arrive, they couldn't be expected to work with the natives—they didn't speak English (yet), and anthropology departments in England didn't teach courses on obscure littoral languages (yet). But like a kleptomaniac left unsupervised in a jewelry shop, the urge to take things over was too strong to resist.

Soon, posters went up in all corners of the Raj, advertising free land waiting to be given to any community that cared to show up. An enterprising pastor, a Karen from Burma, rose to the challenge. Stifled by the hierarchy of organized religion, yearning to be left alone with his parish, he jumped at the opportunity. The establishment was impressed. "Some uncivilized people do live on the islands," an officer told him. "We hope the pastor views it as an opportunity to increase his flock."

Instead of saving their souls, the pastor condemned the tribals to eventual annihilation at the hands of the new colonizers, the Indians, by naming them the Dying Race. His first glimpse of the living tribe, ironically, was the dead bodies floating on canoes with all their belongings. It was a ritual, he soon realized, leaving old and injured people to die on canoes with limited rations. So he named the surrounding sea the Sea of Dying, as a direct warning to avoid it.

Had the pastor been an aristocrat in a colonial empire, perhaps he too would have set sail to other parts to hone his natural flair for naming, but he wasn't. Hidden from the church's controlling gaze, he used his creativity to innovate beliefs instead. In the first four months after the migration, his flock had shrunk by half, consumed by the struggle to cut down the thicket, construct huts, farm, hunt, and make babies.

To boost their morale, he created a new tenet that was mentioned in a secret bible only he possessed. "Thy soul doth not perish," he would repeat each time someone was killed or eaten by an animal. "It liveth on in the devourer." That is how a Karen villager came to have a shark for a brother-in-law. It was also how malevolent creatures became benevolent ones, the pastor believed. By feeding them relatives, they would turn into relatives. That was how a farmer became the father of a centipede. The community's faith in its pastor didn't waver, even after a woman who believed a certain crocodile to be her mother was devoured by it when she went to give her offerings. And that was how an old man came to have the same crocodile for his wife and daughter, and a younger man for his wife and mother-in-law.

"Sickness is a product of worry," the pastor would announce during the funeral when someone had died of disease. "This poor soul was so worried about the completion of the village, it got the better of her. Let her sacrifice not go in vain." The villages were constructed, but two out of three villagers perished in their construction. Much like the prisoners who died building the Cellular Jail in the south.

It would take the Karens five years to build three makeshift villages. By the end, the pastor would be so spent, he couldn't be bothered about proper names. Two of the villages would go on using their site names, Rotten Eggs and Spit Nest. For the third and final village, the pastor decided to have an inauguration at which no one showed up except for his wife and children. "The guests never came," he sighed as he cracked the customary coconut to baptize the site. The lament stuck. The village would be called The Guests Never Came.

Months after the parish had settled in and begun to indulge in the luxury of a normal village life, the pastor's wife confronted him as they slept outside on hammocks, surrounded by stars and mosquitoes.

"You're a stubborn man," she said. "You saw your parish die, but you did not return to Burma."

"I'm a man in love."

"You're a fool. A stubborn fool."

The next day, the pastor took his wife for a walk on a winding trail under an intricate canopy of leaves and branches, where even the sun couldn't impose its will. Between the sounds of birds arguing and footsteps crushing leaves, the pastor's wife could hear another sound.

She could hear gentle raindrops falling on the maze of leaves above, yet there was no water falling down, nor was it raining on the island. The sky was an empty blue.

"How can it be?" she asked him. "Am I hearing right?"

"This place has magic," the pastor replied, and pulled her closer. Among the villagers, the trail came to be known as the Path of Eternal Rain.

Girija Prasad reaches Savitri Nagar only to find that it doesn't exist. Either that, or Savitri Nagar is the only town in India that consists of a work shed, a guesthouse, a post office, and a single road connecting it to three villages—and still makes the prime minister's eyes moist with pride. It may make Girija Prasad livid, but the Middle Andamans have also given him reasons to be relieved.

The air here suits Chanda Devi. She is less pale now. Never before has she seen hens fly higher than crows, or elephants dance on two legs like they do in the circus. She's never seen a man speak to a centipede with fatherly tenderness. Papayas taste like chikoos here, and lotuses smell like magnolias. Chanda Devi herself smells different. Her floral perspiration is swallowed by his earthy smells. It is an eternal cause of arousal, especially when she happens to catch elephants or dogs mating from the corner of her eye.

Like any man proud to be in love, Girija Prasad wants to introduce his wife to his closest friends, the ones who fill him with fondness and curiosity, who compel him to spend a lifetime understanding their behavior.

He begins with the thirty-one caves hidden on a cliff, harboring entire settlements of swifts that build nests from their own spit. In the contained world of the archipelago, their colonies remind him of a bustling metropolis: noisy, filthy, built on the sweat, toil, and spit of its inhabitants. All for unscrupulous humans to crawl into, to steal and profit from. The swifts' nests are coveted ingredients in oriental soups. They will push these birds toward extinction.

Girija Prasad also takes Chanda Devi for a walk along the jungle path locally known as the Path of Eternal Rain, one where the constant sound of raindrops can send your heart racing like the monsoon winds.

"Tell me this is an illusion too," says Chanda Devi. "Tell me that the movement of lands and continents leaves behind memories of raindrops, even when the rains themselves have moved on."

Girija Prasad laughs, though he is secretly impressed. That rains can turn into fossils, ones that can only be heard not seen, is an interesting thought. It is worth dreaming about.

"I am sorry to disappoint you," he replies. "The answer lies not in continental shifts but the opposite. Something humble and ordinary. The sound you mistake for gentle rain is the sound of a thousand caterpillars eating and defecating at the same time, tiny drops of excrement falling on the leaves below."

He shows her a fallen leaf as evidence. It is perforated with holes so small they look like pores and is covered in black flecks. They laugh.

The couple walks through a pathless thicket to reach a patch of miniature mud volcanoes hidden among anthills and trees.

"Had they been bigger, they could have created islands of their own," Girija Prasad tells her. "This way, they take me back in time. They make me feel powerful and gigantic. Like a dinosaur."

He proceeds to stomp around like one, peering into craters that spout bubbles and mud. He is *T. Andamanus,* the most powerful creature to have walked on the islands, bearing a tail so long it could connect two islands during low tide. His teeth will go down in prehistory as saws so strong they can snap the trunk of an Andaman padauk with a single bite. For, despite all its strength, the creature is herbivorous. As the only ferocious herbivore of its time, *T. Andamanus* remains a mystery among paleontologists. How are they to know that the evolution of reptiles, not just humans, depends as much on their mate as on climate and resources.

Girija Prasad looks around, but Chanda Devi has disappeared. He eventually finds her in the surrounding jungle, mesmerized by the sight of a withering palm.

"This variety of palm is documented to flower only once in its lifetime, after which it dies. The yellowing leaves show that the process of death has set in," he tells her.

Chanda Devi is disturbed. "Why?" she asks.

"Some plants have evolved from expending excessive energy and creating numerous seeds with a lower chance of survival to reproducing only once—but ensuring that the seeds have the greatest chance."

"Who are we to take our own lives? How can we?"

"Western intelligence, if it looked at this anthropomorphically, would call it suicide. But you know better than I that evolved souls in our culture willingly leave their bodies when they go into samadhi. I am no authority on morality or spiritualism. But in the world of plants"—Girija Prasad pauses to think—"it cannot be labeled as either. The palm tree has diverted all its growth enzymes and nutrition to the seeds. This saps life away from the tree once it flowers. That is all there is to it. One cannot judge the natural world by human laws."

Girija Prasad's night is punctuated by dreams. It begins early on, when his snoring is so loud it enters his sleep. The unregistered glow that marks the start of a day takes him back to the beginning of time.

He is a prehistoric reptilian that roams around in a hot, parched landscape. He is searching for something but in vain. Fed up with the bleached grass and palm fronds, he is searching for flesh. Living, succulent flesh. And then he sees it. A goat sitting in the shade of a singular tree.

By the time Girija Prasad comes to his senses, it is too late. Excited by the dream, he has bitten into Chanda Devi's arm resting on his chest. She opens her eyes in alarm. Though she wasn't asleep, the unlikely violence has frightened her.

"Sorry! Sorry!" he exclaims. "I was dreaming and got carried away."

She hasn't slept at all. Her chance meeting with the palm tree has unsettled her. The ethereal being was withering away, yet Chanda Devi couldn't sense pain or sadness when she stroked its bark.

The tree responded to her concern. It spoke to her. "Do you know why you speak to trees?"

Chanda Devi didn't.

"Do you know why you sought me out in my final moments?"

"No."

"We are the same. You are one of us."

"And him?"

"He isn't. But you have loved him in many lives. Some spirits bridge the gap between different worlds through love. It keeps us all together."

An incessant and incoherent dreamer, Girija Prasad has classified all the dream states he has experienced. The ones that arrive in deep sleep can be rewarding, filling his passive self with surprises and mysteries. In light sleep, dreams can be manipulated. Seeped with ambient influences, they are not authentic enough. But what he experiences on his return from the Middle Andamans, aboard the *Ocean Whore*, isn't a dream at all. If compelled to, Girija Prasad would classify it as a vision.

He is awake on a moonlit night when an old man enters his cabin. Through his window, Girija Prasad has seen him step onto the deck from a high wave, as if the ocean were solid ground. Despite the dexterous move, he stoops and has an unsure gait—he could do with a walking stick. But each step has a purpose and destination. He sits beside Girija Prasad on the bed. He radiates an aura of calm. In his presence, Girija Prasad feels it too. He doesn't want to question what is happening, for ever since the miscarriage he has forgotten what peace feels like. The old man reaches out and gently strokes Girija Prasad's forehead with his cold, wrinkled hands. The twinkle in his eyes is a sign of life, not ghostliness. Girija Prasad slips into a deep, dreamless sleep.

Girija Prasad wants to tell Chanda Devi, the expert on visions, all about it. But he refrains. He cannot find the right words or the right moment. He knows nothing of the other world, where this one ends and that one begins, or if one tightly sits on top of the other like layers of skin. But he is quick to grasp its sanctity. Visions only appear to the ones they are meant for.

A week after their return, Girija Prasad visits Mount Harriet to place a stone slab on his son's grave. It says, DEVI PRASAD VARMA 1951. If it was a girl, they had decided, she would be called Devi. And if it was a boy, he would be called Devi Prasad. It is only after months of excruciating thought that Girija Prasad went ahead without an epitaph. A blank slab best describes a life that could have been but wasn't.

CHANDA DEVI MET MARY on one of their trips to Savitri Nagar. She first saw the young Karen girl sitting at the entrance to an elephant camp and peeling an unripe mango. It was uncommon to see girls in maxis in these parts, for though the Karens were Christian, they had stuck to the traditional Burmese longyi and blouse for their attire. Her dress had more darned holes than buttons, and the buttons were chipped. There were spots of blood on her feet, probably from walking barefoot on leech-infested paths. Chanda Devi considered it odd. The islands were far from developed, but she was yet to see a poor person here.

On Chanda Devi's last day at Savitri Nagar, the pastor came with Mary to the guesthouse. "She's barely twenty and her life has ended," he told Chanda Devi. Her husband, a laborer from Burma, had died in an accident. The pastor had paid for the burial and transported their eight-month-old son back to Rangoon, for how was Mary expected to look after a child all alone, when she was herself a child? Mary's parents had disowned her, as had the rest of the villagers, for eloping with a Buddhist outsider. But the pastor felt pity. She was, after all, the first child to be born in the settlements. He couldn't forsake a child he himself had baptized.

Chanda Devi understood what the man was implying. "I will speak to my husband," she said, and escorted them out. She was afraid the pastor, a talkative type, would devour her morning whole.

Later that evening, Girija Prasad questioned his wife's decision to keep her. "She needs us as much as we need her" was her reply.

"Not only is she Christian, her family comes from Burma. I can say with certainty that the girl is not vegetarian," he told her. As the master of the house, Girija Prasad felt cheated. Even housemaids elicited more compassion than he did.

Mary left on the *Ocean Whore* with them. No one, not even the pastor, came to wave her goodbye. In Port Blair, Chanda Devi took her to the market, first thing in the morning. From now on, Mary would wear a longyi and blouse like the rest of the Burmese, for Chanda Devi could not risk bare legs walking all around Goodenough Bungalow, especially with its platoon of deprived male ghosts. Once the list of essentials had been bought, she treated the girl to sweets from the mithai shop she had inaugurated.

"Is there anything else?" Chanda Devi asked Mary, who could follow only basic Hindi.

The girl shook her head. Despite the chappals, the sores on her feet still bled. She suffered from sunburn. Her elbows and cheeks were peeling off like a snake discarding its skin.

"Are you Christian or Buddhist?"

Mary nodded in confusion, then smiled apologetically.

"Do you believe in god?"

Mary had tears in her eyes. She covered her eyes with her palms, even as her smile widened.

That night, Chanda Devi asked Girija Prasad to bring home a bible in English for Mary.

"Why?" he asked.

"She has studied up to the fifth grade and can read and write in English."

"Does she want one?" By now Girija Prasad could discern which actions stemmed from his wife.

"She lost everyone and everything too soon," said Chanda Devi. "Without god, there is no purpose to loss. She needs faith to start again."

"But faith is not the birthright of the pious. A virus does not need Jesus Christ to understand the value of adaptation and survival."

Chanda Devi momentarily halted her restless tidying, the monotonous ritual that proclaimed it was time to retire. She looked at him in the dressing-table mirror.

"We are human beings, not viruses. A virus will not mourn the loss of a child or the death of a spouse. A virus will not question the turn life has taken, depriving you of the people you lived for." She sat down on the stool and began to cry.

Girija Prasad put his book down and walked toward his cupboard to pull his handkerchief out.

Mary moved into the larder, with only one instruction from her mistress: "No meat, no rats, no strangers." Overnight, she slipped into the daily rhythm of the house, as silent in her work as she was when asleep.

She follows her mistress like a shadow, mirroring her routine and pre-occupations, constantly pulling out weeds from the garden, stuffing dried neem in the various corners of the house, obsessively wiping the dampness away. When Chanda Devi sits down to meditate, Mary sits with the bible. When Chanda Devi engages with the problems people come to her with, Mary stands in a corner and watches. She never leaves her mistress alone, and Chanda Devi has to send her off on errands to enjoy a private moment. So attuned is Mary to her mistress, their menstrual cycles synchronize. Like a shadow, Mary has the shape of a human and does everything that humans do. Yet she shows no sign of life. Her brow bears no wrinkles from the past or worries of the future. Her expression seldom changes. Nor does her demeanor.

When Chanda Devi enters the larder one afternoon, Mary is asleep on the floor with her head resting against the wall. She notices wet patches on her blouse. Her eyes well up. Her breasts had leaked for months after the miscarriage too.

Twenty-three months and ten days into their marriage, the Varmas have been together long enough to experience one of the most sacred interactions between a man and a woman. She is now a nagging wife, and he a clueless husband.

"Mary, never be fooled by marriage," says Chanda Devi one night, seated at the dining table as Mary serves them rotis. "Men can only be married to their work."

Unlike veterans who can find lyricism and philosophy in their wives' nagging, Girija Prasad is disturbed. It is true that he has been preoccupied with teak nurseries of late. It is his brainchild, after all, to introduce the foreign species to the archipelago's wondrous soil. If he succeeds, he will be a commercial genius. Then there's always that headache called Savitri Nagar—or the absence of it. The shrewd businessman has begun to export matchsticks from the island but has failed miserably in his promise. As the most senior government representative in the Andamans, Girija Prasad is forced to take action. But not right away. Tonight, he must focus on the patron goddess of all his preoccupations, his wife.

He tries to embrace her in bed, but she turns away. "That rose plant you carted all the way from Kalimpong," she tells him, her eyes focused on the wall instead of his face. "One of its leaves has caught fungus."

"It is two years old; how can that be? If it was susceptible, the fungus would have consumed the plant already."

Chanda Devi doesn't have an answer. Of late, the islands seem to be wearing her down.

"Are you awake?" he asks.

"No," she replies.

"Has it been two years already?"

"How would I know? You brought the plant and you ask me its age."

"Has it been two years of our marriage?"

"Has it?"

"It feels longer than that."

"It feels shorter."

As a direct outcome of his wife's nagging, Girija Prasad takes Chanda Devi on a picnic to Long Division Creek, a thread of water that weaves through the jungle at its thickest, ending in the ocean on both sides.

Mangrove trees peer into the ripples, sheltering communities of fish from the sun. Low tide exposes roots larger than their trunks, equipped with hundreds of feet and dozens of toes to encroach upon the creek. This is where mudskippers thrive, walking on stumps instead of legs, pulling along a fish-like body, abandoning one hole in the sand for another, like our amphibious ancestors once did.

The land of mudskippers is where crocodiles meditate. The most ancient of ascetics, they have witnessed evolution play itself out. They have seen gods walking around, enjoying the fruit of their own creation before handing it over. They have witnessed the ammonites come and go, their soft flesh melting into the rocks even as the shells hardened into fossil. They have seen the lands and oceans change places, obsessively sometimes, like a game of musical chairs. "Evolution," they want to tell the mudskippers, if only they were willing to listen, "is just a matter of time."

On the creek's banks, salt water has corroded the limestone, creating passages no one knows the end to. Rock has taken on the quality of water, arrested in ripples and currents. The limestone caves are a living museum of stalactites and stalagmites reaching out to one another.

In their morning expedition to the caves, Chanda Devi finds contours of Shiva, a chain of mountains, and a hammer couched in the oddly textured interiors. Girija Prasad finds nothing. Nothing here can resemble the outside world, for these caves are the nostrils of the giant who created the islands and is now asleep. They are a glimpse of the creator's mind at work.

A painful shriek leaps out from the cave's darkness. Girija Prasad reflexively clings to his wife. Chanda Devi takes the torchlight from his hand and searches for the source. The light falls on a puppy, its scalp ripped apart, exposing flesh, blood, and skull, probably hiding in the cave from whatever caused the injury.

The couple watch the wounded little being scramble to the cave's mouth, which is now a distant patch of sun. Chanda Devi is suddenly out of breath. She feels trapped. She falls on her knees and vomits.

Girija Prasad hadn't known that his wife suffered from claustrophobia. He intends to make it up to her after an extended siesta in the guesthouse. An evening at Parrot Island awaits them. Girija Prasad plans to row the boat himself, allowing only parrots to intrude upon their company.

When the time comes to step into the boat, Chanda Devi holds on to his hand for sheer life, not just balance. This seems to be a day when she can't do anything without holding on to him. In the youth of their marriage, this has been the greatest display of affection between them. Girija Prasad makes a note of it. On his map, he will mark Parrot Island as "the place we held hands for the longest time." For these memories, he suspects, will be the joy of aging together. To remind each other of things long forgotten, and to laugh.

In truth, this is no island at all, just a big rock inhabited by parrots. Five thousand and twenty-two, if his local Karen guide is to be believed. The current is winding down, rocking the boat in a rhythm as gentle as breathing. It is also unwinding his wife, who has removed her hair clip, jewelry, and footwear to sit in comfort.

In the privacy of the creek, she allows the breeze to play with her hair. Although he has observed every inch of her skin, every strand of her hair, and every curve that connects one part of her body to another, the sight of her naked foot peeping out from under the sari, unaware of its glory, is hypnotizing. No matter how hot or humid it is, Chanda Devi has the unique ability to remain ice cool in her extremities. Her feet and her hands are refreshing, like ocean waves. Girija Prasad feels an intense desire to drop the oars, tumble to the other side, and cradle first her feet and then her hands. With the oars gone, it will be hours before they return to the civilized world, if at all. But he is embarrassed. It has been a stressful and strenuous day for him, and he reeks of sweat. Besides, though they are alone, this is the 1950s, and physical distance between men and women isn't imposed by society alone. It is created by the men and women themselves. Affection is the sole privilege of stone figurines in temples and caves.

Above Parrot Island, a red moon has begun to rise. On either side of the creek stand trees tall enough to join moon to water. Hidden in the jungle, a parrot lets out a loud cry to mark the end of the day. It commands the moon to rise farther, the sun to sink lower, and all the parrots in the jungle to return. A handful of parrots call out to one another from both sides of the creek. They join a growing circle. The number of parrots over the island has increased in a matter of minutes.

Girija Prasad has been married to Chanda Devi for almost two years now. His mother sends him a letter each month, urging them to move closer to home. Chanda Devi yearns for motherhood. His department seniors want to see profits, and his juniors better postings. The elephants in the timber camps are exhausted, and the teak saplings in the nursery are malnourished. Yet it is possible for him to call this a state of contentment. For too long, he had been toying with atheism, rejecting religion on scientific principle. In this moment, his reasons are clear. Only when one experiences a moment in its entirety—as a world in its own right, with a unique shape and axis, a sun and moon, laws and philosophies—only when one encounters all the moment's possibilities with contentment, only then is one left with no reason to pray. Like the parrots, he is grateful just to return home each day.

It isn't a lack of courage that prevents him from reaching out to his wife but gratitude for this moment filled with longing and contentment. Chanda Devi leans over to tell him something, but her words are drowned out by the cacophony of birds.

"My lady," he says, "you are competing with more than five thousand parrot residents of this isle. You must speak louder."

"I'm pregnant," she repeats.

Confused by the birds and the words, he asks, "How do you know?" although he realizes it is a silly question. Among the few things he knows about her is that she knows things already.

"It is less than a month."

The flying parrots have divided into two large groups, resembling a yin and yang chasing each other in the sky.

"Then we shall move to Calcutta," he says. "I shall file a case against the businessman and fight it out on behalf of the Forest Department in the High Court there."

"Why?"

"He promised a township in exchange for exclusive felling rights. All I see is a tin shed and a road."

"But why must we move to Calcutta?"

"You need the best medical help this country can offer, not a retired English doctor who also treats elephants. I shall ask my mother to stay with us. You cannot suffer like the last time."

"No one can change destiny."

"I cannot argue with you over metaphysics. My intellect doesn't stretch that far. But what happened to you was my fault. I should have known that pregnancies could be complicated on an island with no infrastructure, only jails and penal settlements. Do you know where our child would have been born, had things gone as planned?"

Chanda Devi had assumed that she would deliver at home.

"I was planning to sanitize one of the cells in Cellular Jail and convert it into a makeshift clinic. Since you are sensitive to ghosts, I chose a cell where no one had died. The prisoner was a poet who made it back to the mainland. It was a happy ending, so to speak, leaving no reasons for him to haunt the cell."

The tide has come in. The boat is swaying like a swing. In front of them, the parrots descend upon the island in waves. Only when one wave settles on the branches does another descend. The sky has emptied of every single parrot before Girija Prasad picks up the oars.

At the jetty, Girija Prasad alights first. He takes his wife by the hand and holds her waist with the other as she steps off the boat.

Many years later, ten to be precise, he will find himself at the same place at the same time of the evening, this time with his daughter, who is light enough to be lifted from the boat to the bank. It is still the land of mudskippers and will be so for centuries to come. Like her father, the girl can distinguish between tadpoles, mudskippers, and salamanders, toying with the idea of evolution as if it were a fairy tale.

"Papa," she asks him as he places her on the ground, "after hundreds of generations, will the mudskippers evolve into frogs or fish? Will they live on water or land? Which way are they going?"

"Child, I cannot look into the future."

"Why not?"

If only he could.

IN 1942, FIVE YEARS BEFORE India gained independence, the bespectacled Poet entered Cellular Jail in Port Blair. Among the inmates, this was a cause for celebration. They sought redemption in his proximity, like the thieves crucified beside Jesus Christ. For he was the youth who had unfurled the flag of freedom inside the British parliament.

"The most dangerous criminals are those who inspire others to commit crimes yet themselves stand back and watch," the judge had proclaimed. The Poet didn't hold a gun, stick, or bomb. Yet he threatened to bring down the empire with his thoughts. He had penned the movement's most popular slogans and lyrics.

When the Poet heard the line, he had laughed. The judge had noted his response. His every verdict was a work of art dedicated to the cause of justice—the text, the performance, the practiced solemnity. Like all artists, he too was insecure. The wig made him self-conscious.

Initially, the Poet spent his time meditating. He banished all memories and, with them, the longing for a world that had gifted him those memories. He narrowed his willpower into a knife-edge, razor-sharp and formidable. At knifepoint, he kept madness at bay.

He cocooned himself in the reality of Cellular Jail. But all he could see was injustice. Inmates made to plow in place of bulls, inmates on hunger strike who died after being force-fed, fetters that consisted of a single iron rod from neck to feet, preventing a person from doing anything but standing erect. The Poet was flooded with inspiration, for nothing inspired him more than injustice. But he was helpless without pen and paper. He didn't even have access to chalk and a slate—court's orders.

He had betrayed his countrymen by getting arrested. He had abandoned his parents in their old age. He had disappointed the dogs searching for stale rotis on his street. Many had been punished for supporting him, and he had let all their sacrifices down. When the judge called him the most dangerous mind in British India, he had laughed at the flattery. But now, three and a half months into his sentence, he had even let the judge down.

Most of all, though, the revolutionary had let himself down. The madness that he kept at arm's length in the day began to enter his cell by night. During a hunger strike that lasted for five days, a new phenomenon visited him. It didn't matter if his eyes were open or closed, lucid visions rose before him. The constellations came swirling down from the absolute darkness of space into the twilit skies. The Poet witnessed the river of stars flood into the prison's passage, dissolving chains and fetters with its brilliance. He saw the constellations reimagine themselves to fit the emptiness within. The stars lived and breathed inside him. They replaced the cells within and without. For it was him they sought.

He witnessed water's birth as ice, as he stood on one of Saturn's moons, enraptured by the blizzards. He blinked with icy lashes as he saw the world through her eyes. Like a newborn who perceives it all as one being, she saw the stars and orbits as her limbs. He followed her journey to earth, couched in the ribs of a meteor. He saw her grow into the mightiest ocean the planet would ever see. Standing on the fringes of an atoll, he was hit by glassy waves, rhythmically drenching his calves, wetting his thighs and waist as he walked in deeper, until he was entirely submerged in her tale. She nurtured life in her womb, parasites committed to the blasphemy of evolution—a ceaseless separation, never to come together again.

When he woke up, the sweltering heat of his cell melted the vision into tears. He wept, surrounded by unknown fragrances. Blood tinged with spices, orange peel mixed with sweat. The unbearable smell of loneliness.

On his customary rounds one evening, the Warden found something scribbled in the dust surrounding the fetters. It seemed like a prisoner had used a sharp object held between his toes to scrawl in Sanskrit. The Warden had served in India for more than a decade as Her Majesty's servant. His linguistic talents made him proficient in Hindi, a skill he used to monitor all correspondence and propaganda material within the prison. Sanskrit was a hobby, especially the study of scriptures and texts. Shocked by his love for the ancient language, the Warden wondered if it was possible that, in a previous life, he had been a Sanskrit scholar on the banks of the Ganges.

Being in charge of the prison, he was both concerned and intrigued. Hiding among the inmates was a pandit of poetry. Later that night, the poem would come to life in his dreams. He, too, would wake up in tears.

Wide awake, the Warden would leave his bungalow to stroll through the moonless darkness, unsettled by the sound of waves and the tropical fragrances, overwhelmed by the vision of an ocean that glistened brighter than starlight. He would end up in front of the Poet's cell a little before dawn. He would stand there, observing the feverish movement beneath his eyelids. The next morning, the Warden would track the Poet down again as he pruned the geraniums bordering the gallows.

"We call her Tethys," he would say. "That mythic ocean."

And so began a lifelong engagement between them, eager to devote themselves to the pursuit of poetry. One morning, the Poet was asked to abandon his chores and report to the Warden immediately. He found him in his garden, collapsed in a cane chair, unkempt and barefoot, and wearing only a pair of khaki shorts. Scribbled with a twig on a flower bed was one of the Poet's verses, rearranged to flow better.

The Warden began to subscribe to science periodicals, sharing new research with the Poet. It wasn't the fossils that perplexed him but the names.

"To accept the Silurian and Ordovician periods is to accept the empire's authority," the Poet remarked. "Who governs time? Why does the meridian pass through England, shunning its colonies?" He had chosen to call the ocean Kshirsagar, inspired by Hindu mythology.

Though the Warden disagreed, he understood the practical difficulty of using lofty Welsh names in a work targeted at the natives. They were unpronounceable. So he spent some time on the problem. Human interest in prehistory was limited to a handful of epochs and periods. As for the names, the Warden had to look no further than the islands. He picked the names of the first five island tribes he could think of and replaced the Welsh ones with them.

Over time, the poem turned into an epic, with a structure and mythology of its own.

To the Poet, the Kshirsagar wasn't just an ocean. It was the entire cosmos, with a geography unlike any found in the Eastern or Western scriptures. The cosmos, in its depth, was an ocean of various realms. At the very top was the Sagar Natraj, or the realm of the octopus. A giant octopus, made of subtle energies, balanced the various islands, seas, and celestial bodies on each tentacle in its ethereal dance. The sun was the octopus's mind, nurturing all life forms and elements with its radiance. This was also the realm of existence. At the greatest depths of the ocean was a peak of ice, untouched by light and time. The Poet called it Sagar Meru. To the Hindus, Buddhists, and Jains, Mount Meru was the physical and metaphysical center of the universe. It was the highest point, beyond human comprehension and measurement.

"Not the lowest!" the Warden exclaimed, bewildered by his choice.

The Poet looked at him with tenderness. A glance was enough. The Warden answered his own question. "In the cosmic ocean, the lowest is the highest and the highest is the lowest," the Warden said.

———

These were unpredictable times, with war leaping like fire across the world. The idea that landed the revolutionary his life sentence had spread like an epidemic. Reports of torture and exploitation at Cellular Jail leaked back to the mainland. Under pressure, a committee was sent to investigate. Since the committee couldn't prove the claims untrue, it recommended the next best thing—releasing a few prisoners to divert attention. The Warden, in an act of kindness, put the Poet's name at the top of the list. "After five years in solitary confinement," the Warden was quoted saying in the committee's report, "the gentleman is bordering on insanity. He speaks to himself all the time and scribbles gibberish on the ground. Such a mind is dangerous no longer. It is deranged."

After his death on the mainland, the Poet attended his own funeral ceremony, standing in a corner with folded arms, and decided to return to the islands. It was time to visit the cell as a free spirit. The Warden too had decided to remain on the islands in spirit. Soon after the Poet's departure, an overzealous inmate had pushed him off the roof as he monitored the repair work.

Freed from the shackles of propriety, the two embraced each other for the first time. So much had changed since they'd last met. They were dead, to begin with. England had won World War II but lost its colonies.

"I wasn't shocked by the bloodshed," the Warden said about the Partition. "Anyone could have seen it coming."

"I wasn't surprised by Gandhi's assassination," said the Poet.

They would spend their time strolling on overgrown jungle paths and beaches, going where their hearts desired. And now that death afforded them the time, the Warden had a literary proposition: He wanted to translate the Poet's work into English.

"Of what use are a dead man's poems to this world?" the Poet asked.

"None. Which is why I can translate them freely."

CHANDA DEVI HAS A REQUEST: She wants to see the sunset from Mount Harriet before they leave the islands. Girija Prasad may have the time to drive them there, but he lacks the will to abandon all worries and sit still. He has planned for and preempted most complications that could arise during the voyage. His mother and brother are waiting for them in Calcutta. Yet he is nervous.

If only one could pull Goodenough Bungalow down and put it back again like a Tibetan nomad's tent, the Varmas would have done so. Instead, they must tear down each memory, hack at each emotion the bungalow has given birth to, and search for that handy, incomplete shred they can decorate their future rooms with. And what of all the dreams still to be dreamed? Who will keep the ghosts abreast of all the changes outside? Who will water the rosebush?

Out of the nine suitcases they will take with them, one belongs to Girija Prasad, two to Chanda Devi, and Mary has only a little bundle. The rest belong to the islands. Bottles of dried and powdered herbs, fossilized corals, an intricate tumor from the Andaman padauk, a miniature replica of the *Ocean Whore*, a glass box with local butterflies mounted and framed, an unfinished map of the islands. Some islands remain half sketched, vanishing abruptly into the ocean. There is also a shard of flint and a coconut shell belonging to the Divine Nangas, a broken French vase found in Ross Island, and an urn of soil from the grave on Mount Harriet.

It is their last night in Port Blair. In the darkness, Girija Prasad can gauge his wife's wakefulness by the distance between them. In deep sleep, she is always drawn to his forearm, pushing him to the edge with her desires.

"May I ask you something silly?" he says.

"You may."

"Who are ghosts? I have never seen one, nor quite understood their genealogy. Perhaps that is why I am not inclined to believe in their existence."

Chanda Devi smiles. His odd obsessions and odder language, they make him all the more endearing.

"They are people like you and me. But they belong to the past. They wear clothes from another time. Their habits are old-fashioned."

"Why don't all corpses turn into ghosts?"

"Death . . ." Chanda Devi reflects on the word as cicadas, frogs, and flies intervene. "Ghosts do not live where they died. They return to the place where they felt the most alive. They have struggled, lived, and enjoyed their time there so much, they cannot let go."

"Do you mean to say that we turn into ghosts in our lifetime?"

"Some of us."

"What's the most haunted place you have visited?"

"Here. The islands. Ross Island."

"Why can't I see ghosts?"

It is your good fortune that you can't see the ghosts that sit beside you when you eat, that you can't see death when it is staring you in the face, Chanda Devi wants to tell her husband. But all she says is "It is your good fortune."

A larval silence precedes the dawn. It is a deliberate pause, a reflection filled with hope and anxiety. Hidden among the cluck and hiss, the croak and chatter outside the window, are songs of the extinct. The epic of evolution, told by bards long gone. Oh, to abandon the labyrinthine shell and shed old skin. To be naked and vulnerable. Free to swim, sprint, and fly without inhibition. To vanish without a trace only to reappear as a mating call, the way the sun sets in the west and rises in the east . . . Can their stories and songs be heard by the living? they wonder. Do they acknowledge their legacy in the fossils?

Lost to the symphonies of the night, Girija Prasad says, "I may return to this house as a ghost. Perhaps then I will hear the ghost of the goat that tormented you on all those nights."

She laughs. "By then the goat would have moved on and so would I. Why would you keep me waiting in another life?"

The sky is exceptionally clear. Sunny blue with white wisps, like indecipherable calligraphy. The sea too is exceptionally calm. A sparkling shroud spread over the earth's grave. The breeze has cooled in a torrential rain somewhere over the Andaman Sea, inciting butterflies to flutter miles into the open seas like migratory birds. A solitary fisherman is surprised to find himself in the company of ivory-white butterflies. And such young ones too—their bodies are covered with caterpillar fur. One of them has fallen asleep on his knee. The fisherman lingers on after the nets have gone in. All it takes is the insignificant company of a few insects to make him smile.

Moments later, when his body plummets into the water, the smile is still frozen on his face. The current is diabolical. It pounds his body like a boulder. He is brought up to the surface as swiftly as he is pulled down again, causing an explosion of air in his ears. He doesn't know what caused the water to churn violently, flipping his boat over like a pebble. But he is relieved to take another breath. His final one, before the hull hits his head and cracks his skull open.

Half an hour later, the butterflies float like leaves over the water. The fisherman's corpse bobs in and out. Though all it really took was a minute. One minute, for the ocean bed to collapse and rise like a phoenix.

No one on the islands recalls how the earth moved—a minute when the ghosts of land and ocean gave in to the struggle. Under the land's pressure, the ocean slipped farther down, only to spring back with twice the force. In the life of a planet, it is a rare moment when a conflict on the crust—the shell of its existence—leaves its entire being rattled. The earthquake of 1954 goes down as the second largest recorded since the invention of the seismograph. Scientifically speaking, it displayed the longest duration of faulting ever observed. Researchers attributed tremors in regions as far as Siberia and several more quakes and tsunamis to the event.

The ones who survived are forever trapped in that minute, one of sheer blankness. It isn't presence of mind that has betrayed them. Nor is it a loss of memory. It is a failure of imagination. No one could have imagined that the solid ground that held the islands, the ocean, the reefs, the forests, the rivers, would be ripped apart in less than a minute. Centuries of wilderness and civilization would crumble into clouds of dust, as vulnerable as an anthill in the path of a possessed elephant.

In some places, cliffs crashed into the ocean, like icebergs breaking off from the poles. Windows rattled in places as far away as the Persian Gulf. In Tibet, cranes abandoned their feeding sites and flew aimlessly into the sky. In Indonesia, volcanoes threw up smoke, commanding those farming on their slopes to kneel in prayer. On the shores, boats crumpled into the water as if they were made of paper. Macaques, birds, deer, elephants, dogs, united in a wave of noise. The human voice went unheard.

In a minute, the ocean bed had jumped up, spewing layers of sediment, coral, and sand in the air. The islands tilted by a few meters, drowning forests and farms. Rice fields, yet to be harvested, would become the future playing grounds of sea cows, dolphins, crocodiles, and rays. No one would light the torch in the lighthouse on the archipelago's tip again, for the ocean had claimed its entrance. Children born in the aftermath would dismiss their parents' stories and ancestral myths as tall tales born from the imagination of fools—the same fools who built a lighthouse in one and a half meters of water and went fishing on dry land. The gap between generations would turn into a gulf between people who inhabited different maps.

For most of those who perished, the final image they carried was of

a summer sky, an indifferent eyewitness. As indifferent to the movement of continents as it was to the sight of a fisherman's corpse floating
in the water, surrounded by butterflies.

At work in Calcutta, Girija Prasad is hidden in a fortress of files, lost in
an essay on Paleo-Tethys, a hypothesized ocean and contemporary of
Pangaea. The centrifugal journeys of the continents, the Swiss author
claims, blocked her oceanic currents and gyres, leading to her disap-
pearance.

Call it the influence of his wife or the presentiment of a father, but
Girija Prasad begins to wonder if elements too have souls. Do they also
worry about their legacies? Do their ghosts haunt the earth, like the
sahibs of Ross Island? If a human being is not reducible to mere bones
and blood, how can an ocean be reduced to its geographical space, the
element of water or the form it takes? Life is more than the sum of its
breaths and tremors.

So deep is he in thought, it takes him some time to notice that the
quake is real. Girija Prasad rushes over to his apartment the moment
the tremors stop. He unlocks the door to an empty house. He looks in
all the rooms and panics. He runs down to the shared garden first and
then up to the terrace. He finds her sobbing and sweating. He embraces her until she calms down. He wipes her dry and holds on to her
as they descend the steps. He seats her on an armchair and goes into
the kitchen. He sniffs around to detect if gas has escaped the cylinder,
then puts the water to boil. He walks around to assess the damage. The
tea set that Mary had left to dry on the dining table has fallen and shattered. The wardrobe and bed in their room have moved by a few
inches. Two buckets, filled to the brim with water, have spilled in the
bathroom. That is all.

He is relieved. He serves his wife the chai with some banana chips
and sits down across from her on the sofa. He notices that one of the
butterflies has fallen off its mount in the teak frame titled "Butterflies
of Nicobar." It lies prostrate at the bottom, a corpse once again.

"Why were you on the terrace?" he asks as he unbuttons his cuffs.

"I knew something was wrong. I could feel tension rise from the ground as I stood in the garden. I knew it would not be placated easily. So I rushed up. I remembered what you had told me—to look out for falling trees, walls, and objects when tremors hit the islands."

Girija Prasad airs himself in his vest as he sips on his tea. Though she isn't lying, her pink nose and swollen eyes tell him what she withholds. Chanda Devi, it seems, has been crying for a while. Her anguish precedes the earthquake. It goes beyond. She is seven months pregnant. Like the last time, she seems to have slipped into a labyrinth of melancholy.

"If you cry so much," he says, "our child will be the crankiest one in the neighborhood."

She strokes her tight belly. She had sensed early on that it is a girl. Now she is discovering her nature.

"You have had enough practice attending to my tears."

"If she is as unpredictable as her mother, practice won't be enough."

Her husband, he always finds ways to make her smile.

Girija Prasad collects all the information he can find, piecing the earthquake together in his mind. For the first time since World War II, helicopters and planes are sent to the islands. All the phone and electricity lines are mangled. There are questions he can't ask without sounding frivolous. For who would check on an empty bungalow and a bush of roses in the face of such devastation? Who would indulge his curiosity to see if the Lilliputian volcanoes were billowing more than just bubbles?

When Girija Prasad left the Andamans, he had no time to look back, even though he'd been standing on the deck. He had been nervous about the journey ahead, constantly checking on Chanda Devi. If only he could have seen what was to come. The old jetty would slip into the harbor and drown. Like the elephant Girija Prasad had ferried from the mainland, it would be too large to recover. A new one would be built in its place. The road spiraling up from the harbor into the mountainous terrain, climbing to the top and sweeping down in all directions, would be damaged in so many parts that the government would be forced to start afresh, to build a brand-new road over the skeleton of the previous one.

He searches for eyewitness accounts, for adjectives that can somehow alleviate the horror by articulating it. He finds none. His life on the archipelago had provided him with clues but no answers. Death on the islands was sudden—as sudden as it was certain. Like a crocodile swimming in the mangrove or a purple sun sinking into oblivion.

Two months after the earthquake hit the Andamans, Devi is born hundreds of miles away from the epicenter. Girija Prasad holds the tightly wrapped bundle in his arms as her mother receives stitches. Devi looks at her father with fresh black eyes. He loosens her swaddle to look at her limbs. She raises her hand to her face, mesmerized by the sight of her fingers. They move with a life of their own, one that surprises both father and daughter.

So spellbound is Girija Prasad by the infant hands and infant eyes, the infinite wonder contained in an infant navel knotted like a balloon, he doesn't notice the life swiftly receding from Chanda Devi's eyes. Sensing it, Mary begins to rub her mistress's hands and feet vigorously, even before the doctor can diagnose the internal hemorrhage. By the time he does, the process has set in irrevocably.

Chanda Devi barely speaks; she barely blinks. She leaves the world with her eyes open, meditating upon the image of father and daughter holding on to each other. If only Girija Prasad had read the warning signs. If only he had looked deep into Chanda Devi's eyes. So deep that he could have seen what she saw.

As her husband, it is his duty to light the funeral pyre, a bed of logs that she sleeps on dressed like a bride. It is her good fortune, the pandit tells him, to have died a married woman and not a widow.

Even after the flames peel the flesh away, Girija Prasad refuses to believe what has happened. The porcelain-like piece of anklebone that refuses to be incinerated reminds him of her naked foot in the boat at Parrot Island. If anything, she is more alive than ever.

Disbelief, it turns out, is belief of its own kind. It is a river that flows against the overbearing currents of time and truth to make the opposite journey. It gathers all the mysteries of the ocean and returns them to their frozen origins. In the form of a glacier, it holds its head high up to look at god hiding behind the mists of heaven.

What is the purpose of belief if even god can't put the world back the way you worshipped it?

THE EARTHQUAKE LEAVES BEHIND a gaping crack where Goodenough Bungalow stands, meandering through the garden and the ground below the stilts like a seasonal stream. The ubiquitous vegetation moves in, hiding whatever the crack may have exposed, turning it into a permanent settlement for slugs, centipedes, snails, snakes, and the occasional visitors—hens, pigs, and ducks.

The bungalow itself survives by tilting to align with the earth's axis. The skeleton of a rosebush stands upright, trying to preserve its dignity as only stubs remain where roses once bloomed.

As soon as his daughter turns one, Girija Prasad fights with his mother to return to the islands. Only Mary, the loyal caretaker, is permitted to accompany them as Devi's nanny. No one else. For no one else was around when Girija Prasad and Chanda Devi had lived there. Why would he tamper with the memories? Like all ghosts, Girija Prasad yearns for the place he had felt most alive in.

Once she sees the decrepitude that has overtaken Goodenough Bungalow, Mary puts her foot down. They cannot live there. As a servant, she knows that she doesn't have the privilege to speak up, but her master is, like the house, precariously balanced over a void himself.

As a parting gesture, Girija Prasad leaves behind a pile of new books and newspapers on the porch. Someone needs to keep its inhabitants updated. Girija Prasad wants to believe in ghosts, but it doesn't come naturally.

On Mary's suggestion, they move into the guesthouse on Mount Harriet.

The British who built the structure had been afflicted by a peculiar strain of nostalgia. They built summerhouses in the Himalayan hill stations to remind themselves of the English countryside. But when they built a guesthouse in the Andamans, it was in memory of the Himalayas—replete with French windows looking onto machans, looking onto the jungle below. All they needed were tigers to shoot and the dream of the British Raj would be complete. Instead, they had to satisfy themselves with squeezing leeches out of their boots. As retired officers, when they strolled in parks back home in England, watching the swans skid over water, marveling at the different colors and flowers each season brought, it was marigolds that they searched for and leeches they feared in their socks. Nostalgia, it seemed, was a being with short-term memory. It yearned for things that were quickly receding but rarely for the distant past. To live in the distant past—the German neurologist Alzheimer would prove—was a sign of premature senility.

Mount Harriet sits across the bay from Goodenough Bungalow, and a short ferry ride separates the two shores. Seawater has encroached where, before the earthquake, the highest of tides never could, forcing the farmers to abandon their paddy fields. The roofs of the bunkers built by the Japanese during World War II have caved in. But the guesthouse, an ode to nostalgia, remains untouched.

Girija Prasad moves into the guesthouse with a resolve. This is where he will witness the final sunset of his life. For this is where he and his wife had held hands for the first time, surrendering to that sinking star.

In the new house, Mary busies herself with pushing and pulling things back together, looking after the infant, and looking out for the father. The curtains and bedsheets she has carried from Calcutta are all indigo blue, in sharp contrast to the green and yellow interiors of the previous house. If they do not start afresh, they may not make it.

Life has shown Mary that grief is like water. Once it seeps into a crack, there is no way of draining it. But routine, daily and monotonous, can prevent it from hardening the days. Girija Prasad is always served tea at six-thirty A.M., and Devi is bathed and ready by eight. Mary is never more than fifteen minutes off schedule, for even half an hour lost is time hardened into grief.

In the house on Mount Harriet, Mary becomes the gravitational center. She is the reason why things move and why things stay in place. Girija Prasad and Devi feel the deepest form of gratitude and love toward her—they take her for granted.

At the age of four, when Devi begins to urinate in the flower bed instead of the washroom, it is Mary who runs out to admonish her, only to find Girija Prasad standing nearby. "It is manure," he mutters apologetically, even when she brings home a dead snake. "Manure" is what he will say again as Devi unloads herself on a beach in full view one evening. She is six then. To the world, she is a young girl. To him, an infant.

By eight, Devi has grown to know no inhibitions. When she eats fruits, she removes her dress to avoid stains. She swims naked in the sea and rides elephants bareback. Her hair is a burnt brown and her skin a scaly pink. Every night, Mary rubs aloe vera on her skin and oil in her hair. It is her way of keeping account of Devi's daily scratches and wounds. Mary knows when Devi skips school to explore jungle paths and ruins, ending up at the beach. If Devi goes out, Mary removes a loose brick from the kitchen wall facing the entrance to keep watch. If she is playing in the garden, Mary sits on the porch under the pretext of chopping vegetables.

One afternoon, the gardener catches almost twenty slugs, with the intention of eradicating them. Devi follows him to his killing field in the thicket. She is transfixed by the sight of slugs crawling over one another, desperate to make it to the basket's rim. Instead, they are lifted by a ruthless hand indifferent to crushing defenseless creatures between rocks. Devi doesn't notice when the hands veer away from the basket and wander under her dress, stroking her thighs and buttocks.

Later in the afternoon, the gardener stops in his tracks as he enters the kitchen, pinned by Mary's stony gaze, the intent of the knife in her hands transformed by the look in her eyes.

"If anyone touches her, I will hack him to pieces," she tells him. "You know I will."

The gardener doesn't come to work again.

It is only by chance that Devi discovers the truth behind Mary. Flipping through the pages of an Englishman's travelogue, she chances upon photographs from Ajanta and Ellora, the two-thousand-year-old Buddhist caves. Mary is a rock-cut figure out of these very caves. Like her, the figures have oriental eyes and slender bones. They've been painted with glowing skin and faded clothes. Despite the hundreds of years and hardships they have endured, their expressions remain serene, their movements fluid. Mary's ancestors, Devi concludes, are the cave people who carved these gods in their own image.

FOR DEVI'S NINTH BIRTHDAY, Girija Prasad takes her on a trek to the salt plains in the Middle Andamans. It is a rite of passage, a lesson to be passed on from one generation to the next. As far as she can remember, he's never missed the chance to educate her about the impact of the earthquake. What happens every few hundred years just happened yesterday and can happen again tomorrow.

The shells embedded in the cliffs bear witness to the violence that also creates mountains as mighty as the Himalayas. The destinies of entire species, not just civilizations, can change with the course of a river and the tides of an ocean. The lighthouse one must swim to was once built on dry land. Now a picnic spot for dugongs and turtles attracted to the grass that surrounds it. The salt plain too was once part of the ocean.

Girija Prasad's biggest ambition, it seems, is to document the past in all its vastness, tracing its roots from the ever-vanishing present to the unrecorded prehistory. The scope of his ambition compels him to live in the past. It is either that or Girija Prasad, like all unsuspecting ghosts, is caught in the shifting sands of a singular moment.

"Papa," Devi asks him as they make their way through a jungle path to the salt plains, "why must we study earthquakes? Why can't we listen to the radio or go to the cinema?"

Girija Prasad has illustrated the breakdown of Pangaea, its journey into the present continents, and stitched it into a flip-book for Devi's pleasure. Each continent is filled with its own unique and interesting characters. He knows that drifting continents are difficult for a child to grasp, and understandably so. Even the most sophisticated of scientists struggle to grasp it. For the world, as Girija Prasad grew up to understand it, is a lie. The land that he worshipped as terra firma—permanent and immovable—seems to be the opposite in nature. The poles that guided ships and sailors through the millennia are prone to wandering.

"Do you consider them unworthy subjects, child?"

"I told a girl in my class that the islands are mountains and all continents are islands. She didn't believe me, so I said my papa said so. She said, 'Your papa is crazy; he went crazy because your mother died.' I didn't believe her. So she said her mummy said so."

He is perplexed.

"You know why the islands are a mountain chain and all continents are ultimately islands," he tells her.

"I know," she replies. "But is it true that you are crazy?"

It has taken them two hours to complete the journey, and they are almost there. At the next bend, they will catch the first glimpse of the salt plains. But he won't change his measured, determined pace. He must persevere for the child's sake.

"When your friend uses the word 'crazy,'" he says, "what does she mean exactly? Is she referring to a form of neurosis, like anxiety or hypochondria? Or a psychosis, like schizophrenia? Or is it a degenerative disorder, like Alzheimer's? A scientific mind is always specific. It doesn't use terms and concepts loosely. It seeks the truth, at all costs."

Devi beams. She is proud of her father—an intelligent, scientific person, just like her. Evidence enough that the crazy ones are her friend and her mother, not them.

In the distance, the salt plains sparkle like snow under the sun. Rising from a turquoise-blue ocean, this is what the polar regions must look like, the father and child conjecture. Pure white and deep blue, unsullied by the green and brown of the tropics.

Before the quake, the salt plains had been part of a bay where flying fish were known to drag entire fishing nets down by laying eggs. So serene was the water here that even butterflies would be tempted to venture far out.

Devi runs down the rest of the way, across the bush and onto the plains, to the part that sparkles the most. It is the entrance to the kingdom of the sun. Each aimless step here is a crackle, crumbling the white crust into powder. Devi tastes it. It is saltier than salt. She digs with her fingers through the crumbling white to an oily layer of dark clay beneath. She presses her thumb against it. It leaves a clear imprint.

Baked by the harsh sun, her thumbprint will remain there undisturbed and hidden. Until a crane lands on the same spot nine years later, and the place begins to attract tribes of migratory birds in search of a safe spot to rest, refuel, and share tales of what they've seen on their travels.

But for the moment, Devi and her father are the salt plain's only visitors. As she rummages through the soil, her fingers encounter something solid. She scrapes through the salt and clay to retrieve it. It is a branch, as long as both her arms put together. She struggles to lift it, bending backward, like some ancient god struggling with his staff and the power that comes with it. She prods the ground with it, hoping a spring will gush forth in the middle of this desert. All religions need miracles, and she is in search of hers. Instead, she discovers pale flesh. Blind, colorless, shrimp-like creatures of the deep sea, thrown out by the earthquake, shriveled yet intact in their shrines of salt. In Devi's world, this discovery is bigger than a spring in the middle of a desert. She wishes she had more hands—or if not that, at least a bucket—to carry these treasures back with her. She struggles with the branch, a gift for her father. She looks around; she can't see him anywhere. She freezes.

"Papa," she says aloud. There's no reply.

In the Andaman Sea, each island is a person and each person an island. Tremors and quakes are common, eager to exact their inch of land and pound of flesh. Everything here, including the sea, belongs to the ocean and will be claimed in due course. There is a possibility that Devi's father has vanished, like the sea, leaving her alone on this salt plain.

"Papa!" she shrieks.

A black speck waves back over the glittering horizon of salt. Perhaps the sun is up to some mischief, for the silhouette resembles that of a man stooped with age. Filled with an urge to run into his arms, she abandons the shriveled sea creatures and rushes toward him. In his arms, she begins to cry. "Don't leave me, Papa, don't leave me."

He holds her tight and wipes her tears. "Child," he says, "I could see you all the while. You spent a long time digging. What did you find?"

"You must come with me, Papa. I found so many things!" she exclaims, her eyes wide with wonder. Her tears have stopped as quickly as they started. "I found a branch for you. Every god needs a staff. I found dead shrimp. And, Papa"—a monster called excitement is devouring her words—"I know what to do with the dead in our religion. Set them free in the sea!"

One night, when Devi confronted Girija Prasad about god, she proposed an alternative. How about they create their own religion, with their very own gods and myths? That way, they would have no one to blame but themselves. In the bedtime world of father and daughter, religion is yet another excuse to create stories.

Girija Prasad nods, hoping to say something. What shocks him isn't her earnestness with fantasies but her emotional wisdom. Devi has understood her father's aversion to burning bodies and burying them, for what you do to the corpse is what happens to your heart. When Girija Prasad returned to the islands, he scattered his wife's ashes into the ocean from every corner, resolving to never leave.

The tragedy of Girija Prasad hasn't gone unnoticed on the mainland. A decade may have passed, but it still makes great conversation, a cautionary tale, a warning against the ill effects of tasting beef. People say he lost his mind when he lost his wife, and now he can't face the civilized world anymore. "The poor child," sigh distant relatives over cups of tea, "she will be raised among tribals and end up marrying one." Chanda Devi's parents take enough interest in Devi to write inquiring letters. If they show any more keenness, they fear, the father will dump the child on them and remarry.

With the death of his mother, Girija Prasad's final bridge to the mainland is broken. His brother is the only one who visits them, concerned about this ghost of a brother who taught him to cycle as a child and made him pay attention to passing slugs and snails, to avoid running over them. Each visit worsens his fears.

He remembers Girija Prasad as a man devoted to the cause of appropriate dressing, sporting a different set for breakfast, supper, office, jungle, golf, and Sundays. But now his clothes are wrapped around him like the worn threads people tie around banyan trees for blessings. Girija Prasad's brother gives up on him when he finds him browsing through the morning papers with his reading glasses upside down.

As for his niece, the cherubic angel he'd cradled at birth, she is now Mowgli. Her hair is matted brown and her skin is patchy with sunburn. For meals, she sits cross-legged on the table instead of a chair. She spends her mornings avoiding school and clothes. Like her father, she doodles in the margins of research papers.

Devi's uncle has secured her admission at a boarding school in Nainital, a town in the Himalayan foothills. The principal, an Englishwoman, was Girija Prasad's classmate at Oxford and is willing to make concessions for the motherless child.

"What is the need?" Girija Prasad asks.

"You went to Oxford. You enjoyed English poetry. But your daughter, she thinks 'the woods are lovely, dark and deep' is an ode that you've written to the Andaman padauk."

Girija Prasad laughs affectionately. "She has a unique way of perceiving things."

"Even if she does, I'm afraid she will never leave the islands if she doesn't leave now. What will happen to her higher education? Who will marry her? Had Chanda Bhabhi been alive . . ." He doesn't complete the sentence.

In Girija Prasad's silence lies his resignation.

"Why don't you come with her?" his brother asks.

"If I leave the islands, I will never know why I came here in the first place."

G IRIJA PRASAD DOESN'T KNOW that incessant advice is how parents display their concern. He doesn't know that the time before Devi's departure ought to be spent tailoring clothes, mending shoes, sticking labels, packing and repacking. For the best way to ignore the moment of separation is to deny the silence that precedes it.

He rows a boat into sheltered coves and bays instead. "The world under water is an undocumented map of the world over water," he often tells her. "To solely inhabit the land limits our understanding. All terrains and forms of life, all the cycles of nature and emotions found on land, increase manifold in water."

Swimming is the closest he has come to prayer. Aches and pains disappear. Nothing can weigh one down, not even regrets and fears. There may be moments of tension in the company of crocodiles, sharks, and manta rays, but fear in the water is a different experience from fear on land. It is a profound form of awe.

Girija Prasad and Devi have identified patches of coral, rocks, and weed that remind them of continents and animals. In the topography of the underworld, Italy is a scar on a turtle shell, and Antarctica a sandbar that surfaces during low tide.

They watch the sun rise over Antarctica, off the coast of the Middle Andamans, and the sun set over the Dead Sea, their name for the salt plains. An elephant trail connects the edges of the day—Devi's final one on the islands. She is eager to follow an elephant on its journeys between the timber camp and the forest site. The workers tell Devi that her mother was a seer who had rescued that very creature from madness. Trailing her footsteps, stroking her trunk, and holding her ears to climb onto her back, Devi seeks signs of acknowledgment in those eyes.

By the afternoon, the heat has sapped them. Girija Prasad can see the liquid sparkle evaporate from Devi's eyes, her mouth gaping with thirst. But they have run out of water, even lemons. He waits for the elephant to walk ahead and stops by a footprint she's left behind. It takes a while to settle. The deep imprint cradles clear water, squeezed from the soft, wet earth. He collects it in his palm and wets Devi's face and throat. For a fraction of a moment, Devi glimpses her father's reflection and her own in the water. It makes her smile. How comfortably her world sits in an elephant's footprint. Like the islands, it is nothing more than a passing reflection in the ocean of time.

Exhausted by the day and frightened at the prospect of leaving, Devi asks her father, "Are you angry with me because I kill insects and broke the porcelain doll in the cabinet?"

"No," he replies. "Do I seem angry?"

"You're sending me so far away."

He strokes his daughter's hair and kisses her forehead. Unlike her parents, Devi has fiercely curly hair. A reminder that she is more than their synthesis.

"I am an aging scientist. The islands are big enough for my research but too small to contain the curiosity of a promising young scientist like you. You must leave so that you can return with the latest discoveries and theories and educate me. . . . You must experience snowfall for yourself."

Girija Prasad talks to her as adults speak to children, not as one scientist to another. Devi doesn't prod him further. Even science has its limitations. Though one can predict patterns of separation by studying the past, the actual moment always comes as a shock.

With her first step on the mainland, Devi's life changes irrevocably. The sight of land as endless and chaotic as this is overwhelming. Seated beside a train window for three whole days, she finds that the landscape is rarely broken by rivers or lakes. If Devi didn't know better, she would be tempted to believe that three-quarters of the world is land. But she does know better. She knows of islands such as hers, undulating, fragmented, and surrounded by the ocean. They bear greater truths than continents.

As her bus leaves the train station to crawl high into the mountains, Devi's intestines knot up. One cannot see the toes of the foothills one set out from. Accustomed to confronting the nothingness that sits over the ocean, spreading wide and far into the horizon, she hasn't confronted the same nothingness from such heights. She feels nauseated.

In the dormitory, students are quick to mark their territory with family portraits, photographs of pets, and other portable items of nostalgia, like toys and greeting cards. Devi has nothing. Besides the shell her father gave her, her bags hold nothing sentimental. He insisted that she leave behind the treasures she had collected on Ross Island, the piece of coral she had chipped off from a museum display or her scrapbook of feathers, leaves, and flowers, even her parents' sepia portrait. Such baggage weighs the soul down, he believes.

"What about your family?" a curious occupant on the neighboring bed inquires. Devi tells her about Girija Prasad and Mary. "Is she your mother?" the girl asks.

"No."

"Where is your mother?"

Devi doesn't quite know how to answer the question. Her mother is an urn of ashes strewn across all the corners of the Andamans. It took her father over a year to journey to the various extremities of the archipelago. Technically, that is where her mother is, or was last known to be.

Later that night, she hears the whispers going around the dorm, like the swirling currents of a whirlpool. All the rumors battle against one another, until one girl has the courage to confront Devi.

"Did your mother run away? Or is your maid your mother?" Devi's answer is succinct: a slap on the girl's face.

In her first week of school, Devi slaps two students on different occasions for calling her an orphan. Despite her skinny build, no one hits back. It's those penetrating eyes. Her mother's eyes. They can arrest an animal in its tracks and compel humans into submission. Devi is nick-named "Red Indian." Not only is her skin burned red, her behavior is also uncouth, like that of the naked tribals living on her island. Some claim Devi's father is a tribal chief with so many wives no one knows which one her mother is.

When she enters the dining hall for lunch one day, a group of se-niors seated nearby instigate her hostility.

"Hey, girlie, will you slap all of us if we call you a Red Indian?" one of them shouts.

They get no reply.

"Will you slap us if we call you an orphan?"

"We don't mind being slapped by a junior," pipes in a third. "It's better than being caned by the teachers."

The whole table is up in laughter.

A few days later, when the lunch break precedes an afternoon in the playground, Devi skips a class to sneak into the dining hall. She pours half a bottle of ketchup on the hidden edge of their bench. By the time they notice, it is too late. The senior students are marching into the playground with what look like period stains on their skirts.

Devi is impervious to discipline. For her, caning or detention isn't pun-ishment. In moments of pain, she escapes to the islands. She clutches on to the shell, a naturally polished conch, that her father had gifted her. It fills her being with the distant sound of waves, transforming the mountains into the highest and mightiest of them. Denuded branches resemble driftwood, and every tear carries within it the salt of the ocean.

It is only when the monsoons are a distant thunder and autumn is retreating from the trees that the tremors of change arrive to alter her course. Devi wakes up to a bleeding nose on a frigid November day, one that marks the sharp fall into winter. On her way to the sink, she senses a movement in the air. Odd, she thinks as she peers out of the window. Something refuses to identify itself.

"Who are you?" she asks.

Bloated grains of salt fill the air. They tease gravity, floating higher and higher instead of falling. They defy the force by gaining strength and size. When they end up on the ground or the window, they disappear. What follows for the rest of the day is a mix of hail, snow, and all the stages in between. To Devi, snow will always be like dust particles, pollen grains, salt, sand, or bits of cloud—something to be grasped only in analogies. For a tropical animal breastfed on cantankerous rains and the incessant heaving of waves, it will feel like a shroud, covering the lands with silence.

Soon, enemies turn into playmates. Fellow students hold one another's hands to prevent slipping, even as they skid on purpose. Some swallow hailstones and offer them around like free candy.

That night, Devi witnesses the snow throwing light back onto the trees, the compound walls, the streetlamps, even the moon and the empty sky. She understands what her father meant when he spoke of the earth's glow. Just as fireflies and plankton generate light, the earth too is bathed in its own light. Her father calls it geo-luminescence. "The ocean floor carries light deep within, and so does snow," he had told her.

The next day, a powerful sun forces the frost to retreat into the shadows of trees and to the edges of the compound. As frost replaces dewdrops over the grass, Devi looks forward to winter.

Her first glimpse of snow is a sight she will hold on to forever, like the spiraling conch. Its sheer presence in her memories will tinge all the moments that preceded it, and all the moments to come, with tenderness.

GIRIJA PRASAD ABANDONS the rocking chair for a stationary one after he realizes that the earth is as fidgety and temperamental as a senile old man. The ground that he took for granted is a superficial crust floating on top of a fluid interior.

With every new discovery in the 1960s, scientists find it difficult to cope. Even though a submersible bears witness to new lands pouring out of the mid-ocean ridges, it still feels impossible. The core of the earth remains a mystery and, with it, the reasons that compel us all to wander, drift, sink, and surface.

Faultlines, not rigid continents, guiding poles, or mighty oceans, hold it all together. For every inch of new land created somewhere on a ridge, an older inch of land sinks into a crack. The cracks balance it all out. The cracked few, not the meek, shall inherit the earth.

When Girija Prasad applies the radical new geological theories to the islands, the conclusions are obvious. The geology of the islands is a history of conflict. The Andaman Islands are part of a subduction zone, like Indonesia to the southeast and Burma, Nepal, the Himalayas, and the Karakorams to the north. It is here that the Indian plate is sinking under the Asian plate. It is probably why the islands are the most haunted place Chanda Devi visited. Like the continents, life refuses to give in. People live on as ghosts, dismissing death as a poetic detail for sentimental folk to fuss over.

Girija Prasad sits in his armchair, wide-eyed. The previous evening, he'd chanced upon a paper titled "Fluctuation in Gravitational Pull in Subduction Zones: A Speculation." Though it lacked rigorous scientific backing, the preliminary research posed too many questions to ignore. Girija Prasad didn't sleep that night. Chanda Devi kept him awake.

In the first few months of their marriage, Chanda Devi didn't openly claim, or even secretly confide to Girija Prasad, that she could talk to trees. She just did. On their walks together, she would often stand next to one, at times laughing, at times surprised or maintaining a solemn gaze. He was intrigued. The possibility of a botanist communicating with a tree was as thrilling as the possibility of a priest chatting with god.

On a short hike together, when Chanda Devi halted to greet an old banyan tree, Girija Prasad asked her about the tree's opinion, if any, on his forestry projects and theses. One by one, he explained his pet projects and ideas, and the tree responded through her. The banyan considered his actions and knowledge largely sensible but shot down his dream of introducing teak, a foreign species, to the islands. Teak was the most profitable timber in the world. If he could grow teak in the Andaman Islands, a perfect soil and climate for its growth, the Forest Department would be rich. But the banyan prophesied that teak would prove vulnerable to fungi the local flora had grown immune to. Girija Prasad considered the banyan's views odd. He went back to his greenhouse and tested all the local forms of fungi on teak saplings. The saplings remained healthy. There was a reason why teak was considered to be the sturdiest timber in the world, exported to make railroads in Alaska and machans in Congo: It was impervious to infection. Backed by science, Girija Prasad would go ahead and order four hundred teak saplings from Burma for the exercise. The experiment would succeed, much to the scientist's relief.

It wouldn't be until five years later, when Devi was a three-year-old toddler and the teak saplings had entered their adolescence, that a mysterious disease would ravage the entire consignment, turning the leaves to mosaic and the bark to shrapnel within a fortnight. The culprit would turn out to be a fungus that had remained undiscovered until then. Girija Prasad would go down, reluctantly, in botanical annals as its discoverer.

With Chanda Devi's assistance, the fuchsia-pink rosebush had talked to him too. As a tender shoot uprooted from its home in the blue hills, it had given up on life, suffocated and undernourished in a wooden box. But when it arrived on the islands and the box was opened, it was Girija Prasad's worried face that it saw. He nurtured the stems with the tenacity of Mother Nature. The roses bloomed for his sake.

He was overwhelmed. "Why can you talk to plants? Why can't I?" he asked his wife.

"In spirit, I am kindred to them."

"But you talk to ghosts too."

Chanda Devi laughed. "Plants are the most sensitive spirits in the web of creation. They bind the earth to water and air, and they bind different worlds together. They make life possible. Which is why they can see, feel, and hear more than other forms, especially humans."

"But you are human too."

"Just who do you think you have married?"

Girija Prasad, a keen observer and scientist of nature himself, could make no sense of it. Chanda Devi defied everything that he had learned.

"Who am I?" he asked her.

"I cannot tell you."

"But you're my wife. Surely, it doesn't count as cheating if you help me out."

"We have been soulmates for several births now. But in each birth, our search for love and struggle for purpose is new. It is why I made my bed on the floor for all those nights. You had to earn a place in my heart."

"This is why I prefer physics to metaphysics," he sighed. "No one talks in riddles, only equations."

"I don't have the time to entertain physics now," said Chanda Devi as she got up from the porch steps. "The dal is on the stove, and if I don't attend to it, it will burn, thanks to the increased gravity today. It makes the water boil as soon as you light the stove."

"Gravity?" he asked, hoping he had heard wrong.

"The islands are so unpredictable. The gravity keeps shifting. The other day when we felt the tremors, remember?"

"Yes, when an earthquake hit Papua."

"Yes, yes. That afternoon, it ruined my dal. It took me almost half an hour to get the water heated—and then it burned up, just like that!"

Girija Prasad was an explorer with a curiosity wide and deep enough to swallow the whole world if it presented him with the chance. He had spent his youth trekking in the Alps and the Himalayas, swimming in the Mediterranean Sea, and yearning to run his fingers through the Arabian sands when his ship passed through the Suez Canal.

But the islands, they were his first love. With only eight elephants and two trunks' worth of books and equipment to offer as bride price, he urged them to give in to his curiosity. They refused.

He moved on eventually, consumed by his wife. Fitted within her contours was a universe entirely different yet linked to his own. Her gaze wasn't otherworldly. It was that other world itself.

Not yet fifty, Girija Prasad finds himself alone again. He courts the islands to give in to his curiosity once more. To reveal the mysteries of gravity, to tell him how it all came about and, when it did, was he created as a solitary peak?

With all the new roads and waterways, Girija Prasad spends his time driving, walking, and swimming aimlessly around the islands. Cellular Jail is a mockery now, and Ross Island is in ruins. Rice fields and hutments have encroached upon the jungle. Mud paths are concrete roads. There are shops. There are strangers. There is garbage. It hurts him to see the islands suffer like this. Girija Prasad—dangling from one day and then another as though from the branches of a tree— may have moved on but only to confront life's biggest irony: What one considered past loves would prove to be life's longest affairs.

Through all his explorations, the islands return his expectant gaze. "Where were you all these years?" they seem to say. Behind the accusatory tone lies a tenacious attachment, for the islands never left Girija Prasad, and he never really left the islands.

On Ross Island, although the ghosts would hold their noses in the air and feign indifference to Chanda Devi's presence, it was just an act. So when they saw Girija Prasad return all alone, they were alarmed.

On piecing the tragedy together, they held a prayer meeting in the roofless church for Chanda Devi. "Her passing," the priest said, "marks the end of an era. Ghosts live as long as clairvoyants live."

An apothecary's ghost empathized with Girija Prasad's pain. His own grave lay broken in the graveyard, next to those of his wife and child. Though he had spent his adult days preparing medicines, when it came to the life of his wife and three-month-old daughter, he'd been helpless. The water on Ross Island was poison for the weak. It had claimed his young family in a single year. Much to the apothecary's despair, even death couldn't reunite him with his family. Their souls had moved to different births, while his remained on Ross Island. It was he who had found out about the Varma tragedy and informed the others, just as Girija Prasad had pieced together the apothecary's story by reading the tombstones.

Two decades have passed, and the apothecary is still in the habit of trailing Girija Prasad. One evening, he walks behind Girija Prasad, halting when the man halts. Girija Prasad turns around and walks toward him. He walks with such purpose, the apothecary wonders if he can see him. Could it be that the lovelorn scientist had invented a way of seeing ghosts?

The two stand face-to-face. Girija Prasad looks into the apothecary's faded eyes. The apothecary senses life reaching out to him. He feels a warm wetness on his feet. He is standing, he realizes, between a man relieving himself and a tree.

———

On a long, solitary walk, Girija Prasad is surprised to find lines of poetry scribbled on the soft sands where the surf breaks. Someone is contemplating verses. Written in archaic cursive is the ocean's epic. It is the washed-out lines and sand-filled gaps that arrest his imagination, seizing him in their eddy.

He searches for the Poet. He runs through the entire stretch, even the path at the bend. He climbs the cliff on the other edge and squints into the horizon. He reflects on them—the ocean, the sky, the verse.

Blessed are the ones who weep,
for her salt flows in their tears.
The ocean lives on in their tales
as they wander in her ebb and flow . . .

Girija Prasad hasn't cried since her death. It may take years, if not decades, for the tears to arrive. One day, they certainly will. The ocean will well up in his eyes.

Mary leaves the house on Mount Harriet when she receives a letter from Rangoon, urging her to return. Her son, the infant she left behind twenty-three years ago, has sought her out.

"You have no family, Mary," Girija Prasad implores when she tells him. He is afraid that Mary too has slipped into the past—like him.

"Devi's future lies on the mainland," Mary says to him. "As soon as she completes her education, get her married."

"And what about your future?"

She looks away. She begins to wipe the crockery left to dry on the dining table. She has persisted with the elaborate ritual of setting the table for every meal. It is her way of drawing him out of his study, reminding him of the practical existence of forks and spoons.

"I had a son," she speaks up. "I had a son for all these years, and now I have a son again. He is a student, but the dictator has put him in prison. . . . Like the inmates of Cellular Jail . . . he doesn't know if he will ever be released."

He helps her clear the table before resuming his solitary hours. Lost among bookshelves, he wonders what Chanda Devi, the compassionate one, would have done in his place.

Later that day, Girija Prasad hands Mary a pouch.

"There is enough money in here to see you through the journey," he says. "There's also a pair of your mistress's earrings and a necklace. Sell the earrings when you get there. Hire a lawyer to fight for your son. If the rule of law doesn't exist, pray. Sell the necklace on your son's release. Secure his passage out of Burma—and your own. The country is going through violent times.

"The dinghy to Burma goes through open waters. Go on an empty stomach, and suck on a lemon if you feel seasick."

When the time comes for Mary to leave, Girija Prasad accompanies her to the gate. Mary stoops to touch her master's feet. He strokes her forehead in return.

"Thank you," he says.

"Thank you," she replies.

Life alone, after her departure, proves to be easier than he thought. The house on Mount Harriet hasn't fallen apart, but an air of decrepitude has wafted in.

Now that he is alone, there is no need for clothes. Girija Prasad can see the tribal wisdom behind nakedness. Elaborate clothing, and a culture that engenders it with elaborate notions of modesty, is a fool's paradise, not a tropical one. He has also begun to bathe and relieve himself in the wilderness, nourishing the soil with his gratitude. Teatime, though, remains sacrosanct. Tea is always to be had on the porch, poured from a ceramic teapot and served with biscuits, since cakes are difficult to procure in this part of the world. He has stopped reading books altogether. He shuffles through them instead, feeling the pulse of a page between his fingers. An ardent artist since childhood, Girija

Prasad was too shy to commit to his art in public. Now that he is alone, he sketches where his heart desires, leaving a trail of pencil shavings and crumpled paper.

He is afraid the face may disappear from his memory if he doesn't meditate upon it daily.

The eyes are impossible to replicate on paper. Chanda Devi left the world with her eyes open, and he refused to let any pandit or relative force them closed. Her gaze remains focused, unwavering, forever. Sometimes, the father meets the mother's gaze again in their daughter's eyes.

Each portrait is a discovery. It is a fossil, retrieved from the gravel of memories and preoccupations. All creation, he is tempted to extrapolate, is a form of self-discovery. The face that he searches for cannot be extricated from the canvas of natural history. Born from an imagination that predates life's splintering into animals, plants, and fungi, she is inchoate. She belongs to a time when life could commune with all its possible forms, because all life was one.

He has submitted to the course of nature—the path crosses his heart, literally. One night, he wakes up to a strange itch on his chest. It is a centipede, one foot long, crawling over him. He holds his breath. The movement of a hundred legs is similar to that of a wave breaking on the shore, foam unraveling itself from one end to the other.

An insect entangled in the web of his own creation, Girija Prasad had suffered all his life. A loner at heart, he feared loneliness. Now, naked and alone, Girija Prasad stumbles across an invisible line. One that doesn't separate this world from the others but instead encloses them all.

On Mount Harriet, Girija Prasad experiences the solitude of an archipelago.

D EVI IS SHOCKED to see her father in the state he is in. Unlike other teens who rebel by moving out, she does so by threatening to return.

She has come home, midterm. And now that she is home, the father and daughter return to their days of exploration, following elephants and floating on their Dead Sea. But Devi doesn't enter the water beyond waist deep. She has given up swimming, after an incident at a picnic some months ago. She had gone to a waterfall with her friends one Sunday. Confident, she swam the farthest. The others followed. No one was aware of the whirlpool beneath the surge. Suddenly she felt a hand clinging to her foot. It pulled her down in panic. The more Devi struggled, the deeper she sank. She kicked and kicked until the hand let go.

Girija Prasad takes his daughter on long drives, not just hikes. He drives her to his recent discovery—an alcove overlooking jade-green waters, soothing and transparent as in a fishbowl. They stand on the cliff together, peering alternately at the clear sky above and clearer sea below.

"Jump with me," he says, offering her his hand.

"With clothes on?" At twenty, Devi cannot be expected to swim naked anymore.

"Child, clothes dry under the sun. It is a fact of life."

Devi hesitates. She cannot do it. Girija Prasad takes her hand. He signals her to take a step forward. Before the tears can breach, she has struck the water below. She doesn't need to swim. Her father's hand pulls her up to the surface, leading her to the rocks.

On the long and wet drive back home, she speaks up.

"When I was drowning, I held on to my breath. My ears could have exploded with the sound of my heartbeat."

"When you were in your mother's womb, I would place my ear against her tense belly to hear your heartbeat. It was so loud, even I feared my ears would explode."

"I was scared," she says. "My eyes were open, but I saw only black. All I could hear was my heart. . . . My classmate . . . did I kill him?"

"No. You may be a good swimmer, but you are not trained to rescue drowning people."

Devi remains silent. The sun has begun to recede. "Papa," she asks again, "did I cause Mummy to die?"

Girija Prasad is upset with Devi's professors. How poor must the teaching be, how callous their attitude toward the students, if they return home with such questions? He is upset with Mary for leaving them. He is upset with himself, for he cannot find an answer.

The road passes through a jungle. In place of words, all he can find are trees, imposing, ancient, impenetrable in the diminishing light.

"It was a time long ago, before you were conceived," he says at last. "We were strolling in the jungle that surrounds the Lilliputian volcanoes in the Middle Andamans. I found your mother stroking the trunk of a palm tree. It was a *Corypha macropoda* in its final stages of life. Once it flowers, it dies. She asked me why it happened. It was how trees had evolved, I explained to her. Some had gone from producing hundreds of seeds with a diminished chance of survival to flowering only once but ensuring the seeds made it by giving them their best. . . . Now I realize why she asked me that question. Your mother wanted me to know the answer. As a human being, I cannot look beyond life and death. But as a botanist, I see how limiting individual life cycles can be to our understanding. Nature is a continuum. That is how it thrives."

Girija Prasad wants to say something more. But he is helpless. His entire life, it seems, is a leap from one word to another, one day to another, one landscape to another. It is fragmented and disjointed, like the islands. Over time he has learned to dredge out meaning, sometimes even faith, from the ocean of emptiness that surrounds him.

Devi understands. She has grown up at the edge of that ocean herself, swimming far, wide, and deep in that very search.

She returns to college at the end of the vacation.

In college, Devi prefers to study flowers and the new sensations youth brings forth, rather than books. She looks at the mirror often and avoids the afternoon sun. On her annual visit to Mount Harriet a year later, Devi places a hibiscus, impeccably preserved, under her pillow each night. Her father asks about it.

"It's from a friend," she says.

"What's his name?"

"Vishnu."

"Where's he from?"

"The mountains. The border of Sikkim and Nepal."

Later that night, Girija Prasad reflects over it, the hibiscus. The shriveled petals will soon crumble. In a humid climate such as this, only the stem will remain by the time of her departure. And what about him, the ephemerist? Will he wait, or will his feelings wither, like the ephemera he bears?

"Why don't you invite Vishnu to Mount Harriet for tea sometime?" he asks his daughter at breakfast the next morning.

"He lives six days away," she replies. "Three days by boat, two days by train, one day uphill on the road."

Sensing her hesitation, he says, "You did your schooling in the mountains. You enjoy snow."

"The islands are our home."

Girija Prasad is silent.

"Papa, you and your trees cannot convince me this time."

But flowers succeed where trees fail. Devi breaks down with the fragrance of magnolia, one that Vishnu has plucked from his garden and preserved as a sapling. He wants her to inhale it as a living plant. He wants their love to grow.

After Devi and Vishnu graduate, they come to the islands to register their marriage, with Girija Prasad as witness. The time has come for him to work on his final portrait, a wedding gift for his daughter. It all comes together, like Pangaea once did in a dream, decades ago.

Chanda Devi has experienced age through Girija Prasad's strokes. Had she been alive, this is how she would have looked at her daughter's wedding. The artist has taken the liberty of dressing her in her own wedding sari. The paper was especially produced for the occasion. It is a mix of Andaman padauk, rose petals, and saffron. Chanda Devi loved talking to plants. He hopes that they will whisper his thoughts back to her.

Life and death are a continuum. No one has studied this as closely as he has. "All of us are burdened by the twin destinies of saying goodbye to our loved ones and departing from our loved ones ourselves," he writes in a letter accompanying the gift. "Let this not obliterate the greater destiny we all share—the fleeting moments we have together."

It is one of those rare moments in Devi's life when Teesta, her four-month-old daughter, named after a river in Sikkim, has no desire to feed, urinate, or cry. Devi is relieved to sleep. In her dream, she sees a man, aged and naked, floating in the ocean. She recognizes the blue immediately. It lies ahead of the beach on Mount Harriet, where the island shelf slips with a sharp fall.

His limbs reach out in four directions. His face is calm, and he has a faint smile. She knows this man. He would visit her in her dreams on the long voyages back and forth as a schoolgirl. Where has he been for all these years? she wonders. Why did he leave her when she grew up? His presence, even in dreams, had always left her calm, but today Devi shouts in her sleep, "Papa! Papa!"

Teesta begins to cry. Vishnu consoles them both, his wife and child. "It's just a dream," he tells her. "Why don't you call him?"

"Child, it seems I was smiling in your dream," Girija Prasad tells her on the phone. "Why are you worried?"

Devi is rattled. She wants to visit him but must wait for Teesta to turn six months old.

"Papa," she says. "Good morning." Words that have anchored his mornings, never failing to pull him out of an abyss of dreams, memories, and despair.

"But it's three A.M.," he says. "'Good night' would make more sense."

"You will not go to sleep, I know. You'll probably make yourself tea and study through the night."

"I can hear my grandchild wailing. Perhaps she would like to join me in my nocturnal research?"

Devi smiles. "She'll make an obstinate assistant. She refuses to co-operate.

"I love you," she adds, in the silence.

"I love you too, my angel," her father replies.

It is the first time Girija Prasad has uttered those words. To him, they are the contemporary shorthand for expressing an emotion that old people like him had invested a lifetime of silence in.

In an hour or less, the darkness will begin to diminish. The crows and the birds will wake the dead and the high tide will recede.

Girija Prasad steps out to pluck fresh mint leaves for his tea. As he sits on the porch, he senses a sudden drop in temperature and an opaque shift in the sky. It indicates the arrival of an unexpected guest. He pours himself a cup of tea in anticipation. Before he can place his lips on the rim, he confronts a bee floating inside. It is in the final stages of its struggle. Its wings are fluttering, but its torso has ceased to move. Girija Prasad scoops it out with a spoon and places it in a potted plant nearby.

He cannot drink the tea anymore. Though he has no qualms about sharing his tea with insects, this cup has been contaminated by a futile struggle. He gets up to make another round, this time with lemongrass and ginger. The sharp taste will suit the new arrival.

By the time he returns, the guest has arrived. It has begun to rain. But the rain is unusual, unlike the tropical melodrama he's accustomed to. It is windless, cloudless. "Mountain rain!" he exclaims. In high altitudes, it is the mist that carries rain.

He stands amidst the fog in his garden. Bamboo-straight drops of rain connect heaven and earth, with him standing in between. They fall in complete silence, so silent that he can hear himself breathe. They have fed the Himalayan rivers since their birth, and now it's his turn. Tender drops wet his forehead, his lips, his limbs.

With a single shower, the mountain rains wash the webs he has built around himself, filling him with an urge to visit the gods of all mountains—the Himalayas. For he is Girija, the child of the mountains.

I T IS A MONTH of longing and frustration. A month of braving incessant horizontal rains that arrive from as far as Polynesia in the east and, increasingly, Zanzibar in the west. Rains that tell you the sun is dead, and with it all the seasons. Rains that are a prelude to the oceans taking over.

It is a month of relentlessly mopping the floors, of opening and closing windows in delirium, of placing buckets under shifting cracks in the ceiling, of wiping moss with bare hands and drying handkerchiefs on the stove. A month of talking aloud to the heavens, lest the monsoons drown out your inner voice.

It is time to acknowledge the reflection in the mirror and join hands with one's shadow. It is the month Girija Prasad brought Chanda Devi to the islands. It is the month of June.

Girija Prasad navigates the thicket, making his way to the beach below Mount Harriet for a swim. He has gone past the Japanese bunkers when a subterranean thunder hits him. The bunkers fly up. So do his feet, before landing beside his head. His nose is buried under his groin as a tree breaks his fall.

The earth falls back into slumber as swiftly as it had woken up. In its aftermath, a crack has emerged on his path. The land ahead has opened like an eggshell. So he folds his lungi and underwear and places his walking stick on them, before crawling into the crack on all fours. He doesn't want to dirty his clothes, for he intends to put off washing until it's time for Teesta, his granddaughter, to visit.

Steam, a spontaneous mix of humidity and mud, rises all around him. The centipedes and earthworms, masters of the netherworld, are as confused as he is. They crawl over one another, hanging on to the ferns and leaves that dangle from the canopy. He looks nervously at his testicles as he contemplates the monsoon leeches.

He is in search of a fossil or evidence of some kind, perhaps a new type of rock. He runs his fingers over the exposed layers. He hunts for the fantastical imprint of an undiscovered species. Though it hasn't been documented yet, he suspects that the seafloor is opening up in the Andaman Sea to the east. It must. It is the push that completes the fall. Yet all scientists seem to know of is the subduction zone to the south.

He gives up. He crawls out. Trees have fallen around him. Trees are still falling, using one another as crutches to break the fall. He can smell the odor of low tide from a distance. He leaves the collective shriek of birds and animals behind as he approaches the beach.

He halts in shock.

The ocean has withdrawn into its shell. Seaweed and coral glisten under an afternoon sun, as stranded fish jump up and down, gasping. Unable to scream, the fish look like they are filled with an irrepressible urge to dance in the sun.

He walks toward the water. He follows its footprints—shallow puddles among the bed of rocks. The force of the receding currents has created a strange universe. It has pushed an octopus, a pipefish, a tiger prawn, and a sea urchin into an inextricable embrace. Predator and prey lie hopelessly tangled. Girija Prasad marvels at the octopus's intelligence as she frees her tentacles one by one.

He moves on. He is distracted by his reflection peering at him from a thin sheet of algae and water. Only days away from turning fifty, he looks older than he imagined himself to be. His skin has been burned and wrinkled by all the tropical excursions. He is balding. His shoulders stoop. Flesh hangs from his bones in shame, hiding the true depth of aging inside.

He has met him on several occasions, this man. During the hardest of times, a vision would crawl out from the ocean to soothe him, stroking his forehead, holding his hand. He didn't know who it was then, although he knew it was no god or ghost. It had been established beyond doubt that he could not commune with either.

But he is not ready.

He is yet to meet his grandchild. He is yet to embrace his daughter and son-in-law one last time. He hasn't even watered the plants in the greenhouse for two days. If he doesn't do it this evening, they may perish. From the spirals of time, Chanda Devi's words return to echo in the spirals of Girija Prasad's inner ear. "That's cheating," she says. For when it is time, it is time.

Based on the volume and distance of the ocean's recession, he estimates that a tsunami should hit the beach in ten to fifteen minutes.

This presents him with two options. He could either sprint back to the beach's edge, begin climbing Mount Harriet, and crawl up a tree—an ideal vantage point—or he could walk straight in. The land falls sharply like a cliff very close to the beach. For how often does a man get to peer into a thriving ocean floor minus the ocean, even though it will go undocumented?

Both these options imply a sprint. And he is in no mood to work up a sweat. This is a moment to be savored, down to every cell and atom. Mid-ocean, the tsunami can only be experienced as an extraordinary undulation. It is on sloping beaches such as this one that it arrives in its full glory: destructive and dramatic.

Drifting between options, he wakes up to the only possibility. He has no time to wander among the exposed mollusks and corals, lyrical distractions from the truth that is about to arrive. He has no time left to blink, least of all to turn back and steal one final glance at his home.

A line stretches from one end of the horizon to the other. For all he knows, it outstretches the horizon—tsunamis are known to circle around the entire world and return to the original crack.

The birds have intensified their cries. They have taken to the skies in panic, like muddied currents heralding a flood.

The water hits the island shelf with a pure and overwhelming silence. The universe may have come to life with a bang, but the possibilities were conceived in silence. With time, it will all vanish. The islands, their civilizations, the coral, the ocean. Only silence will remain.

He straightens himself. Girija Prasad stands upright as it approaches. Up close, the curl ceases to be a mere shape. It is roof and ground at the same time. It is the ocean's very womb, seeking new life to nurture.

A lifetime ago, on a day unlike this one, Girija Prasad had lost Chanda Devi. It was unbearably hot, forty-two degrees Celsius to be precise. He stood all alone in some alien corridor, detached from the rest of the hospital. Yet the overbearing smell of blood prevailed. Like the warmth and tenderness of the skin of his wife, declared dead.

The window in front of him framed a different world altogether. A wind stoked the inferno, rattling the aerial roots of the banyan tree outside. A lone parrot stood guard on the windowsill. "Perhaps Mrs. Parrot has laid eggs on the nurse's headdress," he whispered to Devi, swaddled in his arms. For his baby's sake, he had promised not to crumble. Since her arrival, he had never cried.

Standing face-to-face with a tsunami, he is distracted by a youthful stiffness. He's sporting an erection—a perfect right angle to his legs, pointing straight ahead. He laughs. His eyes well up. Girija Prasad Varma sheds a tear.

And the water carries him away.

FAULTLINE

ON THE MORNING of Plato's arrest, the air is heavy with the possibility of a cyclone. Water has condensed on the walls, dripping onto his straw mat, soaking his ever-shifting longyi. Plato wakes up to his favorite moment: an unexpected drop in temperature, overcast skies, and the smell of wet earth, mixed with citrus and incense.

As he brushes his teeth in the overgrown courtyard, an earthworm crawls onto his slipper, soft, tender, as eager for the rains as Plato himself. He splashes it with water, lest it shrivel. "Wait," he says as he brushes it off. "Wait a little longer."

Later that day, he happens to share his table with a stranger at a roadside tea stall. They don't exchange a single word. Plato looks preoccupied, reading Camus's *The Outsider*, ignoring the samosa and tea on the table, as if he hadn't asked for them. The stranger's eyes wander aimlessly as she whistles a tune, oblivious to where his attention really is. Like all Burmese women, she has painted her face with thanakha in the hope of preserving her fair complexion. Though he isn't close enough to inhale her sandalwood fragrance, Plato knows the peculiar chemistry of her skin has altered it. There is nothing unusual about her clothes or appearance. She wears a pink blouse and a matching longyi, with frangipani pinned in her hair. But she also wears a wristwatch and a pearl pendant—signs, like the pink nail varnish, that she's a city girl.

Plato has never heard a woman whistle before. It comes as a shock, unbefitting of his idea of what a lady is supposed to be like. She taps her fingers with the tune, lost to the affairs of the table. What next? he wonders. Will she have the audacity to pull out a cigarette?

There is something unpredictable about her, the way she whistles and remains indifferent toward him. The ease with which she unsettles the centuries of dust shrouding the pedestrians and plants, the dilapidated teak furniture, the waiting and the waited upon, all to her rhythm. Tonight he will fall asleep thinking of her, even as she will remain oblivious of his trembling hands struggling to hold the book straight.

Plato's friends in university encourage him to approach his objects of desire. He has all the qualities of a worthy suitor, they assure him—an infectious smile, a way with words. He's alert to the existence of beauty all around him. But he lacks the courage.

Hours later, when Plato is alone in his shared room, a plainclothes unit of military intelligence arrests him. He doesn't put his book aside until they put the handcuffs on. He wonders if his roommates had known all along. Why else were they missing from the scene? Even if they had known, he would have forgiven them for distancing themselves. They have parents, siblings, and families to fear for. Unlike him, an orphan.

All the students from the underground resistance group are rounded up in a van, which leaves the city before midnight. Through the uncertainties and darkness, the route seems familiar to Plato. The van crosses a muddy offshoot that leads to the forest monastery his grandfather would frequent.

It takes him back to the days when he would stand at the monastery's edge and stare. He was a child then, conjuring up other worlds to explain this one. The jungle was a place where tigers, crocodiles, Nagas—serpent dragons—and Nat spirits ruled. It was where he belonged. His mother, a Naga, had taken human form for his birth. His father, a Naga too, was a serpent from the sea. Earthquakes, whirlpools, cyclones were all their doing, as they slithered through their serpent holes.

Plato's grandfather had passed away two years ago, eight months after his grandmother. A heart attack had killed his grandmother, but he wondered what killed his grandfather. Was it loneliness? Or the tedium of aging?

His own father, he was told, had died before his birth. His mother had abandoned him to start a new life with another man. For all practical purposes, he was an orphan. With no one else to call his own, he entered a monastery. He shaved his hair off and tried to meditate. Within a week, he ran away from the place. He enrolled himself in Rangoon University. Orphans, he realized, needed human bonds, ordinary distractions, and excuses to hang on to. Not the metaphysical emptiness propounded by a prince who had everything—kingdom, palace, parents, wife, children—only to give it all up.

He joined the underground movement on campus. Inspired by communism, he orchestrated three strikes in two years. As an active member of the students' union, he wrote, edited, and distributed pamphlets under the pseudonym "Plato," a man who believed that philosophers, not army generals, were kings. Soon enough, he stopped using or responding to his real name altogether. His parents, he would proudly tell others, were communist rebels hiding in the Shan Hills. They impressed the girls, his revolutionary origins.

As the army drives them all into the jungle, Plato can't avoid the queer sensation he carries within himself. The cyclone brewing in the Andaman Sea has moved farther west, to the Indian coast. The girl that he'd shared his table with has walked out from his life as carelessly as she had walked in. *The Outsider* will remain unread. The earthworm that was on his foot that morning now has an advantage over him. It is free.

The soldiers stop the van and order them to walk into the dense green. Plato is nervous and excited. In all his childhood fantasies, the jungle was where he belonged. In the faint light of the moon, the handcuffed students stumble and fall as they make their way across streams and ditches, past creepers that hang like empty nooses. Joking and singing to keep their spirits high, praying under their breath.

When they reach an opening among the trees, the vociferous few are lined up. Their leader, a student of medicine, is shot point-blank. More than twenty people are killed that night. The ones left alive are made to dig a large ditch. They're forced to throw in the corpses, heavier than the living. Then they are told to jump.

It happens so quickly, Plato can't believe it. Inside the ditch, his leader's corpse rests on Plato's legs, the teeth digging into his shin. Crushed by the dead, Plato can feel the rigor mortis set in.

Though the soldiers haven't touched him, Plato is bleeding. Leeches prefer the warm blood of the living to that of the dead. Stained by the blood of others, drained of his own, Plato has a vision. He sees a woman seated on a rice sack, swaying in prayer. She is in a pagoda and her back is turned to him. He knows who she is, even though he has never met her. Her mere presence causes tremors within him. Wild and uncontrollable tremors that bring him back to life. He knows it isn't over yet. An unresolved story will keep him alive.

Before dawn, the soldiers pull the living out from the ditch. They are being taken to Insein Prison in Rangoon for interrogation. Plato sits in the van, with more than forty leeches hanging from his body. They suck blood off his buttocks; they cling on to his earlobes and scalp. Two leeches suck blood from his navel.

The van stops for a break. The officers and soldiers get down for breakfast. Only one stays back to monitor the prisoners. He looks like he is in his mid-twenties, a little older than Plato. Alone, the soldier can't bear the sight any longer. He lights a cheroot and begins to burn the leeches off Plato's body. He rubs the open wounds with tobacco-scented water. "The smell of tobacco drives away all insects except humans," he jokes. He tears bits from a newspaper and sticks them on Plato's wounds in an effort to stanch the bleeding. It doesn't help. The soldier smiles in apology each time a drenched scrap falls off.

The sun is out, but Plato sits in darkness. All that his eyes can see is the shadow of a waning consciousness before he blacks out.

Ten days later, he has a visitor in prison. He's had to bribe his way in, as only family, not acquaintances, have the right to visit. He is Thapa, a Gorkha Plato had befriended in a tea shop.

The two would often share their meals, sometimes their entire days. A small-time smuggler thriving in a corrupt regime, Thapa, it turned out, was as alone as Plato. Plato would talk to him about politics and philosophy. An uneducated man, Thapa would in return train Plato in business. He would keep the student updated on the price of things—ivory, teak, jade, pearls, ganja, pistols, even women. For a price, Thapa claimed, he could buy a home, a wife, and respect.

When they ran out of excuses to converse, the two kept each other company in silence. They rolled a joint and walked the historic parts of Rangoon, skimming pebbles on any water surface they could find. If there existed an Olympic medal for such a sport, Thapa would have won it. He could make a pebble glide like a duck over water. He attributed the skill to his upbringing. He was born in one of the poorest mountain villages in Nepal, where there was no electricity, school, road, or concrete structure. Only rocks and pebbles in abundance. "We are, because rocks are," he would often tell Plato.

In prison, Plato inquires about the price of smuggling a letter to the Andamans. "Using the post will be easier," Thapa says. But Plato has no address. All he knows is that his mother lives with another man on the islands, that her name is Rose Mary, and that she is a Karen hailing from a village called Webi. "It means hidden, not lost," Plato explains. That is all his grandmother had told him.

On the night of his arrest, there was a reason why the junta left him alive in the ditch. They wanted him to break down without resorting to the elaborate rituals of torture. They had succeeded. Lying in the ditch, shaking with tears, Plato had a vision of his mother. Never before had she come to him with such longing.

Once he's on the Andaman Islands, it isn't difficult for Thapa to track Rose Mary, now known as Mary, down to a neighborhood in Port Blair. The Karens on the islands are a small community. Surrounded by hostile seas, the archipelago's capital is the farthest they got. In the busy market, a Karen woman points her out to Thapa as she waits for her turn outside a miller's shop.

Her son has sent him to find her, Thapa explains. "He is not a criminal," he says. "He is a university student who masterminded protests against the rulers."

Specters of white escape the grinder, covering them as they watch. Mary's tears flow down like rivers across the white to mingle with the afternoon sweat.

"He goes to university?" she asks.

"He did. Now he has given up studying for teaching. He teaches the rest to revolt, wherever he is."

"Does he get good marks?"

"I don't know."

"Do you study with him?"

"No. I barely went to school."

"Where did you meet him?"

"By Inle Lake, skimming pebbles. He saw my pebble hop on the water more than five times and asked me to teach him. The trick is to not think, just aim. But your son cannot stop thinking."

Thapa helps Mary collect the flour in a brass container. He pays the miller when he sees that she has left without doing so. He finds her again, wandering in the wilderness at the edge of the market.

"Do you have a bidi?" she asks Thapa as she sits on a boulder. He lights one and hands it over. Mary smokes the bidi in silence. Thapa surveys the surrounding thicket for the legendary giant centipedes of the islands. He has yet to see one.

"When was he arrested?" she asks him, before stubbing the bidi under her slipper.

"Six months ago."

Mary tries to recollect what her world was like six months ago. "What was the date?" she asks.

"I don't remember, but it was the month of July."

Devi was home in July. Her visits were the highlight of life on Mount Harriet. Like the wheat grains in the flour mill, Mary is pounded by guilt. She had been fussing over Devi's appetite and complexion at the time of her son's arrest.

"What year is it?" she asks Thapa.

"1975."

"How old is he?"

"Twenty-three."

"Twenty-three," she repeats, affirming the reality of this man and her son. "He must leave prison soon and complete his degree. His father was a fisherman and his mother is a maid. Girls these days are very fussy. They want to marry graduates. My Devi will graduate next year too. I keep telling her father to get her married after that. She is difficult. One has to be careful."

Mary sits up straight, as if she has suddenly remembered something. Thapa is about to tell her that he has paid the miller, when she interjects.

"What is your name?"

"Sharan Thapa."

"What is his name?"

"Plato."

"That's not a Buddhist name."

"He calls himself Plato."

"It cannot be my son's name."

"It is a strange name, but he likes it. He adopted it himself."

"What does it mean?"

"It is the name of one of the fathers of philosophy."

"What is philosophy?"

"It is the art of thinking—thinking and doing nothing."

"Sounds like his father."

When she'd last seen him, he was only eight months old. Each new day, she had hoped, would bring him back. Each new hour, she had hoped, would bring news of him. If she had known it would take this long, she would have given up on life long ago. But how could she, without seeing him again?

Thapa looks around. He wants to console her, but he doesn't know how. And then he sees it, the hundred-legged beast, bigger than any other he has seen. It is his first glimpse of the Andaman centipede. He shrieks.

Mary attacks it with her slipper. She attacks it with such blind ferocity, it disturbs him. She doesn't stop, even after the claw-like legs have stopped wriggling, its body smashed against a rock. Thapa doesn't know who the aggressor is, and who the aggrieved.

She wants to believe the stranger so much, desperation has flooded her with the opposite. She crumbles with disbelief.

"You are lying to me. . . . My brothers have sent you here to take me back to the village. They want to punish me for eloping," she says.

Four days later, Mary leaves for Rangoon with Thapa.

MARY LEAVES the Indian archipelago in a dinghy. Tears, as ancient as life and as young as the rain, push the dinghy toward the Irrawaddy Delta to a place where the river latches on to the sea with nine limbs, creating sandbanks to tighten its grip. Twenty-three years ago, Mary had left an eight-month-old baby on one such sandbank in time.

The dinghy has a motor engine and three boatmen, a luxury for a journey that seldom lasts more than eight hours in the open seas.

Sea gypsies control these waters connecting the Andaman Islands to Burma. Traditionally, the gypsies choose the boatmen on this route for their emotional invulnerability. A seafarer's song glorifies the boat-man who can cross this stretch of the sea—impervious as clay, buoyant as rubber, resilient as gold. For a day spent on the choppy waters can easily turn into a lifetime traversing the faultline. No one, not even the cyclonic clouds and deep-sea currents, can escape its elemental pull. There is a danger of slipping into the earth's cleft. It connects Burma to the islands, like a weeping eye to every disowned teardrop. Not all pain, certainly not all longings, can be swept away by the Indian Ocean.

Once a proud continent, Burma was crushed between India and Asia. India pushed it to the north with its drift; Asia squeezed it to the east in defiance. A weeping eye was all that was left of the face, buried under rubble. Burma's aquiline edges were gouged into unconquerable peaks and gorges. Its complexion had rotted into damp jungle and dry desert. Despair was evident in the rolling highlands and tropical is-lands, a reminder of the beauty that once was. Faultlines ran all along it, from the edges to the heart—the biggest one in the form of the mighty Irrawaddy down the spine of Burma, connecting the islands below to the Himalayas above. As profound as the pressure was, Burma could never be one with the masses that surrounded it. It could only crumble.

The dinghy itself is carved out of a single trunk. It won't come apart, even if the surroundings do. It won't sink. Driftwood never does. The water might fling it around like a feather in a whirlpool, but eventually it will give up and toss it back to the shore.

Years later, the dinghy will lie derelict on a tidal sandbank. The twisted roots of trees, abandoned shells, and eels caught in plastic nets will give it company. During low tide, desperate villagers will walk over to hack at its skeleton and carry it away as firewood. Its forgotten bones will drift back into the sea. No one, besides an inquisitive dog, will notice the shapes on the bark. The holes, knots, triangles, and lines that Mary, years ago, had imagined to be mountains, whirlpools, and rivers.

As she sits trapped in the dinghy, Mary's tears take her back to her childhood, to the days when she, in a fit of crying, would beat her head on the ground and strike anyone who tried to approach her. No one could understand the depths of her pain, least of all the profound sense of betrayal she carried. Hungry ghosts possessed her, her grandmother would claim, amidst attempts to feed her. Many decades had passed since Mary was a child. She had ceased to be one the day she reconciled to hunger.

Engulfed by madness in the dinghy, she pacifies herself with a story, like her grandmother would in the past. The faint triangle visible on the wood, is it a mountain or a thatched roof? Is it a fisherman's hut, the kind they construct on the beach to shelter boats? The circles, are they whirlpools, the sun, or the moon? Could there be more than one sun or moon? Could there be more than one lover?

Drenched in seawater, the dinghy's wood is soft and tender enough for Mary to etch on with her fingernails. She makes a symbolic boat, curved like her fingernail. Below that symbolic boat, she makes a symbolic sea. She draws a circle with limbs around it. Inside, she carves out patches, like a turtle's shell. She gives it a head and two slits for eyes.

She remembers those sorrowful eyes from a lifetime ago, when she cooked turtle soup for an entire week. She names it the *Mourning Turtle.*

As for the lines, they could be anything: snakes, trees, streaks of pouring rain, or ghosts without bodies. They are restless spirits in search of closure.

Undaunted by the wind ruffling her hair, Mary removes her hair clip to carve out her fantasies. She makes faces, hands, and legs around the lines. There are humans in the picture now. A man, a woman, and a child stare blankly from the edge of the dinghy at those who sit in it. Or are they three trees? Or three birds? She thinks she recognizes them, but she isn't sure. Reality seldom bows down to fantasy.

The figures calm Mary down with their tale, as they often will.

"Stand up!" An officer prods Plato's prostrate body with his boot.

"No," says Plato. "I will not."

For an entire week, Plato and his comrades are made to stand in different positions under the direct sun. They are made to imitate an airplane, balancing on one leg, with both arms in the air like wings. They are made to sit on an invisible motorcycle, while their thighs are smacked with a stick. They are made to hold positions from the traditional Semigwa dance. Those who fall, unable to resume their act in this circus of torture, are beaten up.

Plato has escaped the beatings so far. But he is certain his turn will come. It is inevitable. One can only delay it or bring it closer. Idealists call this liberty. Unable to bear the anxiety of waiting any longer, he tells the officer, "It makes no difference if I sit or stand or run. You will beat me anyway."

By the end, Plato cannot walk back alone. Two inmates hold him up, grateful because he'd angered the officer so much that he forgot about the others.

Plato's eyelids are stitched together in pain. His head stoops with the memory of the officer's boots. There is the salty taste of blood in his mouth. He can still smell the coconut oil in the officer's hair and the betel nut spewing from his mouth. He can still hear the seconds tick. The hand that slapped his face had a wristwatch on, reeking of sweat mixed with metal—the acrid stench of decaying time, ten years to be precise. Plato has been sentenced to ten years in prison for participating in three strikes.

He shares a cell of ten by twelve feet with twenty-two other men. Only four people can lie down at any given time, and two have sacrificed their sleep for him to recuperate. Urine rises from the chamber pot in the daytime heat and condenses, along with sweat and spit, on the ceiling, only to later descend as soothing dew.

In the evening, a man wipes the dewdrops off Plato's face as he tries to feed him rice. Head pounding and eyelids bound together, Plato can't place him. Judging by the stench, they are all the same, students and criminals.

"Oh, they have broken your teeth!" the man exclaims as Plato opens his mouth. Plato rolls his tongue around the jagged contours.

"It resembles an Ambassador car's bonnet," someone says.

"Or an oyster shell," another voice pipes in.

Plato's smile inspires poetry in the cell.

When he returns to his senses, he wishes he hadn't sent that letter for his mother. He isn't willing to meet her like this, uglier than ever.

The Shwedagon Pagoda is bigger than any church or temple Mary has ever visited. It is bigger than all of them combined. From the center of the dome, a shrine rises in each direction. Hundreds of Buddhas bless the eight corners of the world.

Mary walks around in circles, undecided. Barely a month has passed since she set foot in Burma. Unknown to her, she arrived at a fishing village on the Irrawaddy Delta on the day Plato's teeth were broken. Thapa settled her in with a Karen family in Rangoon while he waited to hear of Plato's whereabouts.

Every Buddha is different under scrutiny. A thousand lives, a thousand faces, a thousand moods. Only the Buddha has the privilege of being so many, while creatures like Mary are forced to hang on to the only chance they've got.

Mary spots a statue that resembles her. This Buddha has a small tapering chin and a slightly protruding jaw. Instead of a smile, a frown hides behind the placid forehead. Mary can see it in the eyes. She is relieved. Estranged from one another by their own unique sadness, everyone smiles in this land. Except for this statue and her.

She stands by the pillar, unsure of herself. Where does she fit in this sea of seated and chanting people?

An old man looks up at her. He points. She is nervous. She follows his finger to the pillar she is standing in front of. There are mattresses hanging from it on a nail. She takes one and sits at the edge. The voices—ancient, certain, young, quivering—chant foreign incantations. They sway and, in turn, are swayed by one another.

Like them, Mary sits cross-legged. Her lower back still hurts from the journey in the dinghy. The walk here has scraped the skin off her soles. Her blouse is embroidered with threads of sweat. Some hooks are missing too.

The sun begins its ascent over the pagoda's spire. Though she has been seated for almost half an hour, she can't erase from her mind the image of the cat that had crossed her path. It carried a pigeon in its mouth—neck twisted and feathers covered in blood.

Mary had walked for two and a half hours to get here.

The route to the pagoda was like the road to hell. It began in the crowded neighborhoods infested with migrants where Mary lived—tenements up to four stories high. Only centipedes, cockroaches, and snakes could live piled up like this. The city was filthier than the Port Blair market. Mary walked through the darkness with no knowledge of the route and only dogs for company. She walked through boulevards lined with margosa, banyan, and gum-kino, onto narrow by-lanes. At dead ends, it wasn't fear but filth that confronted her. The sight and stench of unresolved filth.

By dawn, she had made it to the pagoda's township. The path cut across the monastery compound and markets that sold everything from betel nuts to quail eggs to brooms to Buddha statues. If only they sold faith. If only she could donate all her secrets to the monks, bald and barefoot, wandering with bowls, and enter the pagoda empty.

She had seen a man selling mynahs at the monumental steps leading up to the pagoda. To set one free from that three-story cage would be good karma, she was told. She had heard of this practice before. The birds were trained to return to the owner. They were trained to experience freedom in flight. As soon as Mary was given the bird, she let it go. The tiny thing trembled in her hands as if it were about to explode.

Seated before the Buddha, Mary prays for the pigeon and the mynah. Keep them safe, she chants. Keep them safe. Keep them safe.

Thapa had come over the previous night to give her the news. Plato was in solitary confinement. It could take days. It could take months.

"There is only one place for lonely people. I may be there sooner than I thought. If I don't give in, they will put me in solitary," Plato had written in the letter Thapa gave Mary in the Port Blair market.

She didn't know if the handwriting really belonged to him, her son. She had carried it in her blouse ever since. It had begun to fall apart at the edges, but all the lines were still intact. "I grew up an orphan, raised by my grandparents," he'd written. "My father had drowned in the sea, they said, and my mother had run away with another man. How ugly must I be, I would think, for my mother to abandon me?"

Amidst the foreign hum, Mary contemplates resorting to the only prayers she knows—verses from the bible. But her mind is blank. She came here, the holiest shrine in the land, to pray for something so ordinary, most mothers took it for granted. When the time comes to meet him, Mary fears, she won't recognize him. To be in his presence and walk past . . .

THE MONTH OF MAY would be marked in the history of the Karen settlement in the Andamans. No one would remember the exact date, except that it was a suffocatingly hot morning when Rose Mary was born. The last in a line of nine children, she was also the first child to be born in the Karen villages. The pastor proclaimed, "She has turned this settlement into home. The Lord speaks to us with the glory of her birth."

Rose Mary, the auspicious one, spent her childhood working on farms, attending classes in the church shed, tending to poultry, cleaning the house, and washing up. The Karens were at the frontier of the war against nature, and she was a child soldier.

Rose Mary's father would take her along on fishing trips to collect sea worms as bait. He instilled in her the patience, skill, and intuition needed to appreciate one's own company. She discovered the most efficient way of consuming the solitude accorded to all life forms early. She began with the marshes in low tide, catching mudskippers in her dress for her mother to pickle. She cut her hair short to avoid getting it stuck in shells and spikes when she dove in to collect edible mollusks. It gave her a sense of purpose, bringing home something to eat. When her father failed to catch bigger things, her mother couldn't forage, and her siblings chased the pleasant breeze, the mudskippers would come to the rescue. By the age of ten, Rose Mary had begun to steal her father's fishing rod and bidis at nights, while the rest of them slept. With only bats, owls, and the moon's rippling reflection in the waters to keep her company, Rose Mary would patiently wait for the subtle tug on her rope, smoking the occasional bidi like her father did. By the age of eleven, she had caught her first barracuda and learned to smoke without coughing.

As promising as her skills were, Rose Mary could fish only on the shore. The deep sea of bigger catches was male territory. She could only dream of slicing through the surf in a khlee—her very own canoe—and burying her harpoon in a fish's heart bigger than her own.

Words gave her a headache, so she dropped out of school and devoted herself to fishing and hunting. By the time her body had begun to soften at the angles, centipedes—the local harbingers of misfortune—had bitten her three times already.

"When animals bite, it hurts," her mother consoled her as Rose Mary sat doubled up, hugging her knees to ride through the storm of pain.

"What about humans?" the girl asked. "What happens when they bite?"

"They don't. Not if they believe in Christ."

Her mother's words had upset her more than the centipedes did. The venomous snakes, the bone-crushing crocodiles, and the strangling creepers, were they not creatures of god too? In the unconditional kiss of a leech, the night-colored bruises left on her skin by the jungle, and a sea urchin's spines lived the will of a god very different from the Christ on her mother's locket. A god whose worshippers had the freedom to bite and hurt without guilt.

As the work grew, so did the workforce. To fuel the enterprise of converting unruly forests into sophisticated logs, the empire brought in boatloads of the unemployed from Burma and India.

Rose Mary was thirteen when the Burman boy arrived on her shores, like driftwood left behind by the tide. The village was a burgeoning family of unrelated members and unacknowledged relationships. It would take almost a year for the two to speak.

The Burman, along with five other men, had caught a human-sized grouper. Too heavy to lift, the fish was left to trail behind the boat in the net until they reached the shore. As the victorious men lugged the giant into the village, the walk turned into a procession. The drunks shouted slogans for higher wages, and the women demanded a community feast. The Burman boy, barely seventeen, had turned into a local celebrity.

The grouper was almost seven feet long and weighed more than three hundred kilograms. Resting in a timber shed for all to see, it was a myth sprawled out against the shoddiness of their lives.

Rose Mary pushed her way to the front of the crowd to have a closer look. It was difficult to imagine the Goliath swimming swiftly in the water. Instead, Rose Mary imagined it sinking to the bottom like a shipwreck. Its opaque blue eyes seemed fashioned from the color of the sea itself. Rose Mary imagined the giant surveying the ocean floor with its bulging eyes. Unmoved. Unmoving. Its belly was as high as her waist. Its mouth, as wide as its stout body, protected by fleshy lips. She gazed into its final gasp for water, its exposed, bloodied gills. She raised a hand to touch it. Her fingers sank into its torso, the texture and color of moss. A faint vibration ran through the flesh. She pulled her hand back immediately.

"Be careful," the Burman said. "You'd fit into his mouth quite easily."

Rose Mary felt slighted. Not only was she not allowed to fish in the deep, but even luck seemed to favor men, especially unskilled foreign boys trained in mere ponds and rivers.

"I can carry what I catch," she replied. "I don't need the whole village to hold it up."

"If I showed up in your net," he asked, "would you carry me too?"

"I cook everything I catch," said Rose Mary, surprising herself.

The men sold the grouper to a visiting Englishman for a grand sum of twenty-five rupees. For the next month, the Burman skipped work to drown himself in toddy. But it was hunger, not thirst, that he felt most acutely. He yearned for a meal cooked especially for him. He didn't care if it was made with love or disgust.

One afternoon, he found Rose Mary wading among the corals, alone.

"Careful," he shouted. "You'll cut your feet."

Rose Mary went on with the business of collecting seaweed in her basket. He sat down on the beach, determined to talk even if she wouldn't. The afternoon, like the toddy, had overwhelmed him. He was afraid he would evaporate like sweat into the air and no one would notice. He mumbled away to prevent himself from disappearing.

Rose Mary stomped out of the water in oversized jungle boots.

The Burman was impressed.

"Where did you get them?" he asked. "Did you rob an English sahib?"

"I don't rob dead people."

He laughed.

It was a long beach, and Rose Mary wondered why she had chosen to walk toward the boy when they were surrounded by wilderness. She rolled up her longyi and removed her boots. She wiped her legs with her bare hands, oblivious to his gaze, stronger than the sun's. She began to sort the seaweed.

"Do you know what I found when I cut open that grouper?" he asked.

"No."

"Inside its belly . . ." The Burman looked at her, searching for a way to bring it all—the approaching waves, his receding consciousness, and her industrious fingers braiding the seaweed—to a standstill. "Inside its belly I found an octopus . . ."

Rose Mary turned to him as her hands continued with the chore.

". . . holding in its tentacles a crab."

She stopped to think. Encouraged by the sight of her hands at rest, the Burman straightened up.

"How can that happen?" she asked.

Rose Mary saw his eyes well up. They too bulged like the grouper's. Unlike the grouper's deep-sea color, though, his eyes were a flash of red. The wind had changed, carrying his stench of rotten coconuts to her.

"I don't know how it happened," he replied. "But I'm afraid that I may end up in someone's belly too."

She smiled and returned to her basket.

"Do you know how groupers hunt?"

"No."

"They suck their prey in with their lips. They have no teeth."

"Then how do they chew?"

"They don't. They swallow it whole."

The grouper was like her grandmother, then. Rose Mary laughed at the thought.

"You don't believe me?"

"No."

"So powerful is a grouper's ability to suck that when it takes in water from its gills, a small whirlpool is created on the surface. I have seen it with my own eyes. That is how we tracked it down."

That night, Rose Mary dreamed of being sucked into a whirlpool.

Two months later, when the Burman asked her parents for permission to marry her, they refused. The reasons were obvious.

Not only did he belong to the lowly, unscrupulous, and lazy lot of Buddhists, he had no family to speak of on the islands.

So they eloped to a nearby village called Webi. She was only fourteen. Too young to have experienced love or desire, she would later think. In fact, she was horrified when she saw him naked for the first time. Under their clothes, men were no different from dogs, elephants, and horses.

She hadn't been unhappy in her parents' home. She had given up on school after the fifth grade and spent all her time fishing. The first-born of the Karens, she also had a special place in the heart of the pastor, the most influential man among the Karens.

Seen from the eyes of an aging woman, the fourteen-year-old's actions made no sense, in the logical way her habit of killing centipedes

did. She would attack them at first sight. She would go out of her way
to kill them, smoking them out, putting herself in danger. In her attempts, she was even bitten. What drove her to kill them indiscrimi-
nately? Surely, it wasn't fear. Fear drove people away from centipedes,
not closer to them.

Vengeance, she realized in her later years, was a powerful thing.

The runaway couple found a patch of wilderness to cultivate. For shelter, they built a thatched shed on stilts. The Burman would look for
odd jobs and Rose Mary would work on the farm.

In 1942, an earthquake arrived. So powerful, it turned day into
night with dust. When the dust settled, the Japanese had replaced
the British rulers. So long as the locals constructed and cultivated
for the imperialists, they were left in peace. But when a cyclone destroyed the harvest, all hell broke loose. Like the elephants, the Japanese thrived on greenery—a diet of sweet potatoes, catfish, and snails
made them constipated. So all the men were forced to work in
the fields to step up cultivation. While the Karens were left alone, the
Burmese were persecuted after a group was caught stealing from the
warehouse. Riffraff like Rose Mary's husband were picked up and
beaten to the rhythm of imperial slogans. They were asked to repeat
them. If they couldn't, they were beaten again.

The island seemed to be closing in on the Burman. He stopped
working and started drinking at home instead. One night, he demanded catfish for dinner. When he didn't find nappi—pickle—on the
plate, he beat Rose Mary.

She was stunned. That men beat women was not a surprise to her.
The worth of a man, her grandmother would often say, was judged by
his ability to hunt, build a roof, and beat his wife. Sooner or later, Rose
Mary was prepared for a slap or a kick. What shocked her was his
strength. Where did it come from, she wondered, in this listless man
who spent his days inebriated?

With each beating, he would leave behind something new on

her body. An imprint of his teeth below her collarbone, like a dis-
placed string of pearls. A bruise on her hip, placed aesthetically like
a flower. Scratches on her cheek and neck, as if she'd been grazed
by a palm frond. And the Japanese slogans—the only time he spoke
to her in that language was when he beat her, shouting out imperial
slogans.

One morning, as she stood in a queue to hand over produce to the
Japanese army, the woman in front of her noticed the scratches on her
neck.

"Does your husband hit you?" she asked. Rose Mary nodded.

"So does mine."

"I thought only Burmese men did. You are from India."

"All men do. English, Indian, Burmese, Siamese, even these Japanese ones."

"What about the naked people?" Rose Mary asked about the island's native tribes.

"They don't. Beating a woman is a sign of civilization, like wearing
clothes."

Rose Mary mulled it over as she stood in the queue. She asked,
"Does your husband shout in Japanese when he hits you?"

The woman laughed. "No," she replied. "He is a freedom fighter.
He curses me in Hindi."

Rose Mary smiled. So clear and repetitive was the Burman's Japanese, she had learned it too. Hakko ichiu. Hakko! Ichiu! The sounds
were alive in her head. They were the rhythm to his blows. Without
them, the beating felt incomplete. Standing in the queue, Rose Mary
chanted the words like a nursery rhyme.

When her turn came, she hesitantly placed one papaya and one
cabbage on the officer's table. It was all they had to spare. He looked
up at Rose Mary. Without a common language, he could only convey
his displeasure by frowning.

She was afraid. "Hakko ichiu," she whispered. The only words of
Japanese that she knew. Eight corners under one roof.

The officer smiled.

———

One night, the Burman lay unconscious on the bamboo steps that led to their home. He had guzzled down toddy for three whole days, until he lost all strength to leave or enter. He lay on the steps like an offering to the lords of the night—the mosquitoes.

Rose Mary tried to wake him. When he didn't respond, she sat down next to him. Such an innocent face, she thought as she admired his features. One day, she hoped to have a son who looked like him. She rested her head next to his. She played with his stubble, newly sprouted on his cheeks. She took a long strand of her own hair and tickled his nostril. He didn't budge. Not only his breath but even his clothes reeked of toddy. She sat there, inhaling the fumes. She pinched his cheeks playfully.

Then she slapped him. The Burman opened his eyes in a flash but slipped back into unconsciousness just as quickly. Strange, thought Rose Mary. Though she had slapped him hard, a faint redness was all that was left behind. How hard did one have to hit someone to leave a bruise? She punched his face to find out. The Burman raised his head, disoriented by the pain. Rose Mary pushed it back down. She patted his head.

"Come back, O wandering soul," she sang to him, as Karen mothers would to wailing infants.

TWO YEARS INTO THEIR IMPRISONMENT, the students go on a hunger strike for exemption from hard labor. They are political prisoners, not run-of-the-mill criminals. Plato hasn't eaten anything for five days. He is the last man standing, drinking his own urine to survive. The prison officer claims he's gone mad. The other students dare not emulate him, lest he start molding dolls from his excrement next.

On the fifth evening, the authorities enter his crowded cell. They wrap Plato in a blanket and carry him away. He doesn't resist. His limbs, like his torso, are ornamental. The soldiers hold a blood-soaked towel to Plato's face the entire time, even as they strip him of his longyi and shirt. He quivers and sweats profusely as he lies naked on the concrete floor. A pair of hands gently take hold of his handcuffs. They twirl a long piece of wire around the metal before piercing his wrists with the exposed end. They do the same to his ankles, forehead, and testicles. The hesitation of the fingers is palpable, like the forced murmurs surrounding him.

With every spike in the current, he experiences life and death as an involuntary spasm. He will have no memory of the exaggerated way in which his body quakes and is flung across the floor, the pool of urine and shit that surrounds him, and the stream of drool that flows down his cheeks.

All he will remember is a voice. A shriek so loud and diabolical, it rouses him from unconsciousness. A cavernous shriek. In the delirium of torture, Plato attributes his own cries to a pig being slaughtered nearby.

———

A caretaker, carrying a plate of half-cooked rice, opens the door to Plato's cell. When the stench hits him, he yells, "Even pigs smell better than this." He leaves the plate and runs out.

Plato gets upset each time his bowel gripes, as his left hand—the one he uses to wipe himself—doesn't listen to him anymore. Paralyzed by the pounding ache in his groin, he wets himself often. He is surprised to see the man scurry away like a mouse. It makes him laugh. This isn't the first time the junta has compared him to a pig. During the hunger strike, an officer had told him that the death of a pig required more paperwork than the death of a political prisoner. The general took more interest in poultry and cattle than in the welfare of students drunk on foreign ideologies.

What if, Plato wonders, the man returns to fetch the empty plate and finds a pig inside the cell? A pedigreed pink one with a perfectly curled tail, wallowing in the stench and company of its own shit. What will his response be? Will he run to his senior and cry, "I swear I don't know how it happened, but the prisoner has turned into a pig"? Will they then be forced to look after Plato? If he dies, will the general institute an inquiry into his death?

Two weeks into the confinement, Plato traces the burnt scabs on his body with his fingers. On his chest, scalp, knees, testicles, ankles, and shoulder blades, permanent hieroglyphs created by the live wire.

His clock stopped ticking the moment he entered prison. He will never be a graduate. The girl stopped her whistle mid-song. The borrowed book was closed shut on page forty-nine. The earthworm on his slipper shriveled up and died. And his mother crumpled the letter halfway through.

This is what death is, he thinks. A moment isolated from everything and everyone else. A moment magnified and distorted beyond comprehension. A moment devoid of all possibility. An ossified moment. Like a shell discarded by a mollusk, the moment resonates with reverberations and echoes. Not life.

Plato goes down on all fours and grunts like a pig. He laughs. The laughter drowns out the buzz of insects. It rips the cobwebs apart with its force. It absorbs the emptiness. It bounces off the cold walls and hits him like a tidal wave. Crouching on all fours, Plato is filled with a crazy urge. He bleats like a goat and yawns like a buffalo. He roars like a tiger and hisses like a snake. He crackles like the pouring rain and flip-flops on the floor like a fish out of water. He raises himself off the floor like a flower in bloom and crashes into the walls like a caged rooster. Through the sounds, gestures, and movements, he hangs on precariously to the slippery world outside.

He crawls to a corner and sits with his back against the damp wall, weeping with drops of humidity. He resumes his laughter. The junta has shown him what the monks in the monastery couldn't. Current, that's all he is. Passing through different bodies and lives.

A prison guard stands in Plato's cell. The orders are simple enough, so Plato can't understand why he must repeat himself incessantly, destroying the silence. Silence is hard work. Sometimes, Plato wishes his heart would stop beating so that his body could stop pulsating and his chest stop heaving. The silence then would be pure.

The guard is ordering him to leave the cell. But Plato doesn't stand up. He can't leave his corner just yet. He has killed only thirty-eight mosquitoes since he awoke. By his calculations, he must kill at least eighty each day to restrict their rate of multiplication. Even four mosquitoes flying in Plato's cell are a protest. Ten, a riot. A hundred, a rebellion. They must be silenced. Each and every one of them.

The guard stands there like a winged insect himself, nibbling on Plato's earlobe, distracting him from his lofty preoccupations. Then he pulls him up by the shoulders and drags him out.

The sun hits Plato's eyes. He has survived the past two months by reading the darkness like braille. By distinguishing the plywood over the ventilator, the bricks that constitute the wall, and the cobwebs on the ceiling from the remaining facts of his confinement.

His pale skin itches in the light. The dead skin that has settled all over his scalp and body like permafrost falls off with every movement.

Plato can't remember the last time he washed himself. He possesses no memory of brushing his teeth, combing his hair, cutting his nails, shaving his face, or using soap. His mind is empty.

He enters the courtyard and is confronted by the hellish shrieks of birds, faceless conversations, the sounds of carpentry, and the threatening howls of dogs. The outside is a vulgar caricature of the tender image he had clung on to. In front of him, a gulmohar tree stands in full bloom. The flaming red, orange, yellow, and green sets Plato's vision on fire. He covers his eyes in reflex.

Surrounded by darkness, Plato had held on to colors. He dreamed in them. He talked to them. He lived inside them. His dreams were often red. He swam in a sea of red, kicking, cycling, flapping his hands, only to sink in farther. At times, he clawed at the color and the color clawed right back at him. At times, the red was a warm sensation. It carried Plato in its womb. Unlike the gulmohar. The barking dogs. The persecutory raps of a hammer. And the familiar fragrance of the golden padauk flooding the breeze.

Never before has Plato considered a morning in April an assault. How can it be? Immediately, he grabs the thought by its throat. In the clarity of isolation, he had stopped categorizing thoughts as friends or foes. What promised insanity also held the calm of enlightenment. He had suppressed all memories, longings, and aversions that would lead him astray in the maze of time, trapping him in the past or future. Yet he knows that Thingyan, the water festival, is around the corner, for the tiny yellow flowers of the golden padauk have blossomed, a sign of the first summer rain.

Plato has stepped out of solitary confinement in the month of April. He will be sent back two more times, once for possessing an English dictionary, later for developing a secret code to communicate through walls. Each time, the knowledge will come as a shock—one can forget one's name, but one can't forget the seasons.

He halts in the courtyard. He stares at each branch of the gulmohar above, the bunched-up flowers, the leaves, the crows. He closes his eyes to inhale the fragrances.

The guard taps his shoulder. He points at the bats hanging from the branches, entombed in their wings. Yawning. Scratching. Dreaming in echoes and whispers.

The two men smile as they stand under the tree.

Dear son,

Thank you for your letter. Your kind friend, Thapa, has brought me with him to Burma. Every day I pray for your safety and release. Until that day, I am working as a maid for an Indian family in the Bahan township of Rangoon.

Thapa inspects the letter as he sits opposite Mary, crouched on the last flight of stairs. It is the only private spot in her overcrowded tenement, reeking of sweaty palms, moldy walls, and clandestine conversations. She clings on to the railing, lest reality give way.

"Did you write this?" Thapa asks.

"No," she replies. "I can only read in Burmese. I asked my landlady to."

For two years, no one has met Plato in Insein Prison. The officials will only allow his family to, and Plato has none. Mary is a Karen woman from India. The Karens are the land's oldest insurgents, and India a loudspeaker for democracy. If they discover his mother's origins, Plato could be falsely accused of being a spy and hanged immediately.

But just yesterday, Thapa found out that Plato has been moved to Sagaing, the monastic town near Mandalay. Plato had spent six months in solitary confinement, and the isolation had served to aggravate his incendiary ways. Fed up with the hunger strikes and demands, the officials transferred him far away from his clique.

The Khamti Prison in Sagaing division is small and easy to bribe one's way into. Thapa plans to visit his friend himself.

He has come here to get Mary's reply to her son's letter. Is this all she wants to say?

"Daw Mary," he says, "the junta may worship the Buddha, but they are not nonviolent or compassionate."

Mary nods as if she comprehends. "He will come out one day," she says.

"We don't know."

"He will be released," she replies. "I have prayed for his long and healthy life ever since he was growing in my womb. It cannot be any other way."

Then why did you abandon him, Thapa wants to ask. Instead, he looks away, at a wall. It is muddy gray and pale blue in patches, the paint peeling off to reveal other shades below—a dull white that gives way to bricks and mortar. Like the mortar, Thapa feels exposed. His thoughts are naked enough to shame Mary.

If I had the courage to tell you the truth, I would, Mary silently screams, deep within herself. I don't even have the strength to lie. I am mute.

I too had a son, Thapa confesses. Once upon a time, I too had a wife. Like you, my voice is silenced. Like you, I am sinking every single day.

But you are not a murderer.

Terrified by what the silence insinuates, Thapa asks, "Have you eaten something?"

"No," she says. "My hunger died years ago."

The British and the Japanese had left the islands. The Indian rulers had introduced something new to the archipelago. Something that had thrived for centuries on the mainland and symbolized the new republic in a way that even the tricolored flag couldn't. Poverty.

The islands were bursting with refugees from East Pakistan, from across the Bay of Bengal. More people were arriving every day. Without a livelihood for them to rely on, and no colonial power or cyclone to blame, poverty grew unhindered like a weed.

Rose Mary was seven months pregnant. She would work on the farm, sell what she could spare, and feed her growing belly. The Burman drank in anticipation. Once in a while, he would bring home something to eat. Mangoes, pomfret, fowl, pineapples. For each of these, she was grateful.

Then the Burman went missing for three whole days. Fed up with sitting at home, he had gone to the coast to fish. He returned home one morning with a sack on his back. Inside it was a turtle, still alive and weighing more than twenty kilos. It was the first sizable quantity of meat he had brought home in a month.

Rose Mary was delighted. Such a big animal would last them a fortnight, if consumed prudently. She borrowed a metal bucket big enough to accommodate the turtle and placed it in a corner. She began by chopping the legs off, consuming only one per day. She made it a point to feed the turtle and tend to its wounds. It was the only way to keep the meat fresh.

One morning, while draining the bloodied bucket and refilling it with fresh water, Rose Mary made the mistake of looking at the turtle's face. It had tears in its eyes.

That afternoon, she killed the turtle. The flesh was consumed in just ten days. All that remained were its bones, left in the open to dry completely.

As the eighth month approached, Rose Mary would feel hunger with such intensity it would make her dizzy. Her spine could barely cope with the weight of the hungry child. In desperation, she took the bones of the turtle one morning and pounded them into a paste. She cooked the paste with tomatoes and ate it.

As she dragged her lopsided body through the farm, the sun ignited a headache within her. She sat in a corner of her room, holding her forehead like a bomb about to explode.

When the Burman arrived home later that night, he didn't notice that things were amiss. The kitchen was a mess. The room wasn't tidied, and the hammocks weren't set out. His wife, a storm of activity otherwise, was crouched in a corner, holding on to different parts of her body as if they were about to come apart.

None of it mattered in the delirium of toddy. The Burman grinned as he threw his cloth bag at the entrance and strode inside with exaggerated steps.

Rose Mary didn't look up or greet him.

"Wife, serve food to your hardworking husband," he said.

"There is none."

"But I'm hungry. I have worked hard today."

"Then cook for yourself."

The Burman halted in his march around the room. In six years of their marriage, his wife had always served him his meals. It didn't matter if there was only gruel to eat or pineapple.

"Serve me," he demanded.

"No."

Like a popular folk dance they both knew the moves to, the beating began. He slapped her. She moved her head away. It was his cue to increase the intensity, so he kicked her.

Rose Mary went numb with the pain. It began in her womb and swept through her bladder, her spine, her legs.

"Don't kick your child," she said.

"Don't tell a father how to treat his child. Unless it is not my child."

The Burman was ashamed to call his wife a whore. It angered him. So he said it out loud. "You whore," he screamed.

He kicked her waist. The baby kicked her womb. Unable to bear the pain, Rose Mary stretched her arm out and picked up the rice pounder lying nearby. She had carved pictures of fish and frogs into it, and her fingers recognized each depression and groove like they did the body of her husband.

The Burman lifted his foot to kick her once again. She hit his ankle with the rice pounder.

He fell down, the demon dancer of the act. He writhed in pain. Rose Mary, the vanquisher, rose from the ground. She walked to her makeshift kitchen and sifted through her weapons. She strode across, crouched over him, and slit the jugular vein in his throat, the same one she brought pigs and fowl and dogs down with.

The beating stopped. The rhythm stopped. Time stopped.

Rose Mary witnessed the blood drain out of his body. She lay next to him and held his face in her hands. She saw his eyes turn white. With him, she struggled, trembled, and then succumbed. Slowly, the vibration gave way to a feeble warmth. She counted his final breaths, four shallow ones in quick succession.

The three of them—husband, wife, and the child in her womb— spent the night soaked in his blood.

At dawn, Rose Mary washed the blood off her body and the floor. She covered the Burman with two sheets. Before she left the house, she noticed a bag by the door. The Burman must have left it there. It held the heads of seven eels. Consuming them promised a smooth labor.

Still in the clutches of the headache, Rose Mary walked for four hours to Spit Nest, the village of her birth. She found the pastor and urged him to drop everything and sit with her, alone. She had a confession to make. Troubled by the state she was in, he complied.

"Every wife fantasizes about killing her husband sometimes, child, but don't confuse it for reality," the pastor told her. He didn't believe what had happened until he saw the Burman's body. Were she not pregnant, he would have urged her to give herself up. But who were they, mere mortals, to destroy the life of one in the womb? The pastor wept for hours. The islands, they made no distinction between ants, centipedes, snakes, and humans. They engaged them all in a primal struggle for survival.

He bandaged the Burman's throat with cloth. The man, Rose Mary would claim, had fallen from the steps of his home in a state of inebriation. He had broken his neck and cut his throat against a rock. The burial took place before suspicions could arise.

Rose Mary lived with the pastor and his wife for the duration of her pregnancy. The couple treated her like a daughter, and her son, their grandchild. But they didn't give him a name. It would mean hanging on to him long after he was gone. When the child was old enough to be weaned, the pastor would go to Rangoon, find the Burman's parents, and hand over their grandson to them. He would then find ways for Rose Mary to start a new life.

Loss. That was all Rose Mary brought with her to the Varma household. She would read the bible out to Devi and take her to church. Slowly, the habit seeped into her own life. The priest, like her master Girija Prasad, mistook it for devotion. Mary was relieved. Her reasons were safe. The more she read the bible and heard the sermons, the more her sympathy for her namesake grew. God didn't ask Mary if she was ready to give birth to his son, nor did he seek her permission before sacrificing him. And as for the son, when he gave up his life to atone for humanity's sins, did he think even once about his mother? Was she not part of the same humanity his heart reached out to?

In a world ruled by men and gods, only Mary had the compassion to understand the Virgin Mother's pain.

Mary began her story at the topmost step. She ends it on the ground. She walks out into the night. Thapa sits curled up on the stairs, reeling at the thought of being kicked in the womb.

Hours later, he stands beside her in an unfamiliar street, drenched by the manic sound of cascades and rapids. The swell of the river echoes through the sleeping lanes and alleys.

They are lost. The present has come crashing down, pulled by the gravity of the past. They stand, unable to move a limb, like the first forms of life that ventured onto land. Nothing in water could prepare them for that first hesitant step. The gravity of a planet made of iron and lead, swirling like a cannonball in space, weighing them down.

"You could have stopped when you hit his ankle." Thapa struggles with the thought.

She could have. But she didn't. Mary was afraid her son might not understand the truth either. His father wasn't a monster. Nor is she a murderer.

"Son, never eat turtle meat with pineapple," she tells Thapa. "It inflames the body and poisons the mind."

W HAT IS THE PRICE OF THINGS THESE DAYS?" Plato asks Thapa with a lisp. Thapa is shocked to see his friend. All ribs and bones. No longer a lovelorn student but a starving madman one pities on the streets. Frayed longyi, clumped hair, grime so deeply embedded in his skin it looks like a disease.

This semblance of a man shook Insein Prison up, Thapa reminds himself. The students had succeeded in identifying themselves as political prisoners, not convicts, and their refusal to do hard labor had been accepted.

"The price of things these days," Thapa says, mulling over the question. "The communists, the Kachins, the Karens—they are all searching for weapons to train with. The market value for secondhand, even damaged weapons is high. But opium is still the king."

Plato nods. "Are you doing well?" he asks.

Thapa is on his way to the Shan Province, at the border with Thailand. He has taken a detour before Mandalay to look up Plato. "As long as there is corruption, I will," Thapa replies. "But there is a force that is defeating inflation and greed. Superstition. The general, I suspect, is secretly collecting white elephants, for their price has suddenly shot up. A single live white elephant costs more on the black market than the ivory from ten. The supply has been cut down by the Thai king. He has been hoarding them for generations."

"To the general, a pig has more value than I do," says Plato.

"Pigs are fat. They have thick skin. That is how he likes his countrymen."

Plato laughs. Thapa is relieved. In the disarming laughter of the madman, he glimpses his lost friend.

"And the price of remaining hungry for five days is four broken teeth," says Thapa.

"My teeth have no value. They are not ivory."

"If humans had ivory for teeth, elephants would rule."

"You should have been a philosopher, Sharan Thapa. I've always told you that."

"What is it your friend Marx says? That philosophers can talk about the world in many ways but no one can change it?"

"No. He says that philosophers have interpreted the world in many ways; the point is to change it."

"Oh," says Thapa. He is relieved that Plato doesn't call himself Marx.

"Did you find her?"

"Yes."

"Where is she?"

"She has been in Rangoon for two and a half years now. It is dangerous for me to bring her here or mention her to you in a letter. The authorities are looking for reasons to trouble you. They can accuse you of being a Karen rebel or an Indian spy."

Plato looks around the table. The prison guard is standing far away, by the door. Thapa had bribed him to look the other way.

"What does she look like?"

"Like you. She sent you this."

Plato's hands tremble as he goes through the contents. Wrapped within a longyi is a shirt, a soap, and a toothbrush.

"Where was she all these years?" he asks.

"On the Andaman Islands. She worked as a maid for an Indian family."

In the sweaty heat of the room, Plato shivers uncontrollably.

"Why did she abandon me?"

"She was afraid you wouldn't forgive her."

"Then why did she leave me in the first place?"

"She left you because she killed your father. He would get drunk and beat her. He kicked her when she was eight months pregnant. She wanted to save your life."

Thapa remembers Mary's agitated face. He remembers her words.

"Plato, your father wasn't a monster. Your mother isn't a murderer."

Plato stares at the table. The trembling gives way to a catatonic silence. He barely seems to be breathing.

Before getting up, he asks, "Then why did it happen?"

Thapa has thought about it a lot. He fears an educated man like Plato won't see the truth, so obvious and simple.

"Why did it happen?" Plato repeats, as if thinking out loud.

"Hunger," Thapa replies.

On a hot, suffocating May night, Plato dreams of red again. It isn't as fluid as a sea this time but thick, like sand. He is a fly caught in tree sap the color of blood.

As the resin grazes his hair, it comes alive for all his senses. It has a bitter taste, a strong, smoky smell, and is viscous to touch. He can't extricate himself from it. His wings tremble under the fluid's weight as his legs buckle under the pressure. Red sweeps his vision. The resin covers his compound eyes. Eyes that reflect light in the colors of the rainbow. He kicks and flails to avoid the petrification, but it is just a reflex. He has already let go.

Plato opens his eyes with a start when he hears someone scream. He has hit his neighbor, another prisoner. He sits up. He moves his hands and legs to rid his body of the paralysis.

A cockroach nibbles on his finger. It must have crawled all over the sleeping inmates, seeking subsistence. A praying mantis jumps in from the ventilator. Once inside, it searches for life to feast on. Plato watches the mantis attack the cockroach. At first, it struggles with the enormity of its kill—then embraces it. The mantis leaves the way it had arrived. It pauses between the bars of the ventilator for a moment. Ahead lie nocturnal struggles and freedom, but no rest.

After getting married, Plato's father had sent his parents a photograph of him and Rose Mary. Inherited from his grandparents, it was the only actual image Plato had of his parents. A sepia-toned one, taken in a studio.

His father had his hair oiled and parted on the side. He was clean-shaven. His longyi and shirt were neat, without creases. He was beaming. His teeth were stained from chewing betel nut. Even his eyes seemed to smile. It was infectious. His father's smile would make Plato smile. Was he comfortable around women? he wondered. Or was he tongue-tied in her, his wife's, company? Did he prefer the kingdom of thoughts to the slavery of odd jobs? Did he also shiver and tremble unexpectedly?

The man remained a stranger. Sometimes he felt like a well-meaning uncle, sometimes an elder brother. As Plato grew older than his father in the photo, he looked upon him as a jovial junior in college. But never as a father.

She stood apart. Her gaze lowered, fixed on a point somewhere between the camera and the ground. She was shorter than her husband. She looked like an adolescent, but her expression was guarded, beyond her years. She didn't smile. She didn't look like a wife, let alone a mother. Plato couldn't grasp her, even in a photograph.

The photograph itself remains pressed between the pages of his notebook, which lies, labeled as anti-national propaganda, in some official storehouse. But the image is gone. The praying mantis ate it up before it left the cell.

Somewhere, in the distant certainties of the future, Plato is a free man, roaming the jungles of Namdapha as an armed insurgent. He confronts his preoccupation with death when he holds a piece of amber in his quivering palm. Embalmed within the resin is a gecko, immune to decomposition. When the Burman had kicked his mother, her womb could have hardened, the amniotic fluid drained out and Plato petrified into a fossil himself, all before he could open his eyes.

The amber belongs to the Kachin rebel who helped Plato cross into India, circling around the Lake of No Return and over Pangsau Pass, into the jungles connecting the two nations. For decades, the border has belonged to the Kachin Independence Army more than it has to any country. The amber is part of the Kachin's heirloom, extracted from a mine in his native Hukawng Valley. Burmite, the Burmese amber, is considered harder and older than all other forms. Yet such pieces, dull in appearance, blemished by fissures and dirt, are only good for curiosity. The Kachin boy's family possesses a trough full of fossil-bearing amber. They contain an entire world as it stood back then. Bees, insects, flies, flowers, dirt, bark, wasps, shells—but nothing human. Humans didn't exist, because humans weren't found entombed in amber.

At the time of World War II, the Allied forces constructed a road to connect eastern India to China, via northern Burma. It brought sun-burned Americans to the Kachin's doorstep. A beetroot-red officer, on seeing the trough full of fossils, offered to give his grandfather silver coins in exchange. The grandfather thought about it. In uncertain times such as this, the silver coins could ensure his family's escape, if not their future. He agreed.

The officer never returned with the coins. He was beheaded and his head strung up on a tree beside the road. His body was chopped into pieces and thrown into the Lake of No Return, it was rumored. Countless planes had already crashed into the lake. Not satisfied with scraps of metal, it demanded blood.

Though headhunting and mysterious vengeance weren't new to the Kachins, this particular instance affected his grandfather deeply. A white man's head, when drained of blood, was the palest thing he had ever seen. The sunburned skin had peeled off, revealing translucent flesh and slippery veins below. What's more, the skull, his grandfather swore, held a pig's brain. Even the bees and wasps trapped within amber were luckier than that bodiless head, he concluded. Death hadn't destroyed their physical integrity. He resolved not to part with the pieces of amber again. "All wars are fought for the right to die with dignity," he would tell his children later.

One summer night, the boy stole a piece from his grandfather's trough. He would have given it back readily, had he been asked. But he didn't inform anyone before he left. He couldn't bring himself to say goodbye before he left to join the insurgency.

The amber on Plato's palm is his favorite, he tells him. It carries within it an infant gecko, probably a newborn. It is the only creature that belongs as much to this world as the one long ago. It makes the past ordinary and familiar, like the matted walls the geckos love to walk on. Somehow, it also makes what the future holds bearable.

Burma, the country they are fighting over, is blessed with all the precious gemstones and metals of the world. Amber, emeralds, jade, pearls, gold, platinum, even the world's biggest sapphires and rubies.

"It isn't human nature that makes us fight," the Kachin boy remarks as he plays with the amber, "but nature itself. It is a fight over resources." His army controls the jade mines and narcotics trade across the northern border. If they lose the mines, they lose the war.

For Plato, these are all excuses—communism, ethnicity, democracy, even resources. Excuses that change with the changing times. As a student, it was communism he'd fought for. As an ex–political prisoner, it is democracy. It is the only way the Indian government will support the insurgents. Perhaps in the near future, he too will fight to control the narcotics trade in the Golden Triangle. To him, the value of gemstones—the consistency of imperial jade, the malleability of gold, the hardness of diamonds, and the vibrant pigeon blood that colors rubies—lies in metaphor. The rocks attain their beauty and hardiness through profound violence. Like the scars on his body, his broken teeth and internal hemorrhages, the gemstones too are evidence of transformations at the core. Purged to the surface from faultlines far below, aren't they scars and clots from the land's deepest wounds?

For the five months of the joint operation, Plato spends all his spare time playing with the amber. When he rubs the piece, the fragrance transports his mind to other lives and lands. At times, it conjures up a lifetime spent decorating altars with flowers and incense, surviving on alms and meditation. Often, the inebriating fragrance brings her, the one who whistled, back to him. Once again, she is seated right next to him, where she belongs.

At first, the amber seems dark red. But when you hold it against the sun, it reveals shades of the morning sun and brown stripes. It is turbid with bubbles. Fractures as delicate as strands of hair pierce it in places. When it's held against a clear sky, the gecko inside is distinct and intimate. Plato imagines it to be deep in hibernation. The head, almost as big as the body. The eyes, disproportionately big. The eyelids seem like they've never opened. If he focuses hard enough, Plato can discern the infant's mouth. It cannot possibly bare its teeth. It is way too tiny. Its tail is the size of a human eyelash.

Tree resin must have trickled onto the gecko only moments after it hatched, which is why the creature didn't struggle. The gecko died without a chance to open its eyes or mouth. With no taste, vision, smell, touch, not even a memory to hang on to, the gecko must have had the most blissful life and death possible on this earth.

What was the world like, Plato wonders, when the gecko was born? Human beings, he had read, were fairly recent in the history of the earth. Did that mean lizards ruled the planet at the time of the gecko's birth? Was this infant destined to be their philosopher king? What will the world be like when the philosopher king finally opens his eyes, ready to rule over the future primordial?

On rare occasions, when crossing a high peak or a narrow pass, wandering lost among ancient trees or rooted to a spot, Plato finds himself in the heart of an unexpected fog. When trapped in a cloud in the mountains, or when there are ripples above him in the valley as if the forest is floating, Plato is seized by an involuntary trembling. His entire being spasms, for this isn't an errant cloud he is amidst. Plato has wandered into a daydream. The land he inhabits is a dreamer like him.

Blinded by the radiance, all he can do is listen. He listens to the barking, shrieking, and clucking. He observes the soft and heavy move-ments, the textures brushing against his skin. He is paralyzed by their emotions, even as they move on. Plato re-creates them with colors, contours, and lives. The flying reptiles, the dawdling birds, the plants that walk and the python-sized worms, the tusk-wielding carnivores and giant wading mammals attempting to swim. He sways in the tur-bulence of the escaping ripples, relishing their high-pitched whistles—love songs composed for him and only him.

Hidden within the voices and sensations is a premonition of what is to come. All evolution is guided by the primordial instinct. The one that set us free to explore the uncertain geographies of longing, only to stumble upon the bliss of mortality. The instinct that leads us all to the primordial lake. Floating as uncomplicated single cells, waiting for life itself to cease.

Perhaps the circumstances of his birth led Plato to such realiza-tions. Perhaps such truths led to the circumstances.

He often goes to smoke opium with his friend, a local Mishmi tribal who cultivates poppies in the valley's recesses. The two sit in silence as they distill and inhale opium over the fireplace. The hut's walls are a gallery of animal skulls collected over decades. Here, Plato can iden-tify every animal that calls this jungle its home—wild gaur, leopard, flying squirrel, gibbon, civet cat. Among them are also skulls of the vanished. Musk deer, tiger, and rhino have been poached to extinction in these parts. One day, they will all return.

In prison, Plato was electrocuted twice a day until he lost count of the days. A bloodstained towel was used to cover his face and stuff his mouth. To him, it was no ordinary blood. Going by the smell and taste of it, it belonged to them—all the tortured and the extinct.

The resin dripped from a tree bark at its own pace, indifferent to the speed of transformation around it. The faster the landscape changed, the slower, in contrast, the resin's journey to the ground looked. Like a rock, the resin seemed unmoved. The insects, leaves, particles of dirt, and bubbles of air trapped inside—magnified debris of the past in an ever-changing present.

The resin found a temporary grave in a layer of chalk-like limestone below the soil. It lay there for centuries, at the northern edge of Burma, then an island surrounded by shallow seas. Gradually, it was pushed onto the seabed as amber. The water's force transformed it from an angular block to a translucent egg. Only an infant gecko remained inside.

Somnolent currents pushed the amber off the bay's shelf, into the ocean, and onto a mass grave of shells and spores, ancient truths, and the recent dead. Buried beside the gecko was an aged ammonite, spiraling in shades of rust and gold. The creator of its own world, the ammonite had once floated blissfully, cherishing the visions of a receding paradise. For India's northward journey had begun to close in on the seas.

Then the collision happened. The amber found itself on land once again, amidst a confusion of shale, sandstone, and limestone. A struggle between the ghosts of land and sea ensued. The sea recaptured it. The land grabbed it back. Eventually, the island's edges all rose in the shape of mountains, sheltering the amber in a valley of imperial jade.

The collision also created rubies, sapphires, emeralds, and diamonds. But the amber predated them by an epoch. Trapped within it, the gecko bore witness to one of the most violent events in prehistory. An event that pulverized, hacked, crumbled, slit, and ultimately transfigured the landscape into the unimaginable. No land or ocean was spared the escaping cracks that grew with a life of their own. Flung from great heights to great depths by tectonic transgressions and regressions, it never once opened its eyes. The amber lay in a valley of faults.

If the evolution of life was guided by survival, the movement of continents was guided by an imagination that no life form would be capable of comprehending.

T HE Sagaing faultline didn't push the land apart, nor did it pull it down. Some say it transformed it, as if after hours of meditative tedium.

Placed in solitary confinement for smuggling an English dictionary into prison this time, Plato, like the gecko trapped in amber, experiences the seismic waves that cause the rice fields to rise and fall in ripples with his eyes closed. The darkness comes to life with a subterranean, gut-wrenching wail. The land, reeling from the horror of having its bones crushed and flesh charred, flings him from wall to wall.

Part of the ceiling caves in, presenting him with an escape route. It is his third time in solitary confinement. By now, Plato prefers silence over the company of others. For he has seen all his fears and faith dissolve into the darkness. In their absence, freedom feels like an unwarranted complication.

This room is his shell. One created from his blood and bones, for him to retreat into. The earthquake leaves him to mend the cracks and nurse his bruises.

Mary would often enter Girija Prasad's library on the pretext of cleaning, only to sift through her master's sketchbook, filled with attempts at bringing Chanda Devi to life. That is all they were—attempts. When he got the nose right, the eyes were too small. Mary could recognize Chanda Devi's silhouette in profile, but she couldn't recognize her face. Chanda Devi had peculiar hair. In the monsoons it would curl up, and in every other season it was perfectly straight. Mary noticed how Girija Prasad had matched the texture of her hair with the color of the sky. But, somehow, the portraits never came together.

Memory was life reflected in a shattered mirror. Ever since the Burman's death, Mary had held on to him only in shards. Though the features were clear enough in her memory, she could never see the face in its entirety. The small sharp nose, the soft lips, the discolored patches of skin on his back, the sunken cheeks, the scant chest hair, the immaculately clean fingernails, the belly bloated with toddy, the unexpected curve of his spine, the ridiculous way his hair stood up even in his shadow . . . In shards, she saw his nervous smile and eyes glazed with sadness. She could hear his whistle, perpetually out of sync with his footsteps. She could see the rolled lips and the carefree hands grazing the branches as he strolled. She could smell the betel nut on his breath and the cool touch of his sweat on her own skin. But she couldn't see him.

Mary yearned for him to return, if only as a dream. The Burman had once told her that everything we took from someone, we owed back—even a breath. Before he'd died, Mary had drawn her nostrils close to his and inhaled his final breaths. The Burman had to return, if only to claim the breaths she had stolen.

Mary finds herself at the Shwedagon Pagoda earlier than usual. There is an empty spot right up front. She approaches the statue's feet. She closes her eyes. Her attempts at praying turn into the obsessive rambling of a madwoman. Injured dogs and birds come before the safety of her son. Often, she has the urge to take a broom and sweep the halls herself, unable to bear the errant balls of hair and dust that float around, grazing her feet.

She has seen mountains crumble into dust and seas rise higher than peaks. She has seen corals grow on trees and trees grow out of corals. She has seen noon turn into night when the earthquake hit the Andaman Islands. She has seen her husband bleed to death and her child leave the islands on a boat, never to return. Nothing can change that. Not faith, not denial.

Yet she spends hours in the Shwedagon, surrounded by people chanting, people silent, people weeping, people swaying. Each one of them struggling with despair. Distracted by a quarrel in hushed tones, Mary turns around to find the hall has filled up. There are at least two hundred people behind her. Some are trying to squeeze in; some stand rooted to the ground. Some chant in unison; some are defiantly out of sync. Some have their eyes closed; some seek conversations, even quarrels. Everyone is united in their resolve to shake the structure down to its foundation, if that is what it takes to be heard. Mary returns to her prayers. She stares at the many Buddhas as she searches for the point she had left off at. Where was she, she wonders, before she got distracted.

A new vibration hits the pillars. Like a bolt of lightning, it travels to the dome and the floor simultaneously. The statues tremble. For a moment, Mary sees the Buddha move. The pleats on his robe sway and his hand, the one raised in blessing, quivers. His head tilts, perhaps in submission to the people.

Mary's thoughts immediately return to the islands. She is concerned about her master, for what she is experiencing is just a tremor. Mary and Devi had been trained by Girija Prasad to drop everything and run into the open when an earthquake hit. But here in the Shwedagon, no one halts in their prayers. No one stands up. No one even acknowledges an event that will change the course of rivers, send shivers down the earth's axis, and claim thousands of lives, altering emotional geographies forever.

The tremors disappear just as they had arrived. Mary leaves the pagoda before midnight. By the time she makes it back, she is exhausted. She doesn't eat. She doesn't even sweep her corner or roll her mat. She falls asleep by the balcony, staring at the full moon. The moon, that night, isn't just a rock in the sky. It is that part of the earth flung so far away and so violently that the crater it left behind could never be filled.

After the Burman died, Mary often searched for him in her dreams. She would walk alone on a beach, search for him in the fields, or cook in the hut in anticipation. But he would never come. She would toss and turn in bed, hoping to bump into his warm body as it trembled with snores.

In deep sleep, a sharp pain runs through Mary's womb as it did that night. She wants to double up, but sleep's paralysis won't let her. In the dream, Mary is as vulnerable as she was that night. But when she hits him this time, there is no anger. As she reaches out for the knife, it is without any remorse. As she holds his face in her hands, love is all that remains. She looks into his eyes that are no longer bloodshot. The toddy has left him. So have the demons. The Burman takes one long breath. Or is it four shallow ones in quick succession? Mary doesn't know. But her nose is below his nostrils, to receive his last breath.

His warm body swiftly loses color. His limbs stiffen up. His fingers, entwined with hers, snap free. All of them are soaked in his blood—the child in her womb, the father in her arms, and Mary herself.

As his body enters an ice age, so does Mary's world. The two lie together in spirit as fossils. Though she will eventually leave the village to start a new life, it has all been a sleepwalker's dream. In spirit, she lies next to him, witnessing the cycles of tropical warmth and polar winter that his body experiences. Billions of years pass. Life evolves from complicated and complex beings to simpler, humbler forms. The sun that shed light on both of them expands. In its quest to illuminate, it evaporates all the oceans and kills all the plants. The earth, in retaliation, cools down and shrinks, wrinkling up into mountains and aging into glaciers. Unable to sustain itself in the battle between hot and cold, life moves on to other places, while the sentimental few attached to the earth choose extinction.

Mary and the Burman remain where they are, frozen in a moment. At the peak of its brightness, the sun begins it slow journey toward annihilation. The light that falls on the earth goes from burning red to shades of yellow, fading into white. Eventually, darkness takes over. Emptiness is all that remains. The emptiness in the Burman's eyes, reflected in all of time and space.

From emptiness, it begins. A weak ray of light escapes his crystal eyes. A warm vibration takes over his being. His fingers tremble with life as he reaches out for her. He clings on to her once again. With his touch, she too returns to life. Blood rushes from her heart to her arteries and limbs. She squeezes his hand back.

Mary blinks. The Burman blinks as well. "Forgive me," he says with a nervous smile. She sheds a tear of reconciliation.

A MONK SEES MARY asleep on the grass, in a clearing among the trees. She lies between empty park benches, with a bag for a pillow. He recognizes her as the woman—worn down and deliberately calm, a permanent fixture at the Shwedagon—who prays alongside him.

The year is 1980, and the monk is here to attend the Sangha Congress, the biggest conference on Theravada Buddhism in the world. He has darker skin than the rest and dreams in a foreign language. He dresses himself in ochre, not maroon, robes, for he is an outsider in Rangoon. He hopes the general will appreciate the gift he has brought, for the madman makes the seniors in his Sangha anxious. He had promised to renovate their monastery last year, and nothing happened. The monastery is desperate for foreign benefactors, especially with a civil war brewing at their doorstep.

The monk blesses her in his thoughts. He sees something move behind her still silhouette. A dark tail slithers beside her feet. Judging by the black and white stripes, it is a venomous krait. Her shadow protects it from the sun, like a humble mountain range. The monk is paralyzed with fear. If he wakes her up, one of them will panic. He stands still and prays for her life.

Mary turns around in her sleep. He can see her eyes blink as she shifts. She now lies face-to-face with the krait, like a lover. She opens her eyes. She doesn't blink anymore. There is no change in her gaze, no fear or panic. It is as if she has woken up to reflect on a dream, a persistent one. She lies awake for a while, eventually drifting back to sleep. She begins to snore. The snake moves on, disturbed by the new vibration.

The monk spends the rest of the day observing her from a distance. She sits right in front of the altar when she prays. She gets up once in a while to splash her face, smoke a bidi, and chew on betel nut. Late in the afternoon, she leaves. Descending the steps of the pagoda, she halts by the man with the birdcage. She pays him to set two mynahs free and walks away with him. The monk follows her to the bottom of the steps, outside the gate, to an isolated corner. Under a tree, she extends her arm for the birds to land on. The man opens the cage and lets them in once again.

Unable to bear his curiosity any longer, the monk walks out of the shadows. The bird-seller, frightened by his sudden appearance, picks up the cage and leaves in haste. She stays.

This isn't his first time in Burma. The monk had completed his education in a Burmese monastery. He may not be fluent in Burmese, but he can convey what is on his mind. He blesses her. She bows down in gratitude, even though she is old enough to be his mother and he, her son.

He is a silent man who avoids looking directly at people. "Daughter, I have seen people free birds for good karma. I have never seen anyone pay to set them free and recapture them," he says.

She too stares at his feet, as she attempts to speak. "I cannot release my son. I cannot change a single bird's fate. I can only see them through the illusion."

Her words don't leave the monk. Nor does the sight of Mary snoring beside a snake. He has seen how the wheel of life spins. He comes from a teardrop-shaped island in the Indian Ocean, Sri Lanka. It shares the fate of the land of the weeping eye, Burma. Covered with open wounds, the lands bleed. With time, even the sun setting over them will bleed. In the wars to come, the young will die, and the old will be spared to bury them.

He would know. Two days before leaving for Rangoon, the monk had performed the last rites for seven young men found in a ditch. No one dared ask who they were or why their flesh was scorched.

The general has gone to ludicrous lengths to organize the Sangha Congress. He has spent a quarter of the nation's annual budget on it already. More than five thousand delegates are expected to attend. He has invited monks and professors from as far as Korea, Mongolia, and the United States. Rumor in the capital has it that the superstitious general has tipped over the edge. In his lifetime, he'll also change the currency to denominations of nine, abruptly implement right-hand driving to counter the leftist rebellion, and even bathe in dolphin's blood to stay young.

The general lives in a mansion by a lake. On some mornings, he yearns for the sublime calm of water to enter his being as he stares at it from his bed. He suffers from erratic sleep and a restless heart. He has married twice already and is afraid he may do it once again. Deep down, he knows it isn't absolute power—over the nation or his lovers—that he seeks.

Before the Congress commences, the general hosts a private audience with the dignitaries. He needs each and every one of their blessings.

A young Sri Lankan monk has carried a bodhi sapling all the way from Sri Lanka as a gift for the general. It is a descendant of the original sapling brought over from India in the third century B.C.

"May the sapling bring peace and prosperity to the soil it is planted in," the monk says.

The general is touched. He is calmed by the monk's gentle and reassuring manner. He fantasizes about giving it all up and joining the young monk's followers. Renunciation has been a persistent fantasy for him, one that will crop up more and more often as he grows older.

Pleased by the gift, the general asks the monk what he can give in return.

"Set them free."

"Why are you alive?" the officer asks Plato.

Plato has spent five years in prison. Though he had been sentenced to ten years, his time has been cut short by half. The general has announced amnesty for certain political prisoners and criminals on the occasion of the Sangha Congress.

The prison is flooded with theories. Is he guided by superstition? Or is it a shrewd political move? Does the general want to win public sympathy, now that the world is watching? Or does he want to earn good karma by setting humans free instead of birds?

This is Plato's final round of interrogation. Out of habit, Plato doesn't answer.

"You are alive because we have kept you alive," the officer answers for him. "You are too old to return to university, but we can give you a job if you want. With a steady job, it will not be difficult for you to get married, even though you are an orphan. It is very important to us— your future."

Plato is touched. Orphans can be the most forgiving creatures in the world.

"The junta looks after all those who support the junta. My mother is paralyzed, and my son had tuberculosis two years ago. Had it not been for my income, how would I have paid for the treatment?"

It daunts him to sit across from the officer like an equal, separated by a table full of files, boxes, papers, and the general's photograph. He wants to feel at ease with the ordinariness, for this could be life after imprisonment, the life of an informer. Talking, even sharing a moment of intimacy, appreciation, or nostalgia with intelligence officers. "Those were the days," they might say. "Pigs mattered."

In anticipation of his release, Plato has requested that the prison guards shave his hair off, to get rid of lice. He is nervous about his appearance. Mary, his mother, will be there to greet him. He catches himself staring at his crescent-shaped teeth, reflected on the tabletop.

"Do you know why I am an orphan?" Plato says.

"No."

"My father beat my mother when she was carrying me. She was afraid I would die, so she killed him instead. Then she ran away. Do you think I should forgive her?"

The officer lifts his cup to sip on his tea, but there is none left. He orders another. He smiles at Plato while he waits. Does Plato want some too? He doesn't. The cup arrives. Before taking a sip, the officer leans forward and whispers something, so softly not even Plato can hear him. He can only decipher the words by reading the lips.

They both laugh. Plato laughs so hard, he has tears in his eyes.

Plato will never meet the officer again. Within a year of his release, he will dodge the intelligence officials and escape into India. He will train himself in guerrilla warfare in the Himalayan jungles at the Indo-Burmese border. He will operate under a new name for twelve years. His life as an armed revolutionary will abruptly come to an end when the Indian military intelligence lures his faction into a trap and throws them in prison on false charges. In India, his mother will resume her struggle for her son's freedom. Human-rights organizations will fight his case.

A visiting lawyer will be confused by Plato's lighthearted demeanor. He will mistake the smile and laughter for dementia. At the same time, he will be impressed by his lucidity and insight.

"What am I to make of your smile?" he will ask Plato. "You speak of death, torture, and anger against your country's regime as if you are sharing jokes."

Plato will laugh once again. That will be his answer.

After ten years in Indian prisons, the year of his release will also be the year of the general's death. Plato will read about his six wives in one of the many obituaries. It will remind him of the final conversation that he had with the intelligence officer in Sagaing.

"I hear the general fears his wives more than the communists," the officer had said.

MARY IS REMINDED of Mount Harriet as she stands on the highest peak in Sagaing. The greenery rolls out in every direction. But the trees are not as high, the thicket not as dense, as on the islands. Golden spires and domes of all shapes and sizes rise up higher than the trees, like anthills over grass. The Irrawaddy is the closest they will get to the ocean, connecting them to the delta, the Andaman Sea, and ultimately the Indian Ocean. Mary has lived her entire life on this very fault, of which Sagaing is the spine. The Karen villages in the Andamans and Port Blair are nerves branching from it. She will always consider herself an outsider here, in the land of her parents, her husband, and her son.

A few hours ago, when she sat next to Thapa on a small boat to cross the Irrawaddy, she saw fishermen standing waist-deep in the water. Some of them had wooden boxes beside them as they stood above the water on stilts. She wondered what the odd arrangement was for. Perhaps this is how the Burman had fished too, before he left for the islands.

At the riverbank, a girl was selling candied flowers. Intrigued by the foreign delicacy, Mary bought some. They were too sweet for her liking and made her thirsty. Her belly began to ache soon after. Though the river was as gentle and calm as a pond, Mary felt seasick on the boat. Her womb throbbed with pain. Once on land, she rushed behind the bushes to relieve herself. She was shocked to see blood on her dress—her menopause had occurred almost three years ago. The period was a flash flood from the past, an obscene reminder of how helpless she was in the face of blood. Unprepared, she used a handkerchief as a sanitary napkin and returned to Thapa. Later that day, the two find themselves at the highest point in Sagaing. By the time they finish the climb, Mary's forehead and cheeks are on fire, and she is sweating feverishly. She lies down on a bench and covers her face with a newspaper.

Thapa returns with ice-lollies. He wipes Mary's forehead with his palms and helps her up. They sit on the bench, licking the bright-orange ice from the stick. It melts onto Mary's hand, dripping over her dress. If another earthquake were to arrive, she wouldn't move a finger. She has consumed all her strength to make it this far.

Tomorrow, Plato will be released. But today she is defeated. A short, breezy trip across the Irrawaddy has drained her of every last drop of dignity and will. It has made her bleed like an adolescent and suffer the hot flashes of menopause. It has filled her with the desire to live but drained her of all hope.

Sitting on a park bench that afternoon, Mary lives a thousand emotions and a thousand lives all at once. Crushed by nine hundred and ninety-nine, finding it impossible to hang on to this one.

How ugly he must have been for his mother to abandon him, Plato had said in his letter. It isn't his but her own ugliness she fears the most.

"Do you have another longyi for tomorrow?" Thapa asks. "We can buy you one." Her bloodstained, disheveled state has him concerned.

"New clothes cannot change what I did," she says. "I left my baby, even before I could wean him off."

The Irrawaddy sprawls in front of them. From the bench, the river looks like two rivers separated by a sandbank big enough to be an island. Despite the low water level, Thapa can see boats traveling upstream. They don't have a choice—the river is the only way to get to many places up north. In the distance are the hills of Mandalay, soft and rolling, like ripples of sand, in sharp contrast to the daunting Himalayas to the west and Tibet to the north. So high and steep are those mountains, the world ends there for most. No man has made it to the top of the peaks and the bottom of the gorges near Namche Barwa. For the longest time, people mistook the Tsangpo and the Brahmaputra to be two separate rivers, for no one could venture across the great bend to see that they are one and the same.

Thapa tries to distract himself with the view, until it isn't possible anymore. Mary's words have transported him back to his own past.

"Not everyone gets a chance in this life," he says, "to start again."

Mary nods. A group of crows catches her attention. They are perched side by side on a denuded branch of a dead tree. They give the illusion of being a happy family. The mother crow grooms the father's feathers, while the adolescent looks around aimlessly.

Crushed by guilt, Mary escapes into the tale she had begun to tell herself on the dinghy from the Andamans to Burma, as she waited, nauseated and anxious, to set foot in the land of her husband and son for the first time.

ONCE UPON A TIME, a turtle lived in the sea. She was so big that the fish and coral below mistook her shadow for a rain cloud. One day, she swam to the nearest shore and dug a deep hole in the sand. She laid a hundred eggs inside and covered it with sand once again, so that no one could suspect what lay below. Then she swam back into the sea. When the time came for the eggs to hatch, she would be waiting for her children just beyond the surf. Together, they would explore the seven seas of the world and the eighth one, of heaven. As fate would have it, she was caught in a fisherman's net instead.

Before her eggs could hatch, her body was hacked, cooked, and the leftover bones piled up and buried in the fisherman's garden. So strong was the turtle's desire to live that a tree grew from her bones overnight. It was a strange tree. Though its wood was as solid as teak, it bore no leaves, let alone flowers or fruit. It was bare from sorrow.

Seeing no value in a barren tree, the fisherman decided to build himself a new boat with the wood. This boat could cut through currents and ride the highest waves with steadfast balance. The fisherman named it the *Mourning Turtle,* for that is who she was in spirit.

One day, the boat noticed a young turtle swimming in the depths of the sea. Immediately, the *Mourning Turtle* recognized that it was her son. Each egg carries within it a glimpse of where it came from. Despite the hundred eggs the *Mourning Turtle* laid, only one had survived. Swimming directly under the boat, the son recognized her too, for in its silhouette, the boat resembled a giant turtle.

So elated were the mother and son at finding each other, they didn't notice the fisherman cast his net to catch the turtle. Swiftly, the fisherman pulled it in. The boat was distraught. With the next surge in the waters, she capsized. Out fell the fisherman and his net. She set her son free.

The fisherman thought it was an accident. He swam to the shore and returned with others to drag the boat back. That night, as the boat lay on the beach, she looked at the sea with longing. If only she could swim back into the open water and be with her son. But the boat could move only in water, not on land. It prayed to the moon to use all its might and incite the sea to swell.

The moon said, "Why should I help you? It will disrupt my routine."

"It is a mother's will and duty to look after her children. If you help me fulfill mine, nature will bless you with offspring too."

A long time ago, when the hours weren't divided into day and night, the sun and moon lived a contented life together. But the bats were blinded by the sun, and the trees needed to rest in darkness. So they urged the two to spend time apart. Over time, discontent seeped into their marriage. One day, the moon stood between the sun and the earth. She reminded him of the love they had shared before a planet came in their way. The sun, angered by the moon's audacity, began to beat her. Even now, he hits the moon and hacks her into pieces.

In the *Mourning Turtle*'s plea, the moon found hope. It found a possibility of happiness. The moon dazzled the night by showing up in her full splendor. The sea responded by surging high. Slipping into the waves, the boat found the open sea. The next night, the moon laid a thousand eggs. In the course of time, they hatched into stars. One can still see them hatching in the night sky, when a shooting star falls out of its shell.

Guided by her instinct, the boat reached the turtle. Together, they fled the sea for uncharted oceans. In a drifting world, they were inseparable. Faced with predators, the boat would hide her son on board, for the mightiest enemies in the water were helpless in the dry world above.

One day, the son swam deep down to forage in a cave. A tentacle shot out from the darkness and caught him. The boat saw it all. Designed to float, she couldn't dive, in spite of her best efforts. In a flash, she made herself disintegrate and sink in the form of shards and splinters. As the octopus brought the turtle to its mouth, a splinter poked it in the eye. Another shard swam into its open mouth and caught in its throat. Writhing in pain, the octopus set the turtle free.

The turtle escaped to the surface, only to find pieces of driftwood instead of his mother. He began to cry. He hung on to all that remained. He drifted along with every piece he could hold on to. Eventually, he lost consciousness.

When he opened his eyes, he was on an island. Not only was this place new to him—he was new too. His body had been transformed into that of a young man. An elderly woman lay sleeping next to him. She was his mother. He was puzzled. On one side there was the jungle. On the other, the sea. By the waves stood a man.

"Who are you?" he asked the man.

The man smiled. "I am your father. I brought you and your mother here."

It was the father, in the form of an ocean current, who had pushed the boat into the sea that full-moon night and guided the mother to the son. It was he who pulled the pieces of wood into the ocean depths to rescue the son from the octopus. He had protected them all this while.

Together, the three of them lived on the island for a while. After resting, they resumed their journey through the different worlds of land, water, and air. One can still see them sometimes, as three waves in the sea, or three trees in a grove, or three birds flying in the sky. . . .

THE PHOTOGRAPHER SITS on a wall, with his longyi doubled up and his shirt hanging beside him. The noon heat has drenched him in sweat, and the shirt needs to last him the entire day. For a prison, the boundary walls are easy to scale, he observes. He has time to look around. The gates of Khamti Prison haven't opened yet, but the compound is crowded already. Family, friends, perhaps colleagues and informers too, wait in the sun.

He has been directed by the editor of the party newspaper to find a small, obscure prison, not a big one like Obo in Mandalay, to cover. The newspaper needs to impress upon its readers the nationwide impact of the amnesty.

He had planned to arrive an hour early and survey the scene for the ideal frame. But the crowds have foiled him. No one will let him stand in front of them. Umbrellas block his view. This seems to be his best and only option—sitting on top of the compound wall for a bird's-eye view.

The gates open.

Smiling faces rush out. The prisoners must have groomed themselves with great care for this moment. The photographer captures men in buttoned shirts and jackets, men with sunglasses and neatly combed hair. He captures them waving their hands like little children, rushing toward their loved ones.

He can hear the sobs and loud greetings. He can taste the sweets being passed around. He can feel the disbelief in the embraces as he views the scene through his lens. He is relieved. Somewhere around him is a good photo.

He lets his camera hang around his neck as he wipes his face. He looks around vacantly. He senses some movement behind him. Two people stand on the other side of the wall, across the narrow road. An elderly woman, dressed in a seemingly new longyi and blouse, with flowers in her hair. She is clearly uncomfortable. Perhaps she isn't used to dressing fashionably. Perhaps she doesn't want to be here. Perhaps she doesn't like the person she is with, a younger man who stands out in the sea of longyis with his Western trousers. He wonders why they are waiting outside when all the action is inside.

One of the just-released prisoners walks out into the street with unsure steps. He looks around. He halts. He waves to them. His smile reveals evidence of his imprisonment—broken teeth. The man waves back. The woman looks like she is about to break down. The photographer has tears in his eyes as he watches them embrace. No words are exchanged. The two of them, equally frail, hold on to each other as if they had never been apart, as if the cord had never been cut.

Who else could they be, but a mother and son?

VALLEY

NOTHING HERE REMINDS HIM OF HOME.

Thapa has spent the past hour walking the streets of Thamel, a district narrow in its entrance, narrower in its escape route. Cycle rickshaws go where the law doesn't. Unyielding desires take a man where rickshaws cannot—to terrace nightclubs and basement bars in choked alleyways. The heart of Kathmandu, a landlocked valley, is submerged. Thamel sits at the bottom, a cesspool of spirits and portents, waiting to suck you in.

The buildings sway like seasoned drunks, with protruding bellies and an unreliable gait. Pushed aside by the ever-busy streets, stooped with ceilings threatening to cave in, the entrances are snake holes. Humans crawl all over the mounds of debris like termites. When the calamity comes, the structures will all sink without a ripple. For the bamboo scaffolds and timber planks that support it all—the tilting temples and sinking courtyards, the crumbling homes and crowded shops, the crutches that keep the beggars upright—they are, in truth, mere consolations. When the calamity comes, the entire valley, not just this neighborhood, will collapse into the contours and depressions of a seabed, setting the vivid colors and currents free to take new forms and lives.

Who are these people, breeding like rodents in a dump? Just last week, he'd heard of a man who walked off the terrace of one of these buildings. He survived, with only two fractures to show for his broken heart. What lives must they lead, Thapa wonders, to have thought a fall from two stories could kill? One needs greater luck to commit suicide than one needs to survive.

Surrounded by foreigners, the locals in Thamel have learned to speak, trek, and fornicate in foreign tongues, reveling in their leftover pasta and cake. Though Thapa can pass off as a local in most places, it is here, in the land of his birth, that he feels like an outsider. Nothing here reminds him of home. Except for that undeniable pull in his heart.

Miles below the dust we tread on, the restless land tosses and turns feverishly. Sounds from the deep underground pierce into the present. People mistake it for a flock of locusts or groaning winds far away. Not Thapa. In the approaching horizon of the future, the calamity is a certain uncertainty, the greatest one there ever will be. It links them all.

Desperate to kill time, Thapa engages in window-shopping. The quality of fake goods seems to have improved since his last visit. The fake pashmina and fake cashmere. Cheap-blond mannequins wearing counterfeit North Face gear by day and faux Tibetan chuba by night. Photoshopped posters of Mount Everest and the rest of the eight-thousanders. Artificial jewelry and fake precious stones. Fake kukris and fake Gorkha bravado. Fake yak hair and fake yeti folklore. Filthy string puppets and secondhand sweaters. Thapa halts mid-step as the smell of cinnamon, freshly baked apple pie, and coffee floods the street. A café packed with foreigners and impeccable locals has taken over the pavement. Seated right in front is a young mountain girl, made attractive by her grooming and tight clothes. She is arguing with someone on her phone. Her cheeks are flushed. Under her carefully cultivated eyebrows, her kohl is smudged.

"He's not worth a single tear," Thapa says as he walks past. The girl turns around in surprise. "No one is."

Definitely not these boygirls. Last night, Thapa went to a popular bar with live music. Though it was on the first floor, a parallel universe expanded from the small stairway. Hundreds were packed into the venue, drinking, smoking, and listening to a group of men with long hair, skinny waists, and skintight jeans. Men with the voice and demeanor of teenage girls.

Thapa crosses a shameless hovel that calls itself a dental clinic. The dentures, crammed into the display window, are oracles. Enviable sets of thirty-two, half jaws, discolored molars, mint-green and flesh-pink molds, they chatter away like possessed spirits. It is not an earthquake, not a tornado, nor is it a flood—it is all of them. The calamity will swallow all life there is and spit out new specimens. Un-toothed and un-jawed ones, searching for spare dentures among the ruins. Thapa increases his pace. "Coward," they call after him. "He is a toothless one," they jeer.

He is relieved to hear gurgling water choking the voices, drowning them out. He follows the sound to the doorway of a sushi restaurant. The soothing cascades of a feng shui waterfall conjure up visions of lotus ponds with wisps of gold swimming in them. Even the plastic cherry blossoms exude a sense of calm.

As he admires this fake world, he hears a woman just ahead of him whisper something. "Thamel," she tells her husband, or that is who he assumes the man is. One can never know with white people, who touch interpreters and strangers like lovers. Hanging on to his elbow, she moves closer to compete with the noise of the crowd. "Thamel," she says loudly. "Sounds like a French perfume, doesn't it?"

Thapa laughs.

A Burmese army officer had once asked him for a bribe. He wanted French perfume for his mistress. It was a time before counterfeit Chanels and Diors poured across the border from China, and the only ones around had to be original. After six weeks, when he held it, he opened the handcrafted bottle to inhale its expensive secrets. It smelled sophisticated in a way flowers and incense sticks didn't.

Sitting in a dance bar later that night, Thapa's thoughts return to her. Clinging to the arms of another, roaming the maze of his mind. He resents her. She could see what he hadn't been able to all this while. Thamel, as fake in its allure as Chanel.

Thapa arrives late at the dance bar. Of late, he has begun to avoid them. There was a time when he would throw considerable money and time in the pursuit of entertainment and sex. A time when he was enchanted by the fake world.

Something unexpectedly snapped inside him when he halted by a Mishmi village at the border. The village chief was a friend, and it was in his grandson's home that he found the photo he'd left behind. After all those decades of amnesia, a buried moment had returned to him with the immediacy of yesterday and the certainty of today. Thapa stopped drinking completely. Drugs, he was never fond of anyway—he didn't need chemicals to hallucinate.

If the photo had a human life of its own, it would be an adult now. An orphan that had survived under many roofs, determined to show the world that there existed more beauty and hope than we could possibly accommodate in our hearts.

Thamel has only exacerbated the photograph's spell. As he sits perfectly sober in dance bars, it isn't a crisis of morality but one of imagination that hits him. Though she gyrates and pouts and pretends to look into his eyes, she is actually checking herself out in the mirror. The artificial smoke is not mountain mist, nor is the ceiling-shower rainfall. The strobe lights are so jarring they could induce seizures. When the calamity arrives, she will be haggling with a client in one of the back rooms. The wall will flop over them, killing the man with his pants down. The girl will remain unharmed, saved by the empty frame of an open window.

Thapa has come here to entertain a potential partner in crime. In two weeks, he will be transporting a consignment of party drugs across the western border into India. Though he hasn't used the route before, he is confident it will work. He will carry the packets inside carcasses of lambs. Transporting meat is a common practice among nomads, especially before winter. It will also mask the scent. Wads of cash may buy a skill, but only one secret can buy another. Thapa knows what secrets involve, especially for men. He had once seen an officer crawl onto the stage of a dance bar and join the naked dancer under the artificial waterfall. The officer is grateful to Thapa even now, after three years, for telling no one.

Beside him, his guest runs his fingers up and down the thighs of a waitress. Earlier that night, she'd tried to squeeze into Thapa's seat on the pretext of taking an order. So he gave her a tip and asked her to leave him alone.

In front of him, a dancer is unbuttoning her dress onstage. If the whimsical elements permit, all nights at a dance bar are fated to go one way. Once the riffraff is sifted from the ones with money, once the moral brigade is sitting inside, pacified by Black Label, it all comes off. One by one. The top. The skirt. The boots. The dress. The bra. The leggings. The panties. Artificial rain begins to fall. In the glare of a spotlight, a naked girl has one of the most ludicrous showers known to man. She covers herself with laundry detergent for the sake of foam. In spite of the bleaching agents, her eyelids remain turquoise blue and her lips plastic pink.

Thapa squirms in his seat. He is relieved to see a dwarf come up next. He is the only one clapping and cheering when the dwarf walks onstage. In Bangkok, one of his friends runs an agency that rents them out. They drink, they dance, they grin, even as white tourists grab at their crotches. Dwarves, not strippers, are the perfect ingredient for a crazy night.

"The whole world teases the Nepalis for being short, and the Nepalis laugh at dwarves," he tells his associate. The butcher smiles half-heartedly.

The lights dim and a song comes on. Thapa recognizes it immediately, incongruous in this sequence of dance and lust. It is an old Bollywood number, one that was released just months after he'd left his village. The dwarf's silhouette brings the lyrics to life. His miniature fingers and footsteps retreat into an eddy of memories, as he searches for the past. His being hangs on to the emotions with sharp jerks. Thapa cannot take his eyes off the face. His brow furrowed, his mouth half open, weighed down by the unspoken.

The dancer slowly crumples onto the stage, relinquishing control over his limbs one by one. Though his eyes glisten, he hasn't shed a single tear.

———

Thapa pays the bill and leaves the bar. As he walks out of the back door, the stench of petrol fumes mixed with roasted flesh wafting from the makeshift kitchen hits him. He feels nauseated—all the undigested bits of the evening rising up. He must do something to get the song out of his head. He walks aimlessly through the alleys, under the balconies that connect all the structures like one giant clothesline, onto by-lanes where the future is churning itself into existence.

Under the cover of darkness, radical transformations are taking place.

One knows a building will crumble when the creepers carpeting the bare brick walls have shriveled, the pigeons have moved out, and vultures hover instead. The creatures living in the walls, they love the mix of salt, lime, and lentils traditionally used for cement. They have eaten it from the inside out, like intestinal worms. They will not stop eating until the bones resemble coral reefs as they once were.

A few hours ago, Thapa had found himself at a congested intersection in Thamel. Six different alleys converged on a miniature square. It was a typical sight in Kathmandu. Rubble, scaffolding, half-dug ditches, and semi-constructed structures, all squeezed into the corners and recesses of the swamp city. There was a grass mound in the middle of the rubble. Standing over it, a man threw grain to feed the pigeons. The birds, large and aggressive, were not interested in the dead seeds. Descendants of raptors, they carried within them a reptilian hunger for flesh—living, succulent flesh, like the man himself. The pigeons, a countercurrent to the evolutionary tide.

Thapa arrives home, a sparse rented room on the first floor of a dilapidated building, a little after sunrise. At the entrance, he avoids a woman throwing garbage onto the streets. A young girl sits with her head between her legs on the steps. His neighbor's door is wide open. The room is cluttered with bright garments, and the television is on. The room yells and shrieks even without anyone inside. Thapa shuts his neighbor's door before unlocking his own. He leaves it open to let the synthetic stink of packet noodles escape as he cooks it. A smell that links his life with Chanel and Thamel.

Before he sits down to eat, he catches her staring at him from the landing. She must be the same girl he had passed earlier on the steps.

"Noodles?" he asks, suspecting hunger to be her morning tragedy. She nods.

He sets the water to boil again. Noodles, tea, and a packet of biscuits are all he has to offer. She must be really hungry. She hasn't refused anything yet.

"Don't you have to go to school?" he asks later, taking a seat.

She is startled. "Are you trying to rub it in?" she asks, holding his gaze. "Like the landlord who spits at my feet and says he won't feed himself on dirty money but increases the rent each month?"

The words hit Thapa like a slap in the face. He cannot understand how such an innocent question could have hurt anyone.

"Why didn't you let me entertain you last night?" she asks.

The delirium of darkness has vanished. Thapa squirms. He is too embarrassed to say anything. This girl quickly scarfing down the noodles is the opposite of the waitress he had asked to leave him alone. Faceless, ageless, glittering with vulgarity.

"Why didn't you let me entertain you?" she asks again, stabbing the silence in its heart.

"Because I'm old enough to be your father."

She laughs. A royal, reckless laughter. "Only fathers come to dance bars," she says.

"I was there to entertain my business partner. Not myself."

Her laughter has vanished, as if out of respect. In all earnestness, she asks, "Are you interested in boys? There are many in Thamel."

It is his turn to laugh. An earnest, ordinary laughter.

THAPA RESIGNS HIMSELF to a wasted day. If he sleeps now, the laughter is likely to stir the sludge of his emotions into dreams.

He begins the day by soaking his clothes. He then does the dishes, before returning to finish the laundry. Having lived alone for most of his life, he is used to the daily rituals of domesticity. No tragedy, emotion, or assault is big enough to let go of the washing.

With the cleaning for the day behind him, he steps out into the throng of trekkers, touts, beggars, bargainers, crack addicts, under-aged prostitutes, and overaged lovers. Thapa cannot lose himself, even in such crowds.

The sharp drop in temperature seems to have come from nowhere. On this bone-dry afternoon, the torrential wind has incited dust devils, returning one to moments the body remembers only as sensations and the mind has lost all memory of.

The glacial breeze sweeps rain from the peaks into the valley. The crowds are given just minutes to prepare. To push the world under ledges and awnings, to leave it aside and kneel before the thunderstorm.

The soil turns moist with anticipation. Dregs of a sea that evaporated epochs ago, frothing with the breaths of those in hibernation—the stubborn few who, in their wisdom, have hung on to gills, preferring the death of sleep to the life of lungs.

The wind hits Thapa on the back. A shiver runs through his limbs, crashing into his fingernails. His skin erupts into goosebumps.

He walks into the nearest entrance to escape the imminent downpour. It is a jewelry shop, no bigger than a phone booth. As soon as he enters, he remembers his clothes drying on the terrace, naked and vulnerable in the acidic rains of Kathmandu.

"Would you like to see something?" the saleswoman asks with an American accent. "Lapis, silver, turquoise, coral?"

Thapa notices he is the only customer. "Nothing," he says, in Nepali. "I don't know what to buy."

"Oh, I mistook you for a foreigner. Who are you looking to buy for? Wife? Daughter?" she asks, switching to his language.

"No one," he says apologetically.

He searches for something to buy, something that isn't meant for women. He looks at the curios. The floor is crammed with artifacts, the kind only foreigners love to buy. Thapa takes a closer look at the dwarf-sized brass figures. They look like gods. Or are they monsters? It is difficult to tell. Some of them are fornicating. A male and female stand facing each other, joined together at the hip like Siamese twins. In another figurine, a woman sits on top of a man as he enters her. His hands hold her waist, while she throttles him. Yet he seems to be in bliss. "Ridiculous!" Thapa exclaims.

And then he spots the monster.

Hidden in a corner, Bhairava, the Tantric deity, sits in the lotus posture, copulating with a beautiful girl half his size. He is bronze, with big angry eyes and a wide-open mouth, baring wolf-like fangs. Her naked body is painted turquoise, her nipples blood red. Her eyes are closed, her head falling back in submission.

He can feel the saleswoman's gaze crawl over his back. His earlobes burn with shame. He casually shifts his attention to the big box of earrings adjacent to the figures.

"They are on sale," she says. "Since you are a local, the discount will be twenty-five percent. For foreigners, it is ten."

He picks the first pair he sees. He doesn't wait for the change. Here he is, tinkering with earrings, while his handwashed clothes are getting drenched. He leaves the place, all too aware of the reflection trailing him in the window. An awkward, aging loner. A monster.

Thunder explodes all around him, and Thapa begins to run, though no one else is. He looks like a man with a purpose. In Thamel, he sticks out. The shadow dance of the dwarf, the clingy white woman, the nubile waitress's innocence, they have all followed him down the street. Unable to bear it, he abruptly turns in to an alley.

It is a dead end, overflowing with the filth of neighboring restaurants and shops. He can't stop panting. He is consumed by an odd feeling. The air here is overbearingly sticky, and the trash smells of rotting coconuts and putrid weeds, like a coastal swamp.

Crouched in the trash is a woman. Inch by inch, her silent presence swallows him, like quicksand. Her hair is clumpy and unruly. Her oversized shirt isn't buttoned right, and her trousers are held in place with a rope. Her body has a maternal fullness. There is a massive black bruise on her left cheek, as if something heavy, like a brick or a pole, fell on her. Her eyes—they remind him of his own after the landslide. A gaze that acknowledges nothing, neither filth nor sorrow. Her blunt mountain features, sunburned skin, and nose ring are all Thapa needs to gauge her circumstances. A survivor of the recent quake that hit the northern districts. A young mother in a family of illiterate farmers.

Thapa curses the superstitious Nepalis for abandoning her. To them, she is a bad omen. Earthquakes and misery trail her shadow. He wants to reach out, somehow. He searches through his pockets. He has only fifty rupees left. He places it by her feet. He hesitates, then takes off his designer watch and pins the note down with it. She picks it up. She plays with the dial, balancing it on her head.

Thapa is encouraged by these signs of life, as childish as they seem. So lost is he in observing her that he could stand there for centuries. Entombed, like a fossil, in the moonlit sands of her sorrow.

The full moon, in its sharp ascent, has devoured the faint evening, revealing the trash in a new light. They are sea creatures, disguised, hiding in plain sight. Curled into one another, hanging on to one another's limbs and tails for comfort. Ammonites and nautiluses that look like bottle caps. Jellyfish floating like plastic bags, entangled with snakes and eels that pass as broken pipes. Sea lilies and starfish that mimic the colors of discarded bouquets. Reptiles that are visible only as textures, lying around like broken tires and bits of metal. Asleep, they look like infants. Innocent. Blissful. Vulnerable.

She sits among them, detached from the game of explosion and extinction that life plays around her. He takes a step closer, in the hope of saying something. Frightened by his movement, she hurls the watch at him. It hits the wall instead. Thapa retreats.

At home, he inspects the watch. The dial is cracked, but it seems to be working. There is also something else in his pocket. The earrings—miniature prayer wheels carved in silver. Thapa spends his time spinning them, grazing the carved letters with his thumb.

The knock comes well into the night, when Thapa is in bed, running through the accounts for his upcoming trip. He hasn't used this route before, and he wants to carry enough money to buy opium if he comes across a poppy cultivator.

As soon as he hears the desperate thumping, he fears it might be who he thinks it is. She calls herself Bebo, after her favorite movie star. He is only two inches taller; their build is almost the same. Yet, when he opens the door, his shadow looms over her like the shadow of a monster twice her size, fangs tinged with the blood red of her nipples.

The winds have left the city, but the rains have lingered. She has paid her obeisance to the forces of nature by staying in bed—she hasn't gone to work.

She hates the rains. More than winter, which dries her skin into parchment. More than the harsh sun, the biggest enemy of college-girl skin. Her skin remains supple and fair in the rains. Yet it is her biggest enemy.

Thapa nods halfheartedly. If he says something, he suspects it may encourage her and this behavior of hers. But, then, why did he open the door in the first place?

"When I walk in the rains, or see it from a window, I get feelings," she tells him. Thapa leans against the doorframe, subtly stopping her from entering. Despite his silence, she is in no mood to leave.

"What kind of feelings?" he finally asks.

Bebo dives under his arm to enter the room. In the darkness, she strides across like someone possessed. She stops by the window, admiring the view. Flooded with rain, Thamel's streets and structures possess the artifice of an aquarium. The edges of the valley, as transparent and solid as glass. Lightning, like the creatures of the night sky, glides through water illuminated by neon colors.

In the submerged terrain of the night, the clock's hands begin to flicker. An imperceptible crack appears in time for colors and forms to escape from. The fluorescence of deep-sea creatures reigns over the darkness. They have traveled through the eras to reclaim what is their right—this valley. It was once a trench where sunlight didn't dare to venture. The predators were blind, impervious to their own electric glory. In the oceanic midnight, only the gullible had vision.

She laughs unexpectedly.

"The rain makes me angry, even as I laugh. It hurts me. I can't do anything. I am trapped by the rain. After a while, it bores me."

Thapa switches on the light. It is the only response he can think of. Encouraged, she sits on the chair she had sat on fourteen hours ago.

"I'm hungry," she says. "Make me something."

When he'd heard the knock earlier, Thapa had no idea what to expect and, more important, what she expected from him. He is relieved to hear she's hungry. So relieved, he doesn't wonder why he's her preferred chef for packet noodles.

The child-shaped thing had almost finished his rations for the day. If she is as hungry as she was in the morning, Thapa knows he will run out. He uses a trick rebels in hiding had taught him: If you deep-fry stale bread and douse it with salt, it stays with you longer. After this signature dish, she stops asking for more.

She looks around, wondering what to demand next. "Tell me a story," she says.

Thapa remains silent.

"You said you were old enough to be my father. So tell me a story," she repeats. "That is what fathers do for their children."

"I don't know any," he says.

"If you don't tell me a story, I will kill myself."

For the first time, Thapa looks at her directly. "Did you drink?" She shakes her head. No. "Drugs?"

No.

"Smoke something?" He gestures. No again.

She is dramatically solemn. She doesn't allow Thapa to look away, nor does he want to anymore. He is curious. Once upon a time, Thapa had contemplated killing himself. But he couldn't settle on the method. When he finally did, the guilt prevented him from stepping over.

He mulls over her options. Jumping off the terrace of any building in Thamel cannot kill; they are too low. Sleeping pills are fatal only to Europeans. If too much sleep could kill Asians, we would all be dead by now, he believes. Slitting the wrist is melodramatic and ineffective. It suits her personality.

"How do you want to kill yourself?" he asks.

"I don't want to jump off a building or slit my wrists, because that will make my corpse look ugly. I want to look beautiful until the end. I don't want to take poison or sleeping pills either, because I don't want to die unconscious. I want to experience it. . . . Can I ask you something? But you're not allowed to laugh."

Thapa nods.

"What if I just stopped breathing? What if I stopped my breath for long enough to kill myself?"

He giggles.

"From what you say, drowning in the Bagmati sounds like your best option. The water will not let you breathe."

Her eyes widen. She is visibly upset.

"How do you know my real name?" she asks, her voice quivering under the weight of tears.

"I don't," he replies.

"You must know my name is Bagmati; otherwise, why would you suggest drowning in that cursed river? You're making fun of me."

No longer a spoiled child, Bebo looks like a woman betrayed. "Why do you want to kill yourself?" he asks.

"Because I'm bored. So bored, I can't see a way out. I have never been outside Kathmandu. I haven't seen snow or Mount Everest, but every stinking foreigner has. Can you believe it? Nothing, no sea or waterfall, only that dirty brown garbage dump of a river. I was saving up to leave. But then a new Japanese smartphone came out, so I bought it instead. At first it was perfect. It made my skin glow and hair shine. It gave me the perfect pout, like a heroine. It made me feel so sexy, I could have fallen for myself. But then I got bored with it. How many pictures can you take? How many times can you call the same friends? They are so boring anyway. The same old rut. Now I have no money left to leave."

Thapa doesn't know how a phone can improve your looks, but he doesn't want to interrupt. He too has felt the high. The best part about gadgets is that they can be bought and sold.

"I can help you sell your phone," he suggests, and regrets it immediately. It is obvious she is not seeking neighborly advice.

The uneven clamor of rain resumes, intensified by Thamel's plastic and tarpaulin shell. Thapa's thoughts drift to the deranged woman, a distant smudge in the rain. She is still where he last saw her. Neither prowling rapists nor dogs, not even a deluge, can displace her. The Nepalis, heartless and superstitious, were right in the end. Survivors of calamities bring the calamity with them, for it dwells permanently within. The earthquake lives inside her. Her memories are the epicenter.

Bebo clears her throat audibly, as if to remind him that she hasn't left the room. She removes her slippers and puts her feet up on the table. She releases her curly hair from its ponytail and begins to comb it with her fingers.

For a brief moment, Thapa forgets why he is here. Alone and alive. It is on rainy days such as this, when the land turns into the sea, that ghosts return to life. Memories, like creatures long extinct, begin to grow flesh and bone.

"Why are you here?" he asks.

"I want to hear a story."

"Look, I have some cash with me. Take it. It's a gift."

"You think I cannot kill myself? Is that it?"

"No. If you set your mind to the task, you can do anything. You are a smart girl."

"Then do you think I'm not worth it? I don't deserve bedtime stories? I'm only good for ogling at and groping?"

"Why do you want to hear a story?"

"When I was a child, I would get bored and give up. My father would tempt me with his stories. I would finish my food, fall asleep, comb my hair, wash the utensils—all to hear a story. Now I miss them. Without his stories, life doesn't make sense."

"It's my fault, not yours," Thapa says, searching for the right words. "I don't remember stories anymore. I am a businessman. I can import and export goods. I can't tell stories."

"Then tell me about you. Tell me your story."

"Will it bring them back to life?"

"Will it kill you?"

Thapa doesn't answer. He is left with two options: tell her a story like she wants, or leave his room and walk for the rest of the night. But they scare him too, the rains. They breed longings like the damp breeds fungus.

There is one more option. But it scares him more than the brass figure he'd confronted earlier in the day. His fingers twitch and his hands gesture involuntarily as he looks around, pleading with the walls. Then he straightens the creases on his shirt and dusts his knees. He takes a deep breath and begins.

The village is very small. There are only twelve families working on ten farms, and they are all related. There are constant fights over boundaries and water, but it's not their fault. The only thing nature has given them in abundance is humans. The men run off to fight other people's wars. The women and children are sold off to escape poverty.

He is a boy. Yes, he is a husband and a father and a son, but he is still a boy. He has seen enough to learn one simple thing. For the survival of his family, he must work hard and be clever. With much planning and help from his family and relatives, he succeeds in building a canal connecting his farm to the glacial stream above. This doesn't make their life comfortable or easy. It just makes survival possible.

With consistent irrigation, they now have two harvests. His son is two years old, and the man is growing ambitious. He wants to sell a portion of his crops. The sowing season is over, as the monsoons have begun. Instead of sitting indoors, he sets off for the nearest town. It takes three days on foot.

"Why are you crying?" Bebo asks Thapa, who slouches in his chair as if confiding to the floor. The tears leave wet patches on his shirt, his trousers, even his socks. "What happened next?"

A cloud bursts over the distant peaks above his home that night. A landslide buries his entire village as it sleeps. Not a single house stands. When he returns, he sits on the rubble for days. He doesn't have the strength to clear the debris. He doesn't speak. He doesn't eat. An aunt from the next village tells him to cry—men who cannot are good for nothing but fighting wars. But he cannot. He leaves the village, never to return.

Bebo had ceased to matter after the story began. She doesn't know how to get his attention. Like a toddler, she crouches by his knees and looks at him. His face, propped up by his hands, is hidden behind a swamp of tears, snot, and tremors.

She places a pink handkerchief and an orange boiled sweet on his lap. "I ate up all your food. This is all I have."

Thapa's fingers hold on to the gifts with the same intensity they had spun the prayer wheels with.

"We cry because of what happened," she tells him. "We cry because we don't know what will happen. Sometimes we also cry because of what is about to happen. Yet we can't let it happen."

"How do you know?"

"I love crying. It's my favorite pastime. I understand people better when they cry."

She takes his hands into her own. His palms, her fingers discover, are rough. The lines of fate meander like dried-up riverbeds. Life evaporated long ago, leaving only this behind.

N O ONE KNEW where the River Bagmati originated, especially among the sukumbasi, the slum-dwellers who lived on its banks. Like all holy rivers, it would have been so high up that no human being—least of all poor, homeless people like them—could have gone there. But they had faith. They believed it came from the land of the gods—why else would kings build kingdoms and temples on its banks? They worshipped the river, even in its emaciated, filthy avatar.

Her parents named their firstborn Bagmati to appease the river, for their home was the last one before the water took over. Their lives rested on sinking ground. Each year, the rains would cost them a tin wall or a tin roof. Sometimes both. To them, the color of blood was the color of rust, and the taste of blood was the taste of rust.

Bagmati, their daughter, sought comfort in her namesake. At night, she believed, fish grew legs and walked around like tadpoles. She could see them practicing in daylight, jumping higher and higher. Little did she know it was the opposite. In the darkness, creatures with legs dreamed about fins and rudders. They weighed the worth of gills and lungs on the scales of survival. When the calamity arrives, it will be wiser to swim than to run.

The river claimed Bagmati's first pet, a stray puppy who followed her into the water. It wasn't the only tragedy it inflicted upon her. Constant waterlogging led her parents to pay more attention to the shanty than to their children. Being the eldest, she was sold as a domestic servant. The master would stroke and fondle her at every chance, as diligently as the mistress would keep the door to the dining room closed. The look of the hungry, when it fell on food, infected it with irrevocable curses.

At fifteen, she found the logic of survival disagreeable. To her parents, the sacrifice of one child for the sake of three others was a humane calculation. But she, the sacrificed one, refused to wash the menstrual blood, the daily lust, and the dirty dishes of others.

So she ran away. She slept on the streets of Thamel until she found a job in a dance bar. She would be a waitress, not a prostitute or a dancer, the manager said—those were promotions.

He was one of the first customers to notice her. Although many foreigners visited the dance bar, he stood out. A fat American, he was the only one who spoke to them, keen to have them sit, flirt, and laugh.

His interest was piqued by her shyness. Unlike the others, she would look away from him when she caught him staring. It was he who held a mirror to her face, showing her the charm she exuded. Her rough curly hair, high cheekbones, button nose, and reticent eyes made her adorable. He would buy her gifts. A digital camera, a handbag, makeup. One night, he told her he wanted to invest in her. She was the only pure thing in all of Asia.

When she refused, he offered her more. He showed her the dozen credit cards he carried. He could pay her in any currency she wanted. Rupee, dollar, baht, yuan. All she had to do was name it. Name the price.

He began with two hundred dollars. Each day he would increase it a little, until he finally got fed up and said ten thousand. He was really drunk that night and slept on a couch in the bar. No one could lift him. He was too heavy.

She cried that night. She hadn't been bargaining. She slept with a male dancer instead. One of those extras wooing the star attraction onstage. She fell for his smooth skin, lithe frame, and false promises of marriage. She left him after five months. She was lucky to have college-girl looks, he would say, the look customers wanted as they lusted after upmarket girls who hung out in malls and sashayed through coffee shops. It would bring her greater luck as a whore than as a wife.

It was only when she gave up on all relationships that she realized she had misunderstood the American. Money was the highest form of respect in the world. While everyone else kept withdrawing from her, he was the rare one who wanted to invest.

From then on, Bebo clung to that philosophy like Bagmati had clung to the tales her father used to tell her, inducing sleep and dreams. Everything in life came at a price. The challenge lay in being able to afford it all.

One night, late enough to be early morning, Bebo wiped her makeup off as she did the dishes. Though her legs ached from the high heels, she couldn't rest in the face of greasy vessels. A cluttered sink, that is what her nightmares were made of.

As she scrubbed a pan, the familiar redolence of detergent took her back to the time when she was a slave toiling in the kitchen. Soon, the mistress would take all the food to the dining room and shut the door behind her, leaving her to wonder what kind of curses the overfed inflicted on the hungry.

Bagmati had been born into simple, uncomplicated poverty. Even a small amount of money was enough to make them smile. But by shutting that door, the mistress banished her to a place where no affluence—not even the new experiences, toys, or addictions it could purchase—would give her happiness. After she began working at the dance bar, the impoverishment would leave Bebo's lifestyle and enter her head.

Only three years separated those two moments. In this short time, Bebo found herself poorer than the family she had left behind. She may have experienced moments of ecstasy, sadness, anger, and laughter, but never the satisfaction of a free-flowing river. For she was infected by insatiety. It had spread from her mind to her body, and from her body to her heart.

She wiped her face clean and combed her hair into plaits. In bed, she decided to save up and leave the world of dance bars before she succumbed to the false love of a pimp and enforced inhumane calculations upon her own children.

But the disease of insatiety, ever so virulent, flared up when she saw the newest version of the iPhone in the hands of a client slyly photographing her derriere. "Show me the picture," she demanded, and admired the sleek new camera apps and the sleeker metal body. To feel prettier, sexier, and happier, she would have to invest in a better phone.

Three months after acquiring it, she was restless once again. Killing herself wasn't such a bad idea. It was as comforting and warm a thought as noodles cooked by a stranger who didn't want to have sex with her. Up until he'd used the word "father" and reminded her of an innocence she thought she had lost long, long ago. Before rivers, mountains, valleys, and glaciers had materialized, and the earth was still flat. As flat and pure as a blank sheet of paper.

The next night, when she told Thapa she hated the rains, she lied. Standing in the doorway, she didn't have the courage to say it was him and not the rains that brought out feelings she had invested a lifetime in forgetting.

THE BOUDHANATH STUPA RISES from barrenness. A white dome higher than all the surrounding catacombs and buildings, higher even than the distant skyscrapers. It sits like a giant egg half buried in the ground. At the stupa's pinnacle, an artist has painted the Buddha's eyes and nose. Eyes painted in flashes of blue and red, stolen from a kingfisher hunting in the marshes of the Terai.

The sun has bleached the city, strewn like rubble under an empty sky. All things vibrant—colors, emotions, sounds, entanglements—have faded into their paler selves. Sitting at a rooftop restaurant overlooking the stupa, Thapa attributes it to the Buddha's eyes, burning themselves up with color.

Kathmandu, through its history, was many prosperous kingdoms on the banks of the Bagmati, fueling trade between the plains and the mountains. The civil war ended a while ago. Someone shot the king at his dinner table. Someone who sat next to him and couldn't digest the absolute tyranny of a king who could abolish monarchy itself.

But indignation burns as it always has. It compels the valley's offspring to migrate—anywhere else but here. Even deserts and deltas have greater dignity, for they follow the laws of nature in a way this highest of lands doesn't. Here, embers sleep on ice.

Thapa can see fissures running through the stupa's dome. When the calamity arrives, the tremors will cause the dome to crack open in parts, like an egg about to hatch. Giant insects, winged reptiles, and amphibians of iridescent colors will be roused from their deep slumber. They will emerge from the crack, feathers and limbs slimy with amniotic sap, trembling from the movement. Not all of them can glide or crawl, or even stumble. There are also the drifters. Starfish and slugs, mollusks and crustaceans, those who rely on the currents. What will they do? he wonders. Will they latch on to others? Or will they wait for the deluge to sweep across the eggshell? In the upheaval of the calamity, rivers will change their courses, ending up in lakes. The valley will be submerged once again.

Eventually, deep in the womb of the future, the lakes will give way to a glacier and the glacier to a sea.

A tornado will mark the beginning. The torrential wind will push the prayer wheels, all hundreds of them lining the stupa's base, in the opposite direction. The hordes circumambulating the stupa to propel those wheels will change direction too. They will retrace their footsteps. Reversing all their failed attempts at evolution—from lake to sea to land to mountains. From the plateau to the plains and, now, the valley. From one cell to one too many. From six legs to four to eight to two. Only to walk in circles, exploding with the desire to return.

From the height of the restaurant, Thapa sees no difference between the chaotic movement of ants and the mindless drift of pilgrims. They all move in the same direction, like one misguided organism slowed down by the exhaustion of a billion years. With those godly blue eyes watching over, guiding each rock and each cell toward death.

It strikes Thapa that both he and Plato, the Burmese friend he is here to meet, are Buddhists, though neither acknowledges it. Faith never featured in their conversations, spanning over three decades.

"Our god has blue eyes," Thapa tells him, pointing at the painted eyes on the stupa, "but ours are black." The difference strikes Thapa as the reason behind their sufferings. He smiles.

Plato obliges and smiles back. He is here in Kathmandu to help Thapa plan his trip to India. It is a risk not worth taking, in his opinion. But who can convince Thapa to relinquish an opportunity to make money?

The two sip on ginger tea, unable to digest loftier things. After spending ten years in an Indian prison, Plato relishes the taste of fresh ginger. It is sharp, like the irony of being free in exile. All told, he has spent half his adult life in prison—Burmese and Indian. He was recently exonerated of all criminal conduct and offered asylum in the distant Netherlands. It is a strange idea. Apparently, people don't eat rice there, only bread. Nor do they drink tea. They prefer coffee. And how is he expected to continue his fight against the junta back home? Through the World Wide Web, his lawyers tell him. While Plato was in prison, some very smart people created a parallel universe, which reflects and impacts this one. It can be accessed through a computer. No, thank you. Plato prefers to communicate with his mother through his thoughts rather than a computer screen.

An iridescent yellow beetle lands on Thapa's plate, distracting both men. Its black body has yellow spots, and orange fuzz covers its three pairs of legs. Mesmerized by the intruder, they watch the beetle use its pincers to pierce through a tea bag and squeeze out some liquid.

"What insect is this?" asks Thapa.

"I don't know. Even the insects have changed while I was in prison."

Thapa laughs. Disturbed by the new tremor, the beetle opens its magenta wings and flies away. The two men follow the streak of kaleidoscopic colors into the air and onto the neighboring roof. Next to the restaurant, an old man climbs a dilapidated sloping roof to pull out weeds. The devout don't mind the clumps of weed falling from the sky, complete with roots and flowers. Bowlegged, he struggles to find footing on the wobbly tiles. Below him is a vertical drop of three stories into the stupa's compound.

"Look after yourself, Father," Thapa shouts. The old man smiles, exposing a string of missing teeth, as he adjusts his handloom cap.

Thapa wonders what his life must be like. Rickety gait, missing teeth, yet willing to climb the sloping roof of a three-story building to pull weeds out for a sum less than their restaurant bill.

"An old man crawls on the roof, risking the only thing he still has, his life, to feed himself. Below him live men much younger, listening to the radio, watching TV, or sleeping. They've sold their wives and children. They can't stand the heat with their shirts on," says Plato. "That's the contrast. That's what turns life into art."

This is why Thapa likes to meet Plato. He is the only man he knows who talks like this. Somewhere in his gibberish lies the possibility of redemption.

Despite everything Thapa's seen, despite himself, Kathmandu still evokes a tenderness and anxiety within him. He cannot get her out of his thoughts, the crazed woman he encountered in the alley. A few nights ago, he saw her again.

It was a moonless night. Thapa had ventured behind the bushes to relieve himself. He was weaving his way out, guided by distant street-lights, when he saw those wolf eyes, ablaze with fire inside. She was hiding in the thicket. Stark naked, bald, and anorexic. He could see the ribs behind her shriveled breasts. Her skin was scratched and bleeding with psoriasis. The bruise on her left cheek had grown from an island to a continent.

On full-moon nights, she was the spirit of a primeval ocean, exploding with life, the mightiest one there ever was. On moonless nights such as this, she was the ghost of a curdled sea, retreating into cracks and faults.

Seated in the restaurant, Thapa faces a peculiar difficulty. If only he could exhume her story from a gaze. If only he could see the world through another's eyes.

"Why can't I?" he asks Plato, struggling to explain his problem. "Why can't I write poems or stories like you? About other people?"

"You're not the only one," says Plato, folding his arms on the table. "Many writers spend a lifetime writing, yet they suffer like you. When they write, it is about their own life. That is art's biggest tragedy. We can imagine god, god's enemies, ideologies to fight over, but we can't tell a single story of which we are not the center. That is the root of all the world's problems, my friend. But you cannot put yourself in someone else's shoes until you remove your own."

On this bleached and dehydrated afternoon, Thapa comes across as a man either in love or high on hashish. But Plato doesn't want to pry. The two have always shared their company, even their demons, in silence.

"What makes you so interested in stories and poems?" he finally asks. "You were the one who teased me . . . The price of a poem is four broken teeth."

"A girl," Thapa replies. "She wants me to tell her a story. I want to tell her a story too. But I don't know how. I don't know what makes an incident or an event a story. For that matter, what makes a story a story? My grandmother told me so many. But were they stories? Or were they just . . ."

Thapa doesn't complete the sentence. He is distracted by a flood of sweat sweeping down his scalp and back. He cannot bear the thought of staining his freshly dry-cleaned shirt.

Had Plato not spent all those years in jail, he wouldn't have understood Thapa's predicament. But he has spent the most promising part of his life in prison. It has taught him to read, hear, and embrace the silence that follows half-uttered sentences.

"It is the same thing that turns life into death," he replies. In jail, Plato was denied stimulation of any kind—pens, newspapers, tea, conversations, hope. He was denied a life, even that of an ant or a cockroach. By the end, it wasn't the isolation that got to him but the sheer waste of time. Wrongly labeled a terrorist by Indian intelligence, he is afraid he may become one, if only to avenge the time lost.

"Change," says Plato. "Something needs to happen. Without it, a story is dead. We are dead."

"I don't think I understand," Thapa says.

"Let's say an unmarried woman gets pregnant," says Plato. "Sorry, a girl . . . She must choose. To marry or not, to bear the child or not, to abandon it or not. Whatever she chooses, she cannot come out of it unchanged. The story cannot end like it began."

Thapa slips into silence, scavenging through Plato's words for something to retrieve.

"Have you changed?" he asks Plato. "Is your life a story?"

"It is a tragedy," Plato replies. They laugh.

Plato's eyes well up. "What about you?" he asks his friend. "Have you changed?"

Thapa sits there, tears glistening on his cheeks. Naked and vulnerable, like a crazed woman on a moonless night.

The old man has crawled down from the roof and is standing below. His legs stick out from the weeds he's spent an hour pulling. He cannot see Thapa standing behind him, staring at him as he stares at the stupa. He flashes a broken smile as he waves to none other than the blue-eyed god himself.

Before they part ways, Thapa hands over the framed photograph to Plato, as he had planned to almost eighteen years ago.

THE LAND OF MOUNTAINS rose from the sea. There are many things outsiders will never understand about it, because they're not born of this soil. It is neither flat nor round. It is neither wide nor long. Depth, that's all it has. That is why we, its offspring, didn't climb its highest mountains, worshipping them instead. From the highest place on earth, when you peer down into the deepest depths, you can see beyond layers of soil, ice, gravel, sand, rocks, and embers. You see the cracks connecting you to the earth's core. And when you do, you cease to be human. You have broken the cycle of births. But most of us want to live on. We want another chance.

This land is a complete land. It has its own desert, sea, glacier, rivers, even its own unique sun and rain, which it doesn't share with the rest of the world. The elements are the rulers. They are the gods, the monsters, the rebels, the revolutionaries, the dancers, the smugglers, the generals, the kings, the poor, the rich, the lovers, the children, the parents. The elements are human.

The mountain air is still and dry. It preserves everything. It preserves the skeletons of extinct beings. It preserves corpses discarded by souls that have moved on to newer lives and lands but may return one day to reclaim what belonged to them. It also preserves laughter, vibrating long after it was laughed through the valleys and caves.

What the rest of the world consumes as breath is, in this land, a musical instrument. The mountains use the air to hum, drum, howl, and sing. They use the air to connect your soul to their own. For once you have breathed in the mountain air, there is no turning back. No matter where you live out your story, the outcome will have been decided by the mountains.

But there are also things that we, the children of the Himalayas, are yet to discover, despite living our lives in their light and dark. Where does the heart of the Himalayas lie? For whom does it beat?

That, dear Bagmati, is the backdrop of our story.

Once upon a time, long, long ago, a landslide swallowed his world. It left him behind to sit on the rubble, even as his soul was trapped below. He sat in this bardo state for days, his soul in between death and birth. He sits like this even now, unable to reclaim the corpses of the past or move on to a new body.

The floods that brought on the landslide have disappeared. One day, a heavy sun comes out. It makes his eyes water. He begins to cry. He cries for days, so many days that even the days confuse themselves for one another, because he looks the same each day, crying in the same position, sitting on the rubble. His tears stream down to create a pond.

And out of the pond walks a little girl. A girl born from his tears. He is her father. She sits on his lap. When she does so, the man's soul comes crawling out of the rubble and reunites with his body. He combs her stubborn curls into plaits. He rolls his tattered shirt into a ball and wipes the turquoise blue of her eyes, the blood red of her lips. He also wipes the gold dust from her body. "You may be a child goddess," he tells her, "but you are human now." The man rebuilds his house from its broken remains.

When he was crying, the gods had watched him. The goddess of rain felt remorse, for the cloud that had burst with sudden excitement, causing the landslide, was one of her devotees. To make amends, she sent down her daughter, a river, from heaven.

Bagmati is a kind river. She volunteered to come down to banish landslides from the Himalayas forever, teaching the clouds and rains to spread happiness instead.

Every morning, the man's house on the mountains is blanketed by clouds. Before setting out, they visit her to seek her blessing. All she has to do is look up for them to rain. When she blinks, they stop.

———

"Does that mean she has never seen the sun?" asks Bebo.

Thapa thinks about it, impressed by her ability to immerse herself in the fantasy world, while he floats above it.

"No," he says.

With her around, the village has enough water for two harvests, not just one.

Bagmati grows into a beautiful young woman. Each day, her father wipes away the turquoise blue of her eyes, the red of her lips, and the gold dust that naturally settles on her. For she lives in the world of humans, and her father protects her. By her grace, he doesn't need to work. So he spends his time telling her tales.

One day, a young nomad comes to their doorstep, selling the usual trinkets that nomads do.

Bebo looks up at Thapa in confusion. "What do they sell?" she asks. She is yet to come across nomads. They don't visit dance bars in Thamel.

As a child, Thapa had spent his summers chasing such visits, besotted by the sunburned foreigners carrying tales and wares from Tibet. The yak-bone jewelry and sweets made from yak milk. The precious stones and ancient bones they picked up while their herds grazed. The memory makes him smile.

Flushed with excitement, Thapa moves closer to Bebo.

"Chanel," he whispers as he clings to her arm. "The nomad sells French perfumes."

They burst out laughing. Far away, at the Everest base camp, a white woman smiles in her sleep.

———

The nomad has unclouded blue eyes. As he stands at the doorstep, not a drop in his being bows down to Bagmati's divine powers. His skin is golden pink, like the evening. His hair is a river of furious black, cascading to his waist. Yet not a strand is out of place. The wind, like the water, dares not touch him.

His nose ring is a mere thread of gold. Yet it glows brighter than anything Bagmati has seen. It is even brighter than the colors on his necklace—a string of corals, bones, turquoise, lapis, and cowries.

"What is coral?" Bebo asks, snapping the thread of Thapa's story. A thread he is discovering, inch by inch.

"They are trees that grow in the sea," he replies, returning to excavate what happens next.

"Have you seen them?"

"Yes."

He has dived into coral reefs, stolen and smuggled them. He has seen reef sharks, turtles, dolphins, and the rare dugong too. Most creatures glisten and glow, their vibrant colors at war with the dark volcanic ash found on many islands. Some blend into the sticky ash, living as smudges.

Here he is, holding the severed thread of his story. He is upset with Bebo for being impatient like a child and interrupting him. He is too old for this. Telling a story has brought back the torment of having sex for the first time. Some things come best with experience. And Thapa isn't a storyteller or listener. He is just a jaded smuggler who prefers to be inconspicuous. He is a stonefish scurrying on the reef's floor, all bulging eyes and barnacled skin.

He gives up. He doesn't know what happens next.

He looks down to tell her the story is over and finds her face eagerly staring at his, hanging on to the silence.

"Where was I?" he asks.

"The colors in the nomad's necklace are brighter than any Bagmati has ever seen. His nose ring shines like the sun, I think."

"Yes. It does."

He holds Bebo's hand and jumps back into the sea of fantasy.

When Bagmati looks into the nomad's eyes, something strange happens. Her eyes grow moist and her lashes wet. The mountain air turns damp with the hope of rain. This has never happened before. Her father notices it. He invites the nomad to spend the night in his home. In the morning, he offers him his daughter's hand in marriage. Bagmati, being the kind girl she is, resists.

"Why are you sending me away, Father?" she asks. "I don't want to leave you. I want to look after you."

But the father has learned so much from his daughter. She has given him the wisdom of a few lifetimes in just a few years. He understands why nature is worshipped. What she takes with one hand, she gives with the other. New life was born from his tears.

"I may not be a god, but I know that you two are destined to be together," he tells her. "Go with him; let him be your guide. Seek the heart of the Himalayas. And when you find it, think of me. This is my gift to you."

Bagmati obediently follows her father's wishes. And so begins the journey to her husband's home.

It is far away from the crowded plains of Kathmandu. So far, it cannot be measured in kilometers or the time it takes. You must leave the ants behind in their anthills, the tigers and elephants in their jungles. You must cross meadows, plateaus, valleys, and ridges, until you reach the peaks. Little grows here, except for moss and lichen. Only ravens and vultures are there to give you company. You have left everything behind. Everything is hidden by mist. Which is why you believed nothing lay beyond these peaks except heaven. The air is thin here. Your heart beats faster. Your breaths are shorter. You don't want to eat, as nausea grips you by the throat.

But heaven lies even higher. Once you learn to see through the mist, you realize that you are only at the knees of the mountain gods. From here on, all your breaths turn into mist and the mist freezes into ice. Skin turns into parchment. Fingers go numb. Most people stop here. But the nomad doesn't. The higher he climbs, the greater is his bride's fall into love.

The two of them enter the kingdom of frozen life. They brave the blizzards that blow like sheets of ice. They spend the nights in caves. Humans cannot spot these caves, disguised to look like walls of ice, the beginning of a glacier, or the opening of a crevasse.

It is he who always starts the fire and melts the ice, washing her feet and hands, alternating between hot and cold water, saving them from the blue death. One night, as he melts the ice that clings to her hair, she asks him, "What is your home like?"

The nomad takes the necklace off his handsome, broad neck and puts it around hers.

"This necklace is made of the things I'd collected as a child," he says. "When you sleep tonight, you will dream of your new home."

That night, she finds herself standing at the center of a flat white land in her dreams, encircled by mountain peaks. Though she cannot see them, she knows they exist. They are higher than the highest peaks known to man. For they are the mountain gods, worshipped by the earthly Mount Everest, Nanda Devi, Kanchenjunga, and other peaks the foreigners pay millions to climb.

A powerful sun makes the land a blinding white. Yet nothing burns here. Her skin feels warm, like it does when her husband lights a fire.

She takes a step forward. The whiteness she stands on crumbles into powder. The sand is mixed with pieces of corals, shells, and bone, exactly like the necklace she is wearing.

For Thapa, the earth is flat. So what if some white people flew to the moon, looked back, and concluded it's a sphere?

"Have you seen any evidence of the earth being a ball yourself?" he had asked Plato three decades ago, sitting below a banyan tree in the compound of Rangoon University.

"Yes. Why else would a boat disappear over the horizon?"

"Because human beings have poor vision. We are not blessed like leopards or owls. On a blazing afternoon, if you stand at one end of the neighborhood, you cannot see the other end. It is your vision that fails, not the road that bends."

"There is no evidence of rebirth, yet you believe in it, don't you?" said Plato, hoping to strike at the weakness of all Buddhists.

"I don't," replied Thapa. "If I don't work, god will not feed me. If I die, god will not resurrect me."

"Long ago in Europe, the people who worshipped god imprisoned a man who said that the world is round and that the sun, not the earth, is the center of the universe. They tortured him until he took it back. But you are neither. You don't believe in god. Nor do you think the world is round. What is your opinion of the sun?" he asked.

Thapa, an earnest country man at heart, didn't see that Plato was merely teasing him. So he thought about it—the sun. Walking on the burning sands of tropical islands, one suspects it is the strongest near the ocean. But it is at its most powerful at high altitudes. An hour spent on a snow peak can give you sunburn and chilblain at the same time.

"What about the sun?" He threw the question back at Plato, without really understanding it.

"Do you consider it to be the center of the universe?" Plato repeated.

"No."

"Have you ever witnessed a sunset that fills you with a sense of peace and beauty, though the rest of your life is far from it?"

"Not yet," replied Thapa. The sun, like all other stars, exacerbated regret. A sky full of regrets.

"If you haven't seen one yet," said Plato, "there is hope for you. There is something still left to discover."

Hope. Thapa liked the sound of it. That would be his gift to the girl in the story, the girl for whom it came to life.

———————

The morning after the dream, Bagmati tells her husband that it is the most magical place she has ever seen. It felt like the sun stood in front of her, yet it didn't burn up the land. "And the sand, where did it come from?" she asks.

So the nomad tells her the story of his home.

In the beginning all land was an ocean floor, hidden from the sun, hidden from air. Then one day a grain of sand had a dream. In it, it was basking under the sun at the highest place on earth. That single dream of the smallest thing—it changed the face of the earth. The grain leaped up. With each leap, it reached higher and higher, and different lands were created.

The home of the nomad was an ocean bed once upon a time. But now that all the water has drained out, it is a desert. It is the land of the white glow. In summers, he collects rocks of salt, gems, bones, shells, corals. In winter, he comes down to trade in them. The villagers, like all other humans, consider them to be objects of fantasy. The nomad enjoys weaving stories around them for all the children he comes across.

To the nomad, these objects are family. Like him, they belong to a timeless world. They carry no memories, no desires, no regrets. They are the creators of it all. They are the suns and moons of their own existence.

A mammoth glacier lies on their journey ahead. For days on end, all they confront is ice, snow, and blizzards. In the land of frozen life, Bagmati would have frozen too, had it not been for the tents her husband made, the fire he lit within, and the warmth of his skin. His gaze falls upon his wife like the sun's rays. She is nourished by his silent heat.

One morning, as they stand over a giant block of jade-colored ice, he tells her a secret. Somewhere below lies the heart of the Himalayas—a grain of sand hidden in the block of ice below their feet. The oceans feared the entire earth would turn into land, so the jade sea leaped up to capture the grain and froze the instant it did.

Bagmati holds on to her husband's hand and peers below into its glassy depths. So many fractures, fissures, and faultlines running through it. She puts her ear against the glacier's heaving chest. A faint rhythm runs through the ice. From the ice, it leaps to her body. It flows into her ears, flooding through her to drown out her own heartbeat. Like the ocean, Bagmati's body explodes with the heartbeats of a million sea creatures.

Her eyes grow moist as she remembers her father's words. Born to the gods, she has received the most precious gift of all from a simple human.

"What do they look like?" asks Bebo. "A million sea creatures?"

Look around you, Thapa wants to say. They are everywhere, crawling out of pipelines, garbage dumps, and cracked walls, hanging on to the scaffolding and planks, falling off trees and swimming in tanks, eating structures from the inside. Blinding the darkness with their fluorescent colors. But he is afraid. Bebo may think him crazy and go away, leaving him alone within these cracked walls and cobwebbed corners.

"I don't know," he replies. "I don't know what they look like."

"Have you ever held a grain of sand?" she asks, lost in the crosscurrents of the tale.

"It is smaller than dust," he says, "and slippery like water. No one has."

They spend the rest of the night in silence, sitting on the floor. Him running his fingers through her curly hair, brushing off the sand and dust that has settled on her during the course of the night. "If a grain of sand is the heart," he says, a little before dawn, "is an earthquake the heart's torment?"

"I guess so," she replies, distracted by the sandcastles she is building on an imagined beach, much like the ones on picture postcards. Wondering how small a grain is and how big she must be.

"What about a landslide?" he asks. The smile on his face may have diminished, but it hasn't vanished.

The morning sun has crept in through the sole window, surrounding Thapa with a temporary halo. Bebo disrupts the sacred aura. She whispers something in his ear, but all he can feel is her warm breath as she swallows up her words in excitement.

In the still air of dawn, the strains of their laughter merge like bodies, gaining life in each other's embrace.

I T IS A FRIDAY NIGHT. Bebo goes up to the manager and tells him she wants to dance. She orders him to switch on the shower. Bebo isn't one of the bar's main attractions. She is an extra who fills the stage during group dances. But dancing under the shower implies stripping. Almost. The manager here is humane—he lets the dancers keep their underwear on, if they wish.

With her favorite song coming up next, she strides onto the stage. It is a song of seduction, dedicated to her favorite star, Bebo. So big is her fantasy, the chorus chants her name. "Take my heart," she sings, "it is the reason I'm here."

Bebo rules the stage tonight. Restless and clumsy in her movements otherwise, tonight she slows down. She flows.

She turns her back to the audience, grinding against an invisible hero.

"What are you on tonight?" a friend shouts. "You're a star!"

"I'm clean," she shouts back. "I'm fasting and praying to find a good husband."

Tonight, she is as irresistible as the Bebo of films. She is a goddess, passing through the world of humans.

The electricity is palpable. A drunk man stands at the edge of the stage, throwing notes at her. Another one dodders to the other side, placing a thin bundle on the stage itself, pinned under a lighter. Bebo walks over from the shower in her drenched miniskirt and bra, teasing the men on both sides. It is war. And she is the promise of liberation.

All they need is a hint of unzipping to send them into a frenzy. With the wad of notes touching her toes, she takes off her skirt and throws it at the man's face. He is ecstatic. Until she walks to the other side, gyrating in her underwear. The night has given the man on the opposite side another chance, and he won't waste it. He pulls out a credit card and shouts theatrically for the benefit of the whole bar, "Twenty thousand for your clothes, whatever is left of them!"

Bebo smiles, a queen lording over her kingdom of lonely, desperate, and ugly men. She has practiced each move in front of the mirror at least a hundred times but lacked the confidence to do it onstage, until now.

She turns away and walks toward the shower. Her mouth and eyes are half open in the water. Not because that is what girls do when they are turned on. It is what Bebo, the Bollywood star, does in her films.

She loosens her bra, hook by hook. Then she turns around, looking right into his eyes, and shakes her head. No. Twenty thousand isn't enough. She begins to do it up again.

"Thirty thousand!" he shouts.

Her smile returns as she strolls across the stage. Her song is long over, replaced by a new, hip-hop number. She hasn't heard it before, but it doesn't matter, for she dictates the rhythm of the night.

"Thirty-five thousand!" shouts a new entrant, too wasted to stand up from his couch. "Fifteen for the bra. Twenty for the panties."

That night, Bebo strips down for the first time. She dances naked and free for the benefit of only one man in a small, dark room behind the stage. The disco lights shine down on them, multicolored stars reconfigured into new constellations. He has paid her seven times the amount he would have paid a prostitute loitering in the same bar that night. The victory belongs as much to him as her. She may have turned him on, but what gives him the biggest erection is the world watching the two of them walking into the room together.

Envy is arousing, as arousing as money.

With many things left unspoken and unfinished, the nomad and his wife leave the glacier. They begin their final ascent to a height where no humans survive.

The land of the white glow is like mist. It is only when you stand there that you gain the sight to see through it. The nomad wastes no time in collecting some of the most beautiful artifacts the land has preserved. Plucking a strand of his hair, he weaves a necklace for his wife. He decorates her body with pieces of coral, turquoise, and the bones of ancient fish. She is now part of the land. The nomad, Bagmati discovers, doesn't live in a house. His radiance cannot be contained in one. This land exists just for the two of them.

He removes his clothing and puts it all away. She does the same. For clothes are the deceit they wear in the world of humans, not here. She glimpses her husband in the light of his land, his true light. "I know who you are," she tells him. "You are a child of the sun. You visited my father's house to search me out, the daughter of the rain."

Bagmati's life is complete. She is back among her own kind, the gods. It makes her both happy and sad. Happy to have the sun as her husband. Sad to have left behind her father, the reason she had come down to earth.

With this, Thapa's voice falls silent.

In three days, his room will be leased to someone else. It strikes him that reality is the worst story ever written. It lacks all rhythm; it has no respect for its characters. That is probably why we worship him, the blue-eyed one, a mortal who achieved divine status by helping people look beyond the ending.

Lying on his lap, Bebo tilts her head up to look at him. She is tired. She has been working hard at the dance bar. She stripped for the first time, earning more than a month of tips in just one night. But flowing is an art that tires even rivers. This ending has left her dissatisfied. The exact opposite of what a story should do.

"Why would the sun and the rain live in a desert?" she asks him. "It doesn't make sense. If they live there, how can it be a desert?"

Thapa knows the answer from his previous life as a farmer. "Everything stems from the soil," he tells her. "The nature of the land, even human nature. The difference between a desert, a jungle, and a swamp is the soil. The difference between us and white people lies in the different soils we come from."

"So why choose a desert?" Her question stands vindicated.

Because that is his idea of heaven. It is what heaven must look and feel like. Of all the landscapes he has passed through, it is only in a snow desert that all thoughts and visions, lives and spirits, evaporate. In heaven, we are all inconsequential. Could there exist a bigger blessing? The place cannot be experienced in a photograph or a film. It must be lived.

"Why don't you see the desert for yourself?" he asks her. It can fall on his route to India if he makes a small detour. "Come with me."

He is relieved. It sounds like a better ending. "You can start another life in India, ending this one, like you want to," he says.

She turns away from him to look out into the dying night, resuscitated by the neon reflections outside.

"It hasn't rained since we met," she says. "I miss it."

"I thought you hated the rain."

"I am the daughter of the rain. How can I hate it?"

She can sense him smile.

"But who are you?" she asks. "Are you the father or the nomad?" Thapa thinks about it a lot these days.

"I don't know. . . . And does it matter? I am still here, next to you." She will think about it, she tells him, over a breakfast of deep-fried bread and noodles. The ending, she will think about it.

Thapa spends the next two nights by himself. Here he is, a man nearing sixty, besotted by a girl young enough to be his granddaughter. An object of ridicule, like the dancing dwarf.

Meanwhile, the Marxists have come into power, defeating both the flailing monarchy and the budding democracy. The old man, no longer pulling weeds from decrepit roofs, has found a job that involves climbing down manholes instead, removing the dead cattle that clog the city's sewers. Somehow, the more he risks his life, the longer he lives. The pigeons in the valley are now carrion-eaters, feasting on half-burned corpses in cremation grounds. The white woman has successfully scaled Mount Everest, with the support of a forty-member crew. It is an achievement, and she is buying expensive perfume from the airport's duty-free to remind her of the kingdom of mountains— a trek to the highest point in the world and a walk through Thamel, holding the arm of another. She knew it would all end. She had waved the affair goodbye from the summit. The summit itself is preparing for the calamity. The sea lilies and feather stars—fossils embedded into its rocks—have begun to stir from their sleep.

But the deep-sea creatures haven't crawled out into the dark. Now that the moment is near, the extinct want to reflect upon what it means to be alive once again. For miles below the valley's floor, a layer of sediment has given way. The land has given way to the sea.

On the third night, Bebo knocks on his door. She knows the end, she yells.

In the story, Bagmati asks the nomad, "Why did you bring me to a desert? You are the son of the sun and I am the daughter of the rain. Even we cannot transform this place."

"Which is why we're here," replies the nomad. "It is the only place in the world where we can live and love undisturbed. If the land becomes fertile, humans will follow, and we will never be alone." Human beings ruin most love stories, the nomad tells his wife. Bagmati nods. She has seen enough Hindi films in her father's home to know this.

Thapa laughs.

"What about India?" he asks.

"I have saved a little," says Bebo. "In a month, I will have enough to leave with you."

"I can support you," says Thapa. "I make double of more than enough. We can both have motorbikes and new phones when we reach India." He pauses. "I can teach you to ride the bike."

Bebo smiles.

"In my new life, I want to have at least one relationship where there is no money involved."

He leaves the next afternoon, with a promise to return. He gifts her cartons of bread, instant noodles, biscuits, chocolates, and a pair of silver prayer-wheel earrings.

"Spin them in your free time," Thapa tells her. "It is how my prayers got answered."

Thapa leaves Kathmandu soon after. Plato accompanies him for two more days, as far as the last official checkpoint. After this, it's just him and the porters.

Soon, a four-year-old boy knocks on Bebo's door, demanding chocolate and a ball to play with. She has new neighbors.

Thapa's crossing into India is uneventful. Only refugees and terrorists use unmanned passes to cross into another country, risking gunshots from the army. Smugglers take the most popular route. They stop by checkpoints like everyone else, where they are welcomed like personal guests. A few bottles of whiskey always work in the independent republic of borders.

Four days into the journey, and everything is unfolding as planned. Almost. On the map, Thapa is where he should be. But he is all alone. Encouraged by the desolation, his helpers had drugged him and made off with the contraband, leaving him only his backpack and a mule.

He is lucky to have found a patch of manicured green through the magnified view of his binoculars. As far as he knows, no village exists in this no-man's-land, trapped between the steep rise of Tibet to the north and the sharp fall of the Indus to the south.

The fields, he discovers, belong to the Drakpo people. Some believe them to be the forgotten army of Alexander the Great. Most consider them a thing of the past, much like Alexander himself. Thapa laughs when he sees their hats, decorated with dried carnations, and jewelry made out of British coins. An odd race with odder habits. A man offers to host Thapa for as long as he pleases in exchange for his sunglasses.

Thapa reflects upon his situation. He isn't too concerned about the missing goods and the porters. He knows they will seek him out soon enough, for they are novices. He prefers to chase the secrets of this village instead—the tall tales of lost fakirs and Mongol marauders, of German tourists seeking Drakpos to father their Aryan progeny. He is better off collecting inspiration for Thamel's neon-lit nights.

The morning after his arrival, Thapa receives an invitation from Apo, the patriarch of the hamlet. The old man wants to meet him immediately. A great-grandfather to all, Apo has made it a point to interview every villager returning from the outside world and every outsider visiting the village. They are few and far between, almost none.

Seated on a chair in his orchard, the decrepit man doesn't waste time on pleasantries.

"Outsider! Did you meet a Kashmiri trader who sells machines to villagers, on your way here?" he asks Thapa in an unusually loud voice, betraying his diminishing faculties. "He roams around with his grandmother. She cooks and cleans for the spoiled child."

"No," replies Thapa as he settles down by Apo's feet.

"Have you seen an old Kashmiri woman who smokes bidis and drinks chhang and rum? She is a grandma too. But she is agile. She can walk without a stick and speaks softly, as if reciting a poem."

"No."

"Will you visit the valley of Kashmir soon?"

"No."

Apo is restless.

"Why do you ask, Apo?" Thapa inquires, disappointed by his inability to help.

"I want to marry that woman. Her family cannot reject a bride price of three yaks and seven sheep. That is fit for a Persian empress, not an old hag." He pauses before adding, "Don't tell her I called her an old hag."

Thapa laughs. "Apo, this is the age to get your grandchildren married, not yourself."

"If only my heart had stopped beating before she arrived," he sighs. "She came here with that good-for-nothing grandson of hers. The man goes from village to village, selling monstrosities in the name of the devil. And she looks after him. 'You are old, Ghazala,' I told her. 'At our age, it is best to sit still. Heaven is not what the Quran tells you. It is a sunset in this very orchard, in the company of trees as ancient as us.' . . . " The man's eyes well up.

"As ancient as our love," he whispers, as if talking to himself. "Yes, Ghazala. It is true. The longing grows. It grows old with us. But it doesn't die. In death, it gives root to lifetimes endured on islands such as these. Islands of sunlight in a lonely orchard."

Thapa is quiet. Centuries of solitude weigh him down, like a sea of sediment on a fossil.

"Why are you sad?" asks Apo. "I am the one with the broken heart."

"I've lived with a broken heart for so long, I've forgotten what it means. . . ."

"Son, a broken heart didn't kill me. Age doesn't kill me. Weak bones and indigestion don't kill me. Pray that the Buddha takes me away."

"After you find her, inshallah," says Thapa, remembering the beautiful phrase his Muslim friends often use. Then something strikes him. He smiles. "When you do find her," he says aloud, still gathering his thoughts, "I can gift you some pills for your wedding night. I have all sorts of pills. It is my trade. Pills that make you happy, pills that make you dance and sing and take all the pain away. Pills that also help you have sex. They work on both men and women."

"Are you a witch doctor?"

"The best in the business."

Thapa removes a pouch from his backpack. "There are two white pills here. You must take one yourself and give one to your empress on your wedding night. There is some white powder in a small packet. You must inhale it through your nose if you just want to have a good time. You don't need anything or anyone else. There is also a yellow pill—" He stops to search for the right words. When the words refuse to appear, he blurts out, "It is the newest drug in the business. It brings dead people back to life. I never found the courage to try it. If all the others fail, this will give you solace."

"Give me one more for Angkung, our lhaba," says Apo. "He lost his mother as an infant and has been trying to create potions and powders to meet her ever since."

"All right. But how will you remember all this?" asks Thapa. "The white pills are for sex. The white powder is for good times. And the yellow pills bring the dead back to life."

Ever since Thapa could remember, he had possessed an indelible knowledge of the future. In his heart, he knew that no matter how hard his father worked, the crops would consistently fail, for no fault of his. As a little boy, he experienced death as an inflamed lump in his throat, one that he couldn't swallow or vomit, articulate or ignore. He knew it wouldn't survive, the ball in his mother's womb. His mother, fearful of his soothsaying ways, took him to a witch doctor to be cured. Gradually, the premonitions faded away.

As an adult, Thapa couldn't just wish away what he saw when he left his home to negotiate crop prices. For the first time, the premonition took the form of a vision, not just a sinking feeling or a ringing in the inner ear. As always, his family wouldn't stop waving from the doorway until Thapa had turned into a distant black dot, his infant son persisting even then. Before the bend in the path, he turned around to look back at them. He saw only rubble. A river of debris coming down the slope, spread like a lake over the village. He sensed the spirits trapped underneath reaching out to him, despite the certain uncertainties.

It didn't make sense. How could the whole village get wiped out like that? Not one or four but all forty houses? Only old people, children, and mothers took otherworldly signs seriously. Thapa dismissed it and walked on. As an enterprising nineteen-year-old, he had more reasons to be hopeful than superstitious.

Of late, the premonitions had begun to resurface, calling out to him in his sleep, crawling out of the woodwork, yanking at his collar as he walked down streets, knocking at his door.

When he let her into his room, he hadn't known what to expect. When she talked about ending her life, he laughed unexpectedly. When she asked him for noodles, he was consumed by loneliness. When she demanded a story, he broke down.

Then she took his trembling, wet hands into her own and looked at him with the innocence of a child. At that moment, Thapa understood that the end of his story did not lie in death, for even death forsakes those who live in despair.

WHEN THAPA CAME ACROSS the photograph in a newspaper eighteen years ago, he was relieved the sheet hadn't been used to wrap something sticky or fragile, like jaggery or eggs, but only dried coconut. He smiled when he read the caption below the photo: "Prisoners released from Khamti Prison in Sagaing division as part of the nationwide political amnesty announced to commemorate the final day of the Sangha Congress."

The photograph was a sea of faces pouring onto the pavement outside the prison gates. Somewhere, floating on the tidal wave, was Mary, holding her son's hand. Hidden from everyone, outside the camera's frame, was Thapa. Standing in a corner, staring at them with moist cheeks.

He kept it pressed below his clothes, to remove the creases on the image. But the lines remained, eventually disintegrating under the weight of time. Within three years of being found, the photograph had to be held together by two long pieces of tape running across it. There was no symmetry to the decay. In a desperate attempt, Thapa framed the photograph behind solid teak and glass—the frame an airtight coffin for the moment it had captured.

With no permanent home, no wall or table to set the photo upon, Thapa kept it buried in his suitcase. Over the years, some things were lost, some left behind. Suitcases came and went. The routes, like the currencies he dealt in, changed at a pace greater than he could keep up with. But the frame stayed on.

After his release, Plato survived as an armed insurgent at the Indo-Burmese border. He also supplied Thapa with raw opium from the eastern Himalayas. Together, they connected traditional opium cultivation with the bigger international nexus.

Despite meeting regularly, Thapa didn't mention the existence of the photo to Plato. It was nothing extraordinary. A boring black-and-white in the time of colored photographs. One that largely captured strange faces in a familiar moment.

He often wondered why he was afraid to part with it. Emotions, he believed, were only cosmetic. They held no value in the face of the commercial transaction most people called life. Yet he was unable to wipe the cosmetic stuff off himself. It was he who convinced Plato to seek his mother out when he slipped into self-doubt. It was he who spent a fortnight on the islands, searching for Mary.

"Not everyone gets a chance in this life to start again," Thapa had said to Mary when she broke down on the eve of her son's release. They weren't words of advice or wisdom. He was confiding in her his own destiny.

After ten years of life in the shadows, trading in opium while claiming to wage a war against the junta, Plato decided to leave. In a rare display of unity and ambition, insurgents from different ethnic armies—the Karens, the Arakkans, the Kachins, and the Burmans— had joined forces to launch an attack from the sea. He would join a collective operation on Landfall Island, the last Indian island in the Andaman Sea before Burmese territory began.

As a farewell gesture, Thapa contemplated gifting his friend the photograph. It traveled with him all the way from Rangoon to a tribal hut in the higher reaches of the Namdapha valley. The oblong shelter belonged to a Mishmi chief, the largest individual cultivator of poppy. The shelter was the only one in the village, which consisted of four orange orchards, twelve poppy fields, and a charred grove.

The friends sat beside a fireplace. Soot hung from the sloping thatched roof like stalactites. A gallery of skulls covered the walls. On one side were the ones they worshipped, their gods; on the other, the ones they hunted.

"They are like the junta and the revolutionaries," said Plato, pointing at them. "No difference."

Plato may have left his days of idealism and poverty behind, but the habit of philosophizing clung to him like a tick. He tapped his fingers to the rhythm of Thapa's wristwatch, an explosion of ticktocks in the afternoon silence. It had three extra dials, to display the time in New York, Paris, and Tokyo simultaneously.

Sometimes, Plato would take the watch from Thapa and bring it close to his ears. Like a seashell that carried within it the sounds of the sea, the watch spilled with the discordant rhythm of time.

"If there was one thing I could have smuggled into solitary confinement," he said, "it would have been a watch. Nothing is more frightening than an undivided stretch of time."

Thapa removed his wristwatch.

"Take it," he said. Somehow, it was easier to part with a watch made in Taiwan than a ravaged photo. "Take it," Thapa insisted. "Women adore it. It's an expensive piece of male jewelry."

The opium pipe was ready. After a few rounds shared in silence, the chief left them alone. As the host, he would have to slaughter the bison himself in preparation for the meal.

The pain Plato carried within him had diminished. The grip of the migraine was easing. Chewing food with the left side of his jaw was a possibility again. His bones were at rest, even the disfigured and fractured ones. Opium was the only cure Plato had found to the pounding pain in his groin. Under its influence, time lost its oppressive quality. The present seemed to glide. Either that or Plato himself grew wings, like the mosquitoes in his cell of solitude. "I can forgive them for everything," he said, crushing years of silence in a second. "The broken teeth, the dislocated bones, the internal bleeding. But not that."

Plato wasn't sure if their paths would cross again. Spurred on by the light-headedness, he continued, "They took away my dignity. . . . I can never be close to a woman. I will never know how it feels."

Thapa reflected on the smoke escaping his nostrils, merging with the smoke pouring out of his mouth. Three distinct streams that rose as one.

If only he had a soothing word or a solution to share, he would have. But lies were all he had to offer. Thapa's talk of brothels and mistresses, lighthearted jokes about the fairer sex, even his obsession with ostentatious gadgets and clothing, it was all a distraction.

The night's blackness had descended into the room prematurely. The black soot that had caked the walls for generations disappeared under a darker shade. If Thapa opened his eyes for long enough, he could identify swirls of dark purple and maroon unfurling within the smoke.

"Can you see it?" he asked Plato. "Can you see the colors?"

"Yes."

Thapa was relieved. It made the illusion real. "Can you also see them?"

The ammonites and nautiluses, drifting out with the smoke, escaping the fire. The starfish and sea lilies crawling in the hut's cracked corners, as if all land was a seafloor.

"Yes," Plato replied. "I see them too."

Thapa began to laugh. Plato joined in. Newborns who had opened their eyes for the first time, glimpsing what humans never could, the two reveled in the magic imbued into the ordinary.

"Why didn't you tell me earlier?" Thapa asked. "I thought I was the only madman around."

Plato's laughter intensified, inviting the skulls nailed on the walls to join in. He tried to say something, but the heaving swallowed his words. He lost control over his bladder, wetting himself. Eventually, the night calmed down into a long, peaceful silence.

"I have seen them ever since I could remember," said Thapa. "Falling off trees and roofs, crawling out of gutters, garbage dumps, and pipelines. . . . I see them in floods and landslides. . . . I saw them crawl all over the rubble. . . . Not a single house remained erect. . . . I lost each and every one of them. My family . . ."

"The creatures live with us," Plato replied. "They inhabit the cracks we live in. Desperate to escape."

"Who are they?"

"Premonitions of our past . . . Ghosts of our future . . . They are us."

That night, Thapa forgot all about the photograph. He left it behind, tucked away beside the fireplace. By the time he returned to his senses, he was already three days away from the hut. In a way, he was relieved. The photograph made him sentimental. The faces in the image filled him with a contagious mix of excitement and fear. On occasions, it lulled him into surrendering to the ghosts of longing, staring at the image for hours, imagining how different his life could have been, had it not been this way.

Plato and Thapa left the Mishmi chief's village a little after dawn, putting an end to an opium-soaked night of celebration and sorrow. The photograph went unnoticed until the afternoon, when the chief's granddaughter, a chubby six-year-old in a tattered dress, pointed out the frame tucked under a straw mat by the fireplace.

The chief was concerned. Though he was tired, he would still be able to catch up with them if he sprinted. It was only when he lifted the frame that he realized how heavy it was. The weight was more than the physical weight of the teak, glass, and paper. The frame had a heavy heart.

Going by the Burmese-style clothing and faces and the squiggly caption, the chief assumed that it belonged to Plato and not Thapa. He was concerned about him—better suited for trading in opium than for ambushing the junta at sea.

On a whim, he decided to hold on to the frame, safeguarding it until his friend's return. How surprised Plato would be on finding the frame hanging with the skulls on his wall! It was a cheerful thought, his return.

The frame hung proudly with the skulls for eight years, until it was time to raze the hut to make way for a concrete structure. The chief was dead, and his children wanted to march ahead with the times. They employed laborers to carry sacks of cement and bricks on their backs for two whole days, across the mountain pass and river, into their village.

It was his granddaughter, the one who'd discovered the frame in the first place, who kept it carefully for the fifteen months they spent in a shed. The frame reminded her of her grandfather and of days spent assisting him in his opium escapades, munching on nuts by the fire. Days when her hair was shaved off every month to keep lice away. Days when no one knew what isolation meant. It was only after the family sat in a vehicle, heard the radio, and visited the nearest town, all for the first time, that she knew she was no longer a child.

The skulls were discarded. Only the frame made its way back to the brand-new concrete wall, along with the grandfather's bow and arrows, his shawl, and his favorite smoking pipe—exhibits of an extinct way of life.

When the time came for her to leave the house, she took the frame along as a memento. She carried the frame with her from village to town while her husband, a Tibetan refugee, searched for odd jobs. The black-and-white faces, all too familiar, were the closest thing she had to family. The girl had given them names and histories so deep in the past, she had crossed the bridge from fantasy into belief. The people in the photograph were her grandfather's friends. They would visit him often and smoke the best opium he could offer, until one went on to fight a war and the other fell in love with three women in three different places, caught forever in an endless loop.

Ten years into her marriage, she found herself conversing with the frame propped up against the wall in a suburban slum. She, a mother of three, unsure about what each day would bring. Her husband assured her it would all be fine, but somehow she wasn't convinced. So she complained to them, the guardians of her tribe, her grandfather's friends. What if her husband's stall didn't sell enough momos that week? How would she run the house? She offered incense sticks and small butter sculptures to appease them. She considered decorating the altar with animal skulls.

One day, in the middle of her heated afternoon complaints, she stumbled upon her grandfather among the many faces. Her eyes lit up.

She had missed him so much for all these years. How she longed to return to his lap and inhale his aura of unbridled opium smoke.

But how could it be? She held the frame so close, it almost touched her nose. She squinted. Without any warning or provocation, the illusion fell apart. The man she took to be her grandfather looked nothing like him; he was darker and shorter. In fact, he didn't even resemble a Mishmi. This simple realization started a chain reaction that would explode all myths.

Her husband and children were as much strangers as the people in the photograph were familiar. For all these years, what she mistook to be conjugal love and maternal anxiety was nothing but a fantasy. As much a fantasy as the black-and-white people trapped in the teakwood frame.

She was relieved. The profound sense of isolation she had felt, ever since she'd stepped out of her village and onto the back of an open-roofed vehicle fumbling over a pukka road, vanished.

She packed her clothes and decided to return to her ancestral home, one of the last isolated places in the world. After two days on a train, half a day on a bus, and two days of trekking over mountain ranges, she caught a glimpse of Dapha Bum, the highest snow peak in the region. She bowed down in reverence.

The world was created by an ancient woman who wove it all into existence. It was why everything—as small as fish scales, snakeskin, and the shapes on a butterfly's wing, and as gigantic as a chain of mountains and the path of rivers—fit a pattern. If humans considered something in nature anomalous or aberrational, it was because they lacked the vision to recognize the pattern.

She lost her way among the groves and valleys. She lived on moonlight and fruits. The consequent diarrhea wasn't a problem, as the whole world was an outdoor toilet once again.

One morning, on crossing the thunderous Noa Dihing River over a rickety bamboo bridge, she saw a poppy flower in bloom. It was a soothing pink, with swirls of white. She removed her knife and made three small incisions on its stem, draining the black liquid directly into her mouth.

With the strength of ten horses and the conviction of a madwoman, she walked for sixteen hours through pathless growth, guided by nothing but instinct, until she reached the end of her journey—the wild fields of poppy.

Had her memory let her down or had the poppies grown in size, with the fields covering the entire sloping expanse like a glacier? She saw more shades than the pink, red, and white of her childhood. She also saw orange, purple, and black.

She broke down when a small girl, much like herself as a child, appeared from among the flowers to hold her hand. It was her niece. She led her to her village, now a group of cement structures fitted with proper toilets, ceiling fans, satellite televisions, satellite phones, sofas, gas stoves, and other pollutants from the outside world.

"How did it all come here?" was the first thing she asked her brother. He had grown older in a predictable manner, but the village had been disfigured unpredictably.

"By road, how else?" answered her niece, amused by her deranged aunt who had walked in from the jungle.

A concrete road now connected all the homes to one another and to the nearest town. Fueled by opium money, each home now possessed a jeep, a phone, and a TV, her cousins too preferred smoking cigarettes and drinking whiskey to the tedious preparation of opium.

The only recognizable things left were the mountains around them, with the Dapha Bum lording over the horizon, the poppy fields, the familiar sound of poultry and pigs running freely, and, of course, the mischief in her niece's smile, the curiosity in her eyes, and the lice in her hair. They reminded her of herself, as she once was.

Years later, when Thapa visited the village again, it was no longer a single hut. The Mishmi settlement was like any other. Among the busy tea shops, clinic, primary school, and village council building were an assortment of shabby homes. The walls may have been cement but the roofs remained thatched. The driver searched for the Mishmi chief's house. Locals led them to a brightly colored cluster of structures in the center of the village.

Thapa sat on an ornate velvet sofa, surrounded by teddy bears and vases of artificial flowers, as he sipped on excruciatingly sweet tea. The current head, it turned out, was his friend's grandson. Where had the skulls gone? he wondered, as he stared at the pink walls. Where was the fireplace?

And then he saw it, peeping out from the last row in a glass display. Among portraits of women, infants flashing toothless smiles, and framed certificates was the teakwood frame he had left behind.

The photograph reached out to him like the ghost of someone he had buried with his own hands. But here it was, arresting his gaze once again with its black magic. How could he forget it? Why did it mean so much in the first place? Why was it still here?

The photograph, his host claimed, belonged to his sister. She had eloped with a Tibetan only to return a few months ago, that too from the jungle. He reckoned the foreign men in the photograph were relatives on her husband's side. Why else would she be so attached to it?

Two hours later, Thapa was sharing yet another cup of saccharine tea, this time with the host's sister. She had a tendency to go missing, but no one seemed to mind. This wasn't a big city. No one got lost here.

"That is a beautiful photograph," he told her.

"Thank you," she replied. She smiled as if Thapa had paid her a compliment.

"You must value it tremendously. How long have you had it for?"

"Ever since I can remember."

Thapa borrowed a pen from his hosts. He took a piece of paper from his pocket and did some calculations. It had been so long, he couldn't remember where the years had gone.

"Eighteen years," he told her. "That is how long it has been. Eighteen years since I left it by the fireplace, when I met your grandfather for the last time."

"Have you come to take it?" she asked Thapa.

"I didn't know it still existed," he said. "Looking at it is like meeting someone from a past life."

She felt the same way about the photograph. "Someone close to your heart?" she asked.

He had no answer. "I am a man of commerce" is all he could come up with.

"Has it really been eighteen years? Because it feels like much longer."

"Actually, it feels just like yesterday," he replied.

"Yes," she agreed with him. "Perhaps that's how time is for some of us. It doesn't fly. It sits still."

SNOW DESERT

A PO, THE GRANDFATHER of the entire village, suspects he is fast asleep even when he is awake. Sometimes, the past is real and the present a half-baked memory. Sometimes, the past is an incomprehensible beast and the future its unrealized shadow. Sometimes, all that Apo can claim to know with any certainty is the ability of clouds to not hurtle away into space and the tendency of the sun to rise day after day.

At the age of eighty-seven, it all feels like a dream. The children, grandchildren, and, now, great-grandchildren. The orchard. The stable. The shed. The crooked mud walls and the rose tree. The row of pearls he wears in his ears, and the turquoise and coral that dangle from his neck—signs of his stature.

It has a strange name, this village. One Mother, One Mule. Each villager can trace their lineage to the original inhabitants: a family of three brothers who shared a wife. So poor were the men, they didn't just share a wife, they also shared a mule. Since it took two beasts to plow the fields, the brothers would take turns to share the load with the animal.

The village exists as a sharp incline on the Karakoram mountains. Geographically, black gravel and vertical rock faces separate it from the Valley of Blood Apricots, though nothing can entirely explain its severance from humanity. The Silk Route too goes to circuitous lengths to avoid it. Only good friends, bitter enemies, and the truly lost venture here. For all the village has to offer is desolation.

Of late, Apo has begun to spin the Buddhist prayer wheel incessantly, a spiritual practice incongruous with the juniper trees, fairies, and ibexes the villagers worship. It is a relic from another lifetime, spent in Changthang, the plateau of his birth. Life there was conspicuous by its absence. Instead, the plateau was flooded with unrealized beings and forms. Spirits without bodies, demons without kingdoms, oceans without water, and seasons so extreme they took the place of deities at the altar. Hiding among them was a stubborn creature called love. Without limbs and eyes, without a torso, without even a shadow to call its own, it survived as ice in the glaciers and as sand grains in the dust storms. It occupied the few inches by which peaks grew and continents drew closer.

Apo can no longer remember his parents' names or how many siblings he had. Their faces, in his memory, have been created anew. How else can his mother resemble his great-granddaughter? Yet he remembers his mother's hand distinctly, spinning the prayer wheel and muttering prayers as she sat on a rock in the snow desert, surrounded by grazing yak and sheep. The half-melted snow that trickled through the meadow, like the wrinkles on her hands and the lilt in her voice, they are all real details.

After the Chinese invasion—the only war he ever fought—Apo had struggled to attain amnesia. The freedom to live, even the freedom to die, was linked to his ability to forget. But now that forgetfulness has set in as a natural process, it hurts him. Back then, amnesia was a deliberate act of hope. Now it is a sign of life unraveling. Flesh peeling off like dead skin. Bones snapping under the weight of the soul. Eyes blinking in the darkness, searching for an image to hang on to.

A widower, Apo is resigned to the loneliness of an empty room. As he sits rooted to the chair, the only piece of furniture around, the sounds of war arrive one by one. Nothing can deter the noise or prevent the visions from enacting themselves upon the bare mud walls. Not his deaf ear, nor the ambiguous fog of cataract.

Apo hears tanks revving up on steep climbs, shells exploding nearby, Bofors guns being fired, sirens going off, helicopters hovering like monstrous bees. He sees entire camps go up in flames. Relieved of his morning chores, Apo sits still, indulging his inner warscape. He tries to isolate the cylinder explosion from the noise of the ammunition as the fire spreads in the camp. With the distance and intimacy only time can afford, Apo has found similarities between the sounds of war and the vulgar display of fireworks.

This morning, the sounds refuse to subside. When they grow louder, Apo gets up and leaves. He can't risk damaging his functioning ear with memories of noise.

It only becomes worse. The blitzkrieg, he realizes, belongs to the present. Apo tracks it down to his own fields. He stands at the edge of the sea of yellow buckwheat in bloom. He gasps at the sight of a gigantic machine pillaging his precious crop.

"What is this monster?" he yells.

"Apo, it's a machine that reaps and threshes at the same time. The Kashmiri trader—you know him, he arrived three days ago—he is renting it out to us this season."

"I don't like it. Stop it right now."

"But, Apo, it does the work of ten people. And we have paid for it already."

"Only monsters do the work of ten people. How dare you, my own flesh and blood, ruin our village? Tell that son of a militant to go back with his artillery. We are peaceful people here. No war!"

No war! No war! Apo stands there and protests. His grandsons treat his senility with utmost respect. They leave him alone.

Eventually, Apo gets tired and resumes his difficult walk home. Everything is either uphill or downhill, an ordeal for the knees. Nor is there a proper path. Instead of alleys, a complicated system of channels connects all homes, orchards, fields, and meeting places. In summers, one just wades through the cold, glacial water. It is a late July morning, and the path is full stream.

Apo struggles with his walking stick through the ice-cold gush. The burning sunlight, checkered by low-lying canopies of apricot, walnut, and almond trees, is in sharp contrast to the freezing force slapping at his feet. The ebb and flow of the rushing water is reflected in the old man's thoughts. They run all over the place, blaming the governments of the world, technology, and sweet-tongued Kashmiris for his current state of misery. That monster is no helpful savior—it is a missionary that has arrived before the invasion.

"What next," Apo mumbles, "a winnowing machine?" Winnowing is one of the most graceful activities mankind—rather, womankind—has indulged in. Women toss the gold husk high up in the air, whistling to summon the winds for assistance. Even the sun will go out of its way to shine on them. His wife, long dead, was the best whistler the village had known. The wind, her friends would tease, was her suitor.

Lost in her memory, Apo pauses to pluck an apricot in his path. He spits the dusty fruit out immediately. It is all that cursed monster's fault, spewing dust for miles, contaminating their souls and fruits alike. Enough is enough. As the Apo of the village, he considers immediate action. He will go up to the Kashmiri, order him to take his monster and return to his homeland.

He trudges on, aided by his walking stick, until his bald head steams with sweat. He halts every now and then, muttering curses under his breath. He removes his headdress, made of cloth and decorated with old coins and pink carnations. Sweat drips onto the furrows of his face. His wrinkles glisten, as if touched by raindrops. The Kashmiri's house is far out, at the highest point in the village.

In keeping with tradition, outsiders are not allowed to live among the locals. Apo had been the last exception to the rule, but no one remembers it, least of all Apo himself.

By the time he reaches the outsider's home, Apo is a red-faced baboon, frothing from the gaps between his teeth. Consumed by all the anger and effort, he walks directly into the living room. He is shocked to find an aged Kashmiri woman in place of an unscrupulous young man. She is poised like a painting by the window. His heavy breaths and grunts don't distract her.

"I am here to meet your child," Apo announces in broken Hindustani, a language he had learned lifetimes ago.

The woman speaks so softly, a breeze could fly off with her words, scattering them among the snow peaks of the Hindu Kush. Apo doesn't want to betray his partial deafness to her. Nor can he order her around like a child, demanding that she come closer and speak clearly. Even though her hair is covered by a pink floral scarf and her body is hidden behind a loose purple kaftan and pajamas, Apo can sense the passage of years on her face.

She senses his confusion and points to a chair in the corner. Apo realizes it is a skeleton only after making the deliberate journey to it. The chair has gaping holes in place of the backrest and seat. It would be rude to keep standing. He doesn't want to disrespect the woman. He is left with no choice but to attempt crashing down upon the carpet.

Ever since his knees stopped complying, Apo hasn't been able to sit down or get up from the floor without assistance. Had she been younger, perhaps his daughter or granddaughter's age, he would have asked for help. But the wrinkled skin and characteristic stoop make her a contemporary. As ancient as they both are, he can't get himself to hold her—a stranger's—hand.

Apo experiences a free fall, broken only by the ground. Once the shock subsides, a greater shame glares at him. His earring, a string of pearls looped around his lobe several times, is caught in the carpet. He can't even lift his head.

She rushes to his rescue. With one hand, she gently lifts his face. With the other, her dexterous fingers untangle the complication.

The earrings are a sign of high status, he wants to tell her. Each pearl has been handed down from generation to generation. No one besides him can wear them here. But she is too close for comfort. Ever since he grew deaf, Apo has forgotten the art of whispering.

He is surprised by her strength as she lifts him by the shoulders and seats him, his back propped against a wall. He is envious. She hands him his prayer wheel. She places his walking stick beside him. She straightens his hat and dusts his jacket. And she leaves the room.

Apo is relieved. It would be worse to relive the embarrassment in her presence by having to make elaborate excuses. If only she were younger, she could have dismissed it all as the unpredictable tragedy of aging, perhaps even pitied him.

Apo's restless hands reach out for the prayer wheel. He tries to regain his composure by squinting and imagining the view from the window. From here, it is possible to see the Lion River, known to outsiders as the Indus, flowing at the bottom of the abyss. One can see her wave goodbye at the bend as she flows into Pakistan. But for a brief stretch, as she moves across no-man's-land, she is fierce and free once again.

When Apo first came to the village, a young man told him he was in Pakistan. But the elders, unaware of Partition and its preceding struggle, admonished the young chap for creating a fictitious country to fool the outsider. "Where is Pakistan?" an old woman demanded. "We have heard of China, Tibet, Kafiristan, Russia, Afghanistan, Iran. But what in the half-moon's name is Pakistan?"

"Pakistan is the land of the pure," the young man explained.

"Then it must border the region of Kafiristan, the land of the infidels," the woman conjectured. "That is farther north and farther west, not here."

Ever since the subcontinent's independence, these mountains had belonged to Pakistan. A postman and a policeman would visit the village once in three months, as a token of governance. In the absence of letters and lawbreakers, the officials spent their time nailing framed images of the Father of the Nation here and there, bartering foreign biscuits, sunglasses, buttons, and ceramics for local goods. The tin boxes carrying the biscuits turned out to be more popular than the biscuits themselves. Just as the Pakistani currency notes made excellent rolling paper, and British coins were ideal for ornaments.

Barely a decade had passed since Apo's arrival when an enterprising Indian army officer trekked to the village. His soldiers carried with them sacks of grain, soap, sugar, and cans of diesel as gifts. "Welcome to Hindustan!" the officer announced. He then proceeded to teach them how to make Indian chai, with lots of milk and sugar. It was the first time the villagers had tasted sugar. They couldn't help feeling fidgety, irritable, and pointlessly exhilarated under its influence.

As the world focused on the creation of Bangladesh from East Pakistan, the Indian army grabbed four mountains from Pakistan in the west. The village was on one such mountain. Greeted by Indian army troops, the elders felt vindicated. Their children had been wrong all along. This was all India. British India, that is. The whole world was British India, including Britain.

Three decades later, the Kargil War changed their fate once again. India retreated from the valley to the peaks behind, even as Pakistan occupied the mountains on the other side, across the Indus. While the village sat on the no-man's-land in between, the two glared at each other from the peaks. Like two dogs growling and barking but too scared to seize the bone in the middle.

Gradually, the world forgot about the village. The Indian army rushed to another corner to fight Chinese incursions, and the Pakistan army followed to watch the fun. Except for some enterprising traders, the village remained cut off.

Apo knows the lay of this land like the shape of his own being. Before his arrival in the village, he had spent two seasons roaming aimlessly in the surrounding wasteland. Murmuring winds, shape-shifting sands, the pregnant silence of rocks, and the sea's ghost were all he had for company. Based on vibrations, Apo had learned to sense nature's fears and dreams and predict the onset of earthquakes, even avalanches and floods.

The invisible political borders are constantly in flux. Apo can sense a shift in their movement, the way a blind man reads the light and dark. From the window, the border looks innocuous. The sun reigns over a clear blue sky, causing the ice-cold water of the Indus to resemble molten lava in its color, igniting the rocks and sands over the mountain with illusory flames. But even senility, the greatest gift of aging, won't allow him to simply marvel at the view. It fills him with sadness instead. Flailing in the web of borders, the earth is a being as fragile as a seasonal moth.

Soon, nostalgia takes over the sadness, making its presence felt as a sweet, delicately spiced aroma. The old woman has placed a cup of kehwa next to him. Apo sets his prayer wheel down. He stares at the cup—white ceramic with a blue pattern. It could be flowers and leaves, geometric shapes, or human beings, it's all the same to his foggy eyes. With slow, deliberate sips, he surrenders to the tender infusion of saffron, cardamom, almonds, and cashew.

Like an arrow leaping across lands and time, cutting through skin, flesh, and ribs to pierce the heart, the taste cuts through almost seventy years, to his previous life as a soldier. Back then, Apo was the designated cook for his regiment. In Srinagar, he was given a box of kehwa powder along with the rations. It was a rich Kashmiri tea, to be given only to VIPs when they visited the camp.

"I have tasted this before," Apo announces to the woman as she walks toward the door. "The special tea of your land. When everyone else was drinking alcohol, I would hide from my seniors and drink a few cups of this. After a few glasses of rum."

She nods like she understands. A few minutes later, she returns to Apo's side, this time with a pitcher full of kehwa.

Apo begins to laugh, exposing a chain of exquisitely broken teeth, as she pours him another cup.

"Madam," he says, "at this age, drinking a pitcher of even water can be dangerous. The body is an animal. It collapses where it is supposed to sit; it urinates when it pleases."

She bursts into laughter. Embarrassed by her spontaneity, she pulls her headscarf to cover her mouth.

"If you insist on pouring more, I insist we share," he adds.

"But what will my grandson say?" she asks in confusion. "Entertaining men in his absence . . ."

"It will serve him right for leaving you alone," Apo replies. "Does a woman leave her jewels or a man his chhang unattended?"

She blushes.

She walks toward the window that dominates the room, spanning one end of the wall to the other, opening up to the immensity outside.

She returns to the reflective state in which Apo had found her when he entered.

"Why do you do this?" she asks, pointing to the prayer wheel on the floor. "What does it mean?"

"Life is wheeling by, swiftly and slowly, slowly and swiftly," he says as he picks it up.

She closes her eyes. The sounds of the Indus intensify. The water gushes with such diabolical speed and desperation, there is no river here, only rapids and whirlpools. She stands there, like a fresco painted upon the mud wall. Then she speaks.

> *Life is whispering in my ears with its irresistible melody, offering me the*
> *water of immortality*
> *and the earth of transformation.*
> *Far, very far, from the depths of the hollow sky, death is calling out to me*
> *in a simple, clear voice.*

The verse stays with them like mist on a winter morning. The silence is eventually broken by footsteps. She rushes to pick up the tray from the floor. Her grandson is surprised to find Apo sitting there like the man of the house.

"There you are, my child!" Apo says, attempting to stand up and greet him. The trader rushes to his side to prop him up. "I was waiting to meet you in person. As the village patriarch, it is my duty to welcome and bless you. May you bring more enterprises to our home; may your business grow!"

The trader, relieved by the unexpected kind words, urges Apo to share a meal with them. But Apo declines. "You are our guests; we are the hosts," he says as he struggles with his walking stick.

As Apo lies restless in his bed that night, the ache in his bones isn't the only reason for his discomfort. He wonders how she must have looked in her youth. She has a big nose, like most Kashmiris, one that grows bigger with age as the rest of the face melts away. Despite her sunken and faded eyes, Apo sees currents of glacial blue in them, just as he sees dignity in her wrinkles. Her gait and voice have such grace, it is as if a Persian empress has descended upon the village from distant fruit-laden mountains, fleeing marauders. The only thing incongruent with the vision is the stubborn smell of tobacco on her clothes, which he attributes to that good-for-nothing grandson of hers.

When she smiled at Apo's words, her thin lips parted to reveal peach-pink gums and a flourishing set of teeth.

Though she spoke of death, her verse has the opposite effect. It sends blood rushing into his veins and floods his night with loneliness.

"Who is your god?" she asks, as she gazes out of the window.

"Time," he says as he stares at her unabashedly.

"And what about life?"

"This life of mine has left me exhausted. When the time comes to be reborn, I will decline. If they don't listen to me, I will make a fuss until they do. A weary man like me has earned his break from living."

"But life is hope."

"What good is hope to dead people?"

"In death, we find the hope we had surrendered at birth."

Apo is moved. He smiles in his dream as he weeps in his sleep.

APO WAKES UP in the morning, teary-eyed. He is relieved autumn hasn't set in yet, or he would have caught a cold.

Ira, his twelve-year-old great-granddaughter, sleeps so peacefully next to him, he doesn't have the heart to wake her up to help him stand. Sleep, my angel, he thinks. Sleep through the wars. Arise in peace. Sleep through the loneliness. Arise to yourself. Sleep, my angel, sleep.

He sits up in bed. He grips his walking stick. Bogged down by the thought of standing up, he reflects on the stick instead. He inherited it from his mother-in-law. The stick was older than him by a generation or two. It has an ibex head carved out of black walnut wood for a handle, complete with eyes, nose, mouth, and horns. Apo feels the head with his fingers to stoke his memories—the grooves on its curved horns, its triangular beard, its shallow nostrils and exposed teeth. He wonders if the ibex is smiling or if it is a sign of aggression.

"Why didn't you wake me up, Apo?" Ira sits up in bed and asks. "I told you, you can slap me. I don't hear people in my sleep."

"Child, on some days I don't find a reason to get out of bed," he says.

"If you don't pee as soon as you wake up, it becomes difficult to control later."

"Who is the grandfather and who is the child?" he asks as he playfully twists her ear.

Later in the morning, Apo summons her once again to his room. Behind closed doors, he makes a proposition. He asks her to spy on the Kashmiri woman. It will be their secret.

"Why?" she asks.

"She knows black magic. As your Apo, I must look out for all of us." She stands still, mouth wide open. "Is she a witch?" she asks.

"You tell me."

As the two lie under the same blanket that night, the girl is bursting with stories to share. The Kashmiri granny appears to be an old woman. But she really is a man. Hidden among the trees in the orchard, Ira saw her pull out a bidi and light it, even as she washed clothes in the drain. She performed the two activities as if they were routine. The girl also found a half-empty bottle of chhang, the local beer, among the spices in her kitchen. Not only that, she had a definite mustache and beard, especially when one saw her under the sun at a certain angle.

"That is what convinced me she is a man."

"The chhang must belong to her grandson." Apo tries to make sense of it. "Women of her faith don't drink."

"I saw her take a few sips before falling asleep in the afternoon. . . . Apo," Ira calls out, sensing him retreat into his thoughts. "You were right. She is a witch." Then she corrects herself, "He is a witch."

"You are too young to judge such things."

"Shh!" she says, placing a finger on his lips. "This is our secret."

"You are too young to judge such things," Apo whispers again. "Now, tell me everything you saw."

"She cleans the house a lot. She exclaims something ending with 'Allah' each time she catches a bedbug. After bathing, she rubs her hands and feet with walnut oil and sprinkles her face with rose water to fool people with a woman's fragrance. She removes her scarf to comb her hair. With her hair loose like a witch's, she reads books. I don't know what she does, but she holds a pen and stares at pages for a long time. She also spreads a mat on the floor and prays again and again. I have never seen anyone pray so much. Strange prayers, that too. She holds her palms together like an invisible book. Anyone who believes in fairies wouldn't pray so much. Devils need more pleasing."

"What is her hair like?"

"It is white and gray, like Angkung's horse. It shrivels into a rat's tail toward the end."

Apo strokes his bald head. "I have lice," he says.

"No, you don't. You don't have any hair."

"Yes, I do. My hair is as dark as Angkung's horse's shit." The two laugh.

Apo kisses the child's hands before placing them over his eyes. With a quivering lilt, he proceeds to sing her a song about a king and his lost queen.

That night, he has a dream. It is a new one too, a rare occurrence at his age. Apo can see and hear clearly in his dream. The landscape is simple and geometric, like carvings found in caves. The mountains are sharp triangles, the animals symbolic in their silhouette. The colors all primary and bright, the shadows uniformly black. On one such bare brown mountain covered with scree, a group of ibexes frolics. They jump so high, they touch the pale-blue sky, casting shadows as big as clouds over the neighboring mountains. At first, Apo doesn't notice the source of their excitement. Then he sees a snow leopard curled up in a corner at the mountain's base, a female. She sits utterly calm, swishing her tail occasionally. The leopard's tail, to Apo's surprise, isn't long, majestic, and furry. It is short and shriveled, like a rat's.

Apo wakes up with a single desire the next morning. He has to see her again.

A young boy knocks on her door late in the afternoon, as she darns her grandson's clothes. Before she can get up, the boy is in her living room.

"Our revered patriarch," he announces with rehearsed solemnity, "the well of wisdom, love, courage, and all that is worth revering, is here to grace you with his presence." Saying this, he returns with a chair and places it at the center of the room.

Apo stands outside. He wipes his face with his sleeves. He removes a small crystal bottle of attar from his coat and rubs it on his wrists. His nose has remained as sharp as ever, even as his other senses have failed him. He inhales the exotic fragrance of jasmine with languorous breaths to gather his strength.

It isn't until he sees her startled face that he realizes he hasn't thought of a reason. He has no excuse to justify his visit, particularly at an hour when she is alone.

"Madam," he begins in his characteristically loud voice, "can you write?"

She nods.

"In that case, will you please write down the verse you recited the other day?"

He senses her confusion and continues, "In this village, I am the eldest. The juniper trees are the only spirits more ancient and esteemed than I am. It is my duty to preserve all beautiful things, to educate our children in winter. Winter, as you may know, is long and lonely here."

"But I am not a poet," she says. "All I did was serve food in gatherings where my husband, may Allah bless his departed soul, or my sons recited."

"Madam, you have lived your life surrounded by fools." Saying this, he places his walking stick by the chair, in preparation to sit.

She cannot contain her laughter. "No one has called my late husband a fool," she says. No one had called her, the universal grandmother, "madam" either.

Apo imagines her face turning pink as she giggles, like a girl in the company of other girls. Relieved by her spontaneity, he joins in the laughter. He laughs until the teeth left in his mouth rattle, the veins on his hand tremble, and his bladder momentarily lets go.

The laughter subsides into silence.

"Winter is the time for telling tales," she says, as if in a reverie. "Tales with no end in sight. It is the season dedicated to Scheherazade, not poetry."

"Winter is the queen of all seasons. The bears and marmots hibernate. We Drakpos celebrate. It is the biggest and longest celebration. A time for marriages, festivals, friendships, epics, and tales."

"In my village, that is spring."

"Spring is the season of the heart. Its arrival and departure are felt in the heart more than in the fields." Apo surprises himself with his lyricism.

She is intrigued. "What is autumn?" she asks.

"Birth. It is the soul resigning to yet another life, even as nirvana awaits."

She has never heard seasons described in this light before, especially not in the drunken gatherings her husband had been so fond of hosting.

"Is that what your faith teaches you?"

"No. When senility sinks in, wisdom rises to the surface."

She smiles as she shifts her gaze from the wall to the window, stealing a glance at him in the process. Apo sits hunched on the chair. His face, especially his nose, is gravely burned by the sun, giving his complexion a beetroot-pink hue. The lines running across his forehead, escaping his eyes and encircling his cheeks, are deeply engraved. Below his hat, Apo has thick sideburns, a wispy mustache, and a beard of gray.

He is different from the rest of the villagers, who have fairer skin and lighter eyes than Kashmiris. She has never seen anyone like him before. A man with earrings made of pearls, a necklace strung with corals and turquoise, and numerous rings. He wears more jewelry than she does.

"What about the monsoons?" she resumes.

Apo can count the number of times it has rained here on one hand. Thirty-five years ago, a cloud burst over the peak and caused heavy rains, flooding the village. All the homes on the eastern edge were destroyed. Villagers ran for their life that night, screaming, "Aan! Aan!" in terror. Angkung, the current shaman, was born that night. It was how he got his name—from the sound of fear.

On another occasion, his wife, wedded to the chore of irrigating the fields by day and the orchards by night, was overjoyed to find it drizzling. She removed her traditional headdress and ran outside to dance in the rain that afternoon.

Then there was the thunderstorm that knocked him out in the wastelands, before he ended up in the village. The drops were so voluminous and mighty, they left his skin bruised.

"The rains," he says, uncharacteristically soft and contemplative. "In Hindustan, the rains are god. Here, they are death."

The landscape reiterates his view. She sees the rocks loosely piled up over the mountains, as unstable as the pyramids of pebbles the nomads erected on each mountain pass, with desert winds battering the rows of red, green, yellow, and blue Buddhist prayer flags in the foreground. A playful breeze is enough to cause a dust storm. A specter of dust is already gaining strength on the other side of the river. The gentlest rain can cause a landslide. A torrential downpour, she suspects, will dissolve all the mud homes.

She peers at the Indus raging far below. In her short time here, she has witnessed the movement downstream of a boulder the size of a truck. So powerful are the currents, she estimates the boulder will be in Pakistan within a week.

"The river, my grandson tells me, is worshipped here."

"They are all spirits. The ancient juniper grove is older than human life. Each mountain has its own fairy. The ibexes work for them like the mules work for us. This is why we carve an ibex out each time we hunt one, so it can live on. Every being, whether a rock or a mountain, a bush or a tree, a cloud or the sky, has a spirit."

"Does this religion have a name?"

Apo gives it some thought. "The Buddhists and Muslims call it a religion of spirits. When I first arrived here, the elders nursed me to health. Once I was better, they asked me to leave. But I wanted to marry and settle down here. So I asked them why I couldn't. They were afraid that the Buddha worshipped by nomads like me would upset their spirits. So I converted to their way. I sacrificed the Buddha for my wife," he cackles. "In the beginning of the world, my father-in-law would say, god gave each religion its own rules. But the Drakpos, the people here, they drank too much that night and forgot all the rules. This really upset god, so all they were left with were fairies and spirits."

He expects her to laugh, but she seems lost in thought. "Is it lonely without her?" she asks.

Apo's eyes well up. An errant artillery shell had killed his wife decades ago. India and Pakistan were engaged in a war over the neighboring mountains of Kargil. Apo had left war behind, but war hadn't left him. He heaves and sighs, but the words don't leave his throat. How can they? Her absence grows more acute even as the memories fade.

Ghazala feels guilty for her impertinence and rushes out of the room. Apo begins to feel nervous, wondering what caused her unannounced flight.

She returns with a tray. She places a pot of kehwa, salted cashews, and dried apricots before him on a stool. She pours him a cup.

"Please excuse me," she says, "while I complete my evening prayers."

"Oh! I had forgotten about the Mussulmans' obsession with praying at each and every hour," he exclaims, impressed by his swift recollection.

"Five times," she corrects him.

Apo tries to imagine her as he sips the kehwa in solitude. Separated only by a wall, doubled up on a mat. Eyes closed, head bowed in submission. Or is it resignation? No one knows. What does her face look like at this moment? he wonders. What does she pray for, five times a day, day in and day out?

Apo's great-grandson returns, eager to transport the chair and his great-grandfather back so that he can return to his friends. Apo makes him wait outside, as young boys and dogs ought to. He knows he has to leave soon, but he doesn't have the heart to. Nor does he know how to, especially after she seats herself in front of him with a cup of kehwa.

"What does one pray for at our age?" he asks.

"One prays for the long life of strangers one has met at sunset and hopes to see again at sunrise."

"A new day begins at sunset for us Drakpos."

She smiles. The two bide their time in silence. She watches him doze, moving in and out of awareness, waking himself up in fits and starts. He stares at her cross-eyed, imagining the full moon from its eclipse. Struggling to piece together an epic that sprawls across millennia, lands, and lives from the shard of a conversation. This isn't the first time the reluctant souls have looked at each other with longing, contemplating a free fall into the abyss. Nor is it the first time they have floundered, out of sync with the other's steps.

Eventually, he speaks. "Forgive me for taking up your time. One must speak the truth. I came here to ask something of you."

She nods her consent.

"What is your name?"

"Ghazala Mumtaz Abdul Sheikh Begum."

"How many names do you have?"

"That is my entire name," she replies with a smile. "People stopped asking me that question when I got married. Wives, mothers, and grandmothers don't have names. Apo isn't your name either."

"No. It means grandfather in our language."

"Then what is your name?"

"After a long time, long enough to be a lifetime, it came to me at dawn. I was afraid I had forgotten it forever, the name my ancestors had given me. My mother called out to me with the first rays of the sun. 'Tashi Yeshe,' she whispered in my ears, 'wake up. The sheep are restless; take them with you.' When I woke up, I wondered what your name was."

CHANGTHANG, THE SNOW DESERT, is no ordinary plateau. Its undulating terrain has confounded the human race ever since they stepped out of Africa and stumbled upon central Asia, unable to fly over the bordering mountain ranges like a flock of geese. What the human mind perceives as an unvanquished distance is all a matter of height, for the Tibetan plateau is higher than the highest peaks of all other continents, and it is still rising. Or so the nomads, the future human inhabitants of this plateau, believe. The snow desert shows no signs of belonging to this earth. It hovers somewhere above.

Within the nomad families, more children perish than survive. Some souls quietly escape the womb even before the mother can realize she has conceived. Compared to all the glorious lives one can lead, the human one is quite a chore.

Tashi Yeshe, for instance, has enjoyed previous lives here, in the snow desert. As the landscape transformed, so did he. He witnessed a lonely dawn at the end of a hundred years, for that is how long the sun didn't rise after an asteroid hit the earth. His life as an earthworm left him humbled. At a time when three-fourths of all life forms perished, from plankton to the dinosaurs, he had lived on as a worm. In the ice ages, he was deeply attached to herd mentality as a woolly mammoth. During the great melt, he grew courage as a whale, leaving land to wade into water.

In human form, Tashi Yeshe had barely completed three years when he contracted brain fever. His mother was anxious. She feared the fever would swell out from his brain, nibble through his tender spine as if it were a twig, and leap out of that magical spot where the base of the tail once was. That was how most children left. In search of their missing tail.

The nomads had pitched their tents by the sulfur springs—beings that spewed out steam from craters of ice. Outside the black yak-hair tents, snow demons danced in the shadow of the surrounding peaks, lacerated by winds, entranced by the amber-colored steam. The winter, in its retreat, had orchestrated a vigorous whirlpool of snowstorms all across the desert.

Desperate, his parents decided to put him in the care of those they trusted the most. For the nomads, there existed no hidden meadow or settled hearth warmer than a crowded sheepfold. The little one's mother held him near her chest as his father wrapped them both, layer upon layer. Outside the tent, she braved the unstable depths and heights of snow to reach the pen, a single sheltered hole into which the community had stuffed all their cattle to create an alcove of warmth. The mother dug a shallow pit at the center of the shed, bedded it with blankets of yak hair and pashmina, and lay her burning son down. As she tucked him in, she prayed that the collective heat of the herd would heal him. The boy would have no significant memory of the fever or that winter, except for one. Sweating and shivering at the same time, he dreamed of the strange inhabitants of different cosmic realms. He woke up to find himself surrounded by a thousand eyes, all glowing in the dark. Eyes unlike his own. Shaped like those of beasts and ablaze with evil, for only evil burned brighter than good in the dark. Eyes above his head, behind his head, below his feet, beside his shoulder, torso, and legs. Eyes that burned above him in the sky, whirling like constellations. Peering into the glowing eyes inside him, for they had taken the place of his organs too.

"The ancestors are constantly watching," his grandmother would tell him. "One day, they will punish us for all the mischief we have committed." Here they were, all of them, he thought. Staring silently, waiting to rip his body apart for all the times he had shrieked into his grandmother's deaf ear and replaced her prayer beads with pebbles. He was dead, he concluded.

The cosmic guardians began to hum and bleat, nudging at his blanket and stamping at him with their hooves. A lamb rubbed its belly on his face, warmed by his burning skin. Far from menacing, his ancestors were a playful and cuddly lot.

This early memory would return to soothe him in his final seasons, like the idea of heaven to a weary Buddhist weighed down by the tedious pursuit of enlightenment.

At the age of seventeen, Tashi Yeshe chanced upon army officials offering sacks of grain at the local monastery. The Indian army was recruiting people from the border to protect the borders. In the past, he had seen his father barter pashmina wool, yak hair, salt, and butter with traders in distant Zanskar. But no one had ever bartered himself. Besides earning a regular salary, the boy would be trained and looked after. In the event of his death, his family would receive more money. Raised on generations of hardship, the teenager considered the barter too good to be true. He left the desolate pastures of Changthang to join the Ladakh Scouts as a soldier.

As a soldier-cook, he was sent to Ladakh for his first posting. It would take his regiment twenty-five days to walk from Srinagar, the verdant capital of Kashmir, to the Valley of Blood Apricots, crammed to the southeast of Changthang. Zoji La pass, the gateway to the kingdom of Ladakh, was higher than any in Kashmir but just an ordinary one in Ladakh, the land of high passes. Some of the soldiers began to suffer from nausea, headaches, and difficulty in breathing, forcing their officer to halt the ascent for the rest of the day. The regiment pitched tents alongside shepherds and their grazing cattle. In the evening, they clung to one another like a human herd, generating collective warmth to fight the bitter tunnel of wind descending from the pass.

As the official cook and unofficial butcher, Tashi Yeshe killed three goats that day to feed his ailing, homesick company. He had developed a reputation for precise butchery early on in his training. You could give him any creature—cow, buffalo, rabbit, hen, goat, sheep, marmot, deer, duck, even the mighty yak—and he wouldn't waste a single feather or fiber. It was as if he could see through the skin and flesh to exactly where the cartilage held the joints together. Under his cleaver, ligaments and tendons remained intact. The skin peeled off from the flesh to reveal hidden designs. Designs that held it all together. Designs where it all fell apart.

As with skin and flesh, the boy had seen through the lush deception of the neighboring Kashmir Valley. The profusion of forests, lakes, people, and pastures was, in fact, a subterfuge. One day, the forests would be a desert and the being, laid bare once again, would reflect upon the spirit.

Two years later, the Chinese army crushed the neighboring kingdom of Tibet and extended the invasion to India. The Indian army was caught napping. Rather than fight a lost battle, some of the soldiers decided to flee. Under his officer's supervision, Tashi Yeshe took to the wild, pillaging corpses and ransacking supplies from abandoned camps. To remain unnoticed, the group had to keep moving. There were no resources or time to tend to the injured among them. Death was the slow and painful conclusion for those left behind. But he couldn't just march forward like his seniors. Once everyone else had moved on, he took his kukri and slit the throats of those left behind.

By the end of the invasion, only two of them, the most junior and senior, survived. So they made a pact. The officer would return to civilization. He would declare the rest dead, killed in brave combat. With the soldier's official martyrdom, his nomad family would benefit from his pension and perks—greater than those awarded to the living. Off the record, the soldier would make his way to Tibet. The land of his ancestors. The land of nomads who migrated from pasture to pasture to accommodate every tribe's needs.

Tashi Yeshe didn't fear the Chinese. Nor was he running away from the Indians. He was restless, that's all. Empty within, restless without. Life, it seemed, could still be rescued, if only he could find himself a shed to sleep in undisturbed.

"Do you know my name?" Ghazala asks her grandson, as she feeds him rice later that night.

Lugging and working the electric thresher was backbreaking. By the time he returned home, he was an exhausted child.

"I know that grandfather called you 'Ghazal' when you two were alone. He was very fond of ghazals. Hearing them, reciting them, singing them, memorizing them. That is the only time I heard you being called something other than 'Mother' or 'Grandmother.' "

"It was his name for me," she says, as she proceeds to eat what is left on the plate.

Ghazala considers the existence of a canal running through a thicket nearby a blessing. Hidden among wild trees, she is free to smoke as the clothes soak in soap.

Back home, her vices were an open secret. Everyone in her house knew she smoked and drank. But no one confronted her—a figure worthy of pity, not punishment. Ever since her husband's death, she had been at odds with herself. Her children attributed it to the unbearable loneliness that follows almost seventy years of companionship. No one could have guessed that they helped her ease a much greater burden. The burden of being free.

Ghazala stops squatting and sits, to rest her muscles, on top of the rocks that prevent the drain from veering. She pulls her headscarf off to feel the breeze, as her hands take a break from scrubbing the grease stains off her grandson's clothes.

She lights a bidi, eager to continue her wishful conversation with the man with the pearl earrings. For the time kept aside for washing clothes is also the time dedicated to daydreams and ruminations.

"What about clouds?" she asks him.

"What happened to them?" he wonders. "Where have they gone this afternoon?"

"Who are they?" she probes.

"The clouds . . ." He mulls over it. "They are visions."

"And the mountains?" Ghazala could have never imagined that mountains like the Karakorams even existed. Stripped of greenery, life, and all evidence of it, each peak exists like a fractured bone or mutilated skeleton, devoid of skin and flesh. She has seen purple, blue, orange, yellow, and pink mountain peaks on her journey here. A few days after they had crossed the Zoji La pass, her grandson took a small detour to show her "the moonscape." This valley resembled the surface of the moon, he told her. She marveled at the gigantic mounds and the squiggles shaped out of rocks, defying geometry and the pressures of aesthetics. Like this landscape, the moon too, she concluded, was dreamed up by a toddler. A riot of colors and odd shapes, all drawn in a hurry.

"The mountains are the truth," Apo says. "They are remnants of the truth behind all creation. Precariously balanced, threatening to crumble."

"And the water that roars in the Indus and sits still in the lakes?"

"Madam, mountains and clouds, truth and visions, all are reflected alike on the skin of water. So are the past and the future. They are all attributes of the present, like the rumbling and the stillness you speak of. Water is an element full of possibilities. It is the present."

Ghazala likes it when he calls her "madam." Why did he ask her what her name was? she wonders. And why did she ask him for his, considering she was too shy to call him anything, clearing her throat or fidgeting with her headscarf for his attention.

"Who am I?" she asks.

The man slips into silence. Ghazala stubs out her bidi and returns to washing. The clothes float in the stream like wild weeds. She rinses her feet and sets off with the clothes. She hangs them on branches under a sun so strong, they will be ready to retrieve in the time it takes to smoke one more. She sits down once again.

"You are not a ghazal or a poem or a song," she hears his voice say. "Nor are you the muse. I know you. You are a poet."

Ghazala forgets to light the bidi. She keeps it on her lap and tumbles back into the reverie.

A PO HOLDS ON to the walnut tree at the edge of the twilight hour. Amidst embers of darkness and memories of the Indus lashing out far below, he presses his deaf ear against the rough bark, listening to the tales settled within its ridges. The tree is his friend. A dear and old one. Many constellations ago, they were both albatrosses, traversing the desert when it was still an ocean. Flying over seas and coasts for years on end, without a break in the solitude. But when they met, they cackled endlessly, exchanging stories and adventures.

When Apo first arrived in the village, he was found under this very tree, sunburned and ecstatic, talking to its fruit. He would spend the nights here, shunned by the villagers as impure, contaminated with outside beliefs and traditions. This orchard was his home.

Then the earthquakes resumed and the villagers discovered his ability to predict them. Apo herded them to the peaks, refusing to be ignored. They survived three debilitating ones, all within a month. Apo adopted their customs and ways. Eventually he gained acceptance and moved into the orchard owner's home. Soon, people forgot he was an outsider. Like everyone else, he wore a floral hat, prayed to fairies, sought the guidance of the juniper trees, and worked on the farms. So what if he looked different: slant-eyed, darker, and shorter. He was a Drakpo now.

Apo married the orchard owner's daughter and inherited the orchard. On suffocating afternoons and warm nights, he would return to sleep there. And now he has returned at twilight.

As he laughs at the tale the walnut tree has just told him, he senses someone staring at him from a distance. The gaze falls on him like the shadow of a rain cloud, expectant and heavy. He turns around.

"Are you real or are you a dream?" he asks. "Or have you found a way of entering my memories now?"

"Dreams only visit dreamers," Ghazala replies, but Apo can't hear a thing. He stares as his daydream walks toward him. Compared to those of the Drakpo women, her clothes are drab. She also looks like a man sometimes.

"At this age, how does it matter?" he says aloud. "Dreams, memories, desires . . . Come closer; let me tell you the marvelous tales this tree tells me. I came here hours ago and couldn't leave."

She presses her ear against the bark. But all she hears is a faint gnashing and grinding.

"Can you hear them?" he asks.

"No."

"Come closer, Ghazala. Don't be shy. This isn't Hindustan or Pakistan. Everyone is free to do as they please here. My friend saw the cheemo last night. He comes for the apricots in the orchard."

"Who is he?"

"He is the bear-man—don't you Kashmiris know? He is a legend, bigger than Alexander and his army. Outsiders revere him as the yeti. For the Tibetans he is lucky, and for the Nepalis a bad omen. The Chinese consider the cheemo's penis an indispensable ingredient of the elixir of youth. The Germans think he is the last pure Aryan, a race that descended from the skies to the highest place on earth. All sorts of people come to these mountains chasing him. But no one knows where he lives. They have only seen his giant footsteps. No one has seen him, except for my friend here. Do you want to hear his tale?"

Apo doesn't wait for an answer.

The cheemo lives all alone in a cave of ice in the Land of Glaciers. It is higher than the peaks above the village. In summers, he meditates. In winters, when bears hibernate, he dances in the snowfall. If one could spy on the cheemo without his knowledge, one would hear him whistle and hum. His tunes bear no relation to human music. Nothing in nature can match his strange melodies. He is so alone, he has discovered the language of the stars.

He is shy. He runs away from all creatures, unless he is hunting them. He eats fleshy animals like marmots, sheep, and yak. He is also tender. Unlike cheemos elsewhere, he doesn't kidnap pretty maidens or kill brave nomads. But ever since the Indian and Pakistani armies began a war in the glaciers, the cheemo started descending to the villages. His home is under siege. The onus of preserving his myths has fallen entirely upon him.

"Where did the cheemo come from?" Ghazala asks. "Why is he all alone?"

To get to the glaciers, one must cross the Winding Pass to the southwest of the Valley of Blood Apricots. Hot springs are the first of the many natural wonders that lie on the uninhabited side of the Winding Pass. The residue from the waters has brushed the soil with bright patches of lime-green sulfur, red oxide, white soda, and yellow urea, giving one the impression of walking over a gigantic fresco painted by traveling monks. The colors attract ibexes, marmots, and, from the sky, seasonal black-necked cranes, who have adopted the hot springs as their breeding ground. The cranes build nests as high and mighty as anthills at the edge of the springs.

For centuries, healers have believed in the springs' curative powers. When a heartbroken trader stepped under the powerful spout of a geyser, a stag and a deer hopped out in his place. His broken pieces had revived and become independent, inseparable beings, just as he had imagined his love and himself to be. But the water can only transform grief. It cannot heal.

There was once a Tibetan princess who arrived at the springs to cure her inflamed skin. Despite living in dark, closed rooms, she wouldn't heal. After a dip in the springs, not only was her skin cured, she also sprouted thick brown hair all over her body and developed a layer of fat to protect her from the sun. She was now a bear-woman. Before anyone could capture her, she escaped into the surrounding wilderness. People say that she is the mother of our current cheemo. He has an air of nobility about him. He avoids commoners.

"Who is the cheemo's father?"

"Only the mother knows that."

Ghazala laughs.

Apo has propped himself against the tree, an old companion and now a support in the diminishing light. His feet ache and his hands tremble, yet he refuses to give in to fatigue. She takes his hands and helps him sit. Her grandson must be home, tired and hungry, awaiting her return. Eventually he will heat the rice himself. Ghazala adjusts her headdress and sits beside Apo. She too has a tale to share.

The village of her birth is in an alpine meadow, above the lakes of her eventual domesticity. As a child, she would wander off into the neighboring forests for hours, returning only when she was hungry. Somewhere in the hazy age between six and ten, Ghazala confronted the greatest mystery of her life, hidden among trees of fir, birch, pine, and free-flowing strands of lichen. Had it not been for invisible nudges from the trees, she would never have spotted the creature. His scrawny black legs were as tall as Ghazala. And his wings looked mighty enough to embrace a cloud. Stemming from a bouquet of white feathers was a slender black neck. The crane's forehead had a curious red mark at the center, like the vermilion of Hindus. He seemed restless and fearful, shifting each time she tried to approach him. For some reason, he was limping. She didn't know what to do. She prayed for the crane and returned the way she had arrived.

A few years later, she married an older, learned man, fond of reading books and discussing intelligent things. Gradually, as he gained her trust, she asked him where the cranes came from, the black-necked ones that cut across the skies at the end of winter. The kingdom of

Ladakh, he replied, where it was desolate enough for them to build nests on the ground. She had forgotten all about them until Apo mentioned that they nested nearby.

"On the other side of the Valley of Blood Apricots," Apo whispers into the night. "Do you know how the valley got its name?"

Apricots in the valley bore a red drop in the flesh, close to the seed— a reminder of a Sufi's quest for his beloved. He had wandered naked and delirious through the valley, ending up on the icy shores of the Lake of Visions. It was here that he glimpsed his true self, dancing like sunlight over the glacial waters. In the alchemic world of reflections, he saw an untamed rhododendron bush grow between his legs. His nails curled into lotus stems and his skin turned into leathery bark. An ocean brimmed in his landlocked eyes, trapped by corporeal dunes. So he stabbed himself in the heart, setting the ocean free.

Apo tries his best to distract her with stories. He has fought valiantly to prolong the inevitable. The moment of separation.

The clouds hide the stars. Apart from the occasional glow of fireflies, the two sit in complete darkness.

"The best stories are the ones that are still to come, Ghazala. Close enough to hear, smell, and admire. Yet out of reach."

Ghazala is silent. If she doesn't leave soon, her grandson will come looking for her.

"Will the cheemo remain all alone?" she eventually asks.

In the land of the imminent present, there is a man who seeks the glaciers like a sleepwalker following his dreams. He is a learned man, a man of knowledge. Yet he believes that the only way he can discover why he is here, on earth and in this life, is by visiting places he isn't supposed to be. Despite injuries and misfortunes, he persists.

When the winter reaches its peak, he abandons the path of good sense. He falters and crawls, tripping over rocks and sinking into the snow, slipping through the glacier's crevasses and cracks. An unseen shadow protects him from the unpredictable moods of the ice.

One day, he sits down, exhausted. He is close to giving up when he hears breathing, longer and deeper than his own, like a melody floating in the air. Someone is sitting right behind him, but they don't turn around to face each other. In the cheemo's company, the man's loneliness turns into solitude. In the human's company, the cheemo's solitude turns into longing. The two of them sit like a being with two hearts and four eyes.

"Some dreams are so beautiful and fragile, Ghazala, they are left unrealized."

Ghazala can't sleep later that night, even after two glasses of rum. The more the old man dreams of her, the further she feels from both wakefulness and sleep, left to wander aimlessly in the world of his dreams.

In bed, she waits for her grandson to start snoring. Then she pulls off her blanket. She wears her phiran and headdress. She goes to the kitchen, stuffs her pockets, and walks out without a lamp or torch.

The clouds have disappeared, revealing the illumination within the darkness. The stars, bright enough to guide her to heaven if she so desires, cluster into a path. But tonight the heavens will have to wait. She returns to the orchards and sits down beneath the walnut tree.

She lights a cigarette. A modern one, stolen from her grandson. It is a precious commodity, made in Indonesia, and has the sweet taste and smell of clove. She inhales too quickly and coughs. Even the allure of distant tropical islands cannot distract her.

Ghazala has witnessed possibilities of love on various occasions.

Love grounded her as she stared at the crane, as afraid of the creature as he was of her. It visited her on nights when her husband recited poems to her as she tidied up the room. It sat with her as she rowed a shikara into the lake all alone, allowing the currents to take her where they pleased. But it is only after hearing Apo's stories—filled with a longing so intense, they know no beginning or end—that she understands its expanse. For love is a realization gained over many lives.

She is distracted by a new glow in the orchard. Besides the odd firefly and the lit end of her cigarette, she notices two golden eyes. Bigger than any yak's or wolf's or human's. The eyes burn like lamps. They don't blink; they don't move.

Ghazala stands up immediately. She sits down again. She removes a handful of dried apricots from her pocket and stretches her hand out.

The harvest season is almost over. If there is ever a celebration of all things transient and inconsequential, this is it. A meadow full of frost-flowers glistening under the slanted rays of dawn. They appear on unusually cold mornings in autumn. The frozen sap oozing from the stems in ripples and waves, unfurling itself like orchids, lilies, roses, conches, waves, spirals, clouds, and crystals. By midmorning, a slushy meadow will be all that remains.

The appearance of frost-flowers marks the inevitable slip into the long winter. Their entire lives, it seems, are a tedious preparation for this season. But the efforts will now gain momentum. The vegetables, apricots, and cheese set to dry on yak-hair blankets spread out on the roofs will all be gathered. The rationing, packing, and storing will begin. All things woolen will be darned and resurrected. The dung cakes, collected over time from the meadows, fields, and sheds, will be weighed and kept aside. Here, dung is more precious than jewelry. It is the necessary fuel for cooking and heating. The hammer and saw of last-minute carpentry will fill the air. The shearing of sheep will end. The women, desperate to pound the last grain into flour, will begin their squabbles over the community grinder.

One of these days, Ghazala's grandson will empty the diesel from the threshing machine, pour it into a jerrican, and screw the lid tightly. It will be his signal for moving on. She won't be prepared for it. She will struggle to write a verse in the solace of an empty room. Yet she will lack the courage to stay.

Two days later, they will leave on hired mules before sunrise. Ghazala won't say goodbye. At first, Apo will be upset. Gradually, age-old experience will dawn upon him.

The departing seldom say goodbye. It is better left that way.

WITH THE ADVENT OF WINTER, snow swiftly covers the land, submerging the soul's afflictions, layer by layer. Ice can't heal the wounds or mend the ruptures, but it numbs the pain.

Apo has no choice but to return to his usual self, laughing at misfortune, cursing the world, telling stories, and demanding walnuts—the traditional price of a story. Stories are the cure to various neuroses triggered by the extremes and hardship. Cooped up in the basement, the grandchildren, relatives, and neighbors are addicted.

Apo tells them all: stories of nomads, snow leopards, devious rabbits, ogres, ibexes, fairies, bears, cruel Chinese, lazy Indians, hairy Pakistanis, Persian empresses, and fools in love. Apo also knows what the crowd loves most—stories of brave yak and wise sheep. The cattle are their children, but their hearth just isn't big enough to accommodate all their loved ones. Their hearts are in their sheds.

He is kept especially busy during a blizzard that lasts for three whole days. The crowds keep pouring in through the bleak hours of daylight, despite the excruciatingly cold winds. At one time, more than sixty-five people are herded together in his basement. They all sit there, sipping on barley tea and trying to imagine Apo's words, brutally conscious of the dozens of lives they will lose to the storm.

Only when the winds quieten and the sky begins to clear does Apo sleep. By then he has collected sixty-two pouches of walnuts for the sixty-two stories that made his audience laugh, smile, and weep through helplessness and loss. He sleeps through the prismatic light reflecting off the icicle gargoyles growing from the roof. He sleeps through the cycles of wailing, disbelief, and silence.

He is finally woken up by Digri, the only boy in the village with a certified degree from the outside world. He has come to Apo's home with two foreigners. They were caught in the sudden blizzard and have ended up here.

"Where have they come from?" Apo asks.

"The Land of Glaciers."

"Who are they?"

"An army officer and a doctor of science."

"Which country?"

"Both Indians."

"Are they here to arrest me?"

"No."

"Tell them the old man is dying. He doesn't have time to entertain uninvited guests."

Apo turns over to his other side and returns to sleep. When he wakes up a few hours later, he finds the two of them sitting in his room.

"I don't like the army and I don't like science." Apo switches to Hindustani as he speaks, before proceeding to urinate in a chamber pot. "Armies fight wars, and science creates reasons to fight wars."

"Religion, not science," the scientist says.

"It is the same, religion and science." Apo impresses himself by hearing the offhand comment not meant for his ears. The snow always makes hearing easier. It shuts all the birds, insects, and industrious humans up. "But how would you know all this?" Apo continues. "You look like you were born yesterday. And science came the day before yesterday. It was made by the same people who created religion the day before that. And do you know what came before even religion and science?"

"I know," Ira pipes up. "Salt!"

"Such an intelligent child. Learn from her, foreigners."

"We did learn a lot from her," the army officer says. "She is wise. If only she went to school. The Indian army has set up schools for the border villages, but this is no-man's-land—"

"We don't want our children to be taught by the Indian army. What will they teach? How to look the other way when the enemy attacks? Your countries kick us around like a ball. Pakistan sits on our head and India on our nuts. What if Pakistan reoccupies our village tomorrow? These same children will be branded traitors. No, no!"

Sensing the foreigners' discomfort, the child interjects. "Our Apo curses only those he likes. He is happy to talk to you. Go on, ask your questions."

Apo's grandson enters the room with steaming tea, biscuits, and dried fruits. They have specially sourced sugar and black tea to make the chai Indians so love.

"Bring me some barley tea," Apo orders him. "I don't drink Indian chai. It makes the drinkers lazy, like them." Saying this, Apo dips a biscuit into a cup of chai and draws it closer.

"I am Mohammed Raza, an officer from the Gond regiment," the officer says impatiently. "And my friend here is Rana. He is a geologist, a scientist who studies the earth."

"Since when did the Indian army start employing Pakistanis?"

"Officer Raza here is an Indian," Rana says.

"All Muslims are Pakistanis. All communists are Chinese. All Buddhists are Tibetan. But one thing unites all Indians—laziness. As for the Bangladeshis, I don't know. I lost touch with the outside world sometime during its birth. They were Muslim, which is why they were East Pakistan. But then they also claimed to be Bengali. . . . I have five toes on each foot. They are all different. What if my small toe begins to fight with the big one over the differences between them? What if they all gang up against me and say none of them belong to me because they are all different toes, whereas I am not even a toe? I will turn into a leper!"

"The villagers told us you can predict earthquakes, which is why we are here," Raza cuts through his rambling. "We were told that you saved all the villagers' lives during the four major earthquakes that hit this region in the past sixty years."

The officer signals Rana to take the conversation forward.

"Yes, tell me, son of science, why do earthquakes happen?" Apo asks him. After finishing the biscuits and chai meant for the guests, Apo has moved on to the barley tea.

Ira says, "There is a giant fish that lives in the frozen sea. When it moves its tail, earthquakes happen."

"The question, then, is how often does it move its tail? And why is it so moody of late?" asks Rana.

Raza continues, "We lost two hundred and twenty men to avalanches last year. The Pakistani side lost one hundred and forty-one barely two years ago. Which is why we have agreed to have scientists present at all times, researching and predicting the patterns of this giant fish—"

"Foreigners," Apo interrupts. "Do you have foreign cigarettes?"

"Our Apo never smoked cigarettes before," Ira says. "He began four months ago, under the spell of a Kashmiri witch."

Rana smiles. "He is very lucky to have discovered cigarettes at this age," he says, as he removes a packet from his backpack.

The girl takes the cigarette from him. She lights it over the burning coals, inhales a puff herself, and hands it over to her grandfather. Rana notices that the man only plays with the smoke in his mouth before exhaling, reminding him of his own college days. "The Karakorams are tilting," Apo says. "They are rising up and pushing the Himalayas down. All the mountains of the world have a new king—Kechu. It is just us humans who refuse to accept it."

"Do you mean K2?" asks Rana.

W HEN I SAY KECHU, I mean Kechu," Apo replies, confused. "It is the highest peak in the Karakorams and stands at the edge of the Baltoro Glacier. It is the beating heart of the Land of Glaciers. There is no escaping it. Even if the gods of machines and technology come down to help you." Apo pauses to think. "Even if India, Pakistan, and China stop fighting over the ice and unite to remain there, the mountains will win. Sons, tell your armies and scientists to leave the glaciers. That is the only way they can be safe."

Rana is spellbound. In one breath, Apo has summarized an outcome he has been struggling to express, in spite of the evidence. "But how can it be?" he asks Apo. The Everest is the highest point on earth. It is a fact of life, not just geology.

"When human bloodshed seeps into the cracks of the land, the earth's scabs and wounds cannot heal. . . ." The old man reflects upon his own words. "They can only fester. Your violence and your wars are like gangrene to the earth's flesh. You possess gadgets that can take you to the moon, yet you are blind to the mountains and rivers right in front of you. We have hacked Hindustan into a hundred islands with our borders, mutinies, and wars. It is crumbling into the ocean. The Kechu is rising because the Himalayas are sinking."

The scientist has tears in his eyes. In the illusory light of the fireplace, Rana comes across as a defeated man. One who has known the truth all along yet lacks the courage to accept it.

For the next few nights, Apo sleeps under blankets that weigh more than his body and soul, both of which ache with arthritic severity. Ira's father lifts the blankets to help her crawl in. "Apo! Wake up!" she says, as she warms her frozen fingers on his cheeks. "You cannot fall asleep without telling me a bedtime story."

"Is it time to go to bed already?"

"You are in bed."

"Child, the bed is a good place for death to arrive. People know where to find your body."

"I will tell everyone where you are when you die."

"Bless you, my great-granddaughter. You are my angel of life." He strokes her forehead. "You impressed me with your knowledge when you told the foreigners about the giant fish whacking its tail in the frozen sea. Such fools, they call it a glacier."

"What is the difference?"

"Ocean, sea, ice, snow, mist . . . they are different states of being. If a girl is dancing, can I describe her as asleep?"

Ira laughs. She pinches his cheeks. "Apo, the spirit is the same."

"Yes. Do you want to hear about her?"

Apo had seen her wandering in the desert. To him, she had the spirit of a newborn. Infinitely lost and vulnerable. Yet infinitely at peace. She was slender and long-limbed, like the Avalokitesvara painted in monasteries—her expression as serene and her movements as fluid. Her eyes were the most remarkable. They revealed her inner fire. Apo dreamed of the ocean each time he saw her. That is how he, a land-locked nomad, grasped her enormity. She came to him as she once was, in all her expanse, depth, intensity, and calm.

Born as ice, she came to life as water when she fell in love with what she wasn't. He arose from the earth's core. She embraced him as an ocean and calmed his fire into land. His intensity burned as a restless continent. In her arms, he began to crumble. He drifted in one hundred directions. The lands trampled over her depths, cutting off her currents and drying her up. In her adolescence, she broke down. Over time, each fragment took on a new life, growing and diminishing at will. To survive, a phantom limb gave birth to a body, a tooth grew a new jaw, and the heart new loves. Her spirit withdrew into a shell, resting in the cavernous bones of the highest peaks on earth.

One day, Apo's mother-in-law had slipped off a ladder as she was mending the roof and injured her spine. She couldn't speak or move. The lhaba, the village shaman, advised the family to bring shells from the glaciers. The fossils, when ground into a paste and mixed with turmeric and butter, were a potent adhesive for binding bone and flesh. A healing womb for wounds, created from the bones of ancient creatures.

It was Apo's first time in the glaciers. He instinctively veered toward Nurbu in the west, a small and dangerous glacier between two larger ones, a deep river of fissured ice that flowed on an invisible layer of water through a narrow gorge. Afraid to walk on the shifting ice, he scrambled over the rocky ridges instead.

And then he saw her.

As she walked on the ice, it shuddered and cracked. With a simple gesture, she expanded cracks into fissures, fissures into crevasses. A prolonged glance caused boulders of ice to topple. Then she raised her hands high to summon the water flowing in the depths of the ice. The water, much to Apo's shock, spouted forth like a geyser, welding parts of the glacier together as it froze.

Apo admired her spirit in that unstable landscape, as she resurrected her past glory. The avalanches and quakes were only incidental to her actions.

"Has the scientist seen her too?"

"Only as fossils and shells."

"Apo, why did he cry? Was he upset with Kechu?"

"Child, the boy isn't upset with the mountains. He is lost to the glaciers."

"Then let us pray to the fairies to protect him."

"Yes, my little Ira. Your kindness is the biggest wisdom."

RANA CLINGS TO A SEASHELL as big as his palm, as he lies in bed in just a pair of pajamas, socks, and sweatshirt. He is inside a cabin-sized capsule set up in the base camp of the glacial complex.

Project Dhruva is an experiment designed to de-stress. Although the human body can be taught to adapt to such inhuman altitudes, the mind has proved more resistant. Despite state-of-the-art weaponry and technology, nothing can prevent a soldier from succumbing to the monsters within. It is an open secret that "death by natural causes" is a euphemism for mental illness.

The temperature in the capsule can be adjusted to a maximum of twenty-five degrees Celsius—though it isn't recommended—in sharp contrast to the forty below zero outside. The oxygen levels are higher as well, making deep, relaxing breaths possible. One can switch on mood lighting and play soundtracks as varied as the sounds of a rain forest or a beach, hymns or sermons, to soothe one's tense nerves.

Sounds of a tropical island flood the cabin as Rana plays with the shell. The anxiety and excitement of returning to the glacier keeps him awake, despite the call of multicolored birds, rustling palm fronds, and a tide gently dragging him with its current.

The rudimentary massage function on the bed needs fine-tuning. Rana feels the vibration like a machine gun drilling holes into his body. He notes this in his feedback to the project team, sitting miles away at the rock-bottom altitudes of Chandigarh. There is something else he wants to suggest but doesn't know how to word it. He had found a stack of pornographic magazines hidden below the bed. While it is a great idea, it caters only to heterosexuals.

Rana had arrived at the glaciers shortly after the official renaming ceremony. The earlier name—Siachen, or the Place of Wild Roses—

wasn't patriotic enough to justify spending half the nation's defense budget on, a sum greater than the one allotted to national healthcare. Global pressure to demilitarize the region had grown after an unprecedented spate of avalanches, tectonic upheavals, and glacial melting, highlighting the political mess the region was in.

As a response to the growing controversy, the government decided to rebrand the glacier. The name Kshirsagar Glacial Complex was inspired by an obscure epic written by an incarcerated revolutionary poet during the Raj. The cosmic ocean, with its realms and celestial beings, had enough mythology to sustain the vast nomenclature associated with patriotic endeavors.

Rana was lucky to be at the right place at the right time. He had just returned from a term at the Indian outpost in Antarctica. While this didn't qualify him for research at high-altitude glaciers, to the government officials approving grants it was reason enough to include him in the team of scientists. As an ode to the poet, he dedicated his geodetic research to the mythical core of Kshirsagar. He called his paper "In Search of Sagar Meru"—the realm of ice where the deepest trenches and the greatest heights are one and the same.

The more Rana thought about it, the more dissimilar his assignments seemed. Antarctica, the biggest, driest, and coldest desert in the world. Compared to it, the glaciers were the size of a neighborhood. But at sixteen thousand feet, the Kshirsagar Glacial Complex—or the third pole, as it was also known—was higher than any peak in Antarctica. The disparity in altitude made them different planets altogether.

Yet, somehow, it was the summer in Antarctica that had made him seek out winter in the glaciers. Rana was at a bar in Christchurch, on his way to Dakshin Gangotri, the Indian base in Antarctica, when he met the avian researcher. The man was on his way to an obscure Pacific island to study nocturnal, flightless, overweight parrots in the twilight of extinction. Like meteoric debris whirling through space, their paths had collided.

The solitary birds were socially awkward, like the researcher himself, he joked. Courtship was a rare phenomenon, and the only time they didn't bite each other to death, but all it led to was a dramatic one-night stand.

Rana thought about them, the birds who preferred dawdling to flight and flings to commitment. "They must like their personal space," he said.

"In their case, an island," the researcher added. "In yours, a continent."

Rana blushed and looked away. His gaze, it unsettled him. He had been nervous when the researcher invited himself over to his hotel room. Rana had glimpsed an uninhibited continent of desire in those glacial-blue eyes.

Rana fell asleep in his presence. When he got up, he was startled to find the researcher wide awake, his unwavering gaze holding them both in place.

Days later, Rana stood all alone in Antarctica's blinding whiteness, with frostbitten toes, a scratched cornea, and heart-wrenching numbness. There was nothing to hold on to, not a shadow, not a horizon. A single gaze had broken him down.

In the Kshirsagar Glacial Complex, a colleague had contracted high-altitude pulmonary edema and had to be airlifted back. Then Rana fell into a crevasse. As he recuperated from the shock and scratches, the two remaining scientists, out on an excursion, were caught in an avalanche. Though they escaped largely unharmed, the trauma had left them in shock.

The Defense Research and Analysis Wing had given Rana the option of leaving with the rest of the scientists. But he refused. The gaze had followed him through time and space. It intensified each time he approached the glaciers.

A week later, he and Officer Raza lost their way on an excursion and were forced to descend. It was sheer luck, surviving no-man's-land by finding that village.

And here he was, waiting to scale the glaciers once again.

Inside Project Dhruva, Rana presses the shell against his ear. It is a gift, passed down from his grandfather to his mother and now to him. When he was a child, few things intrigued him more than the shell under his mom's pillow. Instead of the dramatic sound of waves whipping the rocks, all he ever heard was an overbearing hollowness. The same hollowness is a comfort now, like napping on his parents' empty bed, where their peculiar fragrances lingered.

Rana's alarm will go off in forty-five minutes. With it, his mandatory acclimatization and refresher course will be complete. Research has shown that the process of mental atrophy sets in within a month at high altitudes, and the course is designed to keep the mind and body alert.

Immediately after sunrise, Rana will make his way up the Wall of Ice—nicknamed Balls of Ice by officers. He is curious to see the corpse of a Pakistani soldier who had fallen into a deep crevasse forty years ago, preserved as perfectly as an Eocene fossil. Recent upheavals have brought him deeper into Indian territory, and now he's visible from the glacier's snout.

One of Rana's colleagues suggests tracking the Pakistani corpse via satellite to monitor the glacier's movement, a frightfully expensive affair otherwise. His every movement can tell them volumes about the complex currents operating within the ice. But the government refuses. It is beneath their dignity to take the help of a Pakistani soldier, even if he is a cadaver.

The soldier stands in a hall of mirrors, army lore goes. The ice magnifies his torso and distorts all his features—the arched eyebrows, the closed eyes, the healthy Islamic beard, the lips pursed in quiet determination. Some claim that the soldier blinks if you stare at him for too long. Others claim he smiles at you if you are Muslim, ignores you if you are Sikh, and twitches his nose if you are Hindu. But overall, he is benign. He hasn't caused nightmares or mishaps yet.

Will he meet the soldier's ghost wandering on the glaciers? Rana wonders.

Two weeks ago, he had met his late grandfather in the darkness of a crevasse as he waited to be rescued. A man he had longed to meet his entire life. After all, he was named Girija in his memory.

Rana was the last one to jump across. He looked at the weather reading on his digital watch. A decent seventeen below zero, with precipitation of less than twenty millimeters. He gazed at the sunless, tempestuous skies, a trademark of the Glacial Complex. And then he stared at the transverse crevasse, sizing it up. Five feet wide and seemingly endless in length, the crevasse cut across the body of ice and snow in a determined and unstructured manner. Rana wondered if it held a pocket of water at the bottom, an added source of topographical instability and irrational fear.

"Scientist ji!" a soldier from the other side shouted out. "One doesn't need a doctorate to jump. Stop thinking, remember Lord Hanuman, and proceed."

Even as Rana made the preparatory sprint, he knew he wouldn't make it. The relief of his right foot landing on the other side was broken by his fall into the chasm. The rope that connected him to the rest tightened around his waist, sending him spiraling down.

Dim sunlight vanished almost immediately. Time came to a standstill. His awareness accommodated each moment as if it were an eon and each turn of his body a revolution around the sun. The darkness expanded as the crevasse grew wider.

Rana could look deep into the sky through the crack above, as if he was inside a giant telescope made of ice. Constellations, those man-made optical illusions, seemed to be regrouping into new shapes and patterns. It seemed to Rana that he was now thousands of light-years away, where the stars were. What he saw wasn't the earth's usual perspective of pastness, a sky full of stars long dead and disappearing. He saw the universe as it stood at the exact moment of his fall. He saw the present.

After a thud here and a thud there, the crampon on his left foot caught on the ice and the rope tensed like a noose, arresting his fall.

Since he'd arrived, he had witnessed a few army men slip into the shifty gaps and be rescued within four minutes flat. That was the drill. On the glacier above, the swish of ice axes had begun. Rana had a magical sensation of watching the scene as it unfolded on the glaciers. His spirit had detached itself from his body. It was staring at the soldiers kneeling in single file, counting down to zero before they pulled the rope.

It was as if he was the cinematographer and not the actor of his life. As the cinematographer, he had the ability to press pause and observe everything—from the meteors in outer space to the ice ax lodged shakily above, down to the impenetrable blue far below him, at the bottom of the crevasse. In the ice, Rana could see hints of ash from Vesuvius and Krakatoa, asteroidal debris, and undiscovered fossils from the various mass extinctions, all impeccably preserved like fond memories.

It felt stiflingly hot even as the sweat on his stubble turned to ice. His body trembled violently. But in his heart, he experienced an unwarranted calmness. Weightless, left free to float in an opaque cave of greenish-blue, Rana realized that gravity, like time, had also left him alone. But not entirely.

Rana suspected his heart wasn't the only thing pulsating in this abyss. As he discerned a foreign rhythm, he asked, "Who's there?"

"Girija," a voice replied.

"I'm Girija too. Girija Rana. Does this mean I'm talking to myself?"

"I am Girija Prasad Varma."

"Nana!" he exclaimed. He wanted to hug his grandfather. But being in the awkward position of hanging upside down prevented him.

"Child, I'm sorry I didn't live long enough to welcome you into the world."

"That's all right, Nana. Death is not in our hands."

"How are you?" they both asked at the same time.

"I am fine, child, as you can see."

"Actually, I can't," Rana replied.

"My stamina is as good as yours. A very important and useful thing in this topography and at altitudes as high as this."

"What are you doing here?"

"There is no better way to study the mountains than getting down on all fours and scraping the rocks and ice for answers. If sitting on an armchair and sipping a cup of tea sufficed, I wouldn't have left the islands. But I was itching to verify a lifetime of theories with firsthand evidence. . . . How are you, child? I was worried about you. It took you a while to get adjusted to the thin air and terrain, especially your bowels. But you seem fine now."

"You're right, my body seems to be coping. Now it is the research that's giving me sleepless nights. Either that or altitude sickness. I hope I haven't been badly hurt just now. The last thing I need is a broken bone."

Rana suddenly became tense.

"Am I dead, Nana? Did I just break my neck when I fell down?"

"You are as fit and as alive as you were when you woke up."

"Whiplash?"

"Your medulla oblongata is all right. It's just a small jerk."

"Then why am I talking to you?"

"Your grandmother could speak to ghosts and trees and almost all life forms. I don't think your mother can, much like I couldn't. Perhaps clairvoyance, like diabetes, skips a generation."

"It has never happened before."

"This is the highest human beings can go on earth. Did you expect to ascend to this profound altitude and isolation with your spirit untouched?"

"In that case, I am in trouble. I will be seeing the ghosts of many Indian and Pakistani soldiers here."

His grandfather laughed. "And Chinese," he added.

"Oh! Are they here too?"

"They are everywhere. What are you researching, child?"

"I'm researching geodetics. The axis of the trans-Himalayan ranges and the western Himalayas, especially the Karakorams, is tilting. I suspect this region is the fulcrum. It began with the Muzaffarabad earthquake in Kashmir, where we saw peaks grow by eight to ten feet. Then the Gorkha series happened, where some peaks experienced an increase or decrease of up to sixteen feet. These mountains are on steroids!"

"This is how mountains grow. This is how the Himalayas began their rise fifty million years ago."

"No government will allow a geeky scientist to come all the way up here to study orogeny, as fascinating as the process of mountain-building is. So I had to add a bit of spice. Saffron spice, shall I say."

Rana could hear his Nana chuckle.

"It is apparent that Mount Everest will not remain the world's highest mountain in the next thousand years. Based on the tilt of the axis, we can predict which one it might be. I hope it's Kanchenjunga. If I can prove the highest peak will be in India, I will have enough government funds to sustain my research for a decade," Rana mumbled hopefully. "But for any mountain to grow taller than the Everest, it must defy the laws of isostasy. It is impossible to maintain the equilibrium of the earth's crust in such a hypothesis."

"The Himalayas are an exception. The pressure of the continents colliding gives them greater height."

"That is true, Nana, but a taller peak would be gravitationally impossible, even as an exception."

"Unless the gravity is weaker here."

Rana was about to roll his eyes, until he remembered how NASA had mapped the earth's uneven gravity, highlighting the areas above the Karakorams in the color blue to denote a weaker force. He was impressed.

Sensing his grandson's excitement, Girija Prasad continued, "Nature doesn't adhere to the laws of science in the way scientists do. As a naïve young man, I scoffed at your Nani when she accused the fluctuating gravity of burning up her dal and rice on the islands. It took me decades to realize that we lived on a faultline and that gravity was a whimsical force there."

"Mom tells me you were far ahead of your times."

"Son, I learned more from observing my wife than I learned from science journals. Just like I learned about mountains by studying the islands. If you reflect upon it, you will see connections and relationships illuminating the most disconnected things. Gravity defines time, space, and mortality. How can it not influence our inner state?"

"How fascinating! Tell me more, Nana."

"Well, your Nani would often complain how the islands were the most haunted place she had visited, and I wondered why. In the Andaman Islands, the force of the Indian plate being pushed under a heavier landmass increased the situational gravity. This in turn pulled all forms of dense energy, including ghosts, to it. Subduction zones, as you may know, are intense."

"Then why are you here, a contradiction to your own theory?" his grandson interjected.

"I have the spirit of a scientist. A scientist will go wherever his research takes him."

They laughed.

"Why did you take so long to find me?"

"If I had come to you earlier, I would have scared you. If I came to you any later, you would have dismissed me as a hallucination."

"You are my unconscious talking to me, I think."

"Does that make you my conscious?"

"I am barely conscious myself." Rana smiled. "Sometimes I feel like I have dreamed it all up. The glacier. The ridges. Tectonics. Now you . . . Sometimes I feel like the ice and winds are trying to say something through me. I am just a voice. An expression. A reflection, twinkling light-years away from its source."

"I saw the shell in your hands the other day," Girija Prasad said. "The one I gave your mother."

"Yes. She gifted it to me before I left for Antarctica."

In the isolation of Antarctica, the shell stood for time. Rana would cradle time in his hands, tracing the brown spikes in its white contours with his fingers. He would take solace in the hollow sound arising from its spirals.

"It took millions of years to create each spiral," said Girija Prasad. "The shell belongs to the Eocene epoch, when the collision began."

Rana's thoughts drifted to the pages of a book from his childhood.

It had a whole chapter dedicated to fossils from the Eocene found in a pit somewhere in Europe. Seduced by the fecundity of a crater lake, hundreds of life forms were killed by the poisonous gases rising from its depths. A wide-eyed primate, a pregnant dwarf horse, the predecessors of hoopoes and hummingbirds, beetles with their metallic colors and wings intact. Even a pirouetting frog. As a boy, Rana was most intrigued by the nine pairs of turtles ossified in the act of copulation. The crater lake on Tethyan shores was the Pompeii of the Eocene.

Browsing through the pages in his memory, Rana discovered something new among them. He saw the partial remains of unconsummated loves, footprints of paused migrations, vestiges of failed evolutions, and, now, an epoch trapped in a shell.

He saw himself.

By the time he returned to his senses, his grandfather had disappeared. Rana was being unceremoniously hauled up to the baritone counting of a soldier.

"Till we meet again!" he shouted into the darkness.

Inside the greenhouse—Project Kalpavriksha—Rana has finished adding chemical fertilizers and water to all the saplings, when a blizzard swiftly wipes out the empty skies. He has no choice but to wait. So he fiddles, readjusting the angle of the solar lamps.

Of the four saplings, one has perished, two are critical, and only one has survived. The saplings share the plight of the scientists, Rana laughs. In the absence of company, he has begun to enjoy his own sense of humor.

He heats some snow on his portable stove, makes himself a cup of hot chocolate, and eats an energy bar for lunch. He tries his luck at falling asleep. When he fails to do so, tossing and turning as if he were driftwood on the high seas, he pulls out his Rubik's Cube. But the altitude has killed his concentration. Rana prefers to talk to the plants instead.

"I hope each of you participating in this project makes it," he says. "The entire nation has its hopes pinned on your survival. Even the prime minister asks about you before the soldiers. Yes, each one of you, not just the tulsi," he assures them. The hallowed plant of all Hindu households, tulsi could cure sore throats, improve immunity and heart circulation, and even cure homosexuality, if the babas were to be believed.

After Mars, the glaciers are the most inhospitable place one can expect plants to grow. Should the experiments succeed, the Indian government will use the UN's guidelines on disputed territories to claim ownership over the glaciers. The first person to cultivate a piece of land can stake claim over it, states one of its clauses.

The blizzard worsens. Rana sits down. He leans back and begins to sing old Bollywood songs to the saplings. He whistles the parts he can't recall the lyrics to. He has been here for six hours already, and chances are he will be here for longer. He adds a beat by turning the empty fertilizer can into a drum.

It takes him a while to notice an additional voice in the air, as if someone is humming over his shoulder. At first, Rana dismisses it as the wind. When it refuses to quiet, he switches the tempo of the song unpredictably, speeding through some parts and slowing down through others. It baffles him how the voice keeps up. It is a distinct baritone and similar to Mongolian throat singing.

Rana moves stealthily inside the greenhouse. He climbs up a shelf to peep out of the translucent sunroof. He shudders at the sight of a humungous dark shadow right outside, half covered in snow. All that separates the two is a prefabricated wall. Rana fears a Pakistani soldier has crossed over in the blizzard. One of those six-foot-tall, sunburned, and hairy Pathans from the North-West Frontier Province. Or a distant descendant of Genghis Khan, if one went by the throat singing.

All of a sudden, the shadow looks up. He looks at Rana with yellow eyes that burn through the spindrift.

The soldiers find Rana delirious with fever, after almost fifty hours in the greenhouse. He is airlifted and sent to the base camp to recover. The geologist, it turns out, is severely dehydrated and exhausted. All he needs is rest and freshly cooked, not tinned, food.

Officer Raza, the one in charge of the scientists, advises Rana to return home. Not everyone makes it through winter, and this one is hell-bent on being more difficult than others. This particular blizzard has claimed three lives already. The life of a scientist, the officer jokes, is a thousand times more valuable than the life of a soldier. For though there are more than a thousand soldiers stationed at the Kshirsagar Glacial Complex, there is only one scientist. "Come again in spring," he suggests. "It will still be cold, tectonically unstable, and a military hellhole, I promise."

Rana isn't convinced.

"Do you know what state you were in when we found you?" Raza asks him. "You were weeping. 'Why are you weeping?' I asked. 'These are tears of happiness,' you replied. I needed you to be conscious until we got you here, so I asked you, 'Why are you so happy?' But you kept weeping. You almost fell asleep and I had to nudge you again. 'Why are you so happy, Rana? Come on, share some happiness with your buddies.'

"And then you went on to say the most beautiful thing I have heard. 'It's love,' you told me. 'Faces change and are misleading. Sometimes you may not recognize who the person really is. But love is love. So long as you feel it, give it, and receive it, it is enough. It connects you to everyone and everything.'"

Rana has tears flooding down his chapped cheeks once again. It is the only memory he has of the delirium. Bliss. And the tears that accompanied it.

After so many close shaves, he will be a fool to persist, his sister tells him over the phone. But he needs more time. He needs greater geological evidence to build a watertight case for demilitarization, he pleads with the conflicting voices in his head. He hasn't even said goodbye to his Nana.

And what about him, the mystery that set his body on fire?

I T IS UNUSUALLY FOGGY for a summer morning in June. Monsoon winds have hit the land, creating a vortex of storms and floods. In the shadow of the Karakorams, all the village gets is fog. The trees in the orchards, the buckwheat swaying in the fields, the clustered homes and crooked walls are all specters. The Indus too is a river of rumbling mist.

Apo sits in the orchard. A chair has been permanently placed for him under the walnut tree's shade. His walking stick leans against it. The world outside resembles the inchoate one inside. At eighty-eight, he finds it a chore to pin a thought down, to focus one's eyes and articulate a word.

All of a sudden, his heartbeat becomes erratic. An irregular rhythm takes over. After all those encounters with death, after all those decades of seeking it out, is this how it will end? With an opaque sense of arrival? An ancient excitement flows through his veins.

When he was a child, his grandmother had warned his parents that he was a mischievous one. His soul would attempt to escape from his bum, in search of his missing tail. Eight decades have passed since then. And now, when the moment is finally here, Apo feels a strange sensation all over his body. It is as if his soul is evaporating from all the wrinkled pores and dead roots of hair. His diminished senses, waning consciousness, colors, and memories seep into the mist.

She too has surrendered to it in silence. Her heavy breaths and dragging gait, her softly tinkling earrings and bangles, the aubergine color of her kaftan, and her nervous countenance, all lost to the fog.

He awakens to her presence when she reaches out for his walking stick.

"I saw the cheemo," she says, supporting herself with it. "I offered him apricots and almonds."

"Did you not believe me?" Apo is shocked. "Did you consider me a peddler of tall tales?"

Ghazala blushes. She is afraid her happiness may betray more than she is willing to.

His initial exhilaration swiftly gives way to indelible hurt, nursed in the silence of the rocks, the phantom heaving of waves, and the fractures of the heart.

"You didn't say goodbye," he says. The year apart has beaten his voice into an uncharacteristic softness.

"Who are we to question his wisdom?" she asks.

During the war, Apo had given up on god when he slit a friend's throat just so that he could die with dignity, while his senior officer, unable to see him suffer, had moved on.

"I don't believe in his wisdom."

"It wasn't in my hands."

"What is?"

"Separation isn't in our hands. But this moment is. This moment is evidence of Allah's compassion."

"What about your own?"

"O Saki, pour me a goblet of poison"—Ghazala smiles as she recites the couplet—"and I will gladly swallow it. Death has greater honor than a lover's pity and compassion. All this parched mouth seeks is a drop of heavenly love."

Apo has grown frailer. The farthest he can make it is the orchard next door. It is Ghazala's turn to visit his home, something she does daily. Now that Ira's married and gone, Ghazala gives him his medicines and assists in his movements.

Her grandson joins them for his afternoon meals. He has witnessed the younger and able-bodied relinquish their desires for much less, sometimes nothing at all. Being in the company of his grandmother and Apo is a healthy antidote.

"The village has completed its harvesting," he tells his grandmother one morning as she serves him tea. "The fields that remain belong to people not interested in using the machine."

She had known this moment would arrive. How couldn't it?

"I will leave all my cigarettes behind with you," he says.

"But this place is no-man's-land." She panics. "How can I live here? Even the postman doesn't come here."

"What news do you seek?"

"How will I get my rum?"

He laughs. "You seem to like the local chhang. You finished the whole bottle Apo gifted me."

She giggles. "And what about you?" she asks, as the enormity of his words sink in. "You can barely eat with your own hands. If I don't wake you up in the mornings, you will sleep until noon."

"I will grow up."

"What will your father say? And my other sons and daughters?"

"They will tell the world that you died. They will mourn for a few months. Then they will move on. But if you come back with me, will you move on?"

Ghazala doesn't answer. The winters are harshest here, even more than in Kashmir or the rest of Ladakh. At eighty-four, she fears, it may be too late to adjust to such extremes. Then she remembers what Apo had said when she met him at the orchard.

At first, he thought he was dying. His heart skipped a beat in anticipation. Then he saw her stand before him and the reasons for living returned.

GHAZALA DOESN'T KNOW what woke her up. An artificial silence has flooded the room. Her husband isn't snoring. So she reaches out to check his pulse. He is alive, alhamdulillah.

On a winter's night such as this, the warmest room in the village belongs to the newest bride and groom. The bukhari is brimming with coal, the floor and walls are layered with carpets, and the hot-water bags are a gift from the Indian army.

Apo's children insisted on their marriage, lest it set an unwelcome precedent for others. Decades ago, when Apo first arrived, the villagers hadn't wanted him to settle here. "And now when I cannot leave the bed, you are bullying me to marry," he complained. Ghazala needed more convincing. He was a difficult man to live with. More difficult than the desert winter.

In the conscious moments amidst fragments of sleep, the sound returns. It is a faint call for help.

"Can you hear it?" she whispers in his better ear.

"You? Yes, I can hear you."

"No, not me. A lamb is wailing."

"Lambs bleat. Dogs bark. Birds chirp. I snore," he says. "It is the law of nature."

"Why is a lamb outside in the snow? Is it lost?"

"Ghazala, don't be deceived by the winds. Demons imitate innocent cries to lure women out and capture them."

"I am worried for the child."

"And what about me? I could be dead in the morning."

"Why must you always speak of death? You promised you wouldn't."

Had it been a grandchild complaining, Apo would have turned to his side and resumed snoring.

"Lift me up," he says instead. "Hand me my walking stick."

"What if you slip? What if you catch a cold? It hasn't stopped snowing for three days," she says.

"You wake me with your worries. Then you tell me to go back to sleep. What is an old man supposed to do? I cannot speak of death. Then why should I stop living?"

The night outside is a phantom, a figment of the snow's imagination. As the two of them stand at the door, they forget why they are here. In the garb of snowflakes, infinite possibilities drift onto the earth, sideways and curlicued.

Ghazala walks out. She navigates the white amnesia without leaving a trace. Under the starlight, even a footstep is too heavy a burden to carry. She is transported to her childhood, when she'd run out and dance in the snow, much to her parents' dismay. She sways in the spindrift.

All of a sudden, she stands still. This isn't merely the past. It precedes her birth. It is a time when the spirit and the landscape were one. When tropical rains gently descended as snowfall, and deserts expressed themselves as tornadoes of dust on the moon's surface. When oceans slept as ponds within volcanic craters, lulled by the wind's tales. When freedom wasn't a burden, and love was not compromised. For they were one and the same.

Apo watches her from the ledge. She looks so blissful. He takes a hesitant step into the fresh snow. The walking stick slips on the ice. He is silent as his limbs fly through the air. Above him, the winter constellations are creating new patterns from old. Below him, there's nothing. Apo is light and free, like a feather.

A gentle hand grips him by the wrist. It lifts him higher and higher, then brings him lower and lower. Eventually, it places him in the safety of his porch.

Apo finds himself seated at the foot of the door. He isn't alone. He is in the company of a ghost, naked and hunched. He sits balanced on top of the upright walking stick, staring eagerly at Apo's face. He appears to be younger than Apo, and there is something distinguished about him. He has the manner of someone entertaining a dignitary over high tea.

"Thank you, son," says Apo. "You saved a dying man from death."

"A man is committed to his duty, in life and in the afterlife."

Apo nods. Though he cannot grasp the mysteries of this man, he doesn't want to be rude.

"In the first few months of our marriage, my wife too would hear a goat whimper in the dead of night," says the ghost.

This piques Apo's curiosity. "Wedding nights are for the bride and groom," he says. "To be filled with playful acts of lovemaking. Not dwelling on lambs and goats."

The ghost chuckles. "After all these years as a spirit, I owe a gentleman such as yourself a confession," he says. "We lived in the tropics, my wife and I. After a day spent toiling in the hot and humid jungle, each hour of rest was so precious, it was worth its weight in gold. But the cursed creature would insist on making itself heard in the dead of night . . . when a man is in deep sleep, mulling over his dreams. . . . I had half a mind to leave the bed and search for it, just for the pleasure of throwing a jungle boot at it. I also had half a mind to send her to a doctor. For all we knew, her ears were ringing. But she, the late Mrs. Varma . . . she was such a beauty, I lacked the courage to be rude."

Apo laughs. "For the youth, these are the tragedies of love," he says. "At my age, it is all a comedy, son. One must perform a hundred circus acts before one can embrace the beloved."

The ghost joins him in his laughter. He stands up all of a sudden. "Wait here," he tells Apo, before using the pillar to climb onto the roof.

Apo sits all alone. He wants to tell Ghazala how he escaped death for her sake. As he seeks her out in the snow, his cataract eyes witness something extraordinary.

Each snowflake has grown to the size of a cannonball, flooding his vision entirely. Within a blink, Apo sits at the base of snow mountains, lording over the horizon. Within a blink, the snow has begun to melt. The ice is giving way to crystal-clear waters, and starlight to ripples of sun. Apo is surrounded by pink coral, swaying like a summer field on an ocean bed. He marvels at a rusty-gold ammonite floating above. Its shell, coiled and mighty, like the horns of the ram-god, Argali. And its tentacles, dancing with the currents. He reaches out for it. The ammonite flits up, growing in size and grace as it rises. It drifts away as a cloud into the liquid horizon. Apo rises up to where it is. He erupts into the sky like a volcanic island coming to life.

He finds himself on an igneous peak, surrounded by emerald forests and indigo seas. He has never seen such a beautiful sunset before. The colors of the sky define their beings, their lives, even their gaze. He turns toward her. She blushes. In the flash of a sunset, the warmth of sunrise.

The vision is broken by a noise coming from his lap. The lamb's whimper reaches his ears as an indecipherable appeal.

"Here it is," Apo announces, excited.

"It was on the roof," says the ghost, standing outside in the snowfall. He smiles.

Apo watches him vanish into the night. He cradles the infant lamb in his arms.

"He must have slipped out of the shed," says Ghazala as she sits beside him. "Barely a season old and eager to run away."

"He is my ancestor," says Apo. "He has come from my tribe's sheepfold to meet my new bride."

Once inside, Ghazala warms her hands over the burning coals before rubbing the baby's limbs. Curled up in her lap, the lamb is about to fall asleep. Apo stands around aimlessly, watching them. The room is drastically colder, and his clothes are covered by a thin layer of ice. Yet he has no complaints.

"Don't sleep in wet clothes," she says. In all the years of her previous marriage, she'd never had the courage to give her husband orders. This time around, Ghazala isn't just a new bride, she is a new person. "You didn't take your night medicines either," she continues. "You turned to the other side and pretended to be asleep when I brought them to you."

Her words have fallen on deaf ears. Apo stands in a corner, savor-ing the glow of embers on her face and the graceful way in which she sits on the floor. Forget the night's medicines—he contemplates taking something else.

"I have some pills," he says. "We must both take them."

"Why?"

He is nervous. He cannot tell her the truth just yet, lest she misun-derstand. "They help in relieving aches," he replies.

"But nothing hurts, alhamdulillah. You take them, along with your medicines. Where are they?"

"They will help you sleep."

"Rum works very well for me. I will pour myself a glass before I go to bed."

"Oh, can an old man not even tell a lie? The pills help you have sex," he blurts out.

Though she is taken aback, Ghazala doesn't show it. Nothing can take away her dignity from her, definitely not the overtures of a desper-ate groom. She is a mother of five, grandmother to thirteen, and great-grandmother to so many more. She is as ancient and evolved as the act of procreation itself.

"Why do we need pills?" she asks.

"I do."

"Then you take them. Grandmothers don't need pills for sex."

"That Thapa, he didn't understand women one bit," Apo grum-bles. "Or else he would have given me a pill that makes them stop nag-ging."

He walks toward the trunk by the wall. It contains all of his posses-sions, hemmed in by his bride's encroachments. He is still to wrap his head around how much Ghazala, a previously conservative widow, owns. She may cover herself from head to toe and pray a dozen times a day, but she has more shawls, phirans, bottles of perfumed oils, and rum than anyone he knows.

"If you bend too quickly, you will fall on your face," she warns him as he stoops to open the trunk.

"I have fallen on my face a hundred times. A hundred and one won't kill me."

"So much exertion and strain in winter isn't good for you."

"The snow will not last forever. Nor will we."

His hands emerge from the trunk, victorious. Apo has located the yellow silk pouch he'd stored the pills in. But he cannot straighten up again.

"My back is caught," he finally admits.

She places the lamb on the carpet and rushes to his side. She massages his back with her fingertips until she feels the tense knots give way.

"You talk of transience and sex, and you don't even know you cannot bend."

"Mock away, my bride, mock away. An old man is accustomed to the chorus of laughter that follows his miseries everywhere."

Ghazala moves the lamb onto a shawl beside the bukhari. Then she tucks the groom under two blankets in bed.

I T IS THE HOUR when the moon and the sun are both visible in the sky and the night itself is flirting with the dawn. The Drakpos call it the Hour of Courtship.

The sun and the moon are the most ancient of lovers. Though there are more than a thousand moons and satellites in the solar system, the sun, if truth be told, is drawn to only her. The center of the universe longs to withdraw from it all by crawling into her crater, like an ocean resting in the womb of a shell.

As for the moon, just his love isn't enough. It never will be, if it doesn't precede unconditional acceptance. The moon is a flawed creature. Ultimately, she is just a piece of the earth flung into space. The universe itself is a mute witness. It has seen them spend eons together as inseparable lovers and eras as hostile strangers stuck in the same solar system. Each fortnight, the lovers' quarrels reduce the moon to a quarter of her size. Each fortnight, love gives her renewed strength.

But it is at this hour that everything is in equilibrium. Quarrels are forgotten, pain forgiven, anger and regrets hurled away. The moon and the sun are seen exchanging glances through the snowfall, oblivious to the rest.

It is at this magical hour that a primal thought enters an ancient womb. A new world is conceived, entirely different from this one. And in this new world, there are no stars, satellites, planets, constellations, and celestial dust to litter space. Devoid of tectonics, evolutions, and all other inexorable transitions, emptiness is all that exists. An emptiness outside the reach of this expanding universe and the relentless grip of time.

And within it, the possibility of you and I.

Acknowledgments

This is my first published work, and I am grateful to all those who have supported me along the way. Family, friends, and strangers saw me through, for my muses and taskmasters were often one and the same.

This novel is a collective effort. My family, Sunanda, Govind, Shubhra, Shaili, and Heeraz, are my emotional strength. Happiness is always a ready option, despite the professional hazards of doubt and despair, because of Nikhil, my partner. I am also grateful to all the Swarups, Varmas, and Hemrajanis for bearing with a family member who's either missing in action or lost to the world. I owe a lot to the next generation—my nieces, Kaavya and Sivaa, and my daughter, Kalika Swaraj, soon to arrive. Thank you for being a part of my life.

Receiving the Charles Pick Fellowship was a turning point. I am grateful to Amit Chaudhuri and Henry Sutton for mentoring me. The support I have received from the Pick family—Martin, Rachel, and Sue—goes beyond the call of duty. I also appreciate the unconditional support provided by Manu Joseph, Kevin Conroy Scott, and Rick Simonson for my words.

Latitudes of Longing is set in places where I had never previously been. The contribution of my hosts in each of these places is immense, especially since I consistently found myself in sticky situations. They are: Mr. and Mrs. Syamchoudhury, Tanaz Noble, Mr. G. S. Srivastava,

Mr. Mudit Kumar Singh, Sumati Rao, Promi Pradhan and Sanjay Madnani, Kalika Bro-jørgensen, Col. Smanla and Tahira Smanla, Shubham Saha, Archana Tamang Lama, and Sharmila Ragunathan. The Sangam House and Jayanti residencies, and my ancestral home, Shivdham, gave me much-needed solitude.

A lot of research went into this novel, and I have borrowed heavily from the experiences, guidance, and company of the following:

The Forest Department of the Andaman and Nicobar Islands, the Karen community, and the Port Blair State Library, all in the Andaman Islands.

In Myanmar, I am indebted to Mr. Aung Htaik, Mr. Ko Bo Kyii and the Assistance Association for Political Prisoners, Moe Thway, and all the revolutionaries released from the Leech Trials. Letyar Tun's detailed feedback on my manuscript rescued it from many a faux pas, so my thanks to him too.

I was tremendously inspired by the dance-bar workers I interacted with in one of Shakti Samuha's outreach centers in Kathmandu, the Mishmi families living inside Namdapha National Park, the students of the nomadic residential school in Puga Valley and the families living in Ladakh's border villages, and the various geologists, foresters, army, and ex-army folks who I met, in particular the geologist Mike Searle, Capt. Raghu Raman, and a chance meeting with Sharan Thapa, a man from Sindhupal Chowk.

The inspiration for "Snow Desert" came from the late Maj. Noshir Marfatia, the tales he would tell, and his beguiling company. There is also a verse inspired by an Urdu sher that I had once heard in passing, so thank you too, mysterious poet.

In the publishing world, I am lucky to find people whose belief in the novel goes beyond professional engagement, beginning with Maria Cardona and the Pontas Literary and Film Agency. My editors—Rahul Soni, Jon Riley, and Victory Matsui—have played a significant role in honing the work to its current form, guiding me while retaining its vision. Thank you, Nicole Counts, Rose Tomaszweska, and the entire team at One World and Riverrun for the passion put into publishing this. And thank you too, to all my publishers in translation, for taking the novel to a diverse geography and readership.

Then there are the friends: Conrad Clark, Megan Bradbury and Kate Griffin, Sameera Ali, Minal Patel, Smita Khanna, Mansi Choksi, Ananya Rane, Nazia Vasi, Shivangi Shrivastava, Zasha Colah, Nupur Shah, Shirin Johari, Rhea Bhumgara, Jehangir Madon, and many more. To thank you for any one thing would be unfair to all the others you enrich me with.

The muse of this novel is our unassuming planet, a being that bears more beauty, magic, and resilience than this human mind can fathom. As a writer, I am grateful to the process of writing itself, for this work of fiction has brought me closer to truths I've felt foremost in my heart.

ABOUT THE AUTHOR

SHUBHANGI SWARUP is a writer and educator. *Latitudes of Longing,* her debut novel, was a bestseller soon after its release in India. It won the Tata Literature Live! Award for debut fiction and was shortlisted for the JCB Prize for Indian literature. She was awarded the Charles Pick Fellowship for creative writing at the University of East Anglia, and has also won awards for gender sensitivity in feature writing. She lives in Mumbai.

Twitter: @shubhangisapien

ABOUT THE TYPE

This book was set in Baskerville, a typeface designed by John Baskerville (1706–75), an amateur printer and type-founder, and cut for him by John Handy in 1750. The type became popular again when the Lanston Monotype Corporation of London revived the classic roman face in 1923. The Mergenthaler Linotype Company in England and the United States cut a version of Baskerville in 1931, making it one of the most widely used typefaces today.